PANCHO

PANCHO

A NOVEL OF MEXICO

DON ERIC CARROLL

Matador
9 Priory Business Park,
Wistow Road, Kibworth Beauchamp,
Leicestershire. LE8 0RX
Tel: 0116 279 2299
Email: books@troubador.co.uk
Web: www.troubador.co.uk/matador
Twitter: @matadorbooks

ISBN 978 1785893 650

British Library Cataloguing in Publication Data.
A catalogue record for this book is available from the British Library.

Printed and bound in the UK by TJ International, Padstow, Cornwall
Typeset in 11pt Baskerville by Troubador Publishing Ltd, Leicester, UK

Matador is an imprint of Troubador Publishing Ltd

In memory of my dear friend
Ross Gilhome (1941 – 1999)
Ahua don Ross!

ABOUT THE AUTHOR

Don Eric Carroll left school at 14 and joined the RAF as a Boy Entrant, serving for fifteen years. Since then, he has been a professional chef, a college lecturer in Bermuda, poet and traveller, amateur photographer and muralist, a *ranchero* in Mexico, bartender, EFL teacher, and a VSO volunteer in Egypt. Now retired, don Eric is presently editing and redrafting a string of stories he wrote in earlier years.

BY WAY OF A FOREWORD

I wonder, have you thought of developing the character of PANCHO in a separate novel? I think you have hit on a great character here, and with your experience of life on a Mexican ranch you could perhaps give some insight into his life and escapades (On reflection maybe some of your own experiences could be used.)
John Cooper, Tottington, Lancashire

Thus wrote a friend after publication of my narrative prose poem "From Dust to Flowers", about a day in the life of rural Mexico. The initial chapters of PANCHO are adapted from the same prose poem. This present story concerns the life of a bunch of rancheros during one long hot dusty summer on Mexico's central plateau.

Pancho and his co-workers are composites of characters I came across when I lived in Mexico in the '70s. The Ramos people are near accurately drawn from a certain family that more-or-less 'adopted' me, and whose generous hospitality was unbounded for the whole of my time spent in that wonderfully vibrant country. Many of the events depicted in this novel are partly derived from personal experiences. Any historical references mentioned are in fact true and correct.

PROLOGUE

I

The late springtime sun rose out of the Gulf and seared its mark in the clear Mexican sky. Gradually, it left the castellated rim of the eastern cordillera, spreading golden light over the vast expanse of the meseta – the high central plateau – with its arid blasted landscape of tawny hills and fissures of stark desolate ravines. The sun's fast growing heat and harsh light swallowed shreds of mist hugging shallow agricultural valleys. In one of these valleys lies a modest though typical pueblo. Soon the heat will come on hard and the dust rise.

II

A deep morning stillness melted into a vibrancy of sounds over humble adobe huts in the pueblo. A burst of birdsong spilled out from scattered beefwood trees, echoed among cattail rushes and tall stands of reed grass along a river bank threading the valley floor. Thin voices of insects cried in the air, and a soughing of wind filtered through short ranks of wavering pale gold grasses. Domestic animals and peasants alike stirred from the simple comfort of reed debris and straw woven mats, their bodies redolent of dull warmth, like early morning hearth ash.

The pueblo portrayed a composition of mosaic earthcolours; sienna tiling on the hut roofs, struck copper red now by shafts of sunlight driving between roof-high pipe organ cacti. Beige wattle fencing formed corral boundaries, enclosing rust-brown cattle trampling docilely in a crispness of yellow-ochre ground straw. Furrowed fields, parched from a dry season, presented dark-brown faces to the sun, absorbing its fierce rays. The fields stretched flat to a sand riverbank. Beyond the river – at this time little more than a rock-cobbled stream – rugged hills flanked the valley, throwing back heat shimmers of bronze and sepia and gold.

III

In the pueblo people were out and about, mainly women, wearing blue-grey rebozos, followed by a scampering of cheerful children and mongrel dogs. A record played on a wind-up Victrola and the music flowed with a tinny timbre from its brass flaring horn, flooding the valley with its sound. Roosters crowed belligerently, dogs barked, and cattle roared and bellowed in a melody of madness, as they were driven out to pasture by barefooted boys wielding sticks and throwing stones. And the heat came on hard and dust rose and the pueblo exploded alive to another day.

IV

The forenoon heat came over the land like the calescent breath of Satan. A milpero ploughed his field with a pair of sad-eyed oxen, the beasts' heads yoked with a batten of timber. Reaching a furrow end the labourer let go the plough handle. He wiped his brow with the back of his hand and flicked granular sweat into the dry soil. He rested a dusty foot on a clod of earth, and with blunt calloused fingers tremblingly rolled himself a cigarro.

By the riverside a group of women beat out clothes; the washed garments, ragged with constant battering, spread like tropical blossoms over bushes to dry in the sun. A passel of button-eyed youngsters played about sinkholes stamped in the riverbed, chuntering away among themselves like ground squirrels. One shrimp of a boy, unabashedly naked, played alone at the edge of the stream, skimming flat stones. Insects flew in spiralling configurations above the surface of glassy backwaters. And there was a mellifluous chattering of starlings in the tasselled reeds. While in a clear blue sky the sun beat down on the backs of the women. And grasshoppers jumped and scissored in dry sapless grass.

V

The pueblo boasted a plaza with gardens, dirt yards and corrals, small orchards of lemon trees. The plaza itself, a dusty square of open ground centred by an old bandstand, swarmed with noisy youngsters. There were a few dust-spattered shade trees and cacti scattered about, and tree trunk benches where sat small convivial groups of old men playing dominoes. Facing onto the plaza was a stone chapel, a one-roomed federal primary school, a tiny tienda, a corn mill and a cantina. A man strummed a guitar on the stone step of the cantina, bands of unwashed young ones frothed out from yards and side alleys to join the hubbub, dogs chasing after them. The air trembled festively, for the phonograph music was at its loudest here. A bird warbled beyond the chapel's sun-dipped bell-tower, and there was an unceasing crowing of cocks in the yards.

Two drunken mestizos crashed out through double swing-doors of the cantina. The duo lurched and canted across the inflamed plaza, hanging onto each other for support. Then one halted, tried to adjust the buckle of his belt lost under a swollen paunch. The other man, filthy and derelict, suddenly vomited, and it spurted out as though expelled by a pump, splattered over the ground with a soft slap. A mongrel trotted up on rickety legs and sniffed with hope and greedy eyes. Another dog appeared, then one more. The dogs snuffled and gobbled the thick splay of vomit, incuriously watched by hard-faced rancheros dressed in dusty rawhide and denim. The dogs ran off, and the ground was trampled dry again by a pace of pack-burros.

A dust-devil as tall as a horse galloped over the square, and insects buzzed angrily in a smother of dust. The wind began to blow hotly and the heat hammered down on the land.

BOOK 1

Late Spring

Part One

Part One

1

Ruth and Julia

"Ruth?"

The child's voice was low and melodious. A soft rustle of a bedsheet as the child turned over with a quick fluid movement. She leaned on one elbow, small chin cupped in her hand, gazing with wide eyes at her elder sister half curled and sleeping soundly beside her.

"Ruth!"

The intonation of the voice was now urgent with childish impatience. Bright morning sunshine streamed through a tiny one-paned window, a beam of light probing a red brick floor, dust motes floating and swirling in shifting lemon rays.

A fly alighted on the sleeping girl's cheek, and her cheek twitched and her lips appeared to form a brief smile. The child saw the movement and giggled, then immediately suppressed it.

"R-Rutí!"

But the girl serenely slept on, perhaps subliminally entranced in the last of the night's cycle of wondrous dreams with which the young are blessed.

A mellow light in the room richly enhanced her olive skin as she slept.

The child's voice became persistent:

"Rutí, wake up will you!" and she shook the smoothly rounded shoulder of her sister.

The girl stirred restively a moment, hands locked in the valley of slightly swelling thighs. Her small budlike breasts rose and fell evenly, her long glossy hair unbound over a pillow. She smiled in her sleep, showing perfect pearly white teeth.

The child again giggled. "Ah, you're only pretending," she whispered in amusement, her warm honeyed breath caressing the other's cheek as she leaned over her. "Well, I'm asleep too!" she declared, and with that she turned and dived under the bedsheet, burrowing to the bottom of the bed. She lay there rigid and expectant, breath flowing between open teeth in one long strained exhalation.

Ruth half awakened. "Julia?" she said softly. "Are you up?" and there was no answer. Fully aroused now from slumber, Ruth uncurled and stretched luxuriously. She threw back the sheet to her slim waist, and her hands explored under her shift, felt the softness of a slender body. Her mind marvelled at the silk smoothness of her skin, suffused with bed warmth. Her hands moved on up to barely formed breasts and she tentatively squeezed them, with a brief surge of delight and pride of one recently out of childhood yet still very much a child. A finger crept up and touched her throat, released her breath in a satisfied sigh.

"Julia," she said languorously, "it's time to be up."

"Oh, I've been up ages! Is Pancho coming today?"

"Pancho who?"

"You know, *Pancho*!"

"*Señor* Ramírez? *Sí*, I expect so. I think he said he might."

"Oh, *tambien*. That's good. But when?"

"When what? What are you on about?"

"When will Pancho come, I said."

"Why ask me? Any time I suppose, you know what Pancho's like."

"It must be soon, or else…"

Julia grew restive, as the young usually are first thing of a morning. She put a finger to her lips and secretively whispered, "I'm going to see what's going on," and swung from the bed, a tender lemon light falling on her oval face.

She skipped nimbly to the tiny window and peeked through the dust-streaked pane, and her eyes glittered with impish mischief as they roved fleetingly over the main courtyard of the farmstead.

"*Mamá* looks pleased with herself…"

2

Mamá and Cristina

Woodsmoke billowed in clouds from a stone hearth under a kitchen lean-to across the yard. A huge black cauldron sat like an ancient Indian idol on the flames of the kitchen fire. Supporting beams of the lean-to were thick-limbed logs of beefwood, blackened with age and smoke. On them were nailed and hung iron pots and skillets, jugs and tin pails and plastic buckets, strings of onion and garlic and chilli, a basket of eggs, and rusty cans of dry withered herbs. A tan-and-cream goatskin was stretched on a length of *carrizo* hung on rope tied to rafters, and a black swarm of flies flew in a maddened frenzy about the underskin.

The short plump figure of mamá was almost obscured by a belch of smoke around her as she handscooped beans into a pot, a lively intent look on her homely face.

"I hope Pancho does come today. Oh, he must, he must!"

Julia's eyes darted over the main building of the homestead. Walls of adobe bricks and stones; a roof of weathered broken tiles, a roofed porch of corrugated iron, with a new overhang of fresh-scented thatch, golden in the sunlight. On the walls were hung, like a collage mural, straw sombreros, a Funghan's clock which chimed the quarter hour in musical tones, reed cages of doves and plovers and a parrot. There were coils of rope and rusty machetes and farm implements in advanced state of corrosion; dilapidated leather saddles and harnesses, narrow plywood shelves on which stood gasoline lamps and kerosene lanterns, tins and jars of medical ointments to cure stings and bites and scalds. Squat packets of rifle ammunition, bobbin reels of cotton and balls of wool, candles and bottles and spent batteries; plastic bags containing a miscellaneous jumble of gewgaws, scissors and penknives – and all these things were coated with fine grey dust.

"Maybe mamá will let us go to market later on…"

Against the wall on the porch leaned crates of empty bottles and burlap sacks of corn husks, a bale of sugar peppered with mouse droppings, water jars and a large water barrel, gunny sacks of beans and rice and corn; and a vintage waggon wheel with half its spokes missing – and the sun shone dully on these things.

"But I'm hoping Pancho will come before then…"

Jutting out beyond the porch was a low fencing of lattice boards and trellised reed cane, and it was here where mamá kept her herb garden in tin cans wired to the fencing. Miniature-leafed plants twisted and crept through the trellis, tumbled out of their tins in abundance and cascaded over other plants, sharp scents mingling; yellow camomile drinking sun rays, deep blue flowers shaped like dolls-house soup bowls and named *chía*. Delicate rose-pink flowers with emerald cloaks of crinkled leaves, a flaming mass of red jessamine, platinum-white blossoms hiding behind thick olive-green foliage – and insects worked in a business-like manner about the flora.

"Oh, ooh, Cristina is at it, come and look!"

A young woman, in a white blouse and long full skirt, swept the hardbaked dirt-yard with a rush broom. She raised the broom to scatter a hen and its chicks, and the hen clucked and chuckled and bounced across the yard, chicks following in quick nervous runs, like fluffy yellow balls blown by gusts of wind. A turkey-cock gobbled hysterically, fluffing a canopy of riotous coloured feathers, moving over the yard like a richly ornate Venetian barge. The rush broom stroked the ground, lifting crisp sepia dust, and the dust rose like particles of gold in the sunlight.

The *señorita* worked her way over to shade trees of beech and ash and beefwood, of guava and mesquite and tamarind; and the dust she raised fell as a mantle over dark-green shrubs and bushes. Her ears unconsciously caught a monotonous symphony of droning insects in the upper branches. Crimson-and-black butterflies flitted above her head like scraps of paper teased by a wind. She skirted a hog snorting and grunting and bristling with indignation, its forelegs hobbled in true country tradition.

There was a sudden raucous shriek of the parrot on the porch, sending wild doves flying away in alarm from a peach orchard beyond the compound.

"Ruth! Juan's back from the fields…"

3

Juan and his Dog

*A*bareheaded boy plodded across the outer yard under a beating sun, a grey shaggy dog almost as big as the boy himself following at his heels. The boy was bent forward slightly under the weight of a full round basket of fresh green fodder on his back, held by a soft leather tumpline on his forehead.

There was a flash of sun on steel, the blade of a machete tucked bravely in the youngster's belt. He stopped at an animal pen and swung his load to the earth, and a silent explosion of dust erupted around the basket. He slid the machete from his belt and stuck it in the ground, and the metal whanged ringingly. The huge dog sat on its haunches and thumped its tail; hot dust spurted up, causing the beast to sneeze. The boy then heaved the basket to his shoulder and allowed its contents to gush over the fencing of the pen, and the rich green fodder was instantly savaged and trampled on by the animals – goats, pigs and a yearling burro.

The boy wiped a sheen of moisture from his forehead with the sleeve of his sweat-dampened *camisa*. He peeled off the shirt and draped it over a post. Then he padded across the yard, footsteps lighter now. The dog followed, tongue out panting in the heat but with bushy tail eagerly waving.

The youngster ambled through a wasteland patch of the farmstead dump; an untidy area of loose sandy soil and old ground straw, smashed bottles and chicken feathers, dung and tin cans and shucked corncobs. A heavy putrid stink of garbage attracted flies, ants and beetles. Chicken feathers seemed alive, like butterflies, fluttering restlessly with the dust and a steady ground wind. The dog trotted over an effluvium of waste matter, moist nose down and snuffing about a putrescence of decay, overlarge ears flopping about like two damp dish rags.

Into shifting dappled sunlight by shade trees strode the boy. He paused before a tall clay water jar on the porch. With slow deliberate movements he reached for a pot mug hung on a nail in the porch beam, lifted the lid off the water jar. He dunked the mug into a dark cool well of water and raised it, dripping cold quick silver, to dry, dusty lips. He sipped slowly, as he was in a sweat, and took short breathers. His eyes roved indifferently over a grey-bodied accumulation of junk and paraphernalia on the homestead's central porch.

The mug was again lowered into the shadowed depths of the water jar. He drank his fill and rained the dregs over the ground, and the dog went at once to nosy about dark streaks made in the dust. For the dog's trouble it got its big wet nose patched over with dust. It shook its head and snorted like a horse.

The youngster strolled casually to a rope hammock strung between two ancient thorn trees. He flopped in the hammock with a sigh. His faithful follower turned round and round in a tight circle by his master's side, and at last laid itself down, noisily panting, long tongue dribbling a gossamer thread of saliva.

The hammock swung in gentle arcs. The boy could smell acrid woodsmoke as it drifted over from the outdoor kitchen, and he heard the familiar sound of his mamá hand-clapping *tortillas*.

And a boy who had worked in the fields since first light of day waited impatiently for his breakfast.

He listened, a curl of his lips showing faint amusement – or it may have been mild contempt – anticipating the usual morning hubbub to begin of many females about the kitchen.

4

The Ramos Family

*D*oña María Ramos was known as a warm and affectionate woman. She was a true *mestiza*; face dark-complexioned, with laugh lines running from a wide mouth, lips full and sensual. Lines ran in all directions like a road map over narrow brow and high, angular cheeks, crinkling deeply in a 'V' formation from widely-set intensely avid eyes. Her blue-black hair was parted in the middle, combed back in one natural wave, worn in a braid of beaded cord. It bounced like something alive against the small of her back whenever she moved.

To those who knew her, mamá was a strong woman, not only physically but also in mind and character. A woman of indomitable spirit, and one who possessed a homely sense of humour. Her every gesture bespoke practicality and skill, with an authority of manner worthy of anyone's respect. Her hands were swift-moving and sure; clever, expressive – one might say eloquent. And there was in her a gentle tenderness and a commanding dignity. Such were the excellent qualities of mamá.

A chicken squawked and helplessly flapped its wings, hung upside down, shanks firmly gripped by mamá. The fowl feebly struggled in her strong brown hand. She smiled at the severe face with its gunmetal eyes, for a reason that couldn't ever be explained, had she given the matter any thought.

With a brief light of resolve in her eyes mamá stunned the bird with a sudden knuckle rap, lowered it into a cauldron of furiously bubbling water, and held it there till its shanks stiffened and stilled. She drew it from the scalding water. Moments later, plucked and singed clean, its plumpness and fresh odour attracting a small squadron of flies, the chicken was ready for gutting and the stockpot. Mamá cut into it with deft graceful strokes of a knife, an almost devilish smile of triumph on her face.

Two yard-cats mewed imperatively under her feet as she hand-fanned a glut of flies around a pail of smoking warm-stirred entrails and feathers. One of the cats daringly jumped up and snatched at the booty with small sharp teeth, and pinkish purple entrails slivered over the pail rim. The cook wiped a streak of blood off the chicken's breast with a scrap of gunny sacking, and two cats fought an earnest tug-of-war with a rope of intestine.

"Away with you! ¡Andale!" she snapped, clapping hands, and the cats ran off, dragging the snakelike tube of intestine through the dust.

The chicken was thrust into a stockpot, with an unpeeled onion chopped in quarters and half a hand of coarse rock salt. Some dry herbs were thrown in for good measure. That done, mamá lifted a bucket of corn dough, placing it on a stone slab by the hearth, where stood a three-legged stone *metate*. She rinsed down this grinding stone and slapped half the corn dough on it. Next, she picked up a *mano* – a stone rolling pin – and began to grind her corn, body leaning forward a bit, arm muscles taut; and the dough turned to a smooth light grey paste under the motion of the roller.

Girlish laughter caused her to look up from her task. Julia and Ruth came skipping over the yard, Cristina not far behind them, still sweeping dust and splintered sunlight. The boy Juan sidled over as well, the dog predictably close at his heels. Mamá glanced at her brood with amused affection. Little Julia was first to reach her, and the child threw herself gaily into the folds of her mother's skirt.

"Mamá!" she burst out, fresh-eyed and hardly able to contain her excitement. "Is Pancho really coming to visit today?"

"Who? Ha, Pancho. Sí, he did say something of the sort, but you never know with him," gazing fondly into her daughter's sparkling eyes.

The little one bounced about springily, expressing joyous delight. "Oh Pancho! Pancho Ramírez! Señor Pancho!"

"That's enough I'm thinking, *niña*," mamá remonstrated. "Now get from under my feet."

The child jumped on to another tack: "We're going to pick some flowers for you," she burbled happily. "Me and Ruth."

"Flowers? From where might I ask?"

"Why of course, mamá."

"Of course what?"

"You might ask, of course!"

"Well, where then? For goodness sake," laughed mamá.

"From your garden of course, where else?" which doña María thought very nice indeed thank you very much, and said so.

"It'll be a good market today," said Juan, getting in his piece.

"I wonder at that, Juanito," returned his mother, "what with this dry spell we're having."

"Lots of stuff, mamá – they're coming in from all over, I've seen them," said the boy, casting an eye on Cristina who was pouring water into a can from a large tin bucket; while the parrot on the porch gave her a wolf-whistle, followed by an insane shriek.

"I'll send the girls along presently," mamá told her son, who still watched Cristina, now flicking water over the yard in an effort to settle the dust she herself had raised.

"Sí, mamá," said the boy, and sat himself on a wooden stool nearby, the dog hard by him, vigorously scratching itself.

He ran a hand through his shock of jet-black hair. Like most boys who lived in remote pueblos and *Rancherías*, Juan was mature in his makeup quite beyond his tender years. His face showed an expression indicating a high intelligence; reflected plainly enough in his eyes, which saw everything and missed nothing.

He caught his mother's gaze on him at this moment, and she could sense the emotions thrilling through him. She was aware that he idolised the old ranchero Pancho. She smiled then, not at her son so much, but at the fact that his head was perfectly level with that of the huge dog, as it sat and looked on his master with seemingly old and wise but rather mournful eyes.

The two youngest girls began their morning attack on the kitchen, supposedly assisting mamá …

5

Preparing Comida

Several hours later the Ramos family were again bustling about the kitchen and main courtyard.

"Are we having something special, mamá?" asked Julia. "For Pancho's visit," an unusual seriousness in tone of voice and a grownup look on her little face.

Ruth suggested *enchiladas* with *mole* sauce, and the other countered with chicken *caldo* with mint and lemon.

"Tomatoes and onions too," trilled the little one. "And star pasta. Can we have star pasta?" as she poked at a stack of tortillas by the hearth.

"Ha, *mi madre!*" exclaimed mamá, throwing arms up in exasperation.

"Señor Ramírez likes *tamales*," said Juan getting in his little bit. "I know that for sure – if he comes…" He had it in mind to wander to the shrine beyond the farmland fields, in the hope of catching the old ranchero come riding over the ridge. He's bound to come by that way, the boy inwardly exulted.

"Sí, mamá, and I'll sort it," Julia burst out, poking now at corn kernels in a wooden tub. "You make the tamales, Juan –"

"Put those down and stop fidgeting."

" – and you Rutí help mamá with the tortillas – if we should need more –"

"Will you leave things alone!"

"Sorry, mamá. Well, Cristina can pick the orange leaves for *ponche*, and chop the chilli and sift the beans and cook the stars. No, mamá must cook the stars, she knows best how and – Sí, the lemon-grass, Cristina, you pick the lemon-grass and put the whatsits to soak and –"

"Is that all then!" Cristina almost exploded.

"We shall see what can be done," put in mamá mildly.

She lifted a hand of brown speckled eggs from a basket. The eggs were fresh and still warm from the laying, and mamá felt their warmness in the palms of her hands. Long plumes of bluish smoke rose from the kitchen fire and stickwood spat and crackled in a blaze of orange flames. She fired a blackened skillet, poured in some melted fat, and dexterously cracked in six eggs.

"Sit yourselves!" she called over her shoulder, face enveloped in smoke from the woodfire. "Quickly now. ¡Andale!"

Ruth began to hum a romantic song – *me abandonas* – and Julia tried to whistle but without success.

"Hurry it now!" urged the imperative voice, and mamá swiftly turned, grabbed the little one. She tweaked her ear, to remind the child that an order was an order, and plonked her on a stool before a large wooden table.

"Go and fetch your *papá*, Juanito," mamá commanded lightly, "and have him wash his hands before he sits – and Juanny, put something over the parrot's cage, *por favor.*"

She flipped some tortillas griddling on a *comal*, a spatula reaching over to baste the spluttering eggs. Her eyes glanced dartingly from the bean pot to an earthenware jug of boiling milk. The milk was rising fast to the rim of the jug, and she thrust a free hand in a pail of water and shook drops from her fingers into the jug, and the small crisis was over as the milk sank. She pushed the jug from the heat and skimmed the skin with a spoon, flicked it to the ground for the cats to fight over.

"Where's papá?" asked Julia.

"I'll cut the melon," Ruth offered, rising from her stool.

"*Ay*, Ruth," returned mamá from the kitchen smoke.

"Where has papá got to?" Julia asked obstinately, small voice plaintive, tossing her head to clear hair from her eyes. "Shall I –"

"Stay put, you! Don't dare move!"

"Shall I … cut some lemon?" came the weak response.

Doña María glanced with satisfaction at the pot of beans, and the beans jigged about as beans do in rapidly boiling water. She stirred the pot a bit and moved it slightly away from full heat and the beans settled, simmering gently in their purple-black cooking liquor.

Then papá made his appearance.

6

Don Antonio

Don Antonio was tall for a Mexican and, as if ashamedly aware of the fact, tended to stoop shoulders a fraction when he walked. He had large and round rather staring eyes, and high blackly-etched eyebrows, which seemed to give him a permanent surprised, almost incredulous expression.

"Sit yourself down, *papacito*," his wife pressed him warmly, and he obediently sat on a high-backed reed chair in his accustomed place at the head of the table. "The girls are full of it today," mamá went on, a humorous glint in her eyes, "on account of Pancho coming later on – well, if he shows that is."

"Coming here?"

"Only if or when he shows up."

"Uh-uh," returned don Antonio, by nature a man of few words; and when he did speak it was invariably with religious undertones, for he was a pious man.

Ruth appeared with a giant-sized watermelon and expertly cut into it with a long-bladed knife. And at last the family seated themselves; papá and Juan, Cristina and Ruth, and the mischievous ball of energy that was Julia.

Mamá paused in her work for a snatch of time to look them over, as a hen would with its chicks. A platter of eggs was placed on the rough wooden table, and steaming tortillas wrapped in a towel in a *tule* basket. There was a homely clatter of dishes as the eggs were shared out by Cristina. Don Antonio crossed himself and prayed for a brief spell, the others following suit.

"Pancho's coming over today, papá," piped Julia importantly. She bobbed her small head to get the hair out of her eyes and to let the sunshine in.

"He *might*, that's all we know at present," put in Cristina rather coldly, pushing her young sister in the back.

"If God wills it, child," murmured her father, smiling faintly, "so might it be," and dropped eyes to the dish set before him.

"At what time will he come I wonder?" voiced Ruth, looking across the table at her brother for a possible answer.

The boy felt a rising choke of excitement in his chest, and cleared his throat. "Señor Ramírez could come at any time at all I suppose," he told her. "After this I'm heading for the shrine to look out for him."

"That'll be nice," was mamá's comment.

"Pancho! Oh Pancho!" and Julia was about to rise.

"Sit down, you!" ordered Cristina curtly.

"And button your lip, or else," mamá warned her.

The beans in the pot on the hearth were now cooked good and soft, and mamá heaped a full dish of them and put the smoking dish before her husband. Savoury steam rose to tease his nostrils. With a small knife mamá began to chop an onion, chopped it fine in the palm of her hand over papá's dish, and his nose caught the sharp pungency of the onion as it rained in the dish.

Mamá next turned her attention to Ruth, and said to the girl, "I want you to go to market, Rutí, after you've eaten – no need to rush as there's plenty of time. You can take Julia with you, as I've much to do."

"Sí, mamá," smiled the girl.

"Get some big fat tomatoes, hey, mamá!" squeaked the little one.

"Another tortilla, papacito?" enquired mamá, while Ruth passed wedges of watermelon round the table.

"Round and smooth fat red tomatoes –"

"There you are, niña, asking for a clip."

"Eat your melon, child," papá ordered mildly.

Julia held a huge wedge of watermelon in tiny hands. "Look, mamá," she opened up again, "this is our flag, in this melon."

"Ha, indeed, my precious, and how is that then?"

"Don't encourage her, mamá," said Cristina frostily.

"*Maestra* told us at school. See" – the young one tapped a finger on the dark green rind – "here's the green, for independence, and here is the white for ... it means..."

"For religion," Ruth put in quickly, glancing at her father.

Julia ignored her sister and carried on, her finger pushing into the fruit's flesh. "White is for religion, and the red part, mamá, the red is for the union."

"The union of what?" mamá wanted to know.

"The *union*!" Julia emphasised.

"Sí, you said, but what union?"

"Of the races, she means," Ruth slipped in sweetly, and as sweetly smiled at her sister, who promptly pouted her lips, then sank her teeth into the soft pulp of the watermelon.

"I did say of the races," she mumbled.

"I don't recall you saying that," sniffed Cristina imperiously.

"And what are the little black things?" mamá asked innocently.

"Oh mamá!" cried the child in vexation. "They're the seeds!"

Which managed to cough up a laugh from don Antonio.

"Oh hush! Hush! Listen!"

"What now?"

There was then heard a mighty thudding of hooves in the outer yard and all heads turned in the direction of the sound.

"Who could that be?" asked someone.

"Well, if I'm not much mistaken," smiled mamá, "it'll be that scoundrel of a ranchero – Pancho."

Part Two

Part Two

7

Pancho Shows Up

To most folk for miles around the figure of Pancho was instantly recognisable because of his shape and the way he walked. He was broad in the shoulders and chunkily built, as if roughly chiselled from a block of hardgrained wood. He reminded people of a rough-hewn rock sculpture; sort of squarish with the edges chipped away. Keg-chested, with long, well-muscled arms and large, spade-square hands; and having such immense shoulders he was a dynamo of latent energy, a physical powerhouse.

A history of hardship was plainly scrawled over his dark bronze beaten features, left cheek marred by a livid scar, giving him a wild savage brigand look. This was offset to a point by a continual humorous glint in his eyes; the eyes intelligent and milky-blue, the blue of a tropical sea at first light of dawn.

A most striking aspect of his appearance was evident when he removed his sombrero (on the rarest of occasions), to reveal a bristled thatch of ginger-red hair, looking not unlike what a horse would snatch from a hay-rack.

The old man was also bandy-legged like a horseman – which in truth he was – and walked with a peculiarly lopsided gait, long arms slapping slackly at his sides. He swayed and rocked it seemed in his movements, like an old Spanish caravel caught in a turbulent sea swell.

Francisco Medina Ramírez *el ranchero*, better known by the diminutive Pancho, gimped solidly into the Ramos' courtyard, scuffing up dust and scattering poultry and cats before him.

"¡*Hola!* my friends, it's only me," he greeted the family blithely in customary grating gravelled tones, raising his sombrero high and describing arcs of salutation and respect.

"Señor Ramírez! Pancho!" the children carolled with pure joy and enthusiasm.

"And about time too," muttered mamá under her breath, chuckling to herself. "Now matters will get off the mark I shouldn't wonder," she fancied, eyeing the old ranchero.

Juan was up from his seat like a grasshopper to attend the guest's horse, Julia springing up after him.

With the swift instant energy of the young Julia darted across the yard to the dust-laden rider. "Oh Pancho! You've come at last, ¡hurra!" she cried, eyes happily sparkling as she flung herself at him and hugged dusty bandy legs.

"Ho-hee! My little sun-blossom!" laughed the old man, chucking the child's cheek. "*Ay que caray*, if you're not the loveliest creature in all the state, then I'll eat a dirty dog's dinner, and I'd never lie to you on that score, my springflower."

"But I am!" agreed Julia with that naïve, precocious self-confidence of the very young.

Doña María, arms slack and hands on hips, stared wonderstruck at the ranchero's incredibly dusty appearance, for he was covered in it from the crown of his sombrero to booted feet.

Mamá could be sharp and tart as a lemon with her rural wit, just as Pancho was always downright down-to-earth with his country style wisdom. "Well!" she exclaimed with a hearty laugh, "you do look a sight, I must say. Played with the hogs, rolling in it, eh? Dragged yourself here along the ground is it, eh?"

"Something like that, María," he roared, and in respect once more whipped off his sombrero, sunlight setting ablaze his crop of reddish hair. "We had a kind of stampede, you see – And how goes it with my sweet bush-flower, hmm?" bending low to the child.

"A stampede!" mamá cried. "Merciful heavens! What next, might I ask? There's always something or other when you're around, you rogue! You scruff! You great heap of dirt and filth! Just look at the state of it!"

"The herd stampeded?" asked Juan, head peeping round from the stable door. "What got that started, señor Ramírez?"

"What's a stampede?" Julia wanted to know.

"It's when you run away from the wash-basin," Cristina cruelly cut in.

Said Ruth in defence, "Oh leave off, por favor."

"Well, a kind of stampede as I say," grinned Pancho. "Just a little run really. It was our Gerardo who started it, I reckon. Spooked the beasts he did; he's clever that way you should know. Gave us all a nice merry skip around, I can tell you, hmm."

"Ah Gerardo…" said the boy dismissively, taking the old man's white, rawboned mare by the rein and leading her into the stable, as don Antonio rose from his seat at last to welcome the guest.

"¡Chihuahua!" mamá burst out. "Was anyone hurt then?"

"Only Gerardo's pride I'm thinking. You know, Gerardo very nearly got himself gutted," went on Pancho in rasping tones. "I reckon he was that near" – holding thumb and forefinger an inch apart – "that near to being gouged by a pair of cowhorns."

"Such wild ones, you lot are!" mamá scolded him. "Rascals and roustabouts, each and every one of you and one as bad as the other. Ha!"

"But you, señor Ramírez," said Ruth, wide-eyed and passionately attentive, "are you alright?"

"Me?" the old man grinned ruggedly back at the girl. "Them beasts ran all over me to be sure, but what damage can they do to a ranchero, hmm? Apart from chewing half a kilo of dust, I'm fine I reckon, real fine!" and he went to doña María, took her hand and cavalierly kissed it.

"*Pfoo*! You stink like a skunk," recoiling from him.

"I am a bad one I suppose, and smell so, and don't mind admitting the fact. Well María, am I too late to eat? If so then just throw me a bone and I'll enjoy a chew on that. We can feast on praise but I prefer grub."

"You can clean yourself up first, Francisco Ramírez, that's what you can do," she told him hotly. "You look as though you belong in a burrow."

"*Muy bien*, I'll bury my head in the horse trough for a spell," he winked, speaking in his usual rough rock-crunching tone of voice.

"You will do no such thing, you precious specimen, you sorry sack of sawdust!" mamá's arms akimbo on her broad hips. "Ruth, a bucket of hot water and soap for the señor here, por favor."

"¡Carambas!" Pancho popped out in mock alarm. "I have to wash?"

"Just listen to this filth-encrusted can't-see-its-face half animal!" mamá exploded.

"Okay, fair enough, I'll go wash, if you positively insist on it," and they both split into laughter, heads held back, eyes crinkling with merriment.

The old man savoured the food aromas wafting his way. He slapped his dusty sombrero against his thigh, coughed and spat in the smoke of dust he had created. Don Antonio stepped forward, towering over the ranchero who looked up at him, comradely grinning. The other smiled slightly, stooped a fraction to establish eye-to-eye level, and they shook hands.

"How goes it then, *compadre?*"

"Muy bien, Pancho, and you?"

"Hungry, *hombre*," groaned the other. "That's to say I reckon I could finish off a whole steer."

"Is the herd safe?" politely enquired don Antonio, being as it were indirectly reminded of it.

"Oh sure, tucked in a corral they are, watered down and licking dust off their hides, bless them," and Pancho rose and fell on toes and heels as he spoke, stretching his arms to ease niggly aches and pains.

About to hawk and spit as was his habit, he stopped himself in time as doña María confronted him.

"Here, wash yourself," she ordered with warm and open brusqueness, handing him water and soap and a towel.

"Right! ¡Bueno!" he shouted with rough cheerfulness.

He sluiced hands and arms, splashed and spluttered as his head disappeared in the bucket, slapped dust from himself and washed again. As he dried himself, dirtying the towel in the process, he inhaled the teasing aromas of food and winked shamelessly at mamá. Ruth and Julia watched him intently, cracking *pepita* seeds the while with their teeth.

After his ablutions he searched in a panic for his sombrero, which was lying on the ground behind him. He swiftly returned it to where it rightly belonged, and got himself dusty once more. Straightening himself into a proper upright position and glancing down at his fairly dust-free frontage, he considered himself respectable enough. And ready to eat.

Juan returned from the stable and gazed with boyish hero-worship at the old man : Pancho el ranchero; tough but warm-hearted, strong, solid, dependable; fair and honest in his dealings. And very special to the boy.

Broad sunlight brought out the barbaric ruggedness of the old man's features, deepened the weathered criss-cross of lines on brow and cheeks, struck silvery gleams of light in the irises of merry blue eyes. And there was that ever ready expression of simple humour on his open face.

Then mamá clapped her hands, a signal for everyone to return to their seats, and quickly or else …

8

Family and a Friend

Mamá worked furiously on more last minute cooking. Heat from the fire flushed her face red-brown and perspiration dropped from her. Pots and jugs on the fire bubbled and sang, wreathed in steam and smoke. The inestimable lady worked like a furnace stoker, putting the fuel of her matronly love into the task at hand.

Pancho sat four-square, slowly crushing the flimsy reed chair under him. He wiggled his backside, poised ready to crash on the ground. Turning his head he sniffed the wholesome kitchen smells like a starved dog. He was almost ready to shove a finger up his nose, to investigate dust lodged there – the finger wavered uncertainly below his nostril – remembered in time what he was about, and sniffed again instead, briefly, with a peculiar air of significance, as if he knew something of import the others were unaware of.

Then he turned to grin and shrug at don Antonio with devil-may-care nonchalance, winking and nodding at the children, and accepting from Julia the tiniest hand of *Calabaza* seeds called *pepitas*. The seeds he soon found were simply a tease, for he could not crack them as expertly as the girls, and the thin shells stuck to the roof of his mouth; he contorted lips and jaw. Julia was about to offer him more but was checked by a momentary frown on her papá's face.

The dog woke up and seemed of a sudden very attentive, quite ravenous as it glanced hopefully at the faces above the table, and falling into a sulk when nothing came of it. Juan draped a *poncho* over the parrot's cage, to discourage the bird from screaming abuse at everyone, as it so often did when the family gathered to eat.

Sunlight slipped through shade trees and dappled with gold the unusually silent diners at present at the large wooden table. A cock crowed in the nearby pueblo, and a donkey loudly brayed in a field of alfalfa in the valley. Phonograph music drifted to them, and it seemed as if it were coming out of the very earth of the hills. The village chapel bell pealed from its sun-washed bell-tower, making hollow oscillations which travelled in echoing waves through dustsifted air. The curiously subdued group at the table, in order to hide a faint embarrassment over their silence, took an all-absorbing intensity of interest in a trio of hens ruffling feathers and scratching about in the dust of the yard.

"Well make a start, don't be shy," ordered mamá.

What could be safely described as pandemonium broke loose at the table, with everybody talking at once, Pancho's steel-on-sandpaper voice and rough turn of speech predominant. A clatter of dishes and wisps of steam curling at each place setting, and mamá dashing like a bobcat between hearth and table. Don Antonio lordly splashed a generous mugful of *pulque* for Pancho from a tin jug, and Cristina poured hot lemon-grass tea from a chipped enamel pot into cups for herself and the youngsters.

The family set to vociferously with eyes and teeth and fingers, putting a blizzard of energy into eating and chatting, mamá watching over them with a widening smile of immeasurable satisfaction. Blissful sounds indeed to her, the munching and chewing and crunching, the champing of busy teeth and jaws jogging, gulping, swallowing, lip-smacking – a gastronomic symphony.

"I wonder if this dry spell is ever going to break," don Antonio remarked as his opening piece of conversation to his guest.

"Oh it will, you can count on it," returned Pancho urbanely. "In my experience that's always the case, compadre, and experience is the one thing that only comes with time – that and good or bad weather," his face now dipped to his dish, snorting over chicken *caldo*.

Don Antonio's brows met in a slight frown, as though vexed at something or other. "The dry of last year was bad enough, and now this long drought," he went on with a gloomy air. "The corn store this very moment is low enough –"

"It'll rain soon, compadre, I feel it in my 'water'," Pancho predicted. "We'll have it by the barrelful, you mark my words. *Uy*, I feel soaked to the skin already – or is it the water I washed in I'm thinking on?"

The old ranchero looked quizzically asquint at the bright bold blue of sky, as if his thoughts hung there waiting to be plucked. Then more important matters came to mind and down went his head again, slurping in his soup.

"More pulque?" offered his host.

"Ah sí, that's the stuff," the old man thanked the other warmly. "I could do with a wet, as I'm thinking on it."

He raised his bowl to his lips and noisily finished off the broth. He wiped lips and moustache with a sleeve; then, arms resting on the table, he cupped his pulque with both hands as though it were holy sacrament.

"Eat up there," mamá urged him. "Rice and chillies under your nose, hot *tacos* here see – ¡Chihuahuas! All this food lying untouched," she admonished him. "I thought you were hungry. Come on, get tucked in!"

"Ah sí, María, I'm ready for it of course, as you know."

"Get on with it then," said mamá, and Pancho picked up a taco, face taking on a look of a starveling about to devour a stolen chicken.

Juan was whispering something to Ruth, and the girl glanced over at the old ranchero and suddenly asked, "Is it true, señor Ramírez, that you rode with the famous Pancho Villa?"

"Sí, did you?" Juan wanted to know, the boy's eyes wide with interest.

9

Table Talk

R uth's mild brown eyes gazed shyly across the table at Pancho, and she smiled blushingly, showing lovely white teeth.

"Who is Pancho Villa?" piped Julia.

"Well now," began the old ranchero, "I nearly did ride with him, but as it turned out at the time I didn't," filtering words through a mouthful of food. "I was out of it really in those bandit days, for I was cattle-ranching in Sonora – just got started in fact as a real young one."

He glanced sideways at Juan and saw disappointment there, so said, "A cousin of mine was with him though," and that took the disappointment away.

"A *dorado*?" the boy pumped him eagerly, face lighting up.

"Sí, one of – what's his name? – one of Villa's dorados. Surrendered with him to Obregón in – oh 1920 I think it was," giving everyone a brigandish look.

"Who is Obregón?" chimed in Julia.

"Why he was the *presidente* at that time, my poppy."

"That's very interesting," enthused Juan. "About Villa, I mean."

"Sí. and three years later he got himself killed. Assassinated. Hmm."

"Assassinated, what's that?" Julia wormed in again.

"Your cousin got himself killed?" asked Ruth, picking a fly out of her tea.

"No-o, Villa. Pancho Villa," and Juan wanted to know who did the dirty deed. "The *federales* of course who killed him. Uuy, they had no trust in Pancho Villa you see. But it comes to us all I dare to say. ¡Carajo! And what a man he was."

Little Julia made an '*Ooo!*' sound in mock horror, eyes wide and round as the '*Ooo!*' moulded by her mouth.

"He was a bandit, an outlaw," put in mamá. "Something like you Pancho, you rogue and rascal!"

Young Juan was tickled over his hero being called a bandit, and it was Ruth who then said, "He's a ranchero, mamá."

"Ha! It amounts to the same thing doesn't it?" countered her mother, smiling down on Pancho who was veritably fluffing up like a peacock in his pride. He blew out his cheeks, expanded his keg-like chest – the reed chair creaked alarmingly – squinted his eyes and villainously grinned at all around him.

Don Antonio offered his guest more pulque which the other readily accepted. ";Salud!" and the drink went down very well in the drinking man's considered opinion.

The family chattered and ate in a general mood of well-being, hands continually whiffling at the flies. Julia tittered behind the smoke-screen cover of a tortilla as she watched the steady progress of a fly sucking at chicken grease dribbling down Pancho's jaw. He tore a leg to pieces and noisily chomped away, gnawing like a hound on the bone, meat and sinew sliding between teeth and tongue.

Mamá hovered by, eyes watchful and manner attentive, secretly astonished and pleased at the old ranchero's voracious appetite. She clasped hands before her, bobbed and bounced on her heels with pleasure. A fresh chorale of birdsong entertained the gathering, in harmony with the music coming from the pueblo over the way.

"What would you say to a drop more pulque?"

"I'd say it's an offer I couldn't hardly refuse, compadre. Sí, gracias."

Don Antonio almost gave way to a grin, but settled instead for a weak and polite smile, as the other cleared food debris from between his teeth and smacked his lips.

";Salud!" he sandpapered, and down gushed the Mexican beer.

His host poured again with solemn graciousness, while mamá fetched fresh dishes of tasty morsels and put them before the indefatigable diner. Pancho ploughed on stuffing and cramming, near choking on the pulque as he chugged it down, moustache white with froth. To general approval a loud belch erupted from him, echoed from the rafters.

"Try these tamales," urged mamá. "Juanito suggested I make them for you – Papacito, you're slow today," putting a hand affectionately on her husband's shoulder.

"Rutí, just look at señor Ramírez!" sniggered Julia artlessly, nudging her sister in the side, and referring to his hair sticking up in all directions as if he'd been electrocuted, the red of it on fire as it were with the sunlight full on him. They also noticed – children don't miss much when it comes to observing adults – noticed too his ears jumping up and down as he chewed, jaws jumping like a jackrabbit's, and his moustache white like cotton wool.

"I shall laugh if I look again."

"You shouldn't laugh at all, it's rude."

"But I can't help it…"

"And what are you two chuntering at?" mamá enquired, suddenly appearing behind the girls and wagging her head. They confessed it was nothing in particular, and mamá told them to eat up and be good, or they would know soon enough what was good for them *in particular*.

The object of their mirth nonchalantly tossed half a tamale into his open mouth and washed it down with pulque. A wasp had the temerity to settle on his steaming dish, and Ruth obligingly reached over and gently fanned it away.

"A drop more perhaps, my friend?" don Antonio asked with splendid dignity. His guest gave thanks, but voiced his wondering if the other wished to hog it all for himself.

The table was by now a devastation of torn tortillas, bits of onion, chicken bones, squeezed lemons, chilli and tomato seeds. The family chattered away gaily like sparrows in spring. And Pancho was getting more tipsy, merry and loquacious by the minute.

And music continued drifting over from the pueblo for the enjoyment of all.

10

Impromptu Dance

"There was a time up Durango way once – " Pancho was saying to Juan, after a first quick wary glance at don Antonio out the corner of his eye.

"Another tamale. Cristina?"

"Gracias, mamá."

"I'm feeling full to the top," reported Julia, and Ruth confirmed of the same condition. "Can I leave the table now, por favor?"

"You can stay put for the present, my niña, we've a guest."

" – and this nosy priest came along," Pancho pattered on, touching Juan's knee and winking, "and this priest, he says to me: 'Well, my good fellow, and how long have you been working here on the ranch?' Ah, and wouldn't you like to know, I thought to myself. Ay que caray, I looked up at the sun and then at the man of cloth, and said to him, 'Oh, it must be getting on for three hours now, *padre*,'" and the old ranchero threw back his head and rolled off a mighty bellowing guffaw, fit to wake Juan's dog lying at his feet.

"Don't listen to his tales, Juanito," advised doña María, "he can talk the wheels off a waggon and still make no sense – common sense, that is."

"You are too kind, María. There is a way to make friends, you know, and that's to be one yourself."

"Ha! There he goes again talking common *nonsense*!"

At that moment the popular *El Cuartelazo* was sounding off in the pueblo. This lively bouncy *corridor* stormed loud and clear over the heads of the family gathering. Pancho could not have been presented with a better opportunity. With surprising agility – considering what he'd consumed and at his age – he went cat-wise to Ruth and whisked the girl from her seat.

"¡Baile! A dance! Dance!" he shouted, holding her hand in his great fist and leading her away from the table.

"Oho!" laughed mamá, then told Cristina to quickly run and fetch her guitar.

The old man stood like a monument over Ruth. He raised long arms high and smartly clapped hands. "¡Ahua!" he cried the cry of Mexico, and his spatula paws enclosed the girl's rounded shoulders, and they began to dance.

Pancho's left foot slewed across the dust and slapped into his right – a stomp! Then the right foot skimmed over to meet the other – stomp! Round and round they went, dust boiling up around their knees. His ungainly figure spun dizzily, revolving around his partner with jerks of his massive shoulders.

Meantime, Cristina returned with her guitar, and expert fingers immediately started playing the strings, creating a lively atmosphere of gaiety. The dance now really got under way as Pancho stomped about, raising small clouds of dust.

"¡Ahua!" he roared, lifting himself springily like a playful bear, whirling and pivoting round Ruth, the family beating time by clapping hands or thumping on the table: Clap! – Clap! – Clap! "¡Ahua!" and up came the knees, up came the dust.

Julia's face was a study in ecstatic and irrepressible delight as she followed the movement of the dancers with theatre-glitz eyes. She very soon realised however that she was not herself in the limelight, not the centre of attraction, which needed putting right at once. So, on a daring impulse, the tenderling bobbed up from her stool. Catching the contagious spirit of the melody, she began to tap a *zapateado*, the Spanish tap dance. To the child's credit she acquitted herself with remarkable skill and verve, dust spuming up around her as she smacked the courtyard earth with tiny feet. Hopeful eyes sought the table to see if her efforts were acknowledged and appreciated. And such was the case, for mamá encouragingly wagged her head, beaming with pride, and Julia gained further confidence from this. Her dainty feet pattered faster with inexpressible naturalness.

Cristina twanged heavily away at the guitar strings as though her life was forfeit were she to do otherwise. The dog nosed purposely toward a tempting bone lying near Pancho's feet, then hastily backed off as the old man turned, its paws padding with remarkable time to the beat.

"¡Ayii! ¡Ahua!" voiced Pancho joyfully, the beat even faster now with quickening strains of the music.

"Pick your feet up, Pancho!" laughed mamá, "else you'll drill yourself into the ground."

"Can't help it, María!" he bellowed over from a storm of dust. "Weighed down with your good food I am!"

"Ha! Pulque more like, I would say," retorted the cook. "Digging yourself a hole there, is it?"

There were two possible things he could do, he was thinking; quit now while the going was good, or quit now while the going was good, either choice was appealing and desirable – maybe even necessary.

"Well – Excuse me, Rutí – I've had my share of food and drink, and this dancing bit too I reckon," he puffed, out of breath at last. And it was a sheer fluke that he quit there and then, just as the music did. Only the dust continued on, swirling and dancing about him.

Pancho stayed overnight at the Ramos family's homely farmstead, sleeping on a bed of straw in a cornstore next to a henhouse, with rats in the rafters for company.

Early in the morning of the following day it rained hard and healthily for a couple of hours, which certainly settled the dust for a while, but also broke the drought – a great sigh of relief at this from the country folk.

Welcome news for Juan. Mamá and papá agreed to his staying the whole summer on the horse ranch where Pancho worked. Mamá set about getting her son's things together in readiness for the journey, interspersed with many words of advice on how he should behave among the rough rancheros.

Young Juan could hardly wait to get away.

BOOK II

Summer Tales

Part Three

Part Three

11

El Rancho

"Go easy with that mount, José!" roared Pancho. "He's a reasonable saddler so you don't have to act crazy with him. Ease off, for kindness sake."

A hot malignant sun flared down on the rancheros at don Roberto's *hacienda*. Freshly arrived horses, in the stables and out in sunswamped corrals, were skitterish and irritable, bothered by flies, heat, and their new surrounds. The mounts stamped and snorted, milling about in clouds of dust. An entire morning was spent in sorting out this mixed cavvy of nervous restless animals, mostly duns, bays and a few sorrels. Now it was near noon and the men too were worn down and beginning to feel angry misgivings over this latest draft of horses.

"Take it easy, hombre!" the old man repeated to the rider.

The horseman José ignored him, as was his habit, impetuously urging his mount on with tight rein, biting spurs, and harshly plied whip. Away he went galloping off through the corral gates, leaving a wake of billowing dust.

"God alive! How he burns the wind," commented Cándido, a young man leaning indolently against the corral fencing. "Why does he bother? Whipping the hell out of the beast. That sorrel's okay, you tested him yourself."

"Ay, *amigo*, the poorer the rider the bigger the whip. And it's a wasted spur that's used on a willing horse. He'll learn a lesson one of these days, our José will."

"He's too damned impatient by half, if you ask me. That's his trouble."

"You're maybe right. A little patience is what he needs. Patience and an acorn will make a wooden table – Ah, you're ready at last, Gerardo," the old man threw at another ranchero. "Get on then, and get a grip, you're like a one-armed blind-man." He turned to Cándido. "He's so slow and sluggish, like a drift of dust. He's like a thread-worn screw going round and round in circles and getting nowhere."

"Not getting to grips with things?"

"That's what I mean, sí – Get on then, Gerardo!"

"He's a fair tryer is that one – the mount I'm meaning," commented Cándido, squinting unhandsomely in the harsh glare of sunlight.

"Sí, I know…"

"Gerardo will undo all of that, I reckon."

"Sí, I know that too."

"Look to your cinch," Cándido cautioned the other rider. "It's half hanging off, looks like." He turned a grinning face to Pancho, said, "What's the betting he'll be off and biting dust before the day's a minute older."

"I reckon he will at that," agreed Pancho. "Gerardo has fallen from his horse more often than I've had hot beans – ¡Oye, hermano! A double rig is what you want right now. Didn't I already tell you so?"

"It's only some slack," growled Gerardo. "Too damn long by far. Here, Emilio, out of my way there, por favor," as he nearly rode down a fat heavyset man crossing the corral, leading a rare placid dun by its bridle.

José came charging back in a swelter of boiling dust. He sharply neck-reined his mount to a shuddering halt only inches from the old man's nose.

"A right ridge runner is that one!" laughed Pancho, pulling at his moustache.

"You call that thing a wild stallion?" grumbled Gerardo.

"I don't mean the horse," grinned Pancho. "I mean him – José."

"His fast ride in has upset my mount as well," said the other. "I say, José, my horse is spooked enough without you adding to it."

"He's not listening," Cándido told him.

"The lone, quiet hombre," said Pancho by way of explanation.

"I'd love to boot him right up the backside," grumped Gerardo lowly.

"He'll get a kick out of that," quipped the old man.

A sudden hot wind came on and ransacked the corral with the arrogance of an Alexandrian army. A string of horses tethered to posts began rearing heads and restlessly pawing the ground. The wind died as suddenly as it had come, leaving a smoke of dust in the air.

"Your cinch is loose," Emilio informed Gerardo.

"It's okay," returned the other.

The fat man amiably regarded horse and rider, said, "Well, if you don't fall off you'll get thrown off, is all I can say."

"I was once thrown by a blue roan," confessed Cándido, "on the very outer edge of a deep *barranca –*"

"Bring out the claybank, Julian!" yelled Pancho, amid a commotion of many nervous horses neighing and crashing down hooves. "No, not that way, *muchacho*. The end stable. Sí, this way. ¡Bueno!"

"I'll bring him out for you, señor," tinkled Julian, a thin youth with a girlish voice and a simple smile on his face.

"Fall into that barranca did you, Cándido?" asked José with hopeful malice.

"If he did," said Gerardo grudgingly, "I bet he landed on his feet. He always does."

"No, I was alright," continued Cándido, "because I was thrown from the *other* side."

"Fell into a nice thorny cactus as I recall," grinned Pancho, "and got himself punctured in all the wrong places – That right, amigo?"

"You needn't have told them that bit," scowled 'amigo'.

"Ha! So that was it, hey?" said José with a satisfied smirk.

"Don't you fall asleep there, Emilio," warned the old man. "I want you on the claybank. Cándido here reckons he paddles."

"Like he's wearing flippers," smiled the young man, his good humour instantly restored.

"What's he mean?" asked Gerardo gloomily.

"Splays his forefeet out, like," explained José, removing saddle and blanket from his mount. "A bit like the way you walk, hombre, like a cross-eyed duck."

"Only one cross-eyed here," said Pancho, glancing at Cándido.

"You want me to take the yellow dun?" said Emilio. "I thought Gerardo was going to try him."

"What's fit for the pot is fit for the pan," returned Pancho genially.

He glanced up at the high noon blaze, as a dust-devil whiffled over the ground behind him, then said : "Okay, *mi compañeros*, we've done enough for the present, I'll warrant. We can take a short one, eh?"

The men at once broke into a small stampede, dashing out of the unrelenting glare of the sun-exposed corral to the welcome shade within the main stable. They slapped dust off their *chaparreras* and sank wearily onto straw bales, hands flapping at flies about them.

12

Los Rancheros

Pancho remained for a time in the corral under a flood of light. His eyes strayed upward once more and caught on a hawk in the high clear air, far in the distance and moving so slowly that it appeared as if pinned to the blue backdrop of sky. He dropped his gaze and turned to look at the men through the wide stable doorway; and the milkspot pigments in the blue of his eyes seemed to glint with some secret amusement.

At last the old man gimped into the shade of the stable, squatted nimbly on his hunkers before a rough semi-circle of rancheros, and began to roll gently forward and back on toes and heels. He turned slightly to one side and blew his nose between two fingers to clear dust from there. He continually rocked back and forth on his heels as he inwardly ruminated over his work compatriots, in his mind assessing and nit-picking as it were at their individual traits and personalities.

The rancheros on don Roberto's hacienda, like most of their breed, were lean and wiry men, and swarthy of face – except for Emilio who was none of these things. Pancho's glance fell first on the young man Cándido, who was blowing dust from his saddle, a typical Mexican rig with high pommel and cantle. As he lovingly stroked the highly polished dark leather of his saddle, an intent expression on his face accentuated striking squints he had in his nut-brown eyes – one could be cruel and perhaps more accurately say that he was cross-eyed – though he was nevertheless a handsome looking fellow in spite of the drawback flaw. His squinting eyes actually attracted rather than repelled the females, endeared him to their soft sensibilities. A greater attraction – and asset – was that he possessed like Pancho a lively sense of humour, perhaps more droll and surreal than the old man's. Cándido had idiosyncratic tendencies, outlandish imaginings, uncanny thoughts on anything and everything.

Pancho's scrutiny moved on to Gerardo, an altogether different sort; fussy and finicky and always fidgeting, sensitive to criticism, prone to hypochondria. He had a kind of rubbery, mobile face, the countenance of a toad or an ugly-looking thick featured comedian. It was fleshy and doughy as if you could make a large dumpling out of it. It could be turned and twisted, shaped and moulded into many expressions – mostly sad or sorry – simply by whatever might be going through his head at any time. He could mimic ugliness and coarseness to an extraordinary high degree. In a word, he was not a pretty sight. With tongue out to one side of his mouth, Gerardo sat plaiting some rawhide strips.

The fat man next caught Pancho's roving eye. Emilio was neither wiry nor swarthy, as already noted. His chubby countenance with its open friendly look, showed a clear olive complexion, like a young woman's. He would have appeared handsome too but for a certain unfortunate flaw, seen when he opened his mouth. Emilio had large buck teeth that would make a foal envious. He lounged far back on his bale of straw, his recumbent form stretched out like a beach-stranded whale; and about to doze off, which was one of his abiding characteristics.

José was an inscrutable type, a dark horse, as he would like others to believe. He liked to be regarded as a man of mystery, the lone silent hombre, as Pancho earlier put it, and, moreover, one not to be meddled with. He was an angular, chisel-chinned man, hard-faced and mean-eyed. When he looked at anyone it was with a hot-eyed, resentful, smouldering gaze. As Cándido once commented, José with a stare or a scowl could scare the skin off a snake. Jose rarely had much to say, as though needing to keep any feelings or thoughts to himself. And, as the old man knew only too well, José had a fiery temper and could be dangerous when angrily aroused. With elbows resting on knobbly knees bulging under his tight-fitted *pantalones*, José's fingers scrabbled in the depths of his tobacco pouch, like a family of mice raiding a kitchen larder. He rolled himself an extra fat *cigarro*, a reward for a morning's good work.

Pancho's sea-blue eyes softened as they rested finally on young Julian, but all he could actually see was the top half head of the youth, eyes peeping innocently over a bale of straw, his nose resting on the edge of it. Julian was a simpleton, employed as stable-hand. His was a pure and simple soul; a harmless sweet-natured fool. He was at any rate remarkably clever in his handling of horses. He regarded the animals under his care as fellow human beings; conversing freely with them, decidedly one way of course, speaking in soft quiet reassuring tones. The four-legged creatures somehow understood him, certainly they always felt reassured. Julian got along with his horses far better than he ever could with any person, though he was often successful in his many dealings with señor Pancho. And the simple soul would do anything for the men, and was considered by them their general run-around errand-boy.

The rancheros customarily ate their meals out in the open around a cook-fire. They would sit and eat their supper and watch the sun go down, and chatter on through the dusk and later darkness.

A circle of light around the campfire kept its shape by the heavy fall of darkness surrounding it, giving the men an impression they were sitting in a room of full curved walls. Long shadows danced about them as they moved within the compass of this circle. The fire flared up when fresh sticks of wood caught the flames, lighting their faces. The light dimmed again as the fire settled down to a steady red-orange glow. If a man averted his gaze from the fire for a while, he would see milky-mist shapes of trees, tethered saddle-horses, and the oblong grey mass of the stables. Out of the circle, even on a moonless night, a man might see far horizons, dimly contoured and defined just so by starlight.

Sometimes, angry red sparks jumped up, whirling upward with the heat draught, mingling for a few moments with the stars in the sky, or so it seemed, like fine ruby chippings mixed among diamond dust.

It was a kind of comfort to the men in hearing the familiar spit and crack and hiss of burning wood on the fire, and the occasional pop of boiling sap bursting from the flames. After a usual basic supper of beans and tortillas were heated on the fire, it was kept burning to keep away mosquitoes, to supply light to see by, as a focus point upon which to rest their eyes.

Later, after an evening of idle nattering among themselves, the men then prepared for a good night's sleep. It was customary during the summer months – a point of tradition in fact – for the rancheros to sleep outdoors under the stars, rather than be cooped up in the stifling stuffiness of the bunkhouse. The bunkhouse was far too small for them at any rate, except during a cold winter's night when they found it suitable to lie huddled close together, like puppies in a basket.

Gerardo, the finicky one, was always in the habit of collecting cornstraw from one of the stables, on which to lay his sleeping blanket for a more comfortable repose. The others by and large preferred the hardness of the ground, to sleep on mother Earth herself, as man had done for millennia. But Gerardo appeared uncannily to pick the wrong spot from which to draw his night-straw. The bedding straw he chose was invariably far from fragrant, lying in an almost smoky stink of dung and horse-piss. He did not in the least seem to mind, nor the others for that matter.

So the hardy horsemen ranged themselves about the dying embers of the fire, to take their well-earned night-time rest, sleeping under the silent star-showered heavens.

13

Juan's Arrival

One early evening when the last day of May melted into June, the boy Juan Ramos arrived on the hacienda of don Roberto. Riding his chestnut bay, Chapulín, saddlebags heavy with study books on the horse's flanks. The huge wolfhound-sheepdog – named Salté – as usual for this great beast, trotted on ahead in his inimical high-stepping style.

The boy was as intended to stay with the rancheros for the entire summer, and was expected by them. The men greeted him with whoops and *charro* yelps. Juan felt a rush of heat on his cheeks, but it was a warming glow, as there was mixed with embarrassment a little too of pride.

Old Pancho stumped forward and hugged the boy with bear-like arms. The lost-wit Julian quietly took Chapulín away to be stabled, brushed down and fed. And later, Juan enjoyed his first outdoor supper round the nightfire, as he knew the American cowboys had done in the Old West of the 1870s and '80s.

So here he was at last sitting with real rancheros and sharing their food, it being the normal beans and tortillas; which he would eat every single day, though never tire of them, as long as there were hot chillies or *salsa* to go with them. In his present state of excitement and happiness he raised eyes to a softlight evening sky where a half-phased moon hung palely. To the right of it was the sharp gleam of planet Venus, a hard bright unwinking light. As the youngster's gaze moved on to this familiar evening star, he may in his mind have silently blessed the Toltec god Quetzalcoatl who, among other things, was god of this star, and the morning star – the same planet Venus, also called Hesperus, as the boy had only recently learned from his study books.

That same night young Juan slept out in the open, under the black heavens where silver-coloured stars pulsated on their slowly orbiting galaxy trail. Before he could compose himself for sleep, he exulted in ineffable joy and wonderment, listening to new night sounds : the hooting call of a barn-owl and the pleasant flute-sounding piping of a night plover, the short rapid yelp of a coyote in the near foothills, and the sighing of a soft nightwind eating its way through scrubland. Nearby, was the homely sounds of the saddle-horses chomping feed in nosebags and stamping a hoof; and Gerardo – or was it José? – thunderously snoring away in sleep.

For the boy the language of these coming summer days was heat and light, space and dust – and flies. He would develop a deeper understanding of the equine species, a love of the rugged landscape, an exhilarating sense of freedom and a newfound independence. These times on the ranchlands with the horsemen would prove the happiest and most fulfilling that Juan would ever know.

14

Morning Awakening

Next morning, as a swarm of flies whining about his face woke him, Juan felt fully refreshed, though somewhat disorientated at first by his novel surrounds. He glanced upward. There was the broad, boldly-blue sky, boasting of its own vastness, its clearness, its beautiful blue, and with not a single cloud in sight.

And there appeared to be no one about at ground level, as he took his morning ablutions at the water-butt behind the bunkhouse. After a hasty cat-lick of a wash his mamá would never approve of, he wandered over to the corral and stables.

" ¡Oye, Juanito!" Pancho greeted him jovially. "*Buenos días, mi compañero. ¿Que paso?*" as he sidled from out one of the stables. "The muchachos are away rounding up the horses," he continued on in rasping tones, "which have been out grazing all night – except for this lot in here. They shouldn't be long I expect, as them beasts tend to herd up close like brothers you might say. Though there's one or two, meaning the dun and that damned speckled-grey and they will go wandering off on their own like explorers. Hmm. A devil of a job it is sometimes to find them and steals away your time. Well, *amiguito*, did you sleep okay?" and gently shook the boy's hand in the customary Mexican manner, leaning towards him, smelling of leather and straw and dust.

"Tulia will be giving Julian our breakfast to bring over shortly I expect, and then we can eat – soon as the muchachos return of course and they won't be long now."

"Tulia?"

"Ah, have you forgotten her, then? Sí, don Roberto's cook and housekeeper. A real treasure she is too, takes care of us like our own natural mother − 'Pancho! Wash behind your ears now!'" mimicking Tulia at her best. "A good sort she is − ¡Oye! Is that you in there, Julian? I'd say it's time now to look sharp. Collect the grub, my favourite sunray, ándale!" in his accustomed gentle tone of command when speaking to the half-witted youth.

"I go this moment, señor Pancho," returned the simpleton with a smile, peeping out sideways from a stable door.

"Ah, what timing, the boys are coming now, look," as a thunder of hoofbeats broke the morning silence and a largish dust-cloud rolled towards them.

The old man opened the corral gates. And there appeared the windflayed range-hardened rancheros, cracking whips and yelling commands as they expertly corralled the horses, almost choking in a smoke of dust twenty hands high about them. They were used to it and quite enjoying themselves, each with a wide grin on dust-plastered face.

The boy Juan took in the scene as though savouring an exquisite wine. He watched it all as he stood enthralled, transfixed, like a sun-stunned post.

15

A Question of Religion

In no time at all the horsemen were tucking hungrily into a breakfast of mashed *frijoles* – or beans – and warm tortillas, with wedges of watermelon on the side, washed down with a jug of pulque which was passed from man to man. They grinned rather foolishly, apparently not knowing how to open up with the boy in their presence. But it was obvious to Juan that the men were content after their early morning spell of riding, leathern faces and clothes thick with dirt and dust. They appeared not unlike a gang of kids who have momentarily stopped play in a mud-pit.

"So, hermanos," grated Pancho amicably, and he clicked his teeth and winked a merry blue eye at the boy by his side, "you managed to get up in good time this morning, eh?"

"*Con razon* – small wonder – " said José stiffly, "what with Gerardo here keeping us awake half the night with his infernal snoring. Like a hog with a cold in its head."

"You can talk!" glowered Gerardo. "It's you who does all the snoring around here. They can hear you from over the *casa* itself. Night after night you're at it, the very ground shaking with it."

"I'd swear you're as bad as one another," put in Pancho, "with your noisy snoring habits. And it's only because you lie on your backs, that's what does it you know."

"Hey, just a moment," clipped in Cándido, giving a cockeyed side wink at Juan, "you yourself sleep on your back, I've seen you."

The old man sighed a weary sigh. "Sure I do to start off I do, and can't deny it, I must own. But I soon turn over on my side, right side as a matter of fact – to rest my heart you see and take the pressure off it. If you sleep on your side you'll hardly ever or even be able to start up snoring, take my word for it. As for myself, I slept like a top last night."

"Top of what?" queried Cándido.

Pancho sighed again. "A spinning top is what I'm meaning."

"But a spinning top goes whizzing round and round," said Emilio, having just come out of a light doze.

"I know, I know," agreed the old man testily, "but haven't you ever noticed when it gets going, nicely balanced on some flat surface, you'd hardly think it was moving at all. Like it was sleeping, and that's how the saying came about you see. It's how I slept, how I always sleep, like a top in other words. It goes without saying, doesn't it, that —"

"I slept like a log," interrupted Emilio with a smile, showing his large teeth.

"And you nearly burned like one as well," Pancho sang out sardonically, "for you rolled over onto the fire. Smothered and killed it dead, hmm."

"Oye, don't hog the tortillas, Emilio, you fat greedy lout!" spat José.

"Alright, don't get so all-fired steamed up, José, you puffing locomotive! You young warhorse!" soothed Pancho with a wide conciliatory grin, "there are plenty to go round, more than you think in that pile there." He put on his pious look and went on : "A bit like the story in the New Testament, eh? You know, the feeding of the multitude."

Cándido cut in then on cue : "Imagine it if Our Lord Jesus had been born in Mexico, how different the New Testament would be — the miracles for instance. At the feeding of the five thousand —"

"What's he on about?"

"You mean the feeding of the *four* thousand don't you?" gainsaid Gerardo.

"Five thousand men, besides women and children," broke in Emilio, reaching for another tortilla.

"Sí, he's right," verified Pancho, unable to resist putting in his oar too. "After John the Baptist lost his head on Herod's birthday, as I seem to remember. The *four* thousand you speak of, Gerardo, wasn't that a time later? When Jesus went up into a mountain near the sea of Galilee. Hmm, I'm pretty sure that's how it was."

"You trying to rewrite the Bible, Pancho?" José wanted to know.

"That's what I mean," said Cándido with more conviction, "the feeding of the five thousand, as I said. Well, instead of Jesus having only five fishes and two loaves to dish out —"

An argument was in the air. "No, no!" groused Gerardo with some heat. "Get it right, hombre. It was *seven* loaves of bread and a *few* fishes."

"That was at the feeding of the *four* thousand," Pancho punctured him.

"Are you talking – " began Gerardo.

José lifted a fistful of chaff and flung it at Gerardo, though everybody caught an eyeful. "Just clearing the air," he explained with a titter, and let loose a gobbet of spit.

"Are you talking about the four thousand, hombre, or are you meaning the five thousand, which is it?" asked Gerardo grouchily and heating up like a noonday sun. His ugly face puckered into a repellent shape.

"The five thousand of course as I told you," Cándido confirmed.

"Besides women and children," Emilio could not help adding.

" ¡Claro! You've got it," said Cándido. "Now can I get on? And so Jesus is a Mexican you follow, and when He has to feed the multitude instead of the five fishes and two loaves of bread –"

"Sorry, Cándido," ventured young Juan with a grin, "but it was five loaves and two fishes."

"Was it? ¡Bueno! Right! So instead of that Jesus being a Mexican and all, He hands out five tortillas and a dish of frijoles. And – Shut it Gerardo before you start off again, and just listen – and at that wedding when the ruler of the feast in Cana of Galilee tastes the water from the water-pots, well, he doesn't taste water. Neither does he taste wine –"

"I bet it's tequila," gambled Gerardo.

"No, it'll be *mescal*," said Emilio.

" – instead, he'll taste pulque!" Cándido continued cockily. "And when Jesus tells Peter to go fishing, and Peter casts his hook and comes up with a fish, he won't find a shekel in its mouth but a silver peso!"

"I know there're many versions of the Bible," said Pancho, "but I have never heard of a version that's as *loco* as yours, muchacho. Ay que caray dear God, what will your straw-brain be scheming up next I wonder."

"Can't you imagine it though?" cried Cándido. "Jesus Himself wandering over don Roberto's land for forty days and forty nights."

"Done that a few times myself," Pancho put in.

"And preaching to the multitude…"

"Oh, you mean the don's steers and horses – there's a multitude of them alright."

"Not them, he means the fleas on Emilio," said Gerardo with gleeful malice.

The fat man retorted that he could at least get along with his fleas, if he had fleas in the first place, and not like the other who he considered a miserable excuse for a rat's tail, and too ugly by far. Pancho was glad that Emilio could feel comfortable enough with his fleas – if he had them of course – but that he personally wouldn't entertain them on any account.

"Anyway, I'm not ugly," said Gerardo, "I'm what you'd call 'rugged'."

"Ragged?"

"You heard me. At any rate I wouldn't wish to be like you, I'm happy in my own skin, thank you very much."

"Well said, compañero," Pancho praised him. "We each have our own unique identity."

José spied a cockroach scuttling over a scrap of dung lying between his feet. "Damn you, devil!" he hissed, and crushed the large insect under the heel of his boot.

"Feel better now, hermano?" asked the old ranchero with heavy sarcasm, giving the other a direct condemnatory stare.

"¡Chihuahuas!" chipped in Cándido, "Have you thought what would happen if fleas were as big as cockroaches? Why, they'd be – " He stopped there, sensing a change of mood among the men. He fast realised that he was running along an unknown passageway which could only lead to a dead-end.

"Grab him, muchachos!" cried Pancho. "Throw him in the damned gorsebrush, and that'll be a thorny tale to tell."

But the young man was too fast for them. He was on his feet instantly and haring off. The men gave chase, but would never catch Cándido, Pancho wagered, were they to run after him the whole day through.

16

On the Range 1

It was a splendid summer day, a typical day in fact for this time of the season. Dry and clear and pleasantly warm. No sign of cloud until late forenoon. Then from over the long serrated line of the western *cordillera* came a straggly platoon of cotton-white columns of cloud. They came slowly marching across the blue expanse of this high and wide sky. Followed later by larger rolls of cloud, battalion by separate battalion striding on in slow time, eventually clumping into one mighty mass of blue-white blue-grey ranks, white-tipped on the topmost layers. Blocking out the blue. Passing over and on silently with the Earth's high wind.

Then these ranks broke up again by noon or soon after, scattered far and wide as though routed by an unseen enemy. They stretched and streamed across the sky into long thin streaks, like threads of cotton combed along in one direction. A cavalry of cloud now, smartly groomed in a uniform of silver-white and a whitish blue, with plumes and pennants as it were proudly flying.

On the land small winds stirred, creating coquettish dust-devils, swirling and eddying dustclouds dancing here disappearing there; a slight obscurity in the clarity of the air the only sign that they ever appeared at all.

But these splendours of nature were barely noticed by the rancheros as they rode with a cavvy of thoroughbred saddle-horses over sun-seared dusty grassland.

Pancho rode his favourite mount, a strong white mare named Macha.

The old man sat loosely and comfortably in the saddle, fists resting on the pommel, holding the rein. He appeared a different man on a horse, somehow taller and with a certain element of grandeur.

"Don't herd them there, Gerardo," he called over. "Let them loosen out, amigo, they know where they want to go."

He watched a chestnut mare wander off on her own, followed by her foal trotting a little way behind, its ungainly, awkward, soft-boned long-leggedness amusing the boy Juan, by Pancho's side. The foal veered to right and left, repeating the manoeuvre as though it wanted to catch as much as possible of its mother's scent.

Presently Pancho and Juan reined their horses to a sedate walk, and they began to relax to enjoy the moment, following the herd with keen eyes as it fractured and spread out to placidly graze in their own favoured spots. The old ranchero leaned forward slightly, large hands on the saddle-bow, and finally came to a halt, the boy doing the same.

"Now, you see the blood bay stallion to your left?" he drawled in muted tones. "Sí, that one looking our way – blessed if he knows I'm talking about him – Well, he's a real good eater is that big fellow. You know, Juanito, he must drop – oh, something like fifteen kilos of dung in a day. Why, I tell you no lie but I reckon he could bury you in a week, if you're following what I'm saying."

The old one went on to say how the beasts spend most of the time eating and what a pity it was that horses are not meat-eaters.

"Why's that then?" asked the youngster interestedly.

"Well, they wouldn't need so much time grazing would they? There's a lot more food value in meat than there is in this dry grass. Of course we treat them now and then with carrots and special feed. My Macha is rather partial to chocolate you know, but I don't overly spoil her with that, oh no, if I can't have it, neither can she – Ah see what he's up to, the devil! Look, didn't I say he was some eater, eh?"

"But that's dung he's eating isn't it?" said Juan in surprise.

"Sí, dropped a week ago I'd guess, when they were last here."

"Isn't that dangerous though, eating old dung?"

"For you maybe, if you fancy it and I hope you don't."

No, not for a moment for a horse the old man assured him, meditatively stroking his moustache. It won't do the animal any harm at all. In point of fact it will more likely pick up some nutritious minerals there that it would not normally find in grass-feed.

"Hmm. I'm keeping a beady eye on the grey one – in front of the stallion, you see him? He's two years come this autumn. Quietly grazing there, minding his own business you'd think. Only I know for sure he's got an eye on us too. He knows we're here alright, not so daft isn't that one I'd wager."

It was one reason why horses like him have survived from earliest ancient times, Pancho explained to the boy. It can eat its food and graze the land while at the same time keep a wary eye out for predators – the real meat eaters. It is the distance between his eyes and mouth. That long head of his serves a good purpose, the old ranchero hoped the other appreciated the fact.

"He's also long-headed because of his teeth. He has forty-four of them, the horse does. Quite a mouthful, and has to make room for them. And all that grinding while he's grazing must wear his teeth down, which in fact is the case. But while a tooth is wearing away at one end it's growing still at the other."

"Those horses yonder," observed the boy, "in different groups but all facing the same way. Amazing…"

"Ah, you've noticed that, eh? They've all got their backsides to the breeze." Pancho wet his forefinger, stuck it in the air. "Sí, just as I thought. They can see ahead and to left and right, but can't see behind. The wind wafts scents to them. If they catch an alien scent then they become alert to any possible danger."

He leaned over Macha's withers as though he wanted to whisper to his dear and treasured mare. "Isn't that so, my sweet beauty!" he said endearingly, the boy smiling at them both.

The wind became garrulous, making its intrusive presence known, moaning here and howling there, like a spoilt obnoxious kid not getting its own way, and continually blowing up the dust in gusty tantrums over the light-drenched sunbaked land.

"Shall we move on a little?"

As the mounts loped on the old ranchero and the boy were silent for a while, listening as if to music the squeaking and creaking of leather, the tinkling and jingling of snaffles, soft thudding of hooves and occasional clatter when going over rock or shale. Also, the ubiquitous droning and humming of summer insects, and the odd explosive thunder when one of the horses broke wind.

Pancho rose in the stirrups and looked about him periscope-wise.

"Ay, Juanito, the marvels of nature, eh? Ay que caray, she makes the world and is the world…"

17

On the Range 2

A time later as the two still observed the grazing horses, Juan felt the dust-scented wind on his face.

"I can hear the wind," he said quietly, "like it's talking to me. Can you hear it?"

"Ah sí mi compañero," returned Pancho, "I hear it alright…"

The old horseman spoke on in low tones, of how the land speaks in the voice of these high plateau winds, and to listen to the wind is to hear what the land is saying. That the Wind, like his brother Water, is Time's stone-cutter, Time's sculptor; and his song is in the trees and grasses.

"Birds too, I can hear their calls," said the boy.

"Ay Juanito, the swallows and martins. You know, it's in man's vanity to have him think that birdsong is for his ears only. When a bird calls it's letting you know its territory or defending its young. Maybe it's attracting a mate or calling danger or making a battle-cry. Birds are not around solely for our benefit, that's for certain. Besides, they were flying about and mating and reproducing their species long before man came on the scene."

A time passed. Pancho was beginning to think his young charge was altogether too quiet, so unlike a boy. "Are you missing your sisters?" he asked him.

Juan smiled. "No, I don't think I am," he admitted a little ruefully. "I'm very happy for some reason, glad to be here and I couldn't say why. It's just the way I feel I suppose."

"Ah, so that's it…" said Pancho mutedly. "I miss my little girls, you know, after all these years – and my dearest wife as well, God bless their souls in Heaven," crossing himself with utter sincerity.

Pancho faltered, his eyes moistened; there had been a catch in his throat, a tremor in his voice. Juan saw pain in those blue eyes and it was clear that his friend found this distressing. He instinctively reached over a hand and gripped the old man's shoulder. Thus assured that life was good yet and compassion still around, the ranchero shook his head as though to ward off any further incursions of sorrow. He felt a whole lot better and smiled a touchingly sad but serene kind of smile, and gave a grateful glance at the sensitive-minded boy at his side.

When his children had passed away one after the other, he was able to relate now in stronger tones, he had cried many bitter tears. For those poor muchachas to waste away of a horrible disease was too much for him to bear. It was all over in only a matter of a few weeks, his entire family gone. It is no shame to weep a little at times, he said gently; the crying had been good for him, it let out that monstrous grief he had felt so heavily at the time. It had cleansed his soul. It hurt a great deal all the same, mainly because he would never again see their dear faces, never hear their sweet voices, their laughter, or witness their own small childish tears.

Then as time marched on and time healed his hurts, he began to realise that what he had originally expected was not at all true. For he saw them every night in his dreams, every day in his thoughts. And his visions of them never diminished over time – that was the miracle of it!

"So in a way," he concluded in happier tones, "while I'm still kicking and breathing my family lives on with me, and I draw a lot of comfort from it. Hmm…"

Country fragrances rose up from tussocks of wild herbage and hot amber coloured grass, as the two watched the herd of horses grazing and flattening the grass. The horses performed a low symphonic adagietto with their flickering, twitching ears , swishing tails and champing teeth, orchestrated by swarms of flies.

"What was her name, your wife?" the boy asked diffidently, almost in a whisper. He leaned a little, stroked Chapulín's withers to disguise a shade of embarrassment.

The old man turned to him, looked him squarely in the face, smiled and said, "The same as your mamá as a matter of fact – *María*…"

This surprised Juan. "Was – was she much like mamá?"

In many respects she was, Pancho affirmed. She had the same big heart, the same sort of smile, the same cheerfulness and zest for life and love for her little ones. "Sí, she was very much like your mamá," and the old ranchero looked wistful in saying that.

"You're very fond of mamá, aren't you?" asked Juan somewhat shyly.

"Doña María?" said Pancho in a tone indicating he'd rather be speaking of someone else. "Why, she's the best friend I have I reckon, and that's how fond I am of her, a very dear friend. That's my own opinion mind, not your mother's. Why do you ask anyway?" now grinning all over his face.

"Oh, it's just the way she speaks of you sometimes," admitted Juan.

Doña María thought highly of the ranchero, the boy could assure him of that much, which was why it became easy to allow her son to spend the summer with him. Even though she often passed derogatory remarks about him, this was merely a ploy to hide what she really thought and wished to keep to herself.

"I'd be okay and safe with you, mamá said, in spite of what she says to others," and Juan also broke into a grin.

"Ay well, que bueno, it'll do you no harm being among us *rough* rancheros. Though we've some kind of a bad reputation which goes back to the old revolutionary days, we just have a job of work to do like anyone else, and we get on with it."

Out here in the country they were not tainted or influenced by bad things, Pancho averred, because here they only communed with nature and her creatures. They don't gamble or at least hardly ever, the old man grinned. Or womanize, hurt any other man without due cause, or stir up strife in the world. The men like to drink to be sure, for it helps in this lonely existence. All the same they are up the next day and working hard, and *that* was their true reputation.

"We're just simple souls, Juanito, as you may already have guessed, with simple needs and pleasures – we prefer a game of dominoes to shooting up a pueblo. And we enjoy what we do workwise because we know how to do it well. The essence of life is the work you enjoy doing.

"Maybe we're overly prideful too, which isn't such a bad thing. In a higher calling you might name it professionalism. With us rancheros it's what you'd call – well, being a *man*. Hmm, that's the short of it..."

Their conversation out here on the range, as simple and seemingly insignificant as it may appear, had managed to create a developing and long-lasting bond between the boy and the old man.

A comfortable silence fell between them, a silence of their own and not of the land. They heard the swish of switching tails, a rhythmic grinding of teeth as the horses cropped the grass. They heard a low wind softly nibbling at the grasses and a high drone of working insects in busy squadrons about the grazing animals.

Part Four

Part Four

18

Breakfast for Two

Pancho and young Juan were sat alone by the morning cook-fire enjoying a leisurely late breakfast. The men had earlier rode out with a small drove of chestnut bay mounts to be delivered at the local railroad depot for the army.

"I saw you under the tree at sundown yesterday, studying your book," said the old ranchero in his husky, deep base 'morning' voice. "What're you reading at the moment?"

"I've started on a new book," said the boy eagerly, "about Villa and Zapata and the Revolution. Only read the first few pages so far – very interesting, but I bet you could tell me a thing or two about those days. Pancho Villa and the rest of it."

"I could at that, muchacho. Ay caray, such a man he was, as I've mentioned to you before. I always thought it a pity that he wasn't a drinker – like me!" giving the young one a villainous wink.

"He didn't drink?"

No, not Villa, which was why he had lasted as long as he did, old Pancho reminisced. You had to have your wits about you during the unstable times of the Revolution, and Pancho Villa was always alert and ready for any contingency, and so it didn't do to drink yourself mindless. They were after all unsettling days of vengeance and banditry, with people switching allegiance from one leader to another. They were times of useless fire and slaughter, pillage and treacherous ambuscades. And this went on over the whole country, though mostly in the northern desert states, too near for comfort where Pancho lived and worked.

"You had to tread carefully in those bad days and best to keep your mouth shut or lose your life – just like that!" dramatically snapping a finger.

He reached a hand to a platter of hot cigar-shaped tamales cooked in maize shucks earlier sent over by Tulia. "In his younger days he was known as Doroteo Arango, as I think I've said before," he went on, unwrapping a maize shuck casing, horny finger chopping into steamed chicken paste. Insects hovered about him, seemingly intoxicated by the smell of food. "Then, because of a scrape with the federales, he changed both his names and became known from that time on as Francisco Villa."

"Oh, so that's why he changed his name; I knew it wasn't his real name. But he was a hero all the same, wasn't he?" asked the boy.

"Hmm, he was a hero alright, to a great many people," Pancho concurred, "though he was also regarded as an outlaw, and you can't dismiss that little fact."

"Could he have been both at the same time?"

"I suppose so, sí, like *Robin Hood*."

"I don't know him," admitted Juan.

"That's a shame, you'd like him. Well, he was a sort of outlaw too you see in *Inglaterra* many centuries ago."

"Robin *Húd*…"

"Eventually he became a great general."

"This Robin Húd?"

"No-o, Villa did. He was an outlaw again when Carranza came to power. Carranza was his main enemy and took him out from popular favour. Carranza you see sided as well with the *norteamericanos*, who were once Villa's friends for a time. Like I told you there was much of that going on then, chopping and changing, going from one side to the other as they do anyway during times of revolution."

Pancho paused, gazed over the sunwashed corral yard and noticed some bull thistle growing between the feed-barn and the stables. Then his eyes strayed upward at the vast blue far away sky.

"Well," he enlarged, "Carranza himself got caught in the end, like a lot of them did. Shot to death in the mountains up near Veracruz. Though he had done some good for our country I must admit, after a convention at – What's that place where Cándido's uncle comes from? – Querétaro, that's it – with new reform laws and redistribution of land, not to mention other good social changes and what-have-you…"

Zapata had the same frame of mind of course, Pancho pushed on, of giving the land back to the peasants. ¡Tierra y Libertad!' was the popular cry of his followers, 'Land and Liberty'. Though as it had turned out the *Zapatistas* were not at that particular convention, nor for that matter were the *Villistas*.

The old ranchero was now speedily into demolishing a plate of greasy *chicharrones*, also sent up by Tulia that morning. The high brittle scrunching sound he made could be heard clear across the corral.

"What about Zapata then?" the boy prompted him.

"Ah, Emiliano Zapata." – *S-scrunch!* – "But what about him, amiguito?"

"Well wasn't he the *'hombre muy malo'* – the bad man?"

"Hell no – ayí, these chicharrones are good! – No, Zapata was a very good man I'd dare to say and much devoted to his people; he genuinely held them in high regard." Wagging his head for further emphasis he pressed on: "No, muchacho, and just listen to this. If there was any one real 'hombre malo' it was that Cheche Campos fellow. He was a thoroughly bad lot, a cruel swine he was and no mistake I can tell you. That one put terror into the hearts of everybody with his bloody rampaging, his looting and burning and killing innocent folk. Sí, a nasty devil to be sure." – *S-scrunch!* – The old man was certainly enjoying the chicharrones, Juan could see. "Well, you'll be reading all about it in that there book I dare say," swiftly finishing off the remainder of chicharrones.

The old ranchero customarily took his breakfast seat by the fire on a wooden crate, side-end up. In the crate he kept various small treats such as bottles of *Fanta* orange drink, a tin bowl of tiny hot green chillies – periodically topped up by Tulia from her kitchen garden. There were also a dirty glass beaker and straw basket of eggs, also supplied by don Roberto's cook/housekeeper.

Pancho was sat on his box this morning, as he did every morning, and lifted out his glass beaker and a bottle of Fanta. He prised the metal cap off the bottle between his teeth, and quarter-filled the beaker, passing the bottle to Juan to finish. His hand dropped down again to rummage in the crate, plucked two large eggs out of the basket. With the skill of a cook he deftly cracked the eggs one at a time and one-handedly into the beaker. He raised it to his open mouth and down it all slid almost in one gulp. An impressive loud belch and breakfast was now over.

The wind began a catch-me-if-you-can command performance, blowing and gusting in contrary, quick moving turns, stirring a ready audience of dust and grit and scraps of cornstraw.

"There's not much we can be doing this morning while the others are busy sweating it out at the railroad halt," he gravelled complacently, "so shall we go take a ride? I can show you a place where a hawk is nesting, if you're interested," and the old man got to his feet, ready to tackle another day.

19

Ranchero Antics 1

The men had known one another for a number of years and felt comfortable between themselves. Pancho had worked the longest period on don Roberto's hacienda, and was older than the others. Thus he was readily accepted as the leader of the pack, a foreman-without-portfolio as it were, and almost a father figure to his fellow rancheros. Pancho was in charge. He was the boss. Without undue effort he had established very early on a kind of *Pax Pancho*. The men recognised and mostly respected the old man's wisdom and knowledge. This did not deter them however from making fun of his many foibles. Cándido especially would challenge him at every point at every turn and at every opportunity.

Each man knew that insults and abuse could be thrown around at will without recourse to nasty recriminations, a spate of fisticuffs or – heaven forbid – outright murderous revenge. They felt that anyone in their group could be trusted, to a certain limit at least, because they were members of a close and single clan. Over the years they had cut the rough with the not so rough as Pancho once put it; helped one another in times of strife or crisis and developed what can be usefully called a brotherhood of man. It was the psyche and essence of the Mexican ranchero.

Their individual quirks of personality – and they were bountiful enough – and their habit traits had long been identified, mimicked or ridiculed, generally made much fun of and put to the test. Even the chief culprit of these digs, jibes, bantering and put-downs, the old man himself, did not escape the daily onslaught of *'character assassination'*.

On a par with and oftentimes overreaching Pancho's standards, was Cándido. This young man, with his wild and surreal imagination, was adept at changing a perhaps mundane topic of discussion into one of bizarre and exotic convolutions.

José was the deep silent type as already noted; a dark one as he liked to make out. While Gerardo could guilelessly manage with minimum effort to bring ill-luck and misfortune tumbling on his own head. Besides being a mild and harmless sort of hypochondriac he was also something of a fatalist, possibly because of the bad luck usually hounding his every move.

Emilio, as earlier mentioned, was a bland easy-going relaxed fellow, but one who attached excessive importance to the value and benefits of sleep. At any opportunity and even under adverse conditions he could drop off into an instant doze or sound sleep, depending on the amount of time available. He could sleep standing up according to the others. And naturally they ribbed him unmercifully over his king-size buck teeth.

It would sometimes happen when the character traits of two people coincided in a path of conflict. An example of this was evident when Juan had been with the rancheros a week or so and getting to know the men as they knew themselves. The boy could with some relish anticipate the actual outcome of any particular situation.

Gerardo happened to be the instigator in this singular episode in the ongoing war of clashing personalities. It was a time when Pancho was not around and the men had assumed he was over at *la casa* with don Roberto. This gave Gerardo a rare opportunity to shine in performing his party-piece. To do a take-off of Pancho, a perfect impersonation, in order to amuse the others and thereby gain their approbation. The rancheros as usual in Pancho's absence idly lounged about on bales of straw in the main stable.

"Who's this then?" he said, as he bent his legs and began walking around as if he were holding a barrel between his thighs, convulsively jerking his body from side to side, slapping his legs with exaggerated comicality, just as he imagined the old man would do it.

The men rolled about in the straw, stitched up with laughter. With this triumph Gerardo galumphed into an encore, mimicking the old man's movements even more, bumbling on bowed legs across the stable floor – though not looking where he was going. He slammed right into the old ranchero at the stable doorway.

"Oye Gerardo, I was looking for you," said Pancho affably. "I've this moment come from the bunkhouse, and you'll never guess but that yard-cat has had a real vicious fight with your pet opossum," and Gerardo greyed in shock at this news, after first turning mottled red at being caught on the hop with his 'act'.

"Sí, hombre," continued Pancho in sombre tones, "I fear the worst. Your opossum is surely as dead as a fur collar – must be, for the yard-cat was chewing its head off –"

"I'll kill that damned cat!" growled Gerardo, and galloped off in the direction of the bunkhouse. No one had ever seen him move so fast before.

"He wasn't pleased over that was he?" commented Cándido.

"Oh, the opossum is alright," grinned Pancho, "and the cat is as far as I know safe and sound over at the casa. But maybe that will teach Gerardo to try making a *Pancho* out of a Pancho, eh?"

20

Ranchero Antics 2

At another time, when the men were readying to run a small drove of potential army cavalry mounts out onto the grazing lands, they happily horse-played like boys in the corral yard.

Pearly-white, fat-breasted clouds pushed provocatively across the sky; towering blue-white clouds like fantastical castles, and other lesser stacked multi-shaped formations.

"Well, muchachos, see what that bit of rain we had last night has done," said Pancho, pointing at the sky. "What a grand line-up of cloud that is up there. A magnificent sight and no mistake. See the different shapes and colours. That lot near the sun has rainbow colours skimming through it. Ah, the interesting shapes of them. Why, I can see the head of a laughing elephant."

Gerardo, gawping upward, dared to voice the opinion that elephants were not capable of laughing, but Cándido pointed out that it need only take one look at the other and it would laugh alright, laugh its trunk off. José, also staring up, thought he could make out a crocodile with its jaws wide open – no, he was telling a lie, it was a lion with his mouth wide open. Pancho drawled a contradiction as he frowned and scratched an ear, saying it was his laughing elephant that José saw.

Emilio had it in mind that all clouds looked much the same – like clouds. Though he did concede that many of them appeared remarkably like light fluffy pillows; an idea which Pancho knew only too well was natural enough for such a somnolent-minded creature as Emilio, surely the patron saint of slumber. Had the sky been stark clear empty blue Emilio would still have spotted light fluffy pillows. This was acknowledged as a truism by the men, knowing the fat man's propensities for bed-rest and sleep.

Pancho asked Juan if his young creative imagination had conjured up anything of note. The boy pointed and said he recognised something like a savage wolfhound with huge floppy ears.

"Like your Salté then," said Pancho, following the direction. "It's Salté alright, without a doubt." At the sound of his name the real dog sidled up to him and licked his hand. "Why you great soft cream-and-jelly mutt, so you're here as well are you? Savage indeed! Damned ugly for sure but savage? If you're savage, *perro*, then I'm a horse's harness," knuckling the big beast's head.

"I can see a long-bearded pregnant man lying on his back," contributed Cándido.

"Knew he would come up with something stupid," glared Gerardo in disgust. "How the devil can a man get pregnant? You crazy-eyed coot!"

Which only encouraged Cándido to continue on with solemn-faced conviction, mentioning as an example his uncle in Querétaro who once got himself seriously pregnant. "Well, near pregnant you might say. He had all the symptoms you see; fancied strange foods and such, felt sick in the mornings and kept having real awful stomach pains."

It had gotten so bad that Cándido's uncle was forced to pay a visit to the doctor who happened to live further down in the same street. Quite rightly the physician had refused to examine him. Instead he asked the hapless fellow a pertinent question.

"Is your wife pregnant by any chance?" he had put to him.

"Oh, sí, and I'm her husband. What I mean is −"

"My aunty was eight and a half months gone at the time," Cándido went on, "with my little cousin Eduardo. And when Eduardo was born the doc advised my uncle to take a week off work and rest up in bed, which he did."

"I know of women who have these, what you call false pregnancies," said Pancho, "and I knew of one old crone in particular who was a spinster all her adult life. She had never married, never known a man − if you catch my drift − and of course never had any kids. Yet every time I saw the old crow she put it to me that she was well gone and due any week now − even asked if I'd be godparent after she delivered."

With a smirk Cándido reckoned that Emilio could possibly be pregnant, referring to the fat man's magnificently rotund belly.

"Well if he is," said Pancho, "he's going to make us all rich. So, when is it due, Emilio?" with a wink at the fat one.

"About three months to go," smiled the other happily, revealing his large teeth.

"What!" gulped Gerardo. "He's having us on surely?"

"Oh, didn't you know?" said Pancho. "His Teresa is going to have another baby. If it's a boy they're going to name it Francisco after me. Isn't that so, amigo?"

"That's right," Emilio widened his smile, buck teeth showing in widescreen in the sunlight.

"And what if *you* happen to have a baby, Emilio?" asked Cándido.

"Why," interjected Pancho, hitching up his pants and stretching, "he'll do the right and proper thing and name it after you – Now, hermanos, are we going to idle around here all day? Your feet fast nailed to the ground are they? Come on, open the gate José and let's have the beasts out for a run and a graze."

And the old ranchero trundled over to the stable to saddle the mare.

21

Ranchero Antics 3

Another time it was Emilio's turn to have his leg pulled.

"Well, amigo, they say it's going to happen after all," Pancho said portentously one day, "and none of us guessed it would, though there was always a slight chance of it happening. Hard to believe, isn't it?"

"Hard to believe what? What's going to happen, Pancho? Does it involve us?" asked the fat man with burning curiosity.

"Oh, you haven't been told about it?"

"Told about what?"

"So you don't know anything about it then?"

"About what? Stop asking *me* questions, I'm asking you."

"The others know, they've known for some time. I thought you would have known too."

"Know what? For God's sake!"

"Don Roberto told us weeks ago. You were there weren't you?"

"There you go again asking *me* questions! Where were you? And what did don Roberto say? For the love of God!" The usually good-natured fat man was getting more exasperated at every moment, showing there was a limit to his good nature and general affability.

"It was over by the casa at the time, when he got us together and warned us there and then about it possibly happening. For sure now it *is* going to happen, as I've said, so God help those who know nothing of it. That's their lookout, I say." The old man clicked his teeth in a judicious manner, and rubbed his jaw, to wipe away any sense of responsibility he may have felt.

Emilio was at this stage beginning to pant with frustration, his olive-skin face turning splotchy red, as if he had run a long distance at a terrific pace. "Know of what, Pancho? Just tell me that. I know nothing at all of this and no one else has said anything. What the hell is it? What exactly is going to happen?"

Pancho put on a patient and rather patronising look. "I don't understand you, hombre. How can you deny any knowledge of what I've told you?"

"But, Pancho," pleaded the other, "you haven't told me *anything*! Dear Lord —"

"Are you addressing me? I wasn't aware…"

"What's going on? You must tell me, I've a right to know —"

"I wouldn't dispute that…"

"I have a right to know just like the others," wringing podgy hands in nervous agitation.

The old ranchero fixed a smile on his face, perhaps a shade glibly, and said, "I think you do know, amigo, and you are just kidding me on. Well, you can't fool this wise old owl — I bet you've known all along, eh? You're simply having me on, eh, is that it, you rascal! I advise you to remember that you can only go so far with me. You're pushing your luck, hombre," and swiftly strode off tut-tutting to himself.

Emilio, bordering on panic and with strong forebodings, ran to the nearest at hand — young Julian. But he got no joy there, and cursed himself for even bothering to ask the soft-wit. Later, he managed to collar Cándido and put the matter to him. Not knowing that the other was in on the tease, the fat man was led a merry dance, the *issue* parried back and forth without identification, without substance, and certainly without enlightenment. The poor fellow was left in excruciating suspense and frustration.

Finally, unable to stand it any longer, sizzling and seething, Emilio went storming off to the casa to tackle don Roberto himself. No, he was not going to stand for this any longer.

"I'm not standing for this any longer!" were his parting angry words. He would soon get to the bottom of this, he vowed. A few cowmen stood and idled about the front of the house, to see what results might emerge from this confrontation with the Big Boss.

Moments later the tubby man was seen bowling out from the fly-screen doors on the porch as though propelled by a catapult. He completely cleared the porch, landing heavily in the yard dust. Fierce expletives rang out from behind the fly-screens, and the idle onlookers hurriedly made themselves scarce.

Emilio felt as if he had been run over by a herd of cattle. Nothing hurt so much at this present time, however, as his injured pride and self-esteem. And he never did get to know what was 'supposed to happen'. Such were the dealings and devilry among the men, which shot brief sparks into the dull hard graft during these hot summer months.

22

Suppertime

It was Juan's turn one day to prepare and cook the supper. He had returned earlier than the others in order to light the cook-fire and get matters in hand. Standing on his knees he busily attended to the fire, first feeding it with small twigs, then larger sticks of wood.

The men presently came riding in, making a deal of noise while they were about it. As they unsaddled the mounts they chuntered on like a bunch of school-kids, somewhat agitated, even excited over the prospect of a good hot meal. A black pot of beans hung from a trivet over a cheerful-looking fire, already well heated and steaming away. The men halted their chatter for a brief instant, to smell and to sigh at the aroma of cooking drifting past their noses. Then off they rattled again :

" … He took to it like a hog to a mudpatch, so he did…"

"I told him straight: If poverty were a crime we'd all be in the clinker. After all, every firefly is not a star, I said to him."

"What's that mean, then?"

"My meaning is, all that glitters is not gold." This was a conversation between Pancho and Gerardo.

" … So what happened after that, Cándido?"

"Well, to give it straight from the shoulder – to cut my story short, to put it in a pea-pod or to pare it to the bone –"

" Ayí! Get on with it, you cross-eyed wonder!" That was José in his usual combative frame of mind.

" … And don Roberto, he says, 'Who called that horseman an idiot?' Then José shouts out from the back, 'And who called that idiot a horseman?' which was a good one coming from him." This was Pancho now chatting to Emilio.

"What's that about me?" scowled José suspiciously, spoiling for an argument.

"Just saying, amigo," Pancho smiled oilily, "what a sweet nature you have and no mistake, hmm. If you can get along with yourself, I always say, you can surely get along with others." But Jose was not to take the bit between his teeth on that score; instead, he played his 'lone mean hombre' role, disdainfully regarding the fools around him.

As Gerardo flat-footedly tramped off somewhere, his head almost disappeared in a cloud of evening midges. He caught a mouthful before he was able to shake them off, flailing his arms like a manic orchestral conductor.

Juan's hound Salté managed to flush out a rat from a stack of straw bales and gave chase. The rodent was too quick for the old dog, performing a neat disappearing act. Nonplussed and confused, perplexed beyond imagining, Salté paced up and down a line of bales, sniffing hard and noisily, and sneezing with the dust his nose vacuumed up.

"You stupid scruffbag!" said Juan, clouting him on his ragamuffin ear. Understanding this kind of plain language, Salté gave his master an open-mouthed, tongue-panting ingratiating look.

Now on his knees once more before the fire Juan stirred the pot of beans using a whittled stick. He broke up some wood and threw it on the blaze. He found some dry cattle dung and put that on the fire; the dung burned particularly well to his satisfaction.

Salté trotted up, began to butt the boy's side, acting like a yearling bull. Juan cuffed him hard on the back of the beast's head, telling him to behave – or he would cook him. The dog went slinking away to sulk someplace in peace.

The beans cooked merrily in their little black cauldron hooked over the flames. Steam rose and spread about the campsite. The hungry rancheros sniffed and salivated, their empty stomachs already churning digestive juices. Pancho, it was noticed, had his nose in the air like a pointer dog, following tantalizing aromas. He glanced around him at the others with a rugged grin on his face, as though to say, 'Not long to go now, hermanos.'

The old man could recall taking in this delicious savoury smell of beans cooking for time beyond time, going way back to his youth and childhood. It was the same smell then as it was now, naturally enough; only, each time signified the essence and the passing of time itself, of which he was nostalgically aware. His mind would of a sudden flick back to – say, a campfire night in Sonora. Workaday beans slowing simmering in a pot, Francisco happy with the fresh strength and vitality of a young man. He liked to treat the memories of times long past as a kind of favourite book, to be dipped into at will and at any moment of inclination. So here he was in the present, he ruminated to himself, a considerably older man to be sure, but still smelling the good homely cooking smells of those former years.

Maybe it was just as well that smells don't grow old, he reasoned, but renew themselves continually and evoking the same feelings or emotions in those lucky enough to be familiar with them. Nowadays the smell of beans cooking in a pot gave double the pleasure to the anticipatory hungry eater, for it instantly brought back memories of earlier times. And because its singular aroma was uncannily associated with the best of times – that is, meal times – so the memories it conjured up were likewise pleasant.

The men swallowed their saliva, waited patiently for the beans to be done and dished out. They sat or squatted round the woodfire, in their usual semi-circle facing the western foothills and distant mountains, so as to observe the setting sun as they ate their supper. A low wind drifted in, stirred the scents of dust and dung and horse-sweat, mixing with the food aroma.

Evening. The finest time of the day for the rancheros. To sit over their simple supper and watch the sun slowly drop behind the western cordillera. They usually stared at the sunset in silence, humbled almost by the sheer grandeur of the scene set before their eyes. The light and colour of the evening sky always struck old Pancho as exceedingly special and religious, what he oftentimes called an Old Testament sky.

Then twilight came. It came on silently, treading quietly in on kitten-pussy paws. Stars winking on one by one at first, finally in clusters. They could look up at the eveningsky and see nothing there. The next time when glancing up again there would be myriad stars blinking in their cold colossal constellations.

"I imagine the lights up there," said the boy in hushed tones, "as small holes in the night sky, shutting and opening for stars to see through…"

The cook-fire now became the evening campfire. About the fire a cosy warm ring of light danced delicately against a backcloth of maroon darkening. Burning woodsticks chattered and cracked like a coven of witches.

Gerardo was exploring busily about his nose, retrieving a fingerful of foreign matter. He examined it. Waited until it was hard enough to roll into a ball, and flicked it from him. It landed on the toe of José's left boot. José gave him a look fit to sear his face to the bone. Because he was at this moment 'the lone quiet hombre', José didn't say anything – the 'look' alone would suffice.

The evening air was mild and dry and soothing. Young green wood was thrown on the fire, and its smoke kept at bay most of the pesky sundowner mosquitoes. Sweat had by now dried on the men after their earlier exertions of a working day. Nor was it regarded as an offensive odour. It was to them a manly and ageless scent, a scent not unlike a certain wild bitter herb found in sandy woodland.

After supper the slow-wit Julian got up to wash the pans and canteens as he usually did, willingly and cheerfully, chewing the while on a stem of grass. Later, he would trot over to the stables, to 'do his rounds' of the horses. He would hardly ever sit with the rancheros round the campfire, but spend his time talking sweetly though nonsensically to the animals. When twilight thickened the youth would make an early night of it and sleep in one of the empty horse-stalls – a different one each night, so as to spread his own body smell for the benefit of the beasts, as he saw it. Up again at first light – if not before – Julian would attend immediately to the horses in his good care.

He now put away the panware, ready to take his leave, stumbling over someone's saddle in the fading light.

"Look where you're going, muchacho," said that someone in the shadows, "that's my saddle you're kicking the hell out of." That someone may have been José.

Julian left the men to their woodfire chatter …

23

Musical Evening

The contented rancheros hunched themselves around the fire, several conversations going on at the same time :

"A chicken is sorry it's a chicken when it's going to get plucked for the pot, my mamá always used to say…"

"So you have a mamá? I never knew that."

"According to my papá I have."

"Knowing your own faults is a virtue, and a virtue always has value."

"So has a mouth that can keep itself shut."

"I saw you last night with your head buried in Geronimo's nose-bag, eating his oats."

"No, I wasn't then, I'd dropped my currycomb in it. I was looking for my currycomb."

"Your mouth was smeared with oats."

"Well, oats is good for you, builds up your strength…"

" … And he approaches every man as if he were a dog, wondering if he'll get bitten or barked at. That was him all over … You see every question is like a coin or like a door."

"What's your meaning exactly?"

"Well, they each have two sides to them."

"I see, and there're two sides to every story, I can follow that."

"I found an old horseshoe today."

"Nail it on the bunkhouse door – for luck, it's said."

"Too late now, that old mare is wearing it."

" … He could use his initiative I suppose, but you'd have to push him to it – Oye, Juanito, I believe your Salté is chasing after Tulia's yard-cat again."

"He's one great lump of a fool dog," said Juan, getting to his feet. "I'll go get him and clip his ear for him." The boy loped quickly over to the casa.

"Well, hermanos, do you remember when the don bought that puppy dog?" opened up Pancho, ready to dominate the campfire conversation. "A special breed of dog it was – Ah what is it they call them? – Sí, I know, a corgi, a corgi dog, that's it. Cost him a pretty packet as well. According to what the don told me, it's reckoned that this particular breed is favoured by the British Royal Family." He sniffed significantly. "I don't know but at the time the don had some pretensions to being of the nobility or something of the sort, and such a dog would suit."

"Pre-pretensions, does that mean," guessed Gerardo, "you pretend to be something that you're not?"

"That's right," Cándido confirmed. "Like you Gerardo, pretending to be a ranchero when you're really a carpenter – a wood-chipper!"

"Something on those lines, amigo," Pancho smiled over at Gerardo. "As they say, a proud man is as tall as his pride will allow him."

"What do you pretend to be anyway?" gruffed Gerardo sourly at his antagonist. "Damned cross-eyed cuckoo!"

"Wood shaver! Plank chopper!" retorted the younger man.

"Can I get on, you two?" broke in the old man. "So, this corgi pup kept piddling on the master's polished parquet floor. Didn't train it right obviously – a different package of goods than horses. Anyway, when it dropped a nice wet turd on his best leather sofa, uuy, that was it as far as the don was concerned. From that day on the corgi became a yard-dog. Poor little fellow, imagine it if you will, those short legs that breed has. It tried chasing Tulia's chickens – as Salté's doing right this moment with her cat – but it was never able to catch a chicken."

Pancho put his little finger in one ear, wagged it so violently it seemed as if he were determined to drill into his skull. "Then a rat came along one night and bit the corgi, and that was the end of the poor perro. The don never bothered again about getting a house-dog. He bought instead a damned silly noisy cockatoo – Ah, here's Juanito coming…"

There are many expressions you can read in a dog's face, and especially Juan's dog. When the boy returned from the casa yard with his great shaggy beast in tow, the animal had a decided guilty and not to say shameful look about him. Juan sat himself once more by the fire, Salté sprawled well spread out like a pile of discarded rugs at his feet. He gazed at his master fawningly and ingratiatingly, with total submissiveness and something of adoration in his grey-green wolf's eyes.

"I don't understand why that dog of yours is still around in our modern world, muchacho," said José, expertly rolling a *cigarro* using one hand. "I mean to say he's kind of like a mammoth. He should be extinct by now like all the mammoths." He pulled contentedly at his thin, meanly made cigarro, satisfied that he'd said his piece for the present.

"Our Gerardo's still around as well," cracked Cándido.

The young man softly whistled a tune to himself, absorbed now in polishing his saddle – he was forever polishing his saddle thought the others. Gerardo ignored him and the remark, too preoccupied in scratching furiously at his crotch where a louse was busy exploring him.

And the old west wind rode in like a faithful friend, briefly swept caressingly over the men, though they were not aware it had done so. They fell silent for a spell, usually the way when conversing in the open air; in this case the open, mystery-laden night air. They yawned and scratched and fidgeted, hardly thinking a single coherent thought, minds disinclined to bother. Old Pancho was thinking contrarily that it was pleasant to have no thoughts, but what he really meant were thoughts of interest and consequence.

"By the by, Juanito," he started up a little time later, suddenly perking up from a momentary reverie, "you didn't happen to bring your – what's its name? – your mouth-organ with you, did you?"

"Harmonica," corrected Cándido.

"Which is a mouth-organ all the same."

"But properly called a harmonica."

"Sí," said Juan, smiling, breaking the tension between the other two. "I have it right here," fishing it out smoothly from his pants back pocket. "Do you want me to play it for you?"

"I dare say the muchachos would appreciate a bit of music for a change," said the old ranchero. "Eh, you miserable sinners, are you ready for a tune or two?" The men nodded agreeably, shifted their backsides to a more comfortable position in anticipation of some light entertainment.

"Ay, music is a language all the nations understand," Pancho went on pontifically. "Music is the sound of Heaven."

"Juanito's got his work cut out, then," grinned Cándido.

"And silence is its sister," the old man glared at him. "You go right ahead, amiguito. Let's hear some of your stuff."

Juan blew fluff and dust from his small neat instrument, tapped it on his knee, then rubbed at the gleam of chrome on it to polish it up – necessary preliminaries to the performance he was now formulating in his mind.

He began playing a tune known to them all, *Estrellita Marinera*, and the exquisitely mournful notes flowed in the night air. It soothed the rancheros, made them tranquil and at peace. Even the saddle-horses tethered nearby appeared affected, for they soon stopped snorting and side-pacing, settling down to a placid immobility. It had its effect on Emilio leaning back against a bale of straw, reposing in a state of serene placidity and near-somnolence.

Pancho's face was ecstatic as Juan went straight on into a livelier piece called *El Federal de Caminos*. Gerardo grinned like a wedge of cheese, Cándido observed his feet with acute interest. José looked somewhat vacant, Emilio blissful as he stared dreamily into space. As the melodies became increasingly melancholy the more the men seemed to enjoy it. It said something for the loneliness and isolation they had to endure out here on the ranchlands, remote from road and town and people.

The music moved them to soaring heartwarming heights. Pancho was visibly affected; his mind began to wander : The melodies took him up into mountains, along stony trails, riding through mists of cloud – on top of the world. And to the others their imagination was fired, inspired by Juan's playing. Glancing his way they silently blessed the boy for being here with them, sharing the same hardships, making his own unique contribution to this tiny comradely community.

Juan changed the tempo once again to a faster upbeat rhythm. It acted on Cándido like a large shot of mezcal. He sprang to his feet and raced off someplace into the dark, returning moments later lugging a wide length of duckboard. He dropped the plank flat on the ground and then stepped on it. The young man's booted though nimble feet began to thud out some variation of a Spanish tap-dance. His head was down, concentrating on the intricate steps. The others smacked their thighs in tune to the beat. Juan remained for a while on the pace-setting numbers, eventually exhausting the solo dancer.

"You have a go, Pancho, why don't you," urged Emilio (who would normally have dropped off to sleep by this time of the evening, but was now quite broad awake), as the foot-tapper retired from the board, kicking it away from him.

The old man stirred himself. "Start off again, Juanito!" he spouted with peppery verve, stepping on the 'dance-floor' board. His boots pounded along the length of plank. The men clapped hands and the beat got stronger. Pancho was thoroughly in the throes of it, bending his elbows, strutting and kicking out his heels like a dance-hall girl, going in for short twirling leaps in the air, booted feet crashing heavily down.

Then – *C-crack!*

Pancho's boots went clean through the old buckboard planking and over he went, landing on his backside in a smother of dust. The rancheros doubled up with rousing guffaws at seeing the expression on the old man's face which was a rare tonic indeed. Pancho was showing surprised incredulity, and may also have wondered where his dignity had suddenly vanished to, as he sat flat on his arse in the dust.

To conceal his mounting embarrassment he ruefully explained that he had only been to a board meeting and that the board meeting was now broken up.

"You ought to be more careful at your age," said Gerardo gravely. "A back could have been broken."

"But a back was broken," cried Cándido, "the back of the buckboard!"

Then José heard a quick *whooshing* sound and felt a small draft of air hit his ear. "What the devil! What the hell was that?"

"A night-bird," said Gerardo.

"Goodnight, bird," said Cándido.

"A bat," Pancho told him. "There're one or two set up home in the roof of our bunkhouse, and right welcome to it, seeing as we hardly use it."

"Did it frighten you?" crowed Cándido.

Nothing was sweeter than getting José riled up, and it was all too easy; but this time his provocative taunt was made in such a soft tone that wouldn't offend the prickly, unpredictable José. Luckily, José hadn't heard him anyway. The lone, silent hombre spat neatly into the fire; the gobbet hissed, bubbled and popped and disappeared.

That night late on the rancheros took their rest under a starsplit meteor-showered nightsky, dreaming the sort of dreams they may have dreamed in their younger days, on through and past the dirt-dark midnight hour.

Part Five

Part Five

24

Horse Sense

"Don't go too near the roan mare," Pancho warned young Juan one hot afternoon on the grasslands where a horse herd grazed. "Her ears and tail are going and the neck's sawing away you can see. She doesn't like it I swear. We'll take a look at her later when she's more relaxed and amenable – It doesn't do to offend a female.

"Of course it's not so much you getting too near *her*," the old ranchero went on explaining, "but the fact that you were getting a little too close to her friend, the other roan there. I reckon she was jealous of you, Juanito, how about that! But that's your female for you – Now look at her, the lumping softie, she's resting her head by the other's neck. They'll start to groom one another next if I'm not mistaken – Ah, there they go at it! What did I tell you?" The old man grinned as though he had won a sweepstake.

Juan stood up in his stirrups so as to gain a better view.

Pancho enlarged further: "In fact those two have been friends most of this year. No doubt they'll remain so, as long as we keep them together, mind. Hmm. Their relationship is as lasting as your own mamá and papá's is. Mare friendship is usually stronger than it is with the males.

"¡Újule! Damn these flies! Making a regular meal out of me. Let's cut along that way a bit, follow the outer fringe of the herd. With any luck we'll find a nice breeze in our face, to maybe blow away these whining pests, eh?" The two turned their mounts which broke into an easy canter.

Dove-white tufts of cloud, blue-tinged at their base, silently sailed above the land. There began a wind, a wayward wind, undecided and contrary, first blowing from one way and tired of that veering off into a new direction, dry dead grass whistling and whishing in tune with this wind. "Another kind of female I guess," murmured the old man.

"¿Perdónome?"

"Of no matter, amiguito…"

Slowing down moments later, Pancho pointed over to his left at a young bay stallion wallowing like a hog in a dirt spot. "He's taking his cure I see, Juanny," he grinned. "The flies won't torment him now for a while."

"Masking his scent with the dust is he?" inquired the boy.

"Well a little bit of that I suppose. But a dust-coat is like a suit of armour of sorts, and the insects won't get to him so easily. He's made himself fly-proof or nearly so at any rate."

There were other reasons as well, the old ranchero told him, for the stallion to behave in that way, rolling about in the dust. Juan's dog Salte did it too for much the same reasons, he went on, and it was not intelligence that set them off but was rather on the basis of true instinct. He meant, apart from the fact that the stallion was enjoying his dust-bath, it also got rid of the flies as he already mentioned, and also did away with ticks and other parasites from its coat. The dust-rolling broke up matted bits of loose hair and dead skin, getting rid of that lot too. So there was something beneficial in the whole action.

"The fun might be over for him though because — look! — that older stallion has seen the dirt spot. He's going to investigate, as I knew he would. Now the younger one is off you see because the older bay is the leader of their group — all males you may have noticed. Anyway he's the dominant one and the dust spot's his by right of seniority in their little hierarchy."

Their social make-up, he said, seemed hardly any different than the human one and can be just as complex.

"Damn me if these self-same insects haven't followed us, would you credit it!"

"What makes you think they're the same?" asked the boy with a grin.

"I wouldn't swear to it I don't suppose, but they look damned familiar to me is all I can say. Do you fancy having a dust-bath, muchacho?"

"I wouldn't mind a proper water-bath, I've been scratching myself sore all day."

"Occupational hazard, as the foreign saying has it," Pancho slung over. "Come on, I know where there's a small spring with a pool. You'll like that. You can wash off your itchy parasites. A gift from Emilio is it? From Emilio's grand stable of fleas," the old man smiled good-humouredly.

They rode on at a canter for a short spell of time. The sun flared down on them and the dust in the air smelled like an exotic spice, hot and musky. A dust-devil danced and darted across before them, then disappeared.

"It isn't far," rasped Pancho. "You can see now where it lies, there by that boulder where swallows are doing their aerobatics. Trust our feathered friends to know where water is…"

But then, so did the horses. They crossed a dry water-cut, clipped over wind-fashioned rocks and herb-scented shortgrass, and smelled out that promising water. Juan's Chapulín and the old man's Macha broke into a near gallop without any prompting from their riders.

"Seems maybe these two want a bath as well," said the ranchero, "or perhaps they're only thirsty which is more than likely. Well me too, I could do with a wet." He turned in his saddle to face his young charge. "I hope you'll allow us time for a drink, Juanito, before you plunge in with your fleas and what all," blinking at the blinding brilliance of sunlight.

25

A Question of Life and Death

time later, after Juan's refreshing bathe in the spring pool, the two carried on circling the stretched out herd of grazing horses. It only needed two points more to complete their encircling of the herd, as it only needed the two winds of Timosthenes to make up the twelve that became the points of the compass.

They reached a pleasant patch on higher ground, where a lone mesquite tree stood by a grassy mound. The mound was long and rectangular; it could be taken for a grave-site, but was in fact a naturally featured hump of earth created by nature. The tree threw its shadow on it. A good place to sit awhile, Pancho and the boy agreed, and they dismounted. Chapulín and Macha dropped their heads to graze, their owners sitting comfortably on the grass-carpeted mound.

It was possible for them to see the entire herd widely scattered over the sun-drenched land. The duo gazed appreciatively over the land, listened to the birds and insects and their own mounts cropping sun-crisped grass nearby. To the old man it was a scene of ineffable, timeless serenity. Even the boy could sense it in much the same degree.

The long afternoon wore slowly on. The tree's shadow spread further over the tiny grassy knoll where the man and boy sat in placid silence.

"Pancho?" The name sounded significant and powerful and almost startling after the long silence.

"That must be me," grinned the ranchero.

"You're you alright and none could mistake you," smiled Juan, "but I'd like to ask you a question, *con permiso…*"

"This sounds serious, then," Pancho did not know what to do with his grin.

"It's simply something that kind of bothers me when I think about it," Juan went on with a profound earnestness. "I need to know – I mean, well, is there really a Heaven? Is that where we go when we die? And do the animals go there too?"

"That's three questions, muchacho, and three 'heavies' to be sure," returned his companion by way of a counter-reply, "so which do I answer first, eh?"

"I've heard papá's version," the boy continued hurriedly, "and one or two priests have given me similar versions of the same thing." He had not been entirely convinced or impressed with what they had told him. He needed to know from someone like Pancho who was much older and had really lived and experienced a great deal.

The ranchero was intrigued by this quiet outburst. "What's brought this on so sudden-like on a nice warm afternoon spent on the range?"

"What prompted it? I guess it came to me earlier when I saw a dead jack-rabbit – Did you see it, Pancho?"

Yes, he had seen it, by a large red boulder they had passed some time back. Looked fresh-killed he thought, left by some hawk or buzzard for some reason; maybe they had surprised it away. "So that's what switched your thoughts to Heaven, is it? Why, mi compañero? Tell me." Pancho glanced sideways at the boy, saw dust as fine as pollen coating sunsmitten cheeks and brow.

"Well, I was thinking about that rabbit," Juan began, "and being freshly dead it still looked like a rabbit, a handsome fur-skinned creature made by God."

But before the coming night is halfway through, he realised, it will look nothing like a soft furry animal when coyotes and hawks and ants get to it. By tomorrow, he explained, its bones and bits of its fur will be scattered all over the place. Then no one would ever guess it had once been a lovely warm-blooded animal enjoying its existence in life.

The boy squinted a newly acquired professional ranchero's eye at the searing sun, estimating by its angle the time of day, and went on : "When people die – I mean those who die naturally and are buried in coffins in the earth – well, the worms and time get to them until there's only a skeleton left."

Was that it, then? he wanted to know. A bunch of bones in a box? What about people's minds? Their soul or spirit. How do they function without a body?

"We have no eyes to see with," he said in earnest, "so what are we missing … in Heaven? We have no ears so don't know what's happening. We have no mouth or voice to ask what is happening. We can't touch anything or feel anything, or even sense anything that might be happening around us."

The young one held hands clasped and suddenly cracked his knuckles, just as José had once taught him one Sunday morning in chapel. It sounded like a predator breaking a jackrabbit's neck, which reminded him again of the dead creature.

"So when we get to Heaven – if we do get to go to a heaven – what's the point if we can't see or hear or feel? Or even *think*! How can we think if we have no brain matter to think with? Does our soul think for us? If that's the case, how is it done? Just how is it possible? That's what I've been bothered about, and I needed to know…" And Juan shot a shy, deprecatory look at his old mentor, embarrassed over his outburst.

Pancho sighed, slapped a hand on the boy's shoulder. "Maybe you think too much sometimes," he said in his husky-voiced way.

He could himself spend hours of a day not thinking a single thought, he told the boy. He could look around him and not see anything, cock an ear and not listen or hear anything. All the same he was still a human being, he went on, alive with feeling and feeling well, with good eyesight and sound hearing, plus all the appetites of a healthy living man. During the times when he was not actively thinking or seeing and hearing anything in particular, he was in what might be called a 'state of being', as opposed to a 'state of doing' in his talking now to Juan and the boy listening.

"That state of 'being' is probably the nearest you can get while still alive to being a *spirit* of yourself. That's how it is I reckon. Only the dead know the true role and meaning of spirit and soul. I can only say that it must be something quite beyond our human comprehension, so very far from actual human experience, that merely to see or hear or smell, sense or whatever, is simply unimportant and probably irrelevant – as God willed it in His infinite wisdom. It exists and can only exist beyond death itself, and must so to speak hold dominion over death. In other words, Juanito, we all become a part of God Himself, and God is omnipresent – you follow that?"

"Sí, sí!" said the boy eagerly.

"He is there in us all, in every living and non-living thing on this earth.

"Why are we so obsessed with dying and death? I don't know the answer to that one — except to say it's simply in our nature. But life! Look at life. What is it in essence? How long does it last? Why does it have its own time? There's the rub, muchacho, in the length of life. I'm meaning our span of time, our span of life on Earth …

"Since we first evolved — came into being as Man — and through long centuries of our history on this fair planet, we each lived our allotted lifespan, just as the birds and animals and insects lived theirs. We're lucky — if we're lucky! — and can live threescore and ten and sometimes even longer. But our life-span is also measured as our time-span. At the end of it we wear out and die. We are making room for the next generation. We live on in our children. And if we have no family we live on in the general family of humanity …

"Live your life wisely — live it to the full is best! — then move on out. Because all the unborn generations of the future are waiting their turn … to make their appearance on the 'stage of life', as that Shakespeare fellow put it. Does that not sound sensible to you? Sí, muy bien. Prepare for the future, Juanito, because the rest of your life is there."

The old man threw out a hand, swept it before him, indicating the animals and the land and sky, said finally : "In life, Juanny, God has given us sight to see His works, and ears to listen to our fellow creatures. All the other senses too and brains to think with, to enjoy His good works. Our sense and awareness of Him would in death be there as plain and certain as could be to our spirit, and would be absolute, infinite and forever…"

They sank into silence, gazed over the land and the equine creatures with a seemingly refreshingly new outlook. Noticing that the horses grazed in their little clans and groups; colts and fillies trotted and curvetted about, trying out their long and awkward legs. They saw the earthen colours, like a painter's palette; bronze and sepia, ochre and orange and mauve.

"It's beautiful!" breathed the boy, his now fresh-seeing eyes marvelling at the scene before them.

Over in the southwestern sky a bank of down-white cloud came slowly striding hawk-flight high in the deep dark blue sky. Its shadow followed the land, threw shade over the noble animals which momentarily paused in their grazing, sensing the subtle change around them.

26

Stable Life 1

The long summer days flowed on, each slipping away and blending much into one another. Between noon and mid-afternoon the men did as little work as possible. They often idled about in the haybarn or the stables to escape the blasting blaze of sun. Oftentimes they would take a *siesta*, Emilio taking one was a sure guarantee. On this day they pottered around in the main stable. In the stable could be heard a humming of frenetic insects. Fine dust was sifting down from the rafters, coating the horses with a sheen of grey.

Pancho settled himself on a bale of straw, large hands capping his knees, leaning back against the warm, warped boarding of the stable wall. Infinitely fine flakes of chaff floated about, settling on his shoulders like dandruff. Emilio drowsed on a bed of fragrant straw. The simpleton stablehand Julian, a blade of grass between his teeth, was absorbed in plaiting a red dun colt's tail. José sharpened a machete on a grinding stone, in readiness to chop stickwood for the evening fire, Gerardo generously cranking the handle for him.

The dog Salté lifted a hindfoot, cocked his head, and vigorously pounded at his ear, raising a spurt of chaff and dust.

"Away, perro!" snarled José. "I don't want your damn fleas on me." José was as he was, as he always was, tied to the tyranny of his tiresome temperament. He carried on edging the blade of his machete, Gerardo still grittily winding the handle; at the same time he sucked at a callus on the thumb of his other hand in the hope of softening it.

Gerardo sighed heavily.

"Phew, hombre!" gasped José at once. "Your breath stinks. Been eating raw onions or something?"

"Why, sí," glowed Gerardo healthily. "Pancho says they're good for your heart, raw onions."

"Well," said the knife-grinder, "you smell like my grandmother's under-drawers, for crying out loud!"

"Don't rub him up the wrong way, Gerardo," advised Pancho, "he has sharp teeth and can bite – he may even be hungry right now."

Said José : "You'd think you were talking about a dog, dammit! I'm a person, see?"

"So you are, my mistake, my apologies – Oye, Gerardo, I know of a cure for the smell of onion on your breath," Pancho passed over affably.

"Tell him, then," demanded José, "because I'm fair gagging here."

"You know what you need to do, Gerardo?"

"No, but I'm hoping you're going to tell me."

"Chew on a clove of garlic, amigo, that'll get rid of it – Oye, Julian!" the old man's attention diverted elsewhere. "That pie-bald yonder needs worming, as I said before, which is why the poor beast has a face as long as my arm – And the roan there needs shoeing," he crackled on, like a knife scraping sandpaper.

"That there roan is already shod," called back Cándido, with a cut to his voice. "I did it myself only an hour since."

"I remember now, bueno, my mistake, my apologies – Ay, José, your colt is giving you a hungry kind of look, maybe you should get your hair cut. By the by, where's our Juanito – Ah, there he is, with a book in his hand and no doubt with food in his thoughts…"

"What was that, then?" poked in Emilio, waking dreamy-eyed from his doze.

"Go back to sleep, hombre, I was talking to the plough, not its handle. Sit yourself here, Juanito. Show me the book you're reading … Ah, hmm … *Catriona*. By the Stevenson fellow, eh? The English writer."

"He was Scottish," the boy corrected him.

"Uuy, here I go again, my mistake, my apologies – hopefully taken."

Salté trotted up and rested his chin on Juan's knee. The dog's grey-green eyes were focused steadily and earnestly, not to say tenderly on his young master.

"Why, you great fawning soft scruff," said Pancho cheerily. "Has he been fed today, compañero, for he's after something to eat I'll be bound."

"You're probably right at that," grinned Juan. "He knows I've got some sweeties in my pocket."

"Ah, I knew it, the greedy raggy rogue that he is − Have you read any of his poetry, by the by?" Pancho asked the boy, indicating the book in his hand, for which he received a negative answer to that. "Well, he's written some fine stuff which should interest someone of your age. Ay, Juanito, a book unread is like treasure buried away − Oye, Cándido!" he called to the young ranchero leaning against sun-weathered slats of the stable door. "You promised to make a start on that whistle today. I hope you haven't forgotten already, eh?"

"I've got it in mind, Pancho, so stop your fretting." Cándido threw over his winning charming smile, eyes squint-wise and sparkling with unlimited mischief.

The old ranchero turned to the boy again, said whisperingly, "He's promised to whittle me a whistle, he says. Whether he gets round to it or not, your guess is as good as mine."

"I think you're going to have to whistle for that one," grinned Juan.

"Ayí, you may be right there, muchacho − Now, that Robert Louis Stevenson fellow − You're dead square on, he was Scottish − he once took a journey when he was a young man. In some hilly region of France. He had a donkey for his transportation, a creature that gave him plenty of problems. No end of trouble he had. It was a stubborn beast, as you'd expect of a donkey, almost as bad as a mule. Had a mind of her own, just as a female generally does. Caused strife and mayhem no end to our famous book writer traveller. But at the finish of his journey the man was loath to let her go out of his life.

"These turnabouts in our thinking often happen you know, as I've found out myself many a time − Oh, look at your Chapulín, the coy one. I do believe he's having a little snatch of sleep on the sly. Come on, let's give him the pleasure of our company, eh?"

27

Stable Life 2

Pancho stood and stretched, then ambled angle-wise toward the chestnut bay, the boy following up behind him. As they stood contemplatively before the horse, Chapulín perked alert and whickered, obviously enjoying the familiar scent and closeness of his young master. The bay snuffled his nose against the boy's shoulder, shook his cream forelock from large, intelligent eyes. His flanks shivered, muscles twitching, as flies tormented him.

"Back home," said Juan in quiet tones, "I put him in his stable when the sun's down, and there I leave him standing while he tucks into his feed. Every morning I go to him, he's there in the stable still standing as I left him the night before." He turned to the old ranchero. "Why doesn't it tire him, standing all that time? It would kill me, I know."

"Ay well, Juanito, the horse is a big heavy beast to be sure," returned Pancho reflectively. "It takes some real effort for an animal his size to get up from the ground. But in the standing position he's really comfortable. You see, the four limbs on him lock, so to speak, and in a way where no energy is needed. He's perfectly balanced that way, locked solid as your mamá's kitchen table; it's as if he's carrying no weight or bulk at all. This one's as comfortable as you lying on your *petate*." The boy explained that at home he slept in a bed. "Ah, do you now? Well, that's even better for you I suppose. For myself I couldn't lie on anything that's soft. It does my back no good; I need something hard and flat, for my back's sake," and the old man turned aside and spat in the straw, to confirm his point as it were.

Juan went on to another track. "They can cover such distances too

– horses I mean. *Bucephalus* for instance must have travelled tremendous distances."

"Ah sí, the horse of Hernan Cortes is it?"

"No, you're getting mixed up with someone else. I mean the horse of Alexander the Great – I was reading about him only last week. He conquered millions of square kilometres of the old world. So he must have ridden some vast distances on his *Bucephalus*."

"¡El Morzillo! That was the horse of Cortes, and I got it mixed up," muttered the old man. "It seems I'm forever making mistakes and making apologies for them. Still, when you have faults don't be afraid to admit them, and I must admit I get things mixed up when I don't think things through as I ought – when my brain makes wrong connections, crossed wires they call it," he said with a good-humoured shrug, the weathered lines on his face dancing as he spoke.

A scuttering of dust fell from the cross-beams overhead. Through an angled beam of sunlight a spider on the end of its silvery silk lifeline lowered itself onto the horse's croup. With legs swiftly high-stepping over the chestnut hair, it dropped again to the ground to lose itself in a tangle of matted straw.

Pancho glanced over at Gerardo who had recently taken up leather-tooling. The canny craftsman was at this moment punching holes in a fine broad-banded belt, the tip of his tongue slipped out with concentration. "The belt looks good, hermano," he complimented him.

"You reckon?" said Gerardo, highly gratified. "It's what you'd call pride in craftsmanship, as don Roberto himself once told me. The don installed in me the correct and careful way of doing things."

"He *installed* in you?" queried Juan.

"He *instilled* in him," Pancho translated, leaning toward the boy.

"That's how I know it," said Gerardo grandly, "and will never forget it … unless it slips my memory, like."

Cándido sidled up to them, toting a look that was loaded with mischief. "Oye, hermano," he smiled charmingly.

"Sí?" Gerardo glanced up at him.

"Your belt looks real good. What went wrong?"

"Ah, you!"

José called over, "Tweak his ears for him, Gerardo, why don't you? The twist-eyed taco!"

"And you're supposed to be making me a whistle, hombre," Pancho turned on him.

"I will, I shall, I am!" Cándido crafted his way out of this one. "No, seriously though, Gerardo," he went on smoothly, "it looks fair *wapo*."

"You think so?" returned Gerardo guardedly.

Cándido continued pleasantly and conversationally, telling the other about his uncle in Querétaro who once made belts in an almost mass production capacity. The belts he produced were not of leather but made from marijuana hemp, and proved a popular sell-out with young American tourists. "He used to smoke the marijuana in his pipe, but Aunty soon put paid to that little caper – she was not having him sat stoned on her own front doorstep."

Gerardo gaped at him in astonishment.

"He's having you on, amigo," laughed Pancho, then swung round on the mischief-maker. "Now you, muchacho, when you're looking for trouble you never have far to go, do you? Well you can go and take yourself off to the casa and collect our tortillas from Tulia."

"But it's not my turn," objected Cándido truculently. The old man flashed him a withering, caustic look, and he obediently turned on his heels and headed for the house.

"I'll say this for him," said Pancho of the retreating stiff-backed trouble-brewer, "he's generous in his giving, giving us grief mostly. But he has his uses, like that broken strap-watch of his which stopped at two o'clock. Once in the afternoon and once in the night that cheap strap-watch will give you the exactly correct and accurate time," bursting out a loud guffaw at his own joke.

Another complaint was issued, from Emilio this time, wondering what the racket was which had seriously disturbed his siesta. The fat man heaved himself into a sitting position, opened his jaws in a cavernous yawn, showing the full rows of buck teeth. He painstakingly pulled off tight-fitting boots, and peeled off his socks. It was as though he were peeling off his own skin, so long had they been worn on his feet without a change. He began to pick at loose dead skin between his toes. A rank, foul odour assaulted Pancho's nostrils, causing him to jerk up his head in disgust.

"For the love of our Lord Jesus Christ, Emilio!" he bellowed. "Go and bung your feet in the water-butt, you stink like a corpse!"

"I don't smell that bad, surely?"

"Oh hombre, you're far too modest. You could attract all the damn flies of Mexico, and they've started buzzing round you even as I speak."

"Ayí, calamities!" cried the fat man in alarm. "Look at this flesh coming away here, my toes are dropping off!"

"I'm not a bit surprised. You should wash your feet more regularly, dry them properly afterwards," the old man chided him. "You could also change your socks now and again, then you wouldn't have this problem. As the saying has it, everything in life changes except change itself – and your damn dirty socks. You know, the best words of advice are those instantly heeded and acted on, but you don't even listen to me half the time. Why don't you introduce your feet to water? It would be like, I suppose, like a Martian meeting a marsupial."

"What's one of them?" José wanted to know.

"Tell him what a marsupial is, Juanito."

"It's a kind of primitive mammal," said the boy, pleased he could pass on some knowledge he had only recently gained himself. "The female has a pouch on her stomach where she carries her young."

"A kangaroo then, is it?" said José.

"That's one of the group of marsupials, sí," Juan expanded.

The fat man Emilio joked that with his feet now free of socks and boots he could maybe jump like a kangaroo, which got Pancho up on his high horse. "¡Uuy! You're thick-skulled and no mistake," he grated dryly. "Like an Egyptian."

"Who says an Egyptian is thick-skulled?" asked Emilio.

"Herodotus does, that's who."

"And who's he when he's at home?" clipped in Cándido, having rushed back from la casa.

"Why, Herodotus is known as the Father of History," Pancho pontificated.

"So you'll be knowing him, then?" slipped in José with a deadpan face.

The old ranchero told him that Herodotus had lived in times long before the Birth of Christ, and had written in his *Histories* that all the Egyptians were thick-skulled. This prompted young Juan to ask why he had said that and how did he know.

"Saw it himself," returned Pancho, "after a battle between the Egyptians and the Persians. He saw the skeletons scattered over the desert. And the Egyptians were thick-skulled." He got to his feet and stretched himself.

"There's hope for you yet, Emilio," Cándido coolly grinned at him.

Emilio ignored this, more concerned at the moment over Juan's dog. "Call your Salté away, will you, Juanito?" he implored of a sudden. "He's sat here looking at me with those evil grey eyes. Like a wolf he is, and a hungry one at that."

"He's alright," said José, unusually talkative on this day. "Salté only eats meat, not fat pastry," to which the fat man hotly retorted that he had not asked for his opinion.

"Here, Salté!" commanded Juan sharply. The big amiable, harmless softie got up and obediently trotted to his master, with almost a look of 'Well, what have I done wrong?' The dog had only found interest in a chocolate bar tucked in Emilio's shirt pocket. Juan cracked him one across the head, but the dog didn't seem to mind the humiliation he ought to have felt along with the blow, but was only sorry that he'd offended his master – and missed out on the chocolate.

"By the way, Emilio," said the boy lightly, "his eyes are grey-green."

"So he is a wolf, then," grinned the fat one, buck teeth filling his face.

"That's right," pipped in Pancho, "a wolf in sheepdog's clothing."

He stepped back to regain his seat, but someone had re-positioned the bale. Pancho fell back weightily into space, landing on the straw-strewn ground. This instantly set everyone off into gales of laughter.

The old ranchero jumped hurriedly to his feet. "Ay que caray," he muttered darkly, at a loss to know where his precious dignity had run off to, "life is all ups and downs."

28

Moon Shine

It was well past dusk and a mid-June moon was up; full-phased, large and low and glowing bright. The open country was flooded with its clear silver light, and the land itself could have been a moonscape, showing stark sharp shadows, the inky blue-black of these shadows appearing of limitless depth. The day's settled dust and fine sand was as a fall of snow in the moonlight, blue-white and seemingly frost-sparkled.

The rancheros of don Roberto were sat as usual round the evening cookfire, except for José. He had gone away for the day visiting his family, and was in fact overdue in returning to the ranch; no one seemed to be concerned over his lateness, it was quiet and peaceful and trouble-free without him. As the moon rose a little higher he appeared, riding in hard in his accustomed manner on his dappled grey colt, horse and rider finely silhouetted against the moonglow.

"¡Hola, amigos!" he greeted his companions, reining the colt by the moonwashed corral fencing.

He presently approached the group by the fire, carrying rather bulky saddlebags slung over one shoulder. His moonlit face appeared before them. "I've brought you something," he announced with a grin, sliding the saddlebags to his feet. He squatted over the bags proprietarily, lifted out two full earthenware jugs.

"Pulque?" enquired Pancho with interest.

"No, hermano, something stronger," said José in uncharacteristic friendly tones – he had obviously spent a good day with his family. He passed a jug over to the old ranchero.

"How's Rosaria?" asked Pancho politely, hefting the jug in his hand.

"Okay," muttered José thinly, as though he had no wish to discuss his wife.

"Rosaria, like a rose – thorny," whispered Cándido to Juan. "And she can give you looks that could strip the varnish off your saddle."

"I heard that," snarled José, momentarily flaring up, but allowing it to ride as he was in a rare contented mood. "But you're right anyway about my Rosaria, nasty fat-bottomed bitch that she is." He was always wary of his wife at any rate, who was unquestionably larger than him and taller by a head.

Pancho pulled the stopper from the jug and sniffed at the contents with the air of a connoisseur. "Mezcal!" he exclaimed. "A fine grade too I'll be bound."

"But of course," grinned José, rolling himself a nice thick cigarro on account of his present state of uninhibited bonhomie.

"Muy bien," Cándido cried out. "After you, amigo."

"Don't forget me either," said Gerardo gaily, contorting his rubbery face.

"And who are you when the horse is running!" cracked Cándido.

"Plenty for everybody," said José generously. "Go ahead, Pancho, try it, take a good snort. Let's have your considered opinion. It's top grade alright, just as you guessed. The best I could get."

"I should hope so," smiled the old man, "we have a reputation to keep, we don't drink any old muck, only the best quality, don't we hermanos?" He tilted the jug to his mouth with one hand, using his elbow to rest and steady it. He took a long deep draught of the liquor, smacked his lips in evident satisfaction, loudly burped to show the same esteem, and passed the jug on to Cándido, and said : "A man's body you know is merely a vessel for holding pulque or mezcal or tequila. If you only drink water then you deserve to drown in it – a waste of a fellow's body I'm forced to say, even though water does have its uses."

At that moment Emilio awakened with a startling snort, so loud as to lift his whole fat bulk a clear inch from the bale he was resting on. "What's up?" he asked, blinking bleary-eyed at the moonshine. "Did I hear a horse come in? Is José back, then? – Oh, there you are, hombre."

"Go back to sleep, Emilio, we're only trying out José's soda-water," lied Pancho.

"Soda-water, hey? Well, I wouldn't mind some of that. After you,

Gerardo," and the jug was handed over to him. The fat man gulped at it thirstily, then immediately began coughing and spluttering.

"Not bad soda-water, is it?" grinned Pancho.

"Sí, good fiery stuff," agreed Emilio, his eyes watering, "but you could have said it was tequila."

"Oh my, the man has taste to be sure," said Pancho dryly.

"It's mezcal, top grade, six-star," José told him reproachfully. "You horse's mouth!" He chewed on his cigarro as though it were a big fat Havana cigar.

"How naïve can you get?" Cándido chided the fat man.

"Naivety," began Pancho, "is looking at a red chilli and a red tomato and thinking they both taste the same."

"Well, you said it was soda-water," Emilio pointed an accusing finger at the old man, "and it sure as hell isn't soda-water."

"It's not tequila either," slipped in Gerardo gripingly. "Oye, Juanito, are you not having any?" he asked the boy.

"I'll have just one swig," said Juan, "to wet my whistle. And then if you like I'll play my mouth-organ for you."

"¡Ay que bueno!" enthused Pancho. "And speaking of whistles," turning to Cándido with one upraised eyebrow.

"I know, I know," the young man smiled back disarmingly, "I haven't forgotten, so kindly hold your horses."

"Well then hurry it up, muchacho. I'm looking forward to seeing this whistle – Play *Sentimiento y Dolor* if you will, Juanito. I do kind of dote on that one…" and the old ranchero settled back, one eye on the passing jug, the other trying to outstare the moon, watching it slide up the black backdrop curtain of night sky.

Later, as the first jug was nearly emptied and the men feeling mellow or merry, the fire was forgotten and went out completely. At any rate they could see everything about them clearly as the full of the rising moon lighted up the land.

"I feel'm like I'm g-getting *borracho*," garbled Gerardo, as glassy-eyed as a stuffed owl, his ugly, alcohol-strained countenance pallid in the moonlight.

"You certainly look like you're getting drunk," gravelled Pancho, clicking his teeth and winking a roguish eye at the boy Juan beside him.

"Ha, sí? How do you'm m-make that out, then?"

"Oh, I don't know, maybe it's the way you're blinking at the bunkhouse door over yonder. I'm over here, hombre."

"I know exactly where you are, P-Pancho. I've got my eyes and my facts – my faculties."

"Well then, can't you focus on me properly like a proper sober man? – Ah, that's a real nice tune, Juanito. Come on, Gerardo, let's you and me do a turn, eh?"

"What, right here?"

"Where else, you bent taco!"

In the shake of a dog's tail the two were up and standing facing each other, hands held behind their backs.

"Who's g-going to lead?" said Gerardo.

"I am, by God!" declared Pancho decisively, and they broke into the first steps.

The two rancheros danced in the dust, dancing lightly and sprightly, under the light of the moon, as though touched by it. As they spun and gyrated around one another, raising moonwhite dust which foamed about their knees, the onlookers slapped their thighs and tapped booted feet to the beat of Juan's robust harmonica playing.

Several tunes and a couple of dances later, Pancho was broad awake with the fire of mezcal in him, dipping now into the second jug. "You know, hermanos," he said expansively, "life is like a nut, once you've cracked it, it's nice and sweet."

"Say, why don't we take a walk, eh?" he suggested, raring to wander off someplace, anyplace. "Look, it's as light as day," one arm pointed moonward. "Come on, shape yourselves and get off your backsides, and we'll take the jug with us. I'll carry it for safety's sake – that's if you don't object, José? Right, up you come and follow me…"

Pausing for a second, he gave a little hitch to his pantalones, to make certain sure in accordance with the laws of decency and decorum, that he was indeed still wearing his pantalones in a correct manner. Breathing out alcoholic fumes of satisfaction he stumped off into the moonlit landscape, clutching the jug of mezcal as if it were a helpless new-born babe.

29

Moonlight and Ghosts

For a length of time the merrymakers wandered aimlessly and half-drunkenly over a wasteland, under the illumined moon, stumbling about blue-black rock-shaped cutouts of shadow, giggling idiotically at their own clumsiness. The moon was now riding high, full and bright and sharply defined, like a silver-blue sun, foreshortening the shadows of the men as they sashayed and weaved about, colliding into one another, then drifting erratically apart, but gradually making a general forward movement – to where exactly they would themselves not know nor care.

"Drinking is not so bad in itself, you understand," Pancho was saying to Emilio, as they yawed on ahead of the others. "It's when you overdo it that it becomes a problem. That's what you need to watch. So if we must let's overdo it in an orderly civilised decent manner…"

The precocious moonlight coloured the near landscape bluey-black and silver, shaped the shrubs and rocks, the dips and ridges and hollows of rough ground. It was no wonder the men stumbled at every turn, though they were well on their way to total inebriation, skittling and wobbling in and out dark drops.

"Watch where you're going, José!" complained Cándido. "You're tramping all over my feet."

"C-can't be, I'm going in a s-straight line," slurred the other, his head drooped, a fair deal into his cups.

"That must be it then, I thought *I* was going in a straight line – Got to get my bearings – Shove over and give me space, why don't you, damn it!" He glanced up a moment, in time to see a shooting star cut an arc in the cloudless starry nightsky.

" … So if you drink to excess don't overdo it but do it by slow degrees … A man can be content as long as he allows himself to be content, and contentment is that steady pleasant feeling that helps you relax…"

"If you say so," returned Emilio sleepily. "You seem to know it all."

"What's the old one on about up front there?" said José.

"Argh," said Gerardo genially, "our Pancho's had a skinful and he's g-getting *filly-Sophocle* with Emilio." The strong light of the moon shone fully on Gerardo's face, which looked as if he had been splashed with whitewash.

" … He who drinks hard and well and long, Emilio, is a sure sign that something went wrong in his early years. Now me −"

"Who's got the jug?" asked José.

"I'll g-give you one g-guess," said Gerardo, about to giggle.

" … In my younger drinking days I'd get hard liquor by the litre. You couldn't get very far on the piffling little bottles they sell today, because you kept sobering up every time you went back for another bottle…" The old ranchero was speaking now with forced detachment, as if he wished to infer that he was not in the least 'under the influence' of anything that could be termed intoxicating.

" Oye, Pancho!" called over José. "Have you got the jug by any chance?"

"Sí amigo, I have it, but I'm sharing it as you can plainly see − And remember this, Emilio, you can't wash away your sins with strong drink, though no one can stop you trying…" Pancho took another generous belt of the liquor, his face gleaming in the moon's glow, features clearly etched. "Still with us, Juanito?" he called complacently over his shoulder.

"I'm still around." The boy was amused over the men's alcohol-induced silliness.

The men's moonshadows shortened further as the moon moved on its inching way.

"It's kind of g-ghostly this light, isn't it?" said Gerardo presently, and hiccupped genteelly as he straggled on with the others.

There was a brief silence, except for the sound of boots crunching soft rock underfoot; then :

"My uncle in Querétaro once saw a ghost," Cándido opened up.

"Oh no! Not your mad uncle again."

"But he did," insisted Cándido. "He met up with this ghost on the top of the aqueduct in Querétaro."

Gerardo, who never seemed to learn a lesson, even though he may have suspected a gibe of some kind, nevertheless took the bait : "What the hell was your uncle doing on the aqueduct?" he asked, plunging in.

"Well, he said he'd lived in Querétaro all his life and had never properly seen the aqueduct. So one night he went up there and met this ghost. The two of them started talking, getting along famously. The ghost wanted to know how life was down in town, and my uncle told him about the new buildings going up on *Gutierrez Najera*."

"Argh, I don't believe it!"

"That's exactly what the ghost said to my uncle. He couldn't believe these new changes. And my uncle had taken his lunchbox with him to the aqueduct, so he asked the ghost if he'd like something to eat."

"I can't stomach this," groaned Gerardo with his own disbelief.

"Funnily enough those were the very words the ghost used. They went on chatting real friendly like, as if the ghost wasn't a ghost at all but a proper living person in the flesh."

"I think I'm dreaming," griped Gerardo.

"Exactly what my uncle said at the time, the very same words." Cándido cast a serious expression, squint eyes severely crossed. "The strange thing was he had been dreaming after all."

"Grrh!" responded Gerardo with gritted teeth.

"So he never saw a ghost, then?" said José. "He only dreamt of it, is that it?"

"It was real enough for my uncle, though," Cándido answered him, "like this night is as bright as day, even when it's still night time and late in the bargain. Anyway, at the time I reckon my uncle was smoking too much marijuana in his pipe."

"Don Roberto once saw a ghost, saw it in his own casa," Pancho sang silkily through an alcoholic haze of euphoria, hugging the last jug of mezcal tight to his chest. "As you know, the don is a man of honour and wouldn't lie to me – or anyone. Besides, Tulia saw the very same ghost. In fact she was first to see it. It happened one night a few years back. There was no moon like there is tonight. It was a rough and windy night, which is appropriate I do suppose for such a visitation, hmm…"

"Pass the mezcal, Pancho," José interrupted him, "you've had it long enough."

"Ah sí amigo, here you go – " reluctantly letting loose possession of the precious jug, which now didn't weigh much at any rate – "Well, as I say it was a windy night and the windows rattled in their frames. Everything made of wood creaked like something alive. But the don thought he heard something else, a different kind of sound, a sort of wailing, unusual he thought and got out of his bed to investigate."

The old ranchero paused a moment, possibly for a more dramatic effect to his story, probably sorting out in his liquor-soaked brain what he needed to say next. He gazed up at the brightly shining moon high in the nightsky, and the many stars strewn so haphazardly it seemed across the broad, Bible-black backcloth, then at last went on :

"He crept downstairs in his nightshirt, a loaded pistol in his hand, and in the hall he found Tulia, who seemed upset — It was Tulia who had wailed. 'What's the matter, Tulia?' he said, 'you look as if you've seen a ghost.' 'Well, your honour,' says Tulia, 'and begging your pardon, but I have indeed.' 'You have what?' asked the don. 'I've seen a ghost,' says Tulia, 'only a moment ago, walking out of your library and going on to the kitchen — Oh! There it is, look!' she says, (Pancho was miming all the gestures) pointing to a figure in a long white nightshirt gliding slowly along the far passageway.

"Don Roberto looks hard down the passageway and says, 'Why, it's only my guest señor Vallejo in his nightshirt.' 'But, your honour,' says Tulia, 'if you'll forgive a silly old woman, that señor Vallejo he left the casa two days ago. I saw him leave myself, upon my soul he did indeed.' 'Of course, so he did,' said the don, 'I remember it now. So who is that then wandering over my house?' 'I don't know, I surely don't,' says poor Tulia, half out of her wits, 'I only know I don't like the looks of it.'"

Don Roberto roused up his boys, Pancho continued his tale, and they searched the casa from top to bottom. They did not find a thing, certainly not a man in a nightshirt, except that they themselves including the don were wearing their nightshirts, because they had been comfortably sleeping in their beds. They began to suspect one another, so the don ordered everyone back to bed, and for Tulia to take a tablet, and thought that was the end of the affair. And the wind blew on all the night long.

It was of a certainty not the end of it, for the following day the don received a telephone call from a señora Vallejo in Saltillo.

"You'll never guess the reason for her call," purred Pancho tipsily, "so I'll tell you. She was inviting the don to her *late* husband's funeral. He'd gotten himself killed in a road accident outside Saltillo two days before."

The old ranchero smiled at his companions, ready to deliver the finishing touch to his tale. He said how gentlemanly it had been for the fellow to drop in on the don before his travels on to wherever people go when they've finally done with life. "A decent and proper way of showing appreciation for the don's noted hospitality," he averred. "Muy bien, eh, hermanos?"

The moon stood out clearly and dominant in the sable sky. It's light poured munificently over the wandering ranchero revellers, sometimes throwing a kind of halo over each sombrero'd head.

It wasn't too long later when the men realised that Pancho had vanished from sight. "Where's Pancho?" said Gerardo, gaping around him. "Where the devil has he gone to?"

"He's here flat out on the ground," sighed Emilio blearily. "Dead drunk I'd say."

"How'd he manage to get in that state?" asked José, not without envy.

"You don't know the half of it," returned the fat man. "He was all afternoon with the don, wasn't he? Splitting a bottle or two of the don's first grade."

"He never let on to that, the old horse!" said Gerardo somewhat aggrievedly. "Now what're we going to do?"

"About what?" said Cándido.

"This drunken old man, that's what. We can't leave him out here for the night, can we?"

"Why not?" countered José. "He's gotten where he wants to. Wish I was drunk as that, but what chance have you when he hogs the booze half the time."

"I'm as sober as a cardinal," confessed Cándido with some pride, then immediately hiccupped, glancing quizzically about him, as though to say 'Who was that, then?'

"We're leaving him here, then?" said Emilio, slightly shocked.

"Sure, he'll be alright," José assured him. "It's a warm night, and besides he's up to his chin with fiery mezcal, isn't he?"

"He might get attacked by some wild animal."

"What wild animal? No animal dare go near him, not if it's got any sense."

"Tell you what," began Cándido, an eager note stealing into his voice, "we can get just as plastered as Pancho. We're not too far away from the pueblito, so why don't we go and knock up old Pedro and get ourselves a bottle of the hard stuff – Got any money on you, Gerardo?"

Gerardo said he had perhaps enough for one bottle. The boy Juan volunteered to stay with his *patron*, and settled down for a sober night's sleep. The rancheros, inebriated enough by any standard but determined to drink themselves into total oblivion, set off once more for the lure of old Pedro's cantina – merely a hole in the wall – in a nearby village. Leaving the boy and the inert figure of Pancho, who was by now snoring like a boar.

And summer-wise the June moon shone like a white sun upon the – not dilly-dally wandering now but with a decided route and definite destination – upon the liquor-soaked rancheros . And the stars of the night edged along the way of the universe in their stardrift startide turnings.

30

Bandits!

It was a little after midday and the men were taking a break, hunkered down on their heels ranchero-style at the entrance to the main stable. Emilio had broken off work earlier and was resting – most likely sleeping – in the shade of the stable. Not at all hot today, thought the horsemen; mild and tolerably bearable. A wide swathe of cloud drifted over, partially obscuring a gentle sun, reducing it to an anaemic magnolia-coloured dinner plate in the clouded sky.

Pancho stirred from a bout of lethargy – of late he had been drinking more than was good for him, according to Gerardo, who knew all about ailments that could strike without warning. "What's he got in that bowl? Looks like spinach or alfalfa."

"Who? José? The dark green stuff?" said Cándido.

"Sí, that dark green stuff. What the hell is it?"

"It's marijuana."

"Is he intending to cook it – like spinach?"

"Smoke it more like. You smoke it, don't you?"

"Ah, you smoke it before you cook it, is it?"

Cándido gave the old man a peculiarly pitying, contemptuous glance. "Pancho, don't you know what marijuana is?"

The old ranchero gave out a short barking laugh. "Sure I know. Smoked marijuana joints before you were born."

"So that's why your brain is addled."

José meanwhile put away his 'treasure' in an odd-looking pouch and stashed it away in his saddlebag. The pouch was made from a young bull's scrotum, another 'treasure' of his and excellent as a tobacco pouch – and for preserving his stash of marijuana.

"Ah, the good things in life, eh?" the old man sighed with pleasure. "And Life itself is a God-given gift –"

"My mamá and papá gave me mine," Cándido volleyed back, curving his lips in a sardonic smile.

"Time is a gift too, so make the most of it. We have brains in our skulls to reason out all manner of things." Pancho glanced meaningfully at the younger man, and continued : "Of course a few may have missed out on that – but never mind, muchacho, for even an idiot can make a virtue of stupidity. Now, what else is good in life … ?"

Chirped Cándido, "The ability to shut a big mouth when it says too much?"

"Sí, amigo, there is that," conceded Pancho, his grin embracing the others in an invitation to join in on the conversation.

José said that he was all in favour of an endless supply of *ready-made* cigarros – and why couldn't they grow on trees? Young Juan pointed out that tobacco was in fact a plant, but José wanted properly rolled cigarros on his trees. Had Emilio been in on this no doubt he would have emphasised the infinite benefits of a good sleep every night – and every day too perhaps.

"Gerardo?"

Heads turned to him. Gerardo deliberated, ignoring the silly snide smirks of the others, and at last said : "Well, to have a first-class doctor live near to you would be a good and useful thing, don't you think?"

"Are you in need of a doctor?"

"Not right now, no, but one never knows. It's good to be on the safe side, I always say, and a first-rate medical man living nearby would be mighty handy, I reckon."

"Poor fellow would be worked to death if he lived anywhere near you."

Gerardo rightly ignored this, and began rummaging in a lidless wooden box, muttering to himself : "I was sure those shoeing nails were in here." He next started nibbling at a fingernail as if making a meal of it; his ugly, uncompromising features screwed up with concentration.

"Hey, look at that! Look at him!" suddenly cried José, pointing beyond the corral. "Someone's in a sure-fire hurry."

"He's coming this way."

"Shift over, I can't see."

"Who is it?"

"Can't tell with all the dust he's kicking up."

"Looks like some muchacho."

"It is," confirmed Cándido. "One of the kids from the pueblito."

"Which pueblito?" asked José. "Not mine."

"Where the leprosarium is," said Pancho, "and I know that scruffy scamp. It's little Manuel."

A small dusty figure appeared half-trotting half-staggering in a cloud of dust of his own making. As he neared the corral he frantically waved his arms, yelling something the horsemen were unable to catch.

The youngster was now before the men, looking half-dead on his feet, coughing, gasping, choking. " Señores!" he uttered chokingly, sweat and tears streaming down his brown chubby face. "Bandits! Bandits in the village!"

The men exchanged grins. What prank was this whelp of a rascal up to! Pancho however recognised true naked fear when he saw it. He held the tenderling by his shoulders, sat him down on a bale of straw. He turned to Gerardo and told him to bring a mug of water, then gazed down on the distraught child.

"Now, Manuel, just get your breath back first, then you can tell me all about it, what's happened."

"¡Señor Francisco!" croaked the boy in alarm, "there are bad men in the village…"

"Just take it easy, niño," soothed Pancho. "Bad men, you say. What kind of bad men? How many of them?"

"Four, maybe more, señor. They came in a truck…"

Gerardo returned with a mug of water. "Now sip this, little one – Don't gulp it down, take your time…"

Between gasping gulps and spluttering at the pot mug of water, the frightened diminutive villager opened up. And as the boy babbled on barely coherently Pancho motioned in an unmistakable aside to the men to saddle up the mounts. They didn't stay to hear any more of the youngster's tale.

"Old señor Pedro in the village says the truck was stolen … He says the men are con-convicts … escaped from a federal state prison…"

"What do they want in your village?"

"I don't know, señor Francisco, but old señor Pedro says he knows one of them – one of them bad men."

"Is that so, my fine fellow? Well, that's makes it a bit more interesting, if I may so say – Are we all saddled up then?" to the waiting mounted rancheros, their horses skittering and dancing, eager to be off.

"Except for Emilio," said José. "Excused duties is he?"

"Damn that fat lump of laziness!" cursed the old man, storming into the stable. "Stir yourself, you bed-bug!" he barked angrily, kicking the recumbent fat man in his ample buttocks. "Life isn't quite over yet."

"What's the matter? Has a war started or something?" whined Emilio, disgruntled and not yet fully awake. "Can't a fellow rest in some peace around here?" But for all his heavy bulk and sleepiness he was up like a jack-in-the-box and clear-eyed, ready for action, whatever it might be.

Pancho too was now saddled up, thanks to the stablehand Julian. The old ranchero slapped the flank of his white mare Macha, then reached for a gun-belt that was hanging on a hook near the door. He buckled it on a shade self-consciously. Diving a fist into his saddlebag he drew out an antique .45 Colt repeater; it was not his but on loan from don Roberto's youngest, Jorge. He slipped the heavy gun into its holster; it was already loaded, it was always ready loaded. And he too was ready.

Pancho slow-cantered out the stable. The other riders were bunched up, the mounts milling confusedly. "Let's go! ¡Vamonos!" he roared. "Be back soon I dare say," glancing behind him at the three youngsters.

Moments later Emilio rode out of the stable on a speckled-grey roan. He was instantly on his way, his mount running at a fair fine spanking pace, following the line of raised dust that materialised in the near distance.

As soon as Emilio was out of sight Juan had his powerful bay Chapulín saddled. He mounted the tall horse in one swift movement, Chapulín snorting and grinding at his bit and keen to be off.

"Manuel, stay with Julian," commanded Juan. "I won't be long." Horse and rider were soon lost in dust as the bay at once broke into a gallop as though in a race.

When they reached the outskirts of the pueblito Pancho halted his rancheros. "We'll dismount here and walk in quietly," he told them, leaping from Macha like a young man, adrenalin pumping in him.

The men tethered their mounts to a nearby mesquite tree, glancing warily about them; there seemed to be no one around.

"You stay here, Emilio," ordered the old man, "and keep your eyes open and peeled." The fat rider watched as the others set off stealthily in a ragged line, hugging the walls of adobe homesteads.

At a corner Pancho spied a dark-brown wrinkled face peering at him.

"Pedro? Is that you? Sí, it's old Pedro. Get yourself over here, you old stick, and tell us what's going on around this place."

A figure stepped into full view, small and scrawny and hunchbacked. The ancient sidled forward unhesitatingly, giving a kind of salute with a raised hand. "Glad you came, Pancho," he wheezed in low urgent tones. "It was me who sent off little Manuel – he can run fast."

"Well, what's happening around here? Manuel mentioned four desperados – convicts. Convicts for crying out loud! Is that right?"

"That's it, amigo, and one of them is armed."

"Armed? With what, a machete?"

"Hell, no, a hand-gun of some sort. I seen it. German make I'd say, maybe one of them Lugers."

"Why are these four here, Pedro? What do they want? They're escapees for goodness sake, from a state prison. Isn't that what you said?"

"Ay sí, they're convicts alright. One of them, the one who has the gun – I guess he's the leader – well, he happens to be a cousin or some such kin of our Alfonso –"

"Alfonso?"

"Alfonso Alvarez, he lives here in our pueblito."

"Ah sí, that Alfonso, I know who you mean now."

Old Pedro sidled up close to the ranchero, said, "This convict *cousin* reckons Alfonso has some of his money stashed away someplace."

"Money? What money is that?"

"Dirty money, Pancho, from a bank robbery in Gomez Palacio –   you remember that raid? – It's the reason he's doing time in prison – or was!"

"What does Alfonso say about it?"

"He's not here, and that's the trouble. These four banditos are ransacking the whole pueblito."

"Where are they now?"

"I can tell you exactly where they are right now. See that thick line of organ cacti across the way there? There's a feed-barn sitting on its own behind the cacti. Everyone shares the feed-barn. That's where those bastards are right this moment, in that barn. All four of them. Can't you hear them yelling and cursing?" Old Pedro touched the other's sleeve. "Take care, amigo, these are nasty desperate hombres."

Pancho turned to his rancheros. "Okay, let's go. We'll surround that barn, flush them out of there somehow. Come on!"

They soon reached the barn, a dilapidated affair, tall-ceilinged with double doors at its front and no windows, the men noticed.

"Take a look round the back, José, quietly."

José crept like a cat out of sight. Cándido checked the ropes he had brought, Gerardo feeling for something in the saddlebag he had slung over one shoulder.

José stepped alongside the wood wall of the feed-barn like a jungle predator. The toe of his boot stubbed against something hard. A large and rusty kerosene drum. It felt full, probably rainwater, reasoned the ranchero. As he bent to take a closer look a powerful smell of gasoline snatched at his nostrils. Well, well, the damn thing's full of fuel, he exulted; that'll come in handy, if he had anything to do with it, he thought with malicious joy. José was well-known as an incendiary, he liked nothing better than playing with fire. He would smoke or burn the bastards out of their den, he decided.

"Psst! Pancho!" he hissed, returning to the front of the barn. "I've got the answer right here, look! We'll have them out without a by-your-leave," and José set to with his devilish plan, generously splashing the inflammable liquid against the wooden barn walls as though washing down his horse. The barn was old and tinder-dry and was soon aflame on all four sides, thick black smoke beginning to billow up to darken the sky. Inside, and unsuspecting, the convicts were shouting and arguing over something.

It didn't take long, the burning of the barn, and plenty happened in the next ninety seconds or so.

Cándido had set a snare for the first man out. One side of the double doors crashed open. The canny ranchero snagged a foot, yanked hard on his rope. The victim went flying, falling heavily in the dust. Cándido kicked him where it counted most, putting the man completely out of action. The ranchero went to work with swift deft movements of hands and rope. The man was soon firmly hog-tied.

Pancho dealt with the second desperado, who happened to be the one with a gun. The man was left-handed which suited the old ranchero admirably, a nice convenience he thought with a grim smile. He moved snakelike sidewise and with his own .45 Colt knocked the other's weapon clean out of his hand, following that with a short, sharp pistol-whipping of the man's exposed face, at the same time tripping him as he rushed out from the smoke-filled barn. All of this took just a few tense seconds. José then took over, kicking the man to the ground. He tied up the bleeding-faced ruffian with good strong cattleman's rope.

Gerardo felled the third man in one swift swooping blow. His man literally jack-knifed, folded in two, and crashed unconscious to the ground.

"Good grief, Gerardo!" gasped Pancho. "What did you hit him with?" And Gerardo, grinning like a gorilla, held up his trusty steel-headed *ball pein* hammer.

Cándido, done with his trussing of convict number one, made a start on Gerardo's number three.

"One got away," said Pancho. "He'll be in that there damned truck I expect."

"He won't get far," piped a boy's voice behind him.

"Juanito!"

Juan held up the ignition key to the hijacked truck.

"Well, I'll be…"

The rancheros went tearing off to the truck presumably still parked up a side alley where it had been all the time. Easily finding and reaching the vehicle they found the fourth man, lying flat out unconscious on the ground by the cab. Emilio was standing there with folded arms and one foot resting on the man's chest, much in the manner of a big game hunter posing with his kill. He showed his buck teeth, grinning widely, proudly and triumphantly.

"Emilio! You were supposed to stay with the mounts," the old man charged at him.

"I did," said the fat man, still grinning piano keys, "till Juan showed up. I stayed with him instead. The horses could look after themselves."

This last one of the criminal quartet was tied up like the others, Emilio and Gerardo dragging the comatose fellow by the feet back to the plaza grounds where the four were laid out in a neat row.

The old man Pedro tottered on thin legs up to the rancheros, who were guarding their prey as if it were a haul of gold bullion. "That was an almighty smart piece of work you pulled there, amigos," he cackled, his deeply wrinkled face creased more so in a grin. "I expect you do this sort of thing on a regular basis, is it?"

"That's right, old man," cut in Cándido, "but not on Sundays."

"I can hear crying," said José. "Can you hear crying? Someone's crying. Sounds like it's coming from that place," pointing to a small adobe dwelling facing the plaza grounds.

"That'll be Yolanda," old Pedro told him.

"Alfonso's eldest muchacha?" asked Pancho.

"Sí, poor Yolanda. Those bastards gave her a hard time, roughed her up some. As if a young girl like that would know where that damned bank money is hidden – Pah!"

"I know Yolanda," spoke up Juan. "She's in my class at school. I'll go to her."

Pancho gave a nod to Gerardo. "You got your first-aid pack?"

"I have, right here."

"Go along with Juanito. See if you can be of some help to the muchacha."

The old villager Pedro was still with the rancheros. He turned to Pancho and said wheezily, as though he only had a limited supply of air, "You know, that damned feed-barn is a-burning to the ground." As he spoke José swept a hand over his swarthy, guilty face. "We, everyone, use it, a community thing so to speak," he went on in a high wheedling tone. "Who's going to pay for a new barn and a full supply of feed-grain? That's what I want to know. Answer me that, hey? His eyes, steely and glinting like a buzzard's, were saying ' Don't mess with me, hombre'.

Pancho gazed at him with a commiserating wag of his head. He could almost taste the other, his aged body emanating a pungent smell of dried sweat. "If Alfonso has a bank haul hidden someplace," he told the ancient, "then maybe Alfonso could afford to cough up the pesos and foot the bill. But I don't think he has that swag or even knows anything about it. And if he hasn't a few hundred to throw around … well, Pedro, hear this : There's bound to be a handsome reward for these here jailbirds – " He booted one of them in the butt, simply for emphasise. " – The entire pueblito is entitled to it, and as far as we're concerned you're welcome to it – the reward I mean – That right with you, hermanos?" The rancheros assented, albeit reluctantly. "Okay with you, Pedro?"

" Ayí! Muy bien, of course. A thousand thanks, mi amigos!"

Meanwhile, in the tiny adobe home Juan squatted before the girl Yolanda, who was crouched cowering in a corner of the room. The place was a tip, everything tossed about, turned over, ripped and smashed and discarded. Yolanda, her normally sweet young face now cruelly beaten, smote Juan's heart. Her large eyes were purple-bruised, soft cheeks red-splotched and swollen, with streaks of dust-filled, blood-stained tears coursing down her face.

Gerardo clumped round to the rear yard to find water.

"Yolanda? It's me, Juanny. Juan Ramos."

The girl sniffed and snivelled like a little puppy smacked for some doggy naughtiness. At the sound of Juan's pure, boyishly innocent and familiar voice, she burst out afresh into a flood of tears. Tears of self-pity, tears of pain and humiliation, easily provoked, thought the boy, after what she had so recently gone through. He took one of her hands, held it tenderly in his own, saying no more until Gerardo returned moments later with a basin of water and a somewhat tattered grubby towel, there being nothing else of use at hand.

Yolanda managed to restrain her weeping fit as the ranchero carefully and gently cleaned up her disfigured face; he remembered the clean bandages in his aid-pack, and so put the dirty towel to one side. Juan kept a hold of the girl's hand, smiling his reassurance.

Gerardo went off again to change the basin of stained water for more fresh. The two youngsters could hear him in the rear yard, filling the basin from a rain-barrel. The girl, of a sudden and with surprising agility and energy, threw herself into Juan's arms, wrapping her thin body tightly about him.

"Oh, Juanny!" she cried plaintively in her anguish.

"There, there, it's okay now. It's over with. We have those – those dirty swine safely tied up and gagged," he soothed her with a gentle whispering. He held the girl protectively at the waist, thrilled at her softness which was a new experience for him. He was also relieved that nothing worse had been inflicted on this vulnerable female form. This gave him angry vengeful thoughts. If only he had known and come earlier.

Gerardo had performed a commendable patching up job on Yolanda, and Juan managed to raise her spirits a little. She felt strong enough presently to get on her feet, Juan there with a steadying hand. He held her by her slim waist, and the three of them stepped out into the bright sunlight blazing broadly over the plaza grounds.

A short time later they heard a commotion as of a busy highway. A line of vehicles rumbled into view, fanning out across the dusty square of the plaza. Federal cars, motorbikes and trucks, accompanied by a military array of army jeeps and a troop-carrier.

"My!" gasped Juan in delighted surprise. "The cavalry has arrived!"

"Great timing, wouldn't you say?" commented Cándido.

And it was at this moment that the small pueblito suddenly burst into life. Pouring out from every doorway and side alley a stream of women, old men and children. Out from their humble adobe homes, to stare in utter astonishment at the extraordinary scene over the plaza; Pancho and his rancheros and the four trussed villain specimens, the heavily armed federal officers and army personnel spreading out from their halted vehicles.

Pancho took note of a certain anomaly. He cornered the old man, Pedro. "Allow me to ask you this, you old stick, just where're all the men of the village?"

Old Pedro gave back a wicked grin and said, "They left early this morning by charabanc – specially laid on like – for that tournament affair in Guanajuato. You know the one I mean, Pancho, where no women are allowed, hee-hee!"

"So…" Pancho turned to his co-rescuers, "that's why little Manuel came to us for help."

"The Five Just Men," said Emilio, proudly showing his full range of large buck teeth.

"You never could count, sleepylocks," Pancho grinned back. He snatched Juan's sombrero from his head and fondly mussed the boy's hair. "How about *Six* Just Men, eh?"

The rancheros went along with that, sporting pleased looks. All the same, they still possessively stood guard over their 'bagged game' waiting in the plaza dust to be picked up by the advancing party of federal officialdom and military support.

FIRST INTERLUDE

I

Victor Salazar spooned curd off a dish of soured milk and plastered it on a cold tortilla. He rolled the tortilla into a near cigar shape and began his breakfast. Drawing comfort from the simple fare Victor Salazar fell into a habitual reverie, trying to ignore the noises sniping at him from all sides. Children were screaming with wild abandon in the next room. A baby was whimpering in its cot – a bottom drawer of a decrepit dresser a pace away from his flip-flopped feet. Women were laughing coarsely by a wash-tub in a rubbish-cluttered yard. A scrawny bantam cock crowed on the roof. Dogs were barking all around, as though in need of attention. A motorbike revved up in the street. There were many people passing by in the street, coming and going; women and their kids, fruit-sellers, taco-sellers, tradesmen, workers going off to mill or workshop. Beat-up trucks lumbered along this teeming narrow street, honking impetuously, gears grinding as they negotiated pot-holes and loose cobblestones. More shrieking and shouting out there as folk argued and cursed or laughed without humour. Hammering going on next door as a cobbler who lived within had already begun his working day. And the cock continued to crow, as if it had not been heard or heeded the other times, calling louder and imperatively.

It was undoubtedly the busiest and noisiest street in this particular poor area of Mexico City. Or so thought Victor Salazar who was heartily sick of it; he hated this hot, smelly, noisy cityscape. His only solace was to allow his mind to dwell on a time when he had visited his sister, who had married a fairly well-off farmer and naturally lived out in the country, somewhere near San Miguel in Guanajuato. He wished that he too lived and worked in the countryside.

Breakfast over with Victor Salazar set off at once for work. A ten-hour stint in a nearby factory which made slippers and sandals. He was a cutter, and the only male on his floor. And he was thoroughly fed up with that also, for the women were drabs and sluts and big-mouthed in his opinion. He despised them with such vehemence that he could almost taste the bitterness of it.

He pushed through a dense pack of humanity heaving like one amorphous mass in the ugly trash-littered thoroughfare. His feet kicked broken bottles and rusting tin cans, soft rotting fruit and peel. The dust was black with pollution and hung on hard to his feet. He stepped in dog excrement, attempting to avoid the onrush of a fat woman tanking along with a huge basket of melons resting on her rebozo-turbaned head. Deafened by the bawling and shouting, harried by swarms of scruffy street-kids, hustled aside to allow passage for a donkey and cart, on went Victor Salazar. Thinking of a visit to his sister one autumn time, where he helped in the apple orchards ... *These were fruitful autumn harvest hours, and the windfall applesmell intoxicating the deeper he strolled into the orchard. The trees sang and whistled with hidden foliaged birds, and a full-eyed blue-eyed sky stared the Earth out of countenance ...*

II

Victor Salazar was into a maze of busy, poor and grubby, peopled streets, like ants in a disturbed ants' nest. Street urchins hurled verbal abuse at him.

Transistor radios blared from open windows. There was a stink of rotten vegetables and fruit, unwashed bodies, and raw sewage. He came out of a tortuous labyrinth of alleyways and mean dwellings into a wide main road. A roaring river of traffic; buses and cars, taxis, heavy haulage trucks, all blasting their horns and spewing black exhaust fumes. He crossed the road, dodging between moving vehicles, and entered a side street. His place of work was at the end of it.

He worked all day long on the factory floor, two storeys up, sat on a high metal stool before a workbench, cutting soles and heels for leather sandals. He never saw the light of day because there were no windows on his floor. The enormous square room was lit by strips of fluorescent lighting hanging from bare iron girders in the low-slung ceiling. A couple of battered fans revolved slowly, merely wafting hot stuffy air and flies from one workbench to another. The air was filled with vulgar raucous laughter as the slovenly women entertained themselves. And Victor Salazar daydreamed on … *Wet-winged dew-dropping morning orchard ground, where red-cheeked children happily scampered barefooted under the sun-stippled shadow-rich realms of the orchard trees. And the rising morning sun flushed birds from out the trees, and the shadows died in glorious streams of light …*

III

Victor Salazar wended his way home through a maelstrom of humanity in a dull evening light. Traffic was dense, impatient and angry, roaring in its vehicular fury. Street hawkers shoved their cheap shoddy wares in his face, pestering him, tormenting him, demanding custom. He was jolted and squeezed by a clamorous crowd surrounding him; horns sounding, people calling and gesticulating, heaving and sluggishly flowing like thick sludge in a river. He happened to glance up at the sky. And he saw that the sky was hazy with dirt and dust and exhaust smoke, the sun a dull orange disc, misshapen in its setting, melting over the tops of high-rise office blocks.

In his fevered mind Victor Salazar played again with his sister's children, like that first time he had visited them so long ago it now seemed to him, but the memory of it was clear and sweet, refreshing and choked with happy, homely incidence… *The autumn dampened grasses shivered and rippled as a wind stole in. The children smiled with cupid lips and blackcherry eyes, chubby bare feet flattening wet grass. And their breath was a fruity fragrance of ripe apples as they worked, fresh as flowers, gathering in the harvest.*

Part Six

Part Six

31

Letter of Summons

One Monday morning Pancho was called to don Roberto's casa to pick up a letter addressed to him. He had not received mail of any kind in at least a decade and he was naturally curious to know who had sent it. Trundling from the don's residence with the mystery missive held tight in his hand, he headed for the bunkhouse where he knew he'd be alone and away from nosey prying eyes. He was not willing to share the contents of his letter with the others, at any rate not until he found out what it was all about.

In the dim gloom of the windowless bunkhouse the old man tore open and read his letter. It was disappointingly brief. The writer was a cousin who lived in Tijuana. Moreover he was one who regularly crossed the border with the USA, involving himself in lucrative business deals of some kind in San Diego. He must be, as Pancho had rightly speculated, a man of immense wealth and property.

The gist of the message – which was in reality all it contained – informed him to make a personal appearance at a certain address in a town some thirty kilometres west of don Roberto's ranchland. He should not fail, it expressed strongly, to be there by sundown on the following Saturday. A 'special' surprise awaited him, it declared intriguingly.

There was a postscript, the import of which struck Pancho as an odd thing to say. It asked : *'When are you going to get yourself remarried? Isn't it about time before it is too late?'*

The letter was signed Angel Palacio Ramírez. The ranchero recalled that this particular cousin was a shrewd, clever fellow with his head screwed on right. Possessing brilliant business-sense he was destined for making a mint of money, Pancho had always reasoned, and his cousin had no doubt already achieved his full potential.

Stepping out of the bunkhouse dimness into a drench of sunlight, he joined the men working in the corral. The old man idly wondered what the 'special' surprise could possibly be, but for the present allowed it to drop from his mind. All the same he was conscious of a favourite phrase – 'If opportunity comes your way don't let it pass you by' – and he would indeed make that date.

When the proposed day arrived, when dawn first showed a pale pink light, Pancho was up with the birds. He borrowed don Roberto's spacious zinc bathtub, had it dumped on the 'blind' side of la casa. Don Roberto's housekeeper Tulia supplied hot water, soap and towels. While the old ranchero soaked and soused his body in soapsuds, Tulia sat herself on the back porch, with the don's prized Winchester '73 repeating rifle laid across her lap. This was for added security and guaranteed privacy for the vulnerably naked ranchero. And the night before he had induced Tulia to trim his hair, clean and press his clothes, while he himself polished up his boots, and even cut his nails – fingernails *and* toenails. One had to be ready for any contingency he avowed.

His companions were no wiser than he concerning the summons and 'special surprise' waiting at the end of his journey. At any rate he would know all in good time, and the others considered him presentable enough to face whatever was in store for him in town. There he stood, spruced up, pomaded and perfumed, near like a twin to the boss man don Roberto himself; cheeks gleaming as much as his boots, a fresh clean bandanna wrapped around a well-scrubbed neck. Even his sombrero had been through the dusting and cleansing treatment. It was a pity that he had some dusty riding to do first in order to reach the highway, the men opined judiciously.

"Just take it nice and slowly," Gerardo advised him with un-Gerardo-like geniality, but with typical womanish fussiness. A fly alighted on the end of his nose – a big, buzzing horsefly, stinging hot on his nose. Crossing his eyes and glaring down at it, Gerardo made an angry swipe across his face. The sting from his slap was much hotter, and painful he found, but the fly did condescend to buzz off.

Cándido rode with the old man as far as the westbound highroad, waited with him until an old *autobus* came coughing along and stopping to take on its new passenger. The young man waved to the ranchero, wished him luck, took Macha's rein and cantered back into the wild desolate range-land.

32

Town Cantina

*P*ancho soon became something of a sensation aboard the aging, clapped-out autobus. Whenever he took off on a journey such as this it was his custom to carry a full canteen of fair strong liquor, to fortify himself during the boring spell of travel. Being a natural generous soul in the bargain it was inevitable that he should share this booze with his fellow passengers.

Before the bus reached its destination Pancho had the driver and his passengers singing at the top of their voices. The ranchero went clumping up and down the aisle, passing round his canteen and urging the women to 'loosen up a little', as he worded it.

The bus snorted and chugged into the town's terminal like a holiday coachful hitting a seaside resort. The passengers tumbled out in clotted clumps of humanity, faces aglow with inebriated well-being. The old man shook the driver's hand, and set off in pursuit of a certain street at the further end of town. It took him some time, stopping often to ask directions from the townsfolk.

Late afternoon found him – saddlebags slung over one shoulder, empty canteen clipped to his belt – standing at the address as directed in the letter.

Well, well, he thought, this looked promising. It was a cantina. Hardly pretentious nor even modest, a general workaday rundown joint suitable for the town's habitual drinkers and the usual down-and-outers.

He pushed through the double, half-cut swing-doors and stepped inside.

It was a typical small-town cantina, smelling of sawdust, strong urine and stale tobacco smoke – and alcohol. Scattered about the shabbily decorated room were cheap square metal tables with beer adverts imprinted on their surfaces, along with metal chairs of the kind that make a screeching din when moved about. Squalid would be a compliment here, though the old man couldn't see that; he was surprised that the place was devoid of customers. A bartender stared at him with hard eyes, took the stranger immediately for an out-of-towner.

Pancho strode to the bar counter, his boots picking up damp, smelly sawdust, like two fat bees picking up pollen. Eyeing the bartender in a friendly way he ordered a shot of tequila – No, better make that a double, he amended.

"Señor Ramírez, is it?" enquired the man behind the bar. He had a voice from a throat that had downed too many tequilas in its lifetime; it rustled like last autumn's leaves. He spoke unsmilingly, almost without interest, pouring the tequila into a shot glass, and pushing forward the requisite salt and lemon.

The ranchero returned an astonished look, then realised that this was after all *the* rendezvous, and he visibly relaxed. "Sí, that's me," he rumbled almost cautiously, as though he might be lying to the man.

"She's waiting for you upstairs, señor."

"Who? – What?" Pancho produced an incredulous look, as if this time the bartender was lying to him. He felt so out of his element in this town environment. "Who do you mean?" he managed to add.

"The lady, señor, she came in early this afternoon. Been waiting for you ever since."

"Ah, I see…" Old Pancho didn't see, and reacted in his own fashion by swiftly downing the double tequila in one and ordering another. The next slug was thrown down his throat as speedily as the first. "Upstairs, did you say?"

"Sí, señor." Still unsmiling, voice like a high-pitched strained cough.

"The *lady*?"

"The lady is waiting, señor, waiting for you." A smile was now beginning to form on the bartender's closed-shop features.

Pancho delved into his pockets in search of cash to pay for the drinks.

"This has already been paid for, señor." The fledgling smile burst out broadly into a coarse knowing grin. "Now, señor, up the stairs and it's first on your left."

Strange fellow. Pancho thanked the man and turned resolutely for the staircase.

33

A Lady In... Waiting

Ascending the bare stone steps of the cantina staircase Pancho felt an admixture of foolishness, curiosity, and oddly, a rising throat-choking elation. He knocked on the door at the top of the stairwell.

"It's open, just come on in, you're welcome," floated out a warm feminine voice.

Ah well, such is destiny, he thought, boldly striding in.

It was a fairly small though cosy room, most of the space taken by a king-size bed. There was a dresser with mirror, a deal table with drinks set on it, and a single high-backed chair. Wooden window shutters were partly closed, dimming the early evening light trying to creep in. In the air was a remarkably pleasant scent, powerful enough to send male senses reeling.

Pancho's whole attention however was riveted on a female sitting poised with crossed legs on the edge of the bed. Middle to late thirties he estimated appreciatively; most attractive, certainly comely, definitely alluring. As he plainly saw she was not dolled up like a tart or whore, but looked a perfectly respectable woman, a young mother perhaps. Her breasts were truly magnificent he could not help see or ignore, sportively thrusting against flimsy material of a virginal white blouse. What he really found of immediate interest, because he had never seen anything quite like it before, was the fact that she was wearing *pants*. They were more correctly called slacks, as worn by many a Californian female across the border, though he was not to know this. They accentuated the lovely shape of long legs, exquisitely swelling thighs.

My God! he thought, he was already lusting after her. What if she were a relative? A niece perhaps? One of the family! He tried with a supreme effort to shut his mind to the lewd and lustful desires welling in him.

Meantime the young woman was appraising him in return, looking him up and down with a careful noncommittal expression. Under her close and offsetting scrutiny he felt like a horse at auction. And damn right, he thought, a rampant stallion no less.

"Welcome, Francisco," she greeted him first. "It's good to see you."

"¡Hola!" he croaked back, unable to say anything further.

"Have a good journey?"

"Ah, sí … Sí."

"And you found me alright."

"Ah, sí … Sí."

"Here, you sit yourself here, my horseman warrior, where you'll be more comfortable," she said, in the same warm inviting tones, patting a space close by her side.

The old ranchero slid his saddlebags to the floor, unclipped the canteen and let it drop on the bags, then complied without further ado. He sat on the bed beside the female stranger; a touch bemused, though willing to continue this crazy intoxicating charade. He was totally beguiled by her very presence.

"I expect you'd like a drink?" It was put as a question. She got to her feet. Quite tall for a woman, he reckoned. "No, you stay right there, my handsome one."

"Er, no, gracias – Ah, sí, gracias," he faltered, supremely out of his depth at present in this rather bizarre situation.

The woman poured two generous glassfuls of tequila. "I'm Josefa," she introduced herself at last, gazing on him with melting allure. His drink was handed to him – their fingers touched briefly, giving him a piercing jolt – and she sat herself on the bed again, much nearer to him this time.

This is some kind of set-up, he figured, not unduly alarmed; on the contrary he was beginning to find it pleasantly scintillating. He rested his ranch-weary eyes on her young, not quite beautiful but pretty and perfectly fresh face.

"Where are you from, Josefa?" he asked hoarsely, rapidly converting a naturally sprung leer into a decent and respectable smile. He was further shot with astonishment when she told him that she came from San Diego in California.

"¡Újule! You mean to say you're not Mexican?"

"I'm *American*-Mexican. My folks were born in Mexico – in Guadalajara. You know Guadalajara?" She sipped her drink.

"Not as I ought to," he admitted. "I'm strictly a country man." He gulped down his drink like a man frantic with thirst. "But what's your connection with my cousin Angel Palacio?"

"You are cousins?" The young woman showed genuine surprise at this, Pancho discerned. "He didn't tell me that, the naughty man. He's my boss, by the way," she added, almost as an afterthought. "He sent me down here on this – this *mission*. I'm to take good care of you, if you catch my meaning, and if you're willing too it goes without saying."

She took another dainty sip of her tequila, her other hand moving to rest lightly, casually, but none too innocently on the ranchero's knee. He felt another ecstatic jolt of lightning course through his whole body. The old man was so startled by the woman's bold and blatant move that he actually felt compelled to remove his sombrero. He slung it carelessly to one side, to snag on a top corner bedpost; it swung a couple of revolutions, then settled to stillness. And there it remained till next morning, on that corner bedpost – a thin-faced long-necked ranchero type sombrero'd bedpost.

"Angel tells me you're a ranchman, Francisco," purred the delightful hostess. It was not a question. Her fingers moved expertly and caressingly over his inside leg. "You handle horses, *I* handle men."

"I can well believe it," he muffled behind his drink. He slammed it down on the deal table. He could now hardly mistake the look she gave him. It seemed to the old man an aeon since a woman seared him with such avidly hot passionate eyes.

"Yes dear one, enough for the moment, don't you think?" she said silkily, placing her own glass next to his. Her perfume wafted into him with sweet promise as she leaned over.

34

An Illicit Liaison

The sensual female leaned into the ranchero, their bodies pressing, and kissed him full on the mouth. Her lips were cool, soft, and tasted of tequila he noted, though absently. What more could a man wish for? his heart pulse quickening. One hand gently held his face, the other began wandering.

"This would be the fetlock, is it?" she murmured teasingly. "And this must be the hock, am I right? What do you call this, Francisco?" The palm of her hand rested fully cupping his crotch. "Let's have you undressed, dear one, you seem more than ready to me. Oh my, yes!"

Pancho was wise enough not to rush this blissful business. He had all the time in the world. A long period of celibacy was at last coming to an end, and he intended to make the most of this rare opportunity dropped from heaven, as it were. It was all thanks of course to his cousin, he well knew, but why the fellow had gone to this trouble on his account Pancho could not as yet fathom out.

At this present moment in time his one desire was not to dwell on the workings of his cousin's devious mind, but was essentially of a sexual nature.

They made love for several long delicious hours. Josefa was there solely to provide pleasure to this hard swarthy horseman, though Pancho ensured it was reciprocal. She was sexually aroused and satisfied time and again; amazed at the old man's sexual prowess and staying power. She taught him wonderfully satisfying, exquisite things he had never before heard or dreamed of. Pancho was satiated.

The following day was for them alone. The glut of sex activity had given the ranchero a ravening appetite. Josefa took him to eat at the best restaurant in town, the bill put on Angel Palacio's account as earlier planned. Before they left the cantina to eat Josefa had pointed to a note on the dresser, addressed to Pancho. It read:

Dear Cousin,

I was beginning to get the idea that by now you'd be lusting after don Roberto's heifers, and I wouldn't want you to dishonour the family name by any untoward or unseemly action on your part.

Josefa will set you straight for a spell. I picked her myself. Have fun.

(Angel Palacio Ramírez)

Postscript: Why the hell didn't you marry again? It's later than you think, cousin!

After an excellent meal the twosome – appearing to passing strangers as perhaps a happy father reunited with a wayward daughter – the love duo returned to the room above the cantina. On the large double-bed they once again made love, unhurriedly and uninhibitedly. And never for a moment did Pancho think that there was anything untoward or unseemly in what they were doing – thinking of his cousin's sly comment using those very words.

By late afternoon it was time for Josefa to see her lover off on the autobus back eastward.

"We can do it again in a few months time," she promised, taking his hand and gently squeezing it. "Don't forget that. It's okay, old Angel will be paying – my airfare, expenses, everything. He can well afford it I know. Besides, I've enjoyed being with you and it ought to be repeated. It has been a labour of love for me, I can tell you. You're very *satisfying*, Francisco," caressing him sinuously to the last. Pancho gave a hearty, ringing, young man's laugh.

Josefa gave him one last lingering kiss before he boarded his transport, taking in his male smell and truly regretting this leave-taking.

When Pancho returned to his old working routine he was like a new man, completely rejuvenated. He astounded the men with his apparent youthful energy, his moods of blissful happiness and even exultation. It was as if the whole experience of his trip to town had knocked a clear twenty years off his age.

With the wisdom of his actual age he never divulged to his partners what he had actually been up to on his two-day visit to town. Had they known the truth of it they would have torn him to shreds with ridicule and ribald tormenting. To quell their curiosity he simply said that it was an unexpected reunion with a long-lost cousin, which they readily accepted.

It had certainly done the old man a power of good all the same, they agreed as one. As Cándido so fittingly expressed it, the old ranchero was now acting like the month's lottery winner, the cat that got the cream, a dog with two tails.

35

Lone Coyote

"Oye Pancho, it's here again, look!" called out José one day.

The rancheros were trying out a few saddle-mounts, putting them through their paces a little way beyond the corrals. A warm sun shone down friendly-fashion on them, and there was a steady drone of insects torturing the hides of the horses.

"What is?" asked the old man. "Ah, the coyote, I see it. A brave one, or maybe plain stupid, coming this near to us, just asking for trouble. You'd think it was tame or something, acting in that manner."

"It won't come any nearer though," reported José.

"No, I daresay it won't. A man can pet and pamper a chicken, but that doesn't stop it getting killed, gutted, cooked and eaten. Who'd trust the friendship of man, eh?"

"What is it?" enquired the boy Juan, who had this moment approached them, riding his chestnut bay Chapulín.

Pancho turned to him, said, "It's a lone coyote. She's been hanging around these parts for some time according to José here. Damned unusual behaviour if you ask me."

"You know it's a she then, do you?" asked Juan, dismounting.

"Oh, to be sure, that was already established. And I wouldn't be surprised if she had recently dropped a litter. Like I said she's been loping around a while for some obscure reason. Damned queer behaviour if you ask me," he repeated. He turned and spat in the dust.

"I think I know why," said José darkly, overhearing the old ranchero as he neared them on his mount.

"So, you can give an explanation to this, can you hermano?" rasped

Pancho with a faint speculative glance at the other. "Well then, fire away and tell us, we're all ears and eager to know."

José looked uncomfortable of a sudden. "Don't think I'm misunderstanding the matter," he hedged with a serious face, "but I reckon that it's the ghost of Mariano Cruz you see there. That's what it is."

Pancho grinned at him. "The ghost of Mariano Cruz!" he scoffed. "You'd better explain that one as well, for I've never heard of the like in this real world."

The other stroked his ear, then rubbed his nose with slight embarrassment. He was determined however to plunge in fully and said, "It goes back some time, to when my own grandfather worked on this ranch, in the revolutionary days."

"Hmm … Go on, amigo, we're all attention," urged Pancho with a patronising air, resting hands on hips.

"My grandpapá worked with this Mariano Cruz. They were close friends. He told me this himself – oh, way back when I was just a kid. There was some kind of trouble between this Mariano Cruz and a fellow who herded on don Fernando's ranch, but before don Fernando's time as you'd guess. It was when the first don Roberto ran this place, our don Roberto's own father."

"Thanks for the history. So what happened?"

"The trouble was over a woman."

"It generally is the case. Go on."

There was apparently a fight with knives, not unusual in Mexico in those times – or indeed in any times – and this certain Mariano Cruz was the worst off for it. The man had gasped his last in the arms of Jose's grandfather; and before he died he vowed to haunt this land for generations to come. That was the story which was passed on to Jose by his grandfather.

"But why should he haunt this place?" Pancho wanted to know. "For what possible reason had the fellow?"

"I couldn't say," José went on, face still dark and serious, "because my grandpapá never explained that to me, or if he did I must have since forgotten it. But the woman those two hombres fought over, you'll never guess who she was."

Pancho grimaced, spat again in the dust at his feet. "No, I couldn't guess, not in a score of months. I'm flat sure you'll be able to tell me, so you tell me."

"She was don Fernando's aunty, that's who she was," opened up José, breaking into a smile, as the sun was doing over them. "And she's been dead and boxed these forty years or more," he concluded.

"Maybe the coyote bitch over there is the ghost of Fernando's aunty – Why, look at her," Pancho said, pointing to the animal. "What strange antics she's going through. It doesn't make much sense, does it?"

The creature had adopted a firm and meaningful stance, in perfect outline and in full view on a slight rise in the land a few hundred paces to the westward. She kept dipping her head and swaying her lean shaggy body from side to side, backing a step or two, then coming forward again.

"It's as though it were saying, 'Come on, follow me'," said Juan.

Salté came trotting up, and the two animals caught sight and smell of each other. Then a strange thing happened, or at least failed to happen, as it appeared to the human onlookers. It is a well-known fact that a dog cannot abide the scent of a coyote. Salté was downwind of the alien animal, yet he simply stood where he was, looking non-aggressively ahead at the coyote. She, on her part, ignored him altogether, and continued to dip her head and swing her body.

Juan and Pancho observed this. They glanced at each other in puzzlement. While Salté remained standing his ground as before, tongue out from a grinning face, tail furiously thumping up the dust.

"I shall never comprehend these mysteries of nature," murmured the old man, tugging hard at his moustache, "but then, I don't suppose we are meant to." He turned away from the scene.

Presently, the coyote sloped off and disappeared over the rise.

"Are you testing the buckskin today, muchacho?" José asked the boy, who replied in the affirmative, saying he was supposed to, the task was his alone. "He's a switch-tail sonofabitch but bridle-wise, so mind what I said."

A time later Gerardo came riding in, after checking some cattle out grazing on the range.

"I've just rescued a heifer from certain death," he told Pancho with a touch of the dramatics. "Over by the eastern fencing. Got its right hind-hock tangled in some barbed wire. Must have caught itself like that at least a day ago. Near death it was, poor beast. Half-starved and crazy with thirst." He slid from his mount, slapped dust from him, giving the reins to the dull-wit Julian.

"What a mess its hind-hock was in," Gerardo went on, in the sombre tone of someone relating a terrible road accident. "Trying to get clear of that there wire, only making it worse for itself. I was forced to cut the wire, sorry, no help for it. Then I led the creature to water and it must have spent a good twenty minutes drinking, I'm bound to say. It was a good job I had the first-aid pack in my saddlebag. I cleaned it up and bandaged the hind-hock – stopped the bleeding at any rate. Should be alright now I guess, but it was a near run thing I'd say, and I can tell you why."

Gerardo put a hand to his jaw and cast a perplexed look at the old ranchero. "Strange, but I wouldn't even have seen it," he went on, " – for it was lying on its side in a hollow and almost out of view – but for me spotting a coyote a little ways from the heifer. It was like the damn thing was taunting me, running here and there and otherwhere in front of me. I took a pot-shot at it but I missed I'm sorry to say. It ran off eventually, and that was when I noticed the heifer – What's up, Pancho? Why are you looking at me like that? I saved that cow's life, you know."

"Sí, sí, hermano," sighed the old ranchero. "Don Roberto will be right pleased when I tell him."

He squatted on his haunches, back resting against the corral fencing. Was it simply coincidence, he wondered, the coyote being so near the trapped heifer? He shook his head and sighed once more. The mysteries of nature, he was thinking again.

"I damn near got that wily coyote, you'll appreciate. Sí, I nearly got it," Gerardo gabbled on.

"Sí, hombre, you nearly did," Pancho murmured wearily.

When he considered how cruel and insensitive and stupid mankind could be, he had to wonder at his own humanity. If we don't like animals, he reasoned, then how are we ever to like one another – or even *ourselves*?

36

Rainstorm

*D*on Roberto's rancheros were out on open grasslands with a fresh batch of mixed age and colouring of horses. It was late afternoon and the day had been spent in assessing the potential training qualities of this new drove. Young Juan rode alongside his mentor Pancho, taking in the information the horses gave them by their behaviour, individually and in relation to one another among the herd.

One obvious example was enacting before them. Four dun mares stayed as a close little group in one area. If one moved over to the left to pasture, the others immediately followed, in the manner of sheep. One of the mares, a year younger than the other three, stopped and began to urinate, then trotted on to keep in with her group.

"They're the '*wives*' of the red dun there," said Pancho, pointing at a fine stallion which had been watching the old ranchero this last minute. But now he swung his handsome head and moved on to where the young mare had halted. He urinated also, precisely over the same spot.

"There you have it, you see," grinned the old ranchero, "I needn't have told you, for he's done that himself, eh? The creature, so he is."

"But he's not telling me or you exactly, is he?" queried the boy.

"No-o, you are right and point well taken, he's letting those other stallions over there – that tight knot of them, do you see? – he's telling that lot the mares are his and his alone. Sometimes, Juanito, the behaviour of animals is not so much different from that of man when he thinks no one is looking."

Pancho's attention was taken skyward to the northwest where massive stormclouds were stacking up. The black clouds piled and roiled and tumbled on toward them. Blue-streaked lightning stabbed at the earth, bright flashes appeared in the great mass of clouds. Distant thunder rumbled over the land. He carefully studied the approaching stormhead, said :

"We'll get this lot back to the stables, I'm thinking – ¡Oye! José! Gerardo!" he bawled over the herd.

"Will they become nervous out here when the storm starts?" said Juan.

"It's not so much that but they might go kind of crazy-frisky and silly, like there's a bit of madness in the air or something. Some will go skitterish as well I dare swear."

Although a number of the younger horses began reacting to the coming storm by curvetting and tossing their manes, running at one another in spiralling motions.

José came riding up to them on his dappled grey colt. "To the stables?" he called over.

"Ay sí, amigo, we'll take them on in, and we had better be smart about it, if I'm not mistaken. ¡Uuy! That black mess will be over our heads in no time you can mention."

José spurred on his mount, cracking his whip and shouting to the spread out rancheros to close in the herd and move on fast.

A short time later, as the horses ran on the wide track leading back to the ranch, the first rain fell. Large drops which landed in the dust like small explosions. To the men these raindrops appeared as large and hard as pecan nuts, coming down with heavy force. Lightning flailed and crackled, thunder booming colossally over the open exposed range. The men hurriedly unrolled rain-capes and toggled them up tight to the top. Bubbles of rainwater dropped from the brims of their sombreros like falling strings of pearls, sluicing down their rubber capes. And if that were not enough the horses' hooves were splattering muddy water over them.

The rain soon came down heavier in sweeping torrents. Wet and mud-spattered, the rancheros stabled the entire herd. In the main stable it was necessary to squeeze two horses to a stall to accommodate them all. Rain dripped and splashed down through gaps in the roof, and the crowded body of animals steamed and smoked after their hard run in.

Suppertime was a makeshift hurried affair. Gerardo managed to gear up a windbreak around the fire, and to rig a tarpaulin cover to keep the rain from dousing the flames. The men, still wearing their long rubber capes covering them from chin to ankles, stood in the relative shelter of the stable, spooning into billycans of beans.

While the rain lashed down coldly, lightning flickered across a darkened sky, thunder clapped and rolled overhead. Cold gusts of wind and rain tore across the yards and corrals with biting fury, cutting between the clapboard stable walls. An early night of it was called for, suggested Pancho and the men easily acquiesced on that score, for there was little else they could usefully put their hands or mind to.

"The stables are leaking badly," said the old man, "so if we want a good night's *dry* sleep tonight, then it's the bunkhouse for us, hermanos."

The place was good enough he reasoned for a one-night shakedown, though the prospect of sleeping in that cramped, dirty hut did not appeal to his compañeros.

"I'm not looking forward to that!" grouched Gerardo, voicing what the others were thinking. "The place hasn't been cleaned out since last winter."

"Oh, it's clean enough," piped Juan. "Julian worked on it only this morning; sweeping, dusting, swabbing down the floor and walls. All neat and clean and tidy it is. You could eat off the floor. He spent a fair deal of time on the job."

"Julian did?" said Pancho in surprise. "This morning?"

"That's right. He thought you'd need it tonight, that's what he said to me," grinned the boy.

"Julian did?" repeated the old man. "That's a queer one and no mistake. Why, we haven't used the bunkhouse in months –"

"Since last winter," confirmed Gerardo.

" – Then just when we need it our Julian sets to and cleans it out ready for us. How the devil could he have known? I mean to say, the storm didn't come on till near suppertime, and who would have thought this fine morning that we'd end up catching a storm at the end of the day? A queer business it is too I say again, because our lame-wit knew better than any of us, and he's … well, he's a part-wit, or at least he generally is, ay que caray!"

"So it's to be the bunkhouse then," said Gerardo glumly. "Well, what's the betting that I sleep on the floor in there?"

"Me, too," said José. "I'm not resting up in a damn coffin which is what those bunk-beds are."

"I'm so tired out right now," confessed Emilio, about to yawn and show a full gallery of large square teeth, "I'm so tired I reckon I could sleep upright on a fence post."

Cándido felt compelled to point out that not only could Emilio do exactly that but had indeed done so before – on many occasions.

The rancheros trudged unhappily but resolutely through mud and swirling water, the rain slashing down on them, to the isolated little wooden building that was the bunkhouse.

The evening speedily darkened, with no let-up of the rain.

37

In the Wet

*I*n the poor evening light the bunkhouse appeared ludicrously small and spare; square and squat, like a rundown hen-house. Inside, it smelled slightly fusty, which Julian's severe spring-clean job was unable to eradicate.

Juan lit the lamp and confusion reigned for a spell as the men argued over who was going where to sleep. Capes were finally removed and pegged up behind the door. Their remaining clothing was kept on, as the night soon proved damp and chilly. Only boots and one or two sombreros were taken off. There was an instant outcry when Emilio pulled off his boots. To save the peace he drew them back on. As he did so Gerardo wafted the door to and fro in order to allow the obnoxious fumes emanating from Emilio's feet to eat out into the night air.

The men at last settled themselves as best they could, and Juan blew out the lamp. Their bodies covered the entire floor space, looking like a line of victims laid out from some natural disaster. The rain continued to fall, drumming rhythmically on the wood roof. The lightning and thunder had ceased earlier on.

"Hell!" swore José a time later. "You've had too much pulque tonight, Gerardo. You've gone and pissed the blanket, you niño!"

"No I haven't then," came the indignant reply.

"Well someone has by God! I'm all wet!"

"I couldn't agree more," put in Cándido, slyly smiling to himself.

Young Juan jumped to his feet, adjusted his night vision, and said that it must be excess rainwater flooding in from under the door. Sure enough, dirty, foaming rainwater weeped in under the door and soon began spreading everywhere. This was followed by another curse which fell this time from the old man. "Get up! Get up!" he rapped out.

The rancheros got up in the deep gloom, stumbling into one another, with more cursing going on, trying to save their blankets from getting wet.

"Who's that?"

"Shove over there, will you!"

"My feet are near frozen, so they are!"

"Who's swiped my blanket? Which thieving bastard – Ah, I have it!"

Their bare feet squelched and sloshed through a thick mushy cold soup of mud, straw debris and floodwater. The men collided with one another in the cramped, mine-dark space. Someone bumped against Pancho and bounced right off him like a rubber ball.

"Damn it, this is too much!" cried someone in the darkness.

It was Juan who managed to find the lamp. He swiftly lit it and turned up the wick. The rancheros stared down at their feet almost obscured by scummy floodwater and straw debris. Emilio was the only one with dry feet because he had of course kept on his boots. He was about to give a superior smirk but was instantly quelled by a fiery storm warning glance from old Pancho. He smirked inwardly instead, feeling very superior indeed.

"We'll have to pile into the bunk-beds after all," said Pancho with that same storm-warning churlishness. "There's nothing else for it, and that's what they're there for anyhow," floodwater foaming around his feet.

"Hell!" José swore again, "I hate them bunk-beds. Makes you feel like a baby in a cot, or worse still like a corpse in a coffin."

"They're okay for sleeping in," said Emilio, the acknowledged authority on anything related to slumber.

"I don't care much for them either," said Gerardo grumpily. "It's as you say, José, like you're lying in your own coffin. They're far too deep for a start. We're supposed to have thick mattresses in them – we haven't got anything in them! Empty coffin boxes, that's what they are! The don promised us nice thick mattresses an age ago and here we are still waiting for thick mattresses."

"Ayí, stop your damned stewing," Pancho told him testily, "and get up there, use the top one, you're younger and more the monkey than me. Anyway, the don does care for our welfare, only he doesn't much care how he does it – ¡Ay caray! Hold on a moment!"

"What now?"

The old man suddenly realised something. He turned to Juan and said, "If we're flooded here, then the stables are sure to be flooded as well. Muchacho, go and check on our Julian, if you will. The horses will be okay, but Julian can drown in a hand of water. Just have a look see, amiguito," and the boy splashed out through the corral yard, now one huge mud lake, to the main stable where he knew the simpleton would be this night.

"I bet Julian is drowning himself this very moment," said Jose. "Well, we're all born without wits but some of us stay that way."

"He acts like a half-wit certainly," conceded Pancho, "and we see him as such, though I suspect that at times it's only because we've never allowed him to be anything else."

Moments later Juan returned. "He's alright – and not as silly as you'd think," he grinned. "He's fixed some planks across two stall tops. Snug as a worm in wood he is."

"Same as us, then," said Pancho, calling from a bottom bunk.

The men poked grinning, mud-spattered faces up from each deep bunk, peeping at the boy; to him they appeared like special zoo specimens loaded in cargo crates. "I'll join you, Cándido," he said, "so please shove over."

"What're you holding there, muchacho?" asked Pancho sleepily. He was in a better frame of mind, feeling warm, dry and comfortable.

"I picked up some of those army horse blankets from the harness-room. Anybody want one?"

"Sí, Juanito, I'll have one," returned José, and the others echoed him.

The men seemed largely adjusted to this awkward circumstance, though they would hardly have recognised one another, their faces spackled and crusted with dried mud.

Juan distributed the blankets, then went to the lamp. "Move over, Cándido, I'm turning the lamp out now." He bent to the lamp.

It was very dark in the windowless bunkhouse. "It's kind of nice is this," yawned Pancho tiredly but pleasurably, "resting down with a real roof over our heads. Can't beat that, can you…"

"Strange it is though," responded Gerardo, gaping blindly at the ceiling only a foot from his head, "getting flooded out from our old sleeping quarters. When did that last happen?"

"Oh, I remember," said Emilio, who was now unusually wide awake and not feeling at all sleepy. "It was three years back – no, I tell a lie, it was four years ago – when it rained for two solid days and nights, and very cold it was as well. Cold enough to freeze the balls off a brass monkey."

"Freeze the balls off a brass monkey!" echoed Gerardo. "Why do people say that when there's no such thing?"

"Oh, but there is," piped Juan, ready to show off his knowledge of things once again. "A brass monkey was the name given to a cannon used in olden times."

" Ayí!" exclaimed Emilio. "So the balls –"

"You've guessed it, they're the cannonballs," the boy finished for him.

"Ah, sí," said Pancho, continuing Emilio's reminiscence, "and because of the wicked cold weather the don kindly put us up in his special guest-room no less. We were forced to leave our boots in Tulia's kitchen. She insisted on us washing our feet too – you in particular, Emilio, and why she should pick on you I don't know. And Tulia brought us our breakfast the next morning. Breakfast in bed. Újule, that was real grand…"

"Only Emilio slept in the bed as it happened," added José. "We were on the floor surrounding him."

"Sí, like piglets round a sow."

"It was some comfortable bed though," reminisced the fat man nostalgically.

Yes, it was so, and had taken the best part of an hour to wake him, Pancho snorted. Gerardo had thought he had maybe died in the night or something like it. After repeated shakings and shouting to rouse Emilio, it was José who suggested a stick of dynamite might do the trick. And it was José who eventually awakened the Olympic sleeper, when he took the equally drastic measure of hitting Emilio on the head with a chamber-pot.

"Thank God it hadn't been used – for the other," smiled the fat one, large teeth gleaming, even in the dark.

While the rain relentlessly poured, large drops drummed and pattered on the bunkhouse roof, and the wind moaned and keened and howled like demented grieving widows.

38

Bunking Down

"*I*n Querétaro," began Cándido in what could possibly be another of his bizarre or incredulous tales, "in the street where my uncle lives, it gets flooded every raining season."

And so his uncle had decided to build himself a boat, thus enabling him to get to work without getting wet. He built a nice handy little craft, a row-boat with two long wide oars. Cándido smiled to himself in the darkness and went on :

"He just had it ready in time for that great drought we had which lasted nigh on two years. During all that time he had it lying out baking in his back-yard. Of course the sun warped the planking and the boat opened up in a score of places. Aunty thought it would make good use as a colander for the Women's Society kitchen."

"What about the oars?" asked Gerardo, still gawping blankly at the roof from his top bunk. "They would have been useful too, wouldn't they?" his interest in wood stemming from a first early career in carpentry.

"Oh, Aunty found a use for them alright. One she used as a paddle to stir the washing in her tub, and the other she found handy for cracking Uncle a good one whenever he was up to some mischief. As you'd guess both oars got worn with use."

"There was a bad storm once a few years back in Cancún on the Yucatan Peninsula –"

"We know where Cancún is, José," griped Gerardo.

"I didn't know," said Emilio.

"Uuy, you still awake?" drawled Pancho.

"In Cancún, which everybody now knows of," José almost snarled out, "there were floods and drowning and damaged buildings and roads washed away. It was a proper mess I can tell you –"

"I didn't know you went down Cancún way," cut in Cándido.

"I didn't. I never did. I read about it in a newspaper at the time."

"I remember that now, José, but it was a different kind of storm, though," said Emilio, his mind and body still refusing to drop into sleep. "It was what's called a hurricane."

"Ah sí, a hurricane…" Pancho yawned again languidly. "They often get them down there, I'm told."

"Why do the *norteamericanos* give these hurricanes women's names?" asked Gerardo from his top perch.

"It stands to reason, doesn't it?" José returned. "They're such damned unpredictable things and cause no end of problems. Just like women. They're expensive as well, what with the damage they cause."

"The women or hurricanes?" asked someone in the dark.

"Both the same, aren't they? Both alike, aren't they?"

"What's money got to do with women?" Pancho wanted to know.

"If you were married to my Rosaria you'd know well enough," José threw down from his upper bunk. "Expensive? No one spends my money faster than my old bat does. And another thing, them hurricanes can change direction sudden-like, just as women can and do change their minds."

José at this moment may well have started fuming in his cot; perhaps dwelling too closely on his wife, reputed to be a domineering type as hinted at earlier, who generally ruled the roost when her husband was away, but more so when he was at home.

"So that's how it is, then," said Pancho sleepily. "Any thoughts on it yourself, Juanito? You're not asleep yet muchacho?"

The boy smiled in the darkness. It was a fact that hurricanes are given female names, he informed the others, because he had read about it somewhere. It had started during the Second World War when the weather people went through the letters of the alphabet during any one hurricane season.

"So the first storm might be called Arabella or Alisa," he went on. "The next could be Belinda, after that Cristina, and so on."

"In the old days," drawled Pancho drowsily, "they used to name these hurricanes after a saint's day, whatever saint's day it might happen to be when the hurricane did its worst in terms of damage done. But I reckon one day they'll change back to calling these storms by men's names," he predicted. "You wait and see if they don't."

"Why do you say that?" asked one of the top bunkers.

"Why? Because these hurricane storms are going to get a damn sight nastier as time goes on, and soppy girls' names will hardly suit."

It was his opinion that man was messing about too much with the natural world. Cutting down forests by thousands of square hectares a week, he cited as one instance. For every tree that was cut down and burned, he reckoned, its noxious gas was breathed in by one less tree.

"Well, we're burning trees every night for our supper fire," was shot from a top bunker.

The old man gave a restive sigh. "That's not the same thing, José," he grated harshly. "What little we burn is a bit like you, it's only the deadwood."

"Oh, muy bien! ¡Gracias! Thank you very much!"

"Only kidding you, amigo. Anyway, what I'm saying is this, the world is starting to lose its forests. We don't see it round here because this isn't tree country.

"Now, I'm going to try and get some sleep…" He paused a moment. "But before I drop off to sweet dreamland there's something I can tell you which may be of interest…"

A silence ensued.

"Well, get on with it!" pushed an exasperated Cándido.

"Just collecting my thoughts, you impatient pup! I have it now in my head, I think…"

"Better there than in your boots!"

"He's not wearing his boots."

"That's what I mean."

"Oh, let him get on with it!"

"I once remember," Pancho opened up at last, "I remember a scheduled hanging at the state penitentiary in Durango, on a day much like today – teeming with rain it was. The hangman was leading the condemned prisoner out into the yard, to the scaffold at the far end. And it was bucketing down, it was a regular Niagara of rain – a bit like right now out there. 'To be hanged on a day like this,' moaned the poor soul about to meet his Maker, 'I wanted a last look at lovely sunshine and blue sky,' as the rain lashed heavily down on him. And the hangman said to him, 'You needn't complain, it's alright for you but I've got to come back in this downpour!'"

José tittered over that one.

"Did they hang him then?" asked Gerardo.

"Of course they hanged him, that's what rope was invented for."

"Well," said Cándido, "they didn't hang him out to dry, that's for sure."

In his top tier Gerardo stretched and flexed himself within the confined space of his small deep bunkbed.

"Did you hear that?" said José warily. "Is someone about, do you think?"

"It was only Gerardo. Gerardo has bone joints that creak like barn doors," explained Pancho in sleepy tones.

"Hell!" cried José a moment later, to mask his embarrassing gaff, "I clean forgot to groom the colt after I'd dried him."

"It's too late now, hermano. As the saying has it, 'When the owl hoots it's already eaten its supper – Get to sleep, will you."

"Hush a moment! Hush! Quiet! I heard something," said Gerardo. "Did you hear it? What's that noise?"

"It's the rain dancing on the roof," replied someone.

"No, not that. I distinctly heard a kind of scratching and a whining."

"A wolf is at the door," said Cándido.

"It'll be Salté, we left him out there," said Juan, getting out of his bunk once again. He had full night vision by this time, and he sloshed his way through floodwater to open the door. Salté came splashing in, tail going, throwing out small sea squalls.

"Where's he been, then?" said Emilio.

"You still awake, Emilio?"

"Rat-chasing, I shouldn't wonder," said Pancho. "The rain's bringing them out into the open."

The huge, soggily-furred and mud-bespattered hound shook himself mightily, spreading a showering arc of mud and rainwater over the open bunkbeds.

"Oh hell, perro!" cursed José.

"You should moan," said Cándido, "you're safely up top there."

"I caught most of that lot anyhow," José replied.

The dog caught his master's scent on a lower bunk and he joyfully jumped in. After treading muddied paws all over Cándido he curled himself in a wet, mud-coated dog-stinking ball. Juan pushed him over to one side, got back in under his blanket.

A short time later, within the airless confines of the diminutive bunkhouse, it was literally steaming and reeking from the warm damp body odours of dog and unwashed men. They dropped off into slumber at last. Except for Emilio, that is, who tossed and turned for a considerable length of time, blighted with a rare and uncharacteristic case of insomnia. Someone broke wind, which merely added a piquancy to the stifling atmosphere.

Eventually, snorting rasping noises began as José and Gerardo started up their nightly fortissimo duet.

"Anyone awake?" Emilio whispered anxiously in the fetid, heavy darkness hours later, and for answer received only saw-mill snoring and pig-pen grunting.

And the rain tapped on the roof, gurgled and chuckled in the guttering, amply filling the water-butt outside. The rainstorm ran its course, passed into the night and finally died a natural death.

Part Seven

Part Seven

39

Rats and Longhorns

Pancho gimped toward the main stable, young Juan and the dog Salté at his heels. He glanced over at the grazing land which began directly where the stables and corrals ended. Mostly scrubland to begin with, dusty and stony and well hoof-trodden; then into small hillocks and grassland, wide vistas stretching far and away to the cordilleras. To the south were the rich pasture-lands where don Roberto's prized herd of long-horned steers grazed.

It was the longhorns that were presently on the old ranchero's mind, but he temporarily forgot them as he entered the stable where the men were working, his booted feet disappearing in a flurry of dust and corn-chaff.

The poor-wit Julian held a chestnut bay by its bridle, smiling all over his simple face.

"Well start him, Julian, if you would," the old man said curtly. "Let's see him through his paces – Easy now, muchacho!" as the youth stumbled over a dropped horse-collar.

"Just look at him then, look at those clean pasterns. Have you ever seen the like before?" said Pancho, clearly impressed with this mount. "Nicely nicely my handsome fellow – No, Julian, not you, the bay." He slapped approvingly on the bay's withers. "Lead him through, Julian."

Pancho stumped around the superbly built horse with a pleased look. "By God, there's nothing you could say was wrong with this one and that's a fact, hmm. A noble beast we have here to be sure and certain. I bet you'd love to ride him, eh, amiguito?" swinging on the boy with a stretched smile. "Saddle him up later, Julian. We'll let our Juanito give him a try-out. Sí, and fetch one of the new horse-blankets we've got in there," pointing to the harness-room.

He turned again to Juan with a knowing grin, and said, "A few brand new blankets, a gift for the rancheros, for our saddle-horses, courtesy of the army."

The boy blinked.

"An army horse contractor, you understand, gave them to us," Pancho grinned at him. "Army issue they are, surplus to demand or requirements he told me in good faith. But the fact of the matter is, he was just sweetening us in readiness for the sale – No, not a bribe, I wouldn't in all honesty call it bribery, just showing good-will – Ah, there's Gerardo … Do you happen to have a spare snaffle bit over at your end, hermano?"

"I think there's one here I can let you have," came the reply. "Hold on a moment, I'm loosening this girth, then I'll be at your disposable."

Pancho and the boy exchanged amused glances. "So that's it, is it, you'll be at my *disposal*?"

"Like I said, as soon as I've done this."

The old man threw another look at Juan and winked, then said, "Right, I'll wait till you've finished. Meantime, I'd better tighten my own saddle-girth in case my pantalones fall down."

"What's that?" said Gerardo gullibly, glancing over. "Ah you, hombre!"

The old ranchero plonked himself down on a standing burlap sack of corn-feed. Gleaming yellow sunrays lasered through chinks in the slatted stable wall; a fanwise caste of light beaming in lit a patch by Pancho's feet. There was a rustling and stirring, a clinking and jingling and an occasional thud of a hoof hitting a stall. He sniffed. A dry, musky odour of old straw and ancient leather saddlery filled his nostrils – like snuff he mused pleasurably. His sea-blue eyes twinkled with mischief as they caught on Cándido a few paces away, adjusting the saddle-girth of a dock-tailed sorrel.

"Look to that one will you," rumbled Pancho affably, getting on his feet again, "he's chipped a hind-hoof I'm thinking."

"Find it for me," Cándido casually chirped back, "and I'll stick it back on."

"Hmm. There are those who are wise, and there are those who are otherwise." Cobwebs caressed the old man's face as he moved restlessly about in ink-stain shadows. He was raring to try out more of his mischievousness, but he was beaten to it …

Suddenly, there were gunshots fired in quick succession, the loud reports splitting the air, a noise that could be heard over the entire ranchscape.

"José!" he roared. "Are you shooting at rats again?"

"The damn things are everywhere!" came José's voice from behind the stables.

"Leave them be, hombre, they're living creatures like you and me." He looked to Juan and explained, "If they get out of hand in their numbers I have my own methods of dealing with them. I don't need José blasting their guts out all over the place. I don't want him spooking the stable horses either, the damned fool." He pulled furiously at his moustache. "Well – Ah, I've remembered something I'd meant to say earlier. Oye, Gerardo, you and José are leading the don's longhorns onto the meadow grass tomorrow, aren't you?"

"That's right, as soon as the sun's up. Me, José and Emilio as well – plus don Roberto's regular cowmen. We're helping them, like."

"Ah-ha … by the San Juan Canyon, is it?"

"That's where the don wants them, sí."

"Hmm…" old Pancho was returning to his normal cheerful self, along with a return streak of that special mischief roiling about in his head. "All six-hundred head you're taking?"

"That's correct, Pancho, the whole herd of six-hundred."

And Pancho put on his serious, deliberating expression. "You do know that wild herb is still growing there, don't you? That stuff which makes the cattle sick."

"Well, I don't know – I mean I didn't know, never did know that," replied Gerardo guardedly, pushing back his sombrero and scratching his scalp.

The old man judiciously clicked his teeth, and couldn't resist a crafty wink at the boy beside him. "Those weeds are sure to sicken the cattle I'm thinking. No, it sounds too risky by half, I just don't care for it. I'll tell you what, hermano, you take five-hundred and ninety-five head of the beasts and let's try them out first, as a precaution before committing ourselves with the whole herd, eh? You agree? ¿Claro?"

"Okay, if you say so," agreed Gerardo easily, and without even suspecting anything remiss in a somewhat ludicrous request. He simply stood there, inspecting a nasty red array of rope burns on the palms of his hands.

"Right then, that's it settled and I'll see you later. Come on, Juanito," and the old ranchero threshed through ground straw, out into the corral and a beating sun.

Juan was hard put to it in keeping a straight face, and once they were out of earshot of Gerardo he spluttered into helpless laughter. "Surely you were having him on?" he managed to ask.

"In a way I suppose I was," said Pancho with a grin. "You see, Juanito, I do have a reason. Those Hollywood movie fellows are coming here tomorrow to take a look at the don's steers. Only, I needed a few of them to parade in front of the casa so the don's guests can look them over at close quarters, so to speak. They'll want to be *casting* an eye on them, I expect, see if they've got enough 'star quality'. Later on they'll maybe ride out onto the range and see the herd in its natural habitat, or whatever they call it these days.

"Now youngster, I've got a special strawberry roan tucked away that I want you to see," he went on, storming along through thick corral dust.

Juan shook his head, smiling. "You're incorrigible, Pancho, do you know that?"

"What does that mean, muchacho?"

"It means you're –"

"It's okay, I know exactly what it means. I'm not as dumb as some folk may think, you know."

"I can believe you," laughed the boy. "In fact I'm amazed at the amount of knowledge you come out with, and can't think how you do it."

The stink of cordite from José's pistol blasting drifted over to them as they crossed the corral. A dust-devil ran in front of the pair, then quickly died.

"Well, I suppose I can let you into a little secret," Pancho winked again craftily, moving on with his inimitable rolling gait.

40

Renegade Horse

T he old ranchero began telling the boy how one time a good many years ago don Roberto had once called him an ignorant sonofabitch. From that time on, whenever the don was away on his many social or business trips, and he himself had nothing particular to do in the way of work, the 'ignoramus' would sneak into the don's library and browse through his books; the more interesting ones were 'borrowed' until read. He let the boy know that he had been doing that for some considerable time, and eventually exhausted the don's entire library.

"As you know yourself, amiguito, books open up the mind. A closed mind is a room without windows, an open mind lets in truth along with light. And when you know exactly where you're going you are already halfway there."

Juan's eyes popped as he said, "All those obscure facts and odd bits of knowledge…"

"Sí, muchacho, I get most if not all of them from the don's books. It's the only way of knowing minds other than your own – Now, watch this one, he can kick a bit." Pancho led the youngster to the roan in question when they entered the gloom of the stable, to be hit by the close humid stench of nervous horse sweat and dung.

"Oh, muy bien!" mouthed Juan in wide-eyed surprise as he gazed over a fine spirited horse in the first stall. The beast was big, broad-chested, broad-cruppered. "I didn't know you had him stashed away. Why're you keeping him here on his own?"

"Good point, glad you noticed. He's in here on his own for a very sound reason. As I say he's a kicker and a bit of a wild one. A *mesteno* (mustang) you might say. He won't knuckle under or do as he's told. A fractious beast, balky as hell he is; he will want to do a thing his way when you want him to do it another."

Pancho deliberately averted his eyes from the horse as he spoke. "Emilio is supposed to be training him but is yet to control the animal as we'd want him to. We need this awkward one to be obedient, otherwise what's to be done with him – Sí, you, you precious specimen!" as the old ranchero thumped his fist down playfully on the roan's croup. "Sí, you can stamp your feet, you useless horse-flesh, you stubborn, contrary creature!"

The horse blew hard through its wide flaring nostrils, the force of it almost taking off the old man's sombrero.

"But why keep him in isolation?" Juan still had no sufficient answer to his earlier query.

"Well, this is how we see it, Juanito. If you keep him away from his equine companions long enough he's more likely to be more amenable and responsive to our Emilio – or me, you or anyone else. Have you heard of that quote, 'No man is an island'?"

"No, I don't think I do," admitted the boy. "What does it mean?"

"It pretty well explains itself, meaning that we can't live alone, as a human that is. We need our fellow man, to interact with him – or her. On our own we are nothing. We are shaped by our parents and friends and strangers too; shaped by our circumstances and experiences with others. Well, it's something like the same with a horse – or a dog for that matter. The horse needs the herd, or an owner, to form an attachment to. This wild one here thinks he can do it alone, happy with his own company. But no, that can soon get tedious and lonely. He will in the end learn his lesson and know what he ought to be doing – for us and for himself too."

Old Pancho and Juan backed a little from the roan. "But look at him though," smiled the veteran horse-fancier, "he has such a fine conformation. Only, he has too a poor attitude that's not going to get him anywhere. We can spoil him later when he begins to behave, spoil him with good grain, the very best oats."

The roan, obviously a shade stressed over its present state of solitariness, was also as a consequence suffering a nervous, upset stomach, its digestive system plain to hear. Its stomach heaved, gurgling, sloshing and rumbling within.

"Listen to him, amiguito, going like a cement mixer, is it? Well, we can't have him stressed out too long, we can get Julian on the case with a hand of something nice – which should settle him and sweeten him up a bit, I dare to say. We can do that soon, I'm reckoning."

They moved back toward the roan, and as Pancho spoke, sidling closer to the recalcitrant animal, inch by inch, it looked at him now with imploring eyes, as though it had already decided to accept him. "Every day or so," he talked on in low tones, pretending not to notice or show any interest in the roan, "I bring in your Chapulín to this rascal. Only for a short spell, mind, to let him know what he's missing. Chapulín of course gets along with anyone or any other creature. When I take him away again our roan here really kicks up a hell of a fuss, I can tell you. But he'll learn. He'll come round to our way of thinking eventually. A few days more of no contact, no companionship, no interaction, and then you just watch. That roan will be so eager for company I shall walk in one fine day and find him making friends with a barn-mouse."

Pancho glanced over at Juan, eyes locked on a slight movement in the boy's shirt pocket. "On the subject of mice, muchacho, would that be one of the little creatures tucked away in your top pocket?"

"Sí," smiled Juan, a hand coming across to gently pat the wriggling soft bulge in his pocket. "I found him only yesterday near the bunkhouse. You won't believe it but he just came to me as tame as a pet hamster."

The boy carefully lifted a brown-furred mouse from his pocket, allowed it to nosy about in his hand, the small creature's black-bead eyes blinking in the harsh sun-glare pouring through the open stable doors.

"One of Julian's friends, is it?"

"No, I asked him, because it seemed so tame." Juan broke into a knowing grin. "Told me that he didn't recognise this little fellow, so must be new to the ranch."

"A perky one isn't he? Nosey too, sniffing all around … Well, let's get on to the cow-barn. One of the don's cows is due to calve. We can see if Julian is making any progress with it."

Juan tenderly popped the small furry mammal back in his pocket. He felt the wriggling form of it, vibrant against the palm of his hand, and warm as a tortilla at suppertime.

He followed as the old man turned and strode out of the stable, both of them slitting their eyes at bright sunlight.

41

A New Birth

"Why is it that he's so tame, a creature of the wild?" asked Juan, loping along beside the ranchero and still feeling the mouse's movement against his chest.

Pancho, by way of an answer, could only suppose that the tiny mammal and its ancestors going back several generations probably had hardly any or no contact with the usual predators or with the world of man. Therefore it knew of no threat of danger from man and so had no fear of him.

Pancho ploughed on, kicking up dust, and said, "How are you going to feed him and what all?" The boy thought he could perhaps scrounge some titbits from Tulia. "Hmm, that's alright I guess, as long as she doesn't see him. There's something I've learned about our Tulia. The smaller a creature is the more frightened she is of it. Without a doubt she's afraid of mice and rats, terrified of spiders and scorpions and such. Like I say, the bigger the animal is the less she's afraid. You can never figure women out, can you, but then you're too young anyway to know their mystery."

He recalled one incident when Tulia had gone into don Roberto's bull corral. This particular bull was a big black aggressive beast, he told the boy, a real mean and nasty-tempered one. He was failing in his duty however in servicing the cows. Tulia was actually in the bull corral, along with a waiting cow. She boldly stepped right up to the massive animal, smacked him hard across the snout, and aimed a vicious kick at a hind-hock. The bull reacted uncharacteristically to this humiliating treatment and dropped his head in submission. He could smell no fear in Tulia, only somehow sensed her strange feminine power and strong will. The brave – or perhaps foolhardy –

woman then grabbed the great bull by the ear and led him on to the patient expectant cow.

Nothing happened.

"She thumped and kicked and fair tormented that huge hairy beast until he finally got the message and realised what was required of him – Ah, it sounds quiet inside," as the two paused at the threshold of the cow-barn to accustom themselves to the dim light within.

The cow had already dropped her calf and the limp-wit Julian was stroking the pair of them, a smile of delight on his face. "You've only just missed it, señor," he shrilled in his high girl's voice. "It came out slow but easy. A good-looker, hey?" patting the newborn calf.

"Ay, Julian … And so we missed it then."

The barn sounded like a sawmill with the whine and buzzing of insects. Salté trotted in at that moment. He went straight for the newborn calf and began to lick the mucus still adhering to its flank, as if he were the creature's rightful father.

"Your Salté has an identity problem," grinned Pancho.

"Oh, he's forever doing that kind of stuff," returned Juan. "Back home a while ago one of the yard-cats had three kittens. *Nightstar* I think it was, who's always having kittens." He paused a moment, patting the calf on its neck. "As I've maybe told you before, Salté sleeps with me at night, at the foot of my bed – He's my protector, or so he thinks. Well, anyway, he picks up one of the kittens by the scruff of the neck, holding it gently in his jaws, and drops it on my bed. Each kitten was picked up and plonked on my bed. Then he jumps on the bed and curls himself around them, licking their fur just as a cat would."

"Sí, I knew it, an identity problem – the great big softie." Pancho turned his chunky frame and looked speculatively at Julian. "Are you alright, my clever young vet?"

"Sí, señor!" smiled the simpleton.

"You've done a fine job here I can see," Pancho praised him, then broke into one of his countrywise sayings : "When the sun's hard by, the sun will shine, and hope springs eternal, as they say. Come on, Juanito, things to do and no rest for the likes of us," and he headed once more into the brilliant light of the corral grounds.

He felt hot and sweat dropped from him. Daringly lifting his sombrero he finger-scissored his damp red hair. His sweatsalt mixed with the earth's salt.

Turning to the boy and hooking a thumb back at the cow-barn, he said, "A little bit of kindness – kindness in praise – can be a great thing, and I don't mind bestowing a sample of it on that unfortunate youth." With a sideways wink and grin he went on, "Mind you, he can get my temper up at times. And once you've thrown a tantrum it's hard to catch it! Well, let's get on, things to do as I say, eh? A wasted hour, a wasted day are lost forever…"

And as the old man clomped along in the heat and dust there was a kind of halo of bright light around him, which Juan had noticed. It jolted the boy with a spasm of profound feeling.

42

The Coyote I

One sweltering hot morning Pancho and Juan had ridden their mounts away from a herd of don Roberto's cattle in the grazing region and found themselves in a desert wasteland. There was scarcely anything growing in the area, only a few prickly pear cacti and scrubland brush. Even insects appeared few and far between around here, and there was little or no wind. It was eerily silent, thought the two riders, their horses' hooves kicking stones and loose shale sounded loud to their ears.

After a while Juan slowed Chapulín to a walking pace, pointing ahead to something he noticed in the heat-shimmering distance. "If I'm not mistaken," he said in a kind of cautious whisper, "that sure looks like our coyote friend – by that large grey rock there, you see it?"

"Uuy, it's her alright," Pancho readily agreed, "and she knows we've spotted her too I reckon. Well, I'll be blessed if she isn't up to her same old game, look at that!"

The animal was behaving exactly as before; that is, continually lowering her head and swaying from side to side, backing off a pace at a time and coming on forward again to repeat the odd performance.

"You know, Juanito, I ought to have known it the last time, but I believe she actually wants us to follow her somewhere. Do you see it that way as well?"

"Sí, I do," the youngster responded earnestly, "and didn't I say so before when José brought her to our attention? Shall we carry on to her?"

"But easy like and angle off a bit, lest we cause her some alarm and runs off like a rabbit." The two riders urged their mounts on at a steady walk.

The fawn-grey coloured creature ahead stood like an Aztec idol on the crown of a ridge. Waiting there. In a shimmering haze of heat. She then turned and loped on springily, stopping at short intervals to turn her head and observe if she was being followed. Far above and in the distance a pair of hawks circled in the vast brittle blue of sky.

"She's so much like a bitch dog," Juan commented as they rode on several hundred paces behind.

"So much like a wolf you mean," countered the old man. "A prairie wolf is what a coyote is. And there's not as many around as there once used to be. Why, when I was a young man –"

"She's slipped into that gully," Juan interrupted him of a sudden. "We've lost sight of her."

"That's okay, no problem, I know where the gully leads to. We'll head around it this way, it's quicker in fact. Follow me, mi compañero, and we may yet surprise the canny beast."

They rode on past huge rocks and boulders. Then, a fearful *Crack!* rent the air, blasting the silence. It was a rifle shot, they recognised – or at least Pancho did – followed by a brief agonised yelping sound. The silence fell back, heavier than before.

They rounded the area of rock formations and came out into the open, saw a rider on a raven-black horse immediately before them, directly under the southern path of the sun. He held a smoking carbine casually in one hand.

"Who is he?" whispered Juan.

"I can't make him out for the sun in my eyes – Ah, it's Octavio I think, one of don Fernando's men. What the hell is he doing here?"

"Pancho! Is it you?" called the lone horseman. "I've just shot me a damned coyote. Skulking over yonder way, see?" The man pointed eastward to the prone body of an animal, lying on its side as still as death.

"Why did you have to shoot it, hombre?" Pancho shot out at him, anger in his voice. He impaled the horseman with a devastating basilisk stare of contempt.

"Hell, Pancho, they're as bad as vermin – they *are* vermin," grinned the man. "You know that."

Young Juan flinched when the man's gaze fell on him. The boy stared with some revulsion at shifty, slightly slanted obsidian-black eyes in a hard, pock-marked, leathern face with cruel lines marking the length of an evil grin. Even Chapulín laid back his ears as though he too sensed this man's malignancy.

"All the same, vermin or not, hombre," said Pancho with acid heat, "it's not as if there's too many of them – like *rats* for instance!" He glared meaningfully into the man's remote, steely eyes. The old man considered the other as nothing more than a brute, a savage.

"Sorry you feel that way about them," replied the lone rider truculently, a cold granite glitter in his eyes. "They're still damned vermin whichever way you look at it, and ought to be gotten rid of. What do you say, amigo?" he ended, grinning malevolently.

"Don't 'amigo' me, you arse-end of a burro!" fired back the old ranchero. "What're you doing around these parts anyway? This is don Roberto's land, as you well know – And take that damned stupid grin off your ugly face!"

"Hey, hold on old man, all I did was to get rid of a pest," said the other sullenly and unblinkingly. "As for me being here, well, I'm looking for a pair of strays. Sorrel colts. You seen them around maybe?" he asked in a hard-cracked indifferent voice.

Pancho ignored him, looking over the lay of the land. He was silent for a short spell, thinking … A dawning suspicion crept into his mind. He turned to his young companion, said, "I think she intended on heading that way, Juanito, do you agree?"

"Sí, it could well be," returned the boy, keeping a wary eye on the evil-looking stranger who still casually and loosely held his rifle in one hand, and staring fierce-eyed back at them both, his face stamped with the print of a chronic malefactor.

Pancho clicked his tongue, a judicious gesture. "There're patches of quicksand over that way. Let's go – Octavio! I reckon I know where your colts might be. You'd better follow me. We must hurry, and hope we're there in time…"

The old ranchero put heels to Macha, breaking into an immediate gallop.

43

The Coyote II

A short time later the old man's fears were realised. There ahead of them was one of the sorrel colts, pawing at the ground one instant, backing away at the next. The other colt was near to its withers deep in quicksand. Its eyes wildly rolled and it whinnied in sheer terror.

Pancho and the man Octavio knew exactly what they had to do, got on to it without further delay. They carried sufficient rope between them with which to lasso and haul out the trapped colt. They used their mounts for better leverage and for the pulling of the harnessed ropes. Juan held and steadied the other colt, assured the creature with strokes of the neck and soft whisperings in its ear.

Once the colt was safely out of the quicksand the man Octavio gruffly thanked Pancho and hastily went on his way, taking the stray horses in tow. Juan and the old ranchero returned to where the dead coyote lay. They remained seated on their mounts, gazing down on the animal that had intentionally or deliberately, or at any rate effectively, led them to this place; they were firmly convinced of this in their minds.

"Do you think we should give it a decent burial?" asked the boy in muted tones.

His older companion hesitated only a moment, after first glancing at the sky and seeing the hawks still circling as he had earlier observed. He said, "Juanito, we shouldn't deny nature her normal course. There's food here for those hawks hanging about. In every crease and crevice of the land there's bone dust of man and animal." He rubbed his jaw reflectively, eyeing the youngster. "I'll tell you what we can do. We'll come this way again in say a couple of days time, when our friend here is picked clean. You and me can collect her bones – scattered they may be – and bury them as if it were a proper Christian burial. Isn't that the best thing to do?"

Juan agreed with a nod and an understanding though sad half-smile. "I sure didn't much like that Octavio," he said lowly.

"Ah, I know him of old, the evil-faced villain, with no respect for anything or anyone, and can never say a piece that's even half decent. Those are his claims to fame – notoriety, I should say – nothing less than insolence and malevolence, in any order. Come on, mi amiguito, let's ride on back…"

A cheeky juvenile kind of breeze sprang up. A yellow-orange dust-devil curled itself in an upward swirl, then suddenly disappeared. The old man filled his nostrils with the fresh peppery scent of sun-warmed grass. The grasses stirred and murmured, swishing one way and then the next as the young upstart breeze tugged and teased at the small sword-like stalks.

Later in the same day Pancho felt compelled to take it up further with José over this business of a ghost.

"Why did you say straight off that the coyote was the ghost of this Mariano fellow?" he asked him, as they sat around the campfire.

"I remember my grandfather telling me," José opened up. "He said that his friend was pure Indian. He was known among the rancheros of the time as Mariano *Coyotl* Cruz. That's what my grandpapá said and I never forgot it."

"Hmm…" murmured Pancho, reflectively stroking his moustache. "The old Nahuatl name for the prairie wolf, or *coyote* as we say in these times."

"Did you see it today?" asked José with interest. "Is it still around?"

The old man turned half-way about to face Juan, giving an almost imperceptible sideways nod of his head, and said, "Sí, hermano, Juanito and me saw her near that spot where the quicksands are. I reckon she's lost her pups somehow – I'm sure she recently dropped pups – and was out searching for them."

"Ha!" responded José with a grin, "so is that what you think? I tell you straight it's the ghost of that Indian fellow from my grandpapá's time."

"Well, each to his own opinion, amigo," returned old Pancho levelly, "and yours may perhaps be the correct one."

Pancho began to wonder why he had lied to José. Did he suspect that there could after all be some substance to José's declaration? And then, had not that wily creature led man to where an animal was in distress and in need of him? On two counts, for he couldn't forget the cow trapped in barbed wire.

He shrugged philosophically and decided to let it rest, put the matter out of his head.

On the following day close to evening Julian came to him, with something or other nestled in each arm.

"Señor, look what I've found!" he gloated happily.

Old Pancho stared in astonishment. "Where did you find those two, muchacho?" he asked, a certain wonder in his voice.

"Over by the big black rock, you know, over there to the west. I found them in the shade of the big rock. No sign of the mother, I looked and waited and looked and waited ever so long. Crying they were, these two. Sure look hungry, don't they, señor?" holding out a pair of under-nourished coyote pups.

We can all get stuck in the quicksand of life, reflected Pancho soberly, and some of us – many of us – look up at the sky instead of trying to find where we put our feet …

44

A Severe Case

The rancheros had enjoyed a good fruitful day, the highlight being a sale of some twenty very fine cavalry mounts to the military authorities. This was further enhanced by the promise of a bonus to be paid by don Roberto in person. Supper was over and they lounged around the woodfire, already chattering like magpies:

"If you share your problems they no longer become problems."

"But I don't have any problems, do I?"

"Well, you would if you were not married."

"But I am married, you know that."

"Ah, say no more…"

"…'The lord will give a hand to those who help them themselves,' he said to me, then came out with his great horse laugh."

"You mean he laughed like a horse? Is that possible?"

"No, no, hombre, I mean a rough sort of laugh. That's what a horse laugh is."

"My uncle in Querétaro —"

"Oh my God, don't you start!"

"Sí, amigo, fickle is the female." This was Pancho attempting to dominate the conversation once again. "Take for instance that chestnut mare José was making love to – meaning grooming – earlier on. You can shove a handful of nice sweet hay right under her nose and it's no thank you very much; you drop the hay to the ground and she goes for it like she hadn't eaten in a week. I tell you straight there's nothing so fickle and contrary as a female, whether it be a mare horse or a woman."

"Well now," cut in Cándido, "you wouldn't offer a handful of hay to a woman for a start, would you?"

"Oh, I don't know," began José, with a smirk on his face indicating a possible witticism was about to emerge, "Emilio's mamá must have been fed on hay, and Emilio too was probably weaned on it. You only have to look at his horse teeth for proof of that."

All of which went over the head of the affable fat man, who was more concerned at present with arranging bales on which to lie on.

"Where's our Juanito, then?" Pancho wanted to know.

"He's over by the haybarn," said Emilio amicably, settling into a comfortable recumbent position, ready to snatch at least forty winks of sleep. "Reading his book in peace and quiet – which I'm hoping for around here."

"Some hopes," was Cándido's careless comment.

"A strange one is hope," mused Pancho, gearing up for a philosophical response. "Like infinity, never known nor ever seen but often wondered at – Ah, here's Gerardo, with a face as long as a fiddle. What's eating you, hermano? You look as happy as a man about to be hanged. Come on, out with it."

Gerardo could contort and distort his countenance so facilely that he was like many different characters, but every impression he made was effectively ugly.

He groaned slightly, his mobile, rubbery face creased apparently in pain, and said, "I'm constituted. Haven't been now for three days."

"He's what did he say?" queried Cándido.

"I'm a bad case of constitution, that's what I am," griped Gerardo pitifully.

"He means," said Pancho dryly, "that he can't shit. That's what he's saying."

"Oh, constipated. Now I've got it."

"Didn't I always say he was a tight-arse?" José dropped in.

"How many times have I told you to eat more vegetables and fruit?" the old man chided the sufferer. "Beans on their own only bung you solid. Now get yourself over to the casa while it's still light, go round the back and see Tulia – Don't frighten her, mind, try not to smile. Tell her I sent you, and can she spare a handful of those dried prunes she keeps in a big glass jar."

"Oh, right!" Gerardo said gaily, relieved and pleased at this promising development. "Prunes is fruit, I know that much, and so if I eats them I'll be okay, hey?"

Pancho looked at him pityingly. "Not in their dried state, you precious pecan, else you'll be tighter than a kettledrum for the next week. No, amigo, you bring them back here and we'll soak them in cold water for a while. Then we slowly stew them in the same water over a good fire. Then you can eat them. ¿Claro?" The old ranchero sat back with some satisfaction. "After that you'll be so regular your back passage won't ever be shut but always open wide – OOO! like that, see? Off you go then, hombre, before the dark comes on and you getting lost or something."

"Ah gracias, Pancho. My head you know is spinning and my belly's bloated. It feels like I'm carrying a gutful of horseshoes. I'm off then," and Gerardo carefully sloped away with short mincing steps, looking for all the world like a severely constipated man indeed.

"Well, that's that, then," said Pancho complacently. "¡Que horitas! – better late than never as they say, hmm."

"He's rarely happy, is he?" remarked José.

"Our Gerardo? Well, it's a fleeting thing anyway is happiness. Happiness is the little bit that you don't know is there until it has passed; then you realise. It's like strong medicine, only to be had in small doses."

This was the opening Cándido had been waiting for. "My uncle in Querétaro was once constipated, for a whole week –"

"Hold it right there, Cándido," flew in Emilio, having only just dragged himself from a light doze; and like a child who's sleep has been disturbed, felt irritable and bad-tempered – his usual affability flown to the winds. "Is this a genuine story or another of your weird fantasies?"

"It's genuine alright," confirmed Cándido in a neutral tone, "and as true as I sit here. He hadn't been for a full week, my uncle as I say, and he started to worry about it. Got so bad he went along to see the doc who happens to live in the same street in Querétaro. The doc examines him and guess what? He finds a wine cork bunged firmly up his backside."

After an almighty outburst of laughter died down, the young man continued with his tale : "It was my aunty who did it. She was fed up with my uncle when he kept getting drunk on cheap beer, falling asleep, and farting in bed all night long. So one night when he was as sozzled as a sailor my aunty rammed a cork tight up his arse. My uncle never even knew what had been done to him. In his mind he was firmly convinced that it was a case of constipation.

"And the doc told him that if he had left it any later, the accumulating gases would have made a human .88 calibre cannon out of him."

The others were again convulsed with laughter louder than before.

45

Campfire Story

"Ah, there's somebody coming. Who could it be?" said Pancho, after the others had finished rolling about and slapping knees, helpless with mirth. "It's our Juanito at last. ¡Oye, mi compañero!" he called over to the boy. "What have you got there? A book, is it? Come and sit down here and tell us the story you're reading. Curiosity may kill a cat but it keeps a man a man and on his toes, so tell us your tale. We all like tales and the telling of them," glancing at Juan with that ever-humorous gleam in his blue eyes.

"It's about a soldier −"

"Ayí, a soldier!" said José, interrupting. "That's what I wanted to be, you know, a soldier. Just like my papá."

"Your old man was a soldier?" asked Cándido.

"No, but he did want to be one."

"Can Juanito get on!" muttered an exasperated Pancho.

"It's about a soldier returning from the wars in olden times," started up the boy once again, marking his book with a blade of cornstraw and closing it, "and he's lost an arm in the last campaign. When he arrives back at the village where he comes from he finds his house has burned to cinders, for the war even touched as far as his homeland. But his wife is well and safe he discovers with relief − and his two young sons. They're living with his wife's sister in another village nearby."

Juan made himself more comfortable between Cándido and the old ranchero, and went on : "So there he was with only one arm, his home burned to the ground, and the army has forgotten to start paying his war wound pension."

"He's in a sorry state sure enough," perceived José, daring to interrupt once again. "It's like a situation I knew of myself. My brother-in-law you know lost a thumb in a threshing machine, and his chicken-house caught afire one night, roasting his chickens –"

"¡Újule, hombre!" Pancho ejaculated crustily. "We're listening nicely to Juanito's story and this half-baked taco has taken hold of the reins. Clamp up José if you will and let the muchacho get on with it. You carry on, Juanito." He smoothed down his moustache with a spatula paw, as a sign indicating his own readiness to hear the story.

"I hope it's going to get better," slipped in Emilio, roused from a temporary stupor. "It's as sad as a one-sided *centavo* so far. Is it going to be more cheerful, Juanito? I do prefer a happy story."

"Will you let the boy tell his tale," pushed Pancho, glaring at the fat man. "It's like drawing teeth trying to keep you lot quiet."

"Well, the story takes many twists and turns," the youngster continued on, "because it's about life itself for humanity, with all its ups and downs."

"And don't we know it," cut in Cándido.

"I shan't tell you again," Pancho warned him.

"But I've only just opened my mouth!"

"And put your foot in it," tittered José.

"Anyway," Juan battled on, slightly raising his voice, "the soldier manages to get a job on a farm nearby. Feeding pigs, tending sheep, chopping wood, that sort of work. Because he's strong and labours hard, even with a missing arm. But his wife is unhappy, for she hardly ever sees him –"

"Just like mine," murmured someone quietly.

" – She thinks her husband might as well be fighting in the war as before, the little she sees of him. Then the war ends, a victory for this ex-soldier's country, and his pension payments start to come through at last. With something like eight months back-pay in his pocket the soldier starts to build a home for his family on the farmland where he works. Once the house is built he sends for his wife and children to join him, and they work together for the landowner."

The young storyteller has been observing his audience as he speaks, and is satisfied that he has gained their interest. So with fresh force he goes on, putting more confidence and dramatic power into his words.

"Twenty years pass by and the one-armed ex-soldier has grown old, while his two boys have developed into sturdy and manly replicas of their father. There is another war and the two full-grown sons go off to fight. Only, it turns out that they're not as brave as their father once was. They're cowards and run from the field of battle. Because of their cowardly act a great shame falls on the family.

"The veteran soldier is hurt more than the time when he lost an arm in combat. He feels that he has also lost his two sons, he can't in all conscience claim them as his own flesh and blood. He turns them away from his home, tells them to redeem themselves by returning to the fighting.

"But this the two sons can't do, because they're fearfully afraid of ever fighting again. Then an uncle – the old soldier's brother – manages to persuade the young men to go back to their regiment and give themselves up, to face what punishment might be meted out. They know that to flee from the enemy in wartime means execution by a firing squad, drawn from their very own battalion of soldiers.

"So they return to their regiment, though with heavy hearts, because they know for certain that death will be the only outcome of it. At the bivouac they are arrested at once and tried by court-martial, sentenced to be shot. It happens though that they take this with a deep calmness. A different kind of courage is shown in the way they accept their fate."

The men now listened to Juan's narrative with respectful and unflagging attention, wholly absorbed in the tale. They began to show signs of restlessness and not a little anxiety, shuffling their feet and wringing hands in a nervous tension, eager for the next plot development. Juan held them spellbound as though they were children.

"The execution then is set for the morning. The two soldier brothers sit in the condemned prisoners' tent under guard, and they are still calm and ready for death. But that same night the camp is attacked by the enemy and there's total confusion everywhere. The guards have disappeared – the ones supposed to be looking over the two condemned brothers. Here is an opportunity for them to escape and gain their freedom. Meantime, the fighting is fierce and desperate all around them. It doesn't look good for the army encamped in their bivouac.

"Without even thinking about it, but acting as they had been trained to do, the two brothers quickly find and take up arms, and fight desperately in what is the thick of it. They know that this is their one real chance to make up for their earlier disgrace and to fight with sheer courage and daring. They fight so well, turning events to such good advantage, that it puts fresh hope and determination into their comrades-in-arms. In fact their brave action saves the day, for the attack has failed and is called off, with the enemy retreating as fast as they could run.

"The brothers are later reprieved, because honour has been restored to the regiment, and another victorious campaign is over. The war soon ends, the brothers praised as heroes of their country. They return to their homeland and the farm.

"And it happens that they find their father had died only days before their return. The grief and regret over this home tragedy is so much that they can hardly bear it. The old veteran never knew of their redeeming actions in battle. Yet another form of courage is needed of them to get over this sad matter. The old uncle arrives and once more he goes to work on his soldier nephews, trying to bring out that other kind of bravery now required of them. This they somehow do which pleases the old uncle. Only time itself can lessen the grief they feel, but at least they are made to realise this and their grief becomes bearable.

"In the meantime they both marry and start their own families. They teach their children well, because they never cried or ran away from any kind of trouble. Then a famine hits the land … well, that's as far as I've got with the book," the boy gazing at the others almost apologetically.

The rancheros had remained silent during the relating of the tale once it was in its stride, and they were quiet now, as if in deep contemplation. Then Pancho broke it.

"You can see hermanos where the story's at. These varied faces of bravery and courage. If you want my opinion on the matter it is this : I think you're born with bravery. It's part of basic human makeup. Something you have inside of you. Though you're just as liable to lose it. Very easy in fact. Bravery is a thing you have to maintain and hoard so to speak, an investment in human life."

"Can you get it from the bank, then?" joked José facetiously.

"You're a braver man than me if you rob one," Cándido countered.

"No, amigo," said Pancho, "it's there in you. You sometimes have to use it – in times of calamity or war or some tragedy – and then it'll be necessary to build it up again. In its many forms, like in Juanito's story. Bravery – or courage, which amounts to the same thing – well mostwise, in having courage you also have a kind of freedom.

"And you might say, well, what exactly is it, this something that you can't see? To my mind I'd say that courage is having the power to hold back fear, for even the brave feel fear."

The old man stroked his moustache meditatively, and went on : "You would think that courage belongs only to men, but not so, not so, because women also can be courageous and often are. A quiet kind of courage they have, without show or *machismo*; a very special kind only found in the female, which men can never know." He threw a glance over at José, lips curling with humour. "Certain it is your mamá had it, José, the moment you were born. Stands to reason she must have had that special backbone when you popped out to surprise the world. Otherwise she'd have surely shoved you back in where you came from, to try again another time."

Pancho also hinted that there might possibly have been a mix-up at the birth, with the newborn baby José getting thrown away and nurturing the afterbirth instead. The men joined in with the old man's gut-wrenching laughter; even José appreciated the putdown.

It was not long before Gerardo came gambolling back, looming out from the darkness beyond the campfire light, carrying a small saucepan.

"¡Oye, Gerardo!" called José slyly, drawing himself up in readiness for a steel sharp witticism, "have you taken the cork out from your backside?"

Gerardo, completely mistaking what he had heard, said :

"No, no, Tulia got these out for me. Just look at them! A lovely pan of prunes!" and the men took one look into the pan, then suddenly burst out roaring again with side-splitting laughter.

Part Eight

Part Eight

46

Out on the Land

One high noon in late June Pancho and young Juan were out riding the ranchlands, to be on their own for a change and away from the men's idle chatter and bickering. Salté too had been left behind, skulking to the haybarn with his tail between his legs, a face of dejection and sad neglect, determined to have a long sulk over his uncaring abandonment.

The old ranchero and the boy cantered easily over a hot-rock brown-grass plain, under a blue-brushed open sky. The distance danced with waving walls of heat, and despite the aridity they still noticed the odd sandflower or a gathering of rock-flowers. They tilted their sombreros low over their eyes against the glare of the sun and talked quietly, voices harmonising with the tinkling of snaffles, a slight creak of a saddle, the snorting of the mounts as they tried to back off from huge angry sounding horseflies.

Pancho loved this land as a young suitor loved his betrothed. Every aspect of it appealed to his singular senses : the scents of peppery dust and wild herbs and hot stones; its ruggedness of terrain and wildness of tough desert flora such as cacti and mesquite and maguey. He enjoyed the dryness and rare thin air that exists on this high central plateau. He took pleasure in viewing the wide and open vistas of distant mountains, and the magnificent vastness of the sky. The old ranchero had always felt uncomfortable in an urban space; to him it was not space at all but a choking, stifling imprisonment. But out here on the land ... the stillness, the emptiness, a tangible mystery both enchanting and irresistible.

As they continued conversing in muted tones their keen eyes gazed about this Mexican wildscape with its sharp-ridged hills and deep-cleft *arroyos*.

"I noticed on the lintel above don Roberto's front door," Juan was saying, loosely holding Chapulín's reins, "there's a date on it. 1769 as far as I could make it out. That's an old casa of his, certainly." Chapulín's flanks shivered, muscles twitching, as flies tormented him.

"Sí, sí…" murmured Pancho musingly, "and an old hacienda it is as well. The very earliest haciendas you know go back as far the 1620s, and they were up north along the Rio Bravo."

"Don't you mean the Rio Grande?" smiled Juan, with a sidelong questioning look at the old man.

"¡Rio Bravo del Norte! Whatever, same difference," Pancho was not fussed. "At that time they were about centre of our country, so you can imagine how big it was then. Because Mexico and the Spanish Territory stretched further north than it does in these times. Well past the Colorado River and up beyond a little way of Great Salt Lake," he went on, their horses' hooves negotiating a loose-stoned declivity. "All the land west of what the norteamericanos call the Rocky Mountains – Ah, look at that sky, Juanito…" he broke off. The old man appreciated that the deepest darkest blue was to be seen in this present near-midsummer highsky. As he gazed upward splashes of sunlight played on his weather-grained, amiable, relaxed features.

"But we didn't colonise our country then as we ought to have done," he went on, "as the Americans did in a later time. How different history would have been … Of course, amiguito, when I say 'our' country it wasn't our country at all then. In fact it wasn't our own country until we won our independence from Spain, and that was in – ah,–when was it now?"

"In 1821?" Juan supplied him in an instant – he had been reading about it only a day or two before.

"That's it, muy bien, muchacho, well done. But I was only testing you," he returned in a warm expansive tone.

"Okay," grinned Juan, "I believe you." He took a tighter grip on the reins as he glanced ahead of them where a dust-devil sprinted itself into oblivion. "Didn't you once tell me of a connection you had with the Americans?"

"Sort of I suppose," replied Pancho, stroking his moustache with one free hand. "My family originally came from Sonora as you know. But my great-great-grandparents left for the goldfields of California in 1849 or 1850. Hmm. Other families went as well from our pueblito. They all came back to Sonora eventually, at least my family did, no richer than when they left. They returned on account of the Yankees who were taxing them, and very heavily too, right out of all proportion. And why? Because they were not considered citizens of the United States. The poor devils were hounded and forcibly driven out."

Old Pancho talked on, absently combing the white mare's mane with his fingers. The two riders began to climb higher ground. The air here was clean, clear and unsullied by dust or flies. It brought the distant hills closer on account of its crystal clarity. And the now *afternoon* sun burned down on them.

"One moment, Juanito," said Pancho presently, dismounting from Macha.

He kneeled in ground-dust and burnished-bronze grasses, and put an ear to the ground, the back of his camisa patched granular-white with dried sweatsalt.

"An American Indian trick," said the boy.

"You're right. And African tribesmen do it too, did you know that?"

Juan looked ahead and around him, said, "I don't see anything or anyone. Can you hear something at all down there?" Pancho was sure that he could. "Horse's hoof-beats?" No, Pancho was sure it wasn't horse's hoof-beats. "What, then?"

The old ranchero grinned up at the boy. "I hear ants and beetles busy about their tiny lives, and I hear the earth breathing. Nature is happy with herself because she is ever growing, ever constant but ever changing," prompting the boy to shake his head and smile at this ever-wonderful old friend, companion and mentor.

The ranchero got to his feet, slapped dust off his knees, swarthy sunbitten face broken in a friendly grin. A hot wind began to blow. The two shortly rode into a sea of grassland, dogtown or needle grass which waved and swished in the hot wind, soil-anchored and root-deep in hard solid earth. A distant heat shimmer wavered, freely flowing thermals melted the air, distorting the outline of sunflayed foothills, like a mirage from a hot-fevered dream.

Presently they pulled in their reins and paused at a scattering of miniature earthen volcanoes.

"Jackrabbit burrows?"

"No-o," drawled Pancho, scanning the horizon, "they're prairie dog burrows. There're still a few live around here."

"Are they really dogs, then?" asked the boy. "I've never actually seen one."

"The creature is more of a squirrel than a dog. In fact they belong to the squirrel family, but they're reckoned more as rodents than anything by most folk."

"Then why do they call it a 'dog'?"

"Why, that's on account of the doglike calls they make. Mind you, the prairie dog chatters as well as barks like a dog, but when it does bark you wouldn't really take it for a dog – I wouldn't at any rate."

"They're handsome little creatures and I've nothing against them, for what harm can they do out in this empty wilderness, eh!" The old man glanced behind him, running a hand over the cantle of his saddle. "Shall we call it a day, then? They're not going to pop up while we're around. Next time we'll sneak up on them by foot, and maybe we'll get a good look at them. Ah well, muchacho, time marches on. ¡Vamónos!"

They wheeled their mounts round and headed back in the direction of the hacienda. Back on lower ground hot-itch insects flew through the windings of the wind, the pliant grass pointing to where the wind was pointing. And the old ranchero liked the way of the wind, the wind now in his face and setting square his sombrero, the wind with its searing scented breath.

The two riders had no sooner covered half a kilometre or so when young Juan's keen eyes began to track a lone figure on the landscape before them. A slow-treading figure walking half a pace ahead of its own dust trail.

47

Bizcocho

"Who would that be, I wonder," said the boy. "I've never seen him before."

Pancho squinted his eyes and steadily gazed ahead of him. "Why, it looks like Bizcocho. I'm sure that's Bizcocho I'm staring at, it must be him."

"Bizcocho? Is that his name?"

"Sí, *Bizcocho* – Biscuit – Everybody calls him Bizcocho. No one knows what his real name is; might not even have one. People know him as the 'Wanderer of Chihuahua', the state he originally came from. I've known the fellow these five and thirty years. Ever since I was a cattleman in Sonora. All his family were murdered by the federales, by the by, but we needn't bring that subject up any more; no mention of it, eh?

"¡Oye, Bizcocho!" he shouted over to the nearing figure. "¿Que paso, amigo? ¡Újule! But it's good to see you again, and strapping fit I see." The two riders trotted forward to meet up with the man.

Pancho and Juan quickly dismounted, the boy taking Macha's reins as the old ranchero barrelled toward the newcomer to shake him by the hand. There was a fanfare show of back-slapping and roars of laughter for a while, then Pancho got a grip on his sensibilities and introduced his old friend to Juan.

What the boy saw before him was an utterly disreputable-looking character, a *picaro* or vagabond. The man was dressed in tattered shirt and near-shredded pantalones, well-worn *huaraches* on dirty feet, and a ragged straw sombrero tipped angle-wise on his head. The experience of a life spent totally outdoors had carved his face into hard, heavily-lined features, his food-starved indrawn cheeks the colour of cinnamon. His only redeeming asset, from the boy's point of view, was his extraordinary eyes. They were like topaz gems, like the eyes of a jungle cat. All the same they were friendly eyes, the boy realised, as the stranger genially screwed them up at him.

Because of his wandering habit men generally shunned and turned him away. They could never trust a man of his singular aspect, without a home, without roots. Sometimes they would resort to violence and soundly thrash him, before sending him on his way again. Which explained his punchbag battered appearance, and the few remaining teeth in his jaw – a couple of grinders and two front teeth top and bottom.

He appeared evil, cruel and dangerous, but he was none of these things. He was in truth one of God's gentlest creatures. He possessed a laid-back placid disposition, with a charming sweet-natured childish innocence, as though he knew nothing of the world and the many wayward ways of men; though he knew well enough and more.

He was a man of his nation and its rugged geography. The land he walked on was his whole dominion, but only where he set his feet at any time, or where he gazed. It was his homeland, all of it, for he was a truly free man.

Bizcocho treated the animals of the wild with respect and honour. It was his way and he was one of them. Like them he distrusted and feared men, for his ways were not their ways. He always reckoned that most of his good friends had more than two legs. In the sight of God, Whose presence he consciously sensed, he was a creature of humility. As he would tell others wherever he found them, he was merely 'a flea on the skin of this land'.

In consequence of his unusual lifestyle he could count his human friends on the fingers of one hand. Pancho was one of them, their friendship going back a fair number of years, as the old man himself had pointed out.

"So, Bizcocho, what have you been up to this year? For it must be a twelvemonth since I last saw you."

"Oh, I've been here and there and around," the vagabond replied vaguely. "You know me, Pancho." He dug a toe of his huarache into the dust, contemplated his big toe for a moment, glanced shyly over at the ranchero. "I got a job for a while, you know, up in Coahuila…"

"A welcome change for you I should imagine, some spice in your life. What doing?"

"Oh, a bit of this and that and the other –"

"Come on, amigo, what doing?" pressed Pancho.

"I was a cowman of course on a nice ranch. A fine boss who treated me decent. But I quit after a while. Hell, old friend, time was passing too quickly. What with their schedules and timetables, meals at set times, this job to be done by such a date and all that carry on. Time was racing on like a runaway horse. I could stop a stretch and see myself growing on fast, as a mushroom will in the dark and damp of night. No-o, I needed the freedom again of walking the wilds in my own slow foot-walking time. So I quit. Well, you know me…"

He glanced again at his old ranchero friend, a grin spreading over his man-beaten weather-worn face. "I did save my wages this time, as you kindly advised me last year, for when the bad times came. And the bad times nearly did, but for the pesos in my pocket."

"Ay que bueno, amigo, that's the stuff of sense. Did you take better care of yourself too, as I said you ought for your own good and well-being? Eating okay and the like, did you, eh?"

"Sí, compadre. I'm sound as a new-season pistachio, fresh as a shower of rain – well, as you see me, heh! The food was everywhere I roamed; fruit of the prickly pear I found, pecan nuts and honeycomb; easy pickings they were, and free of charge of course. Even wild flowers! I like to eat wild flowers, eating from the very Hand of God it is. Nopal cactus I found as well which I shaved and sliced and fried in a pan."

Pancho eyed the man dubiously. "Did you now, and how did you manage that, then? A frying pan?"

Bizcocho returned a simple and innocent expression. "Why, I take one from someplace, you know me, and when I'm done I return it, as you advised me once a long way back."

Having not spoken, or at least hardly uttered a word to a living soul in many days of his travels, Bizcocho was keen for conversation with his old friend. Indeed, as they walked on, the lone wanderer was loquacious – even garrulous – putting Pancho on his mettle. But he was at any rate a source of entertainment for young Juan, who instantly warmed to him, interested and amused in turn. When this stranger spoke it was almost as if he were singing. Juan listened with pleasure, charmed by the sing-song, slightly hoarse inflection and unique tone colouring of this remarkable man's speech.

Bizcocho agreed to return with them to the ranch. Juan lent him Chapulín to ride, while he sat behind the ranchero on Macha. The trio continued resolutely on their way. Macha and Chapulín, so used to one another by now, walked on side by side, companionably and with a certain sedate style.

It was time for some gossip to make up for lost time :

"How's Gerardo these days with his phantom aches and pains?" to which Pancho was happy to relate that Gerardo at present was as fit as a bat with four wings, maintaining that good health is money in the bank – and earning interest.

Bizcocho enquired next if young Julian was still with the rancheros, receiving a positive nod. And was the fat one Emilio still there too, sleeping his life away? He was indeed and he maintained that lots of sleep was good for your complexion, a notion which was of little consequence to one of Bizcocho's rough-cut, battered countenance. "Ay, amigo," said Pancho, "our Emilio would suit fur rather than fat, with the amount of sleeping he gets through, like a bear in hibernation."

"The silent one, José, will he be alright with me, do you think?"

"Ah sure, he won't harm you, amigo," Pancho promised. "He's mostly wind and piss at the best of times is our José. Besides, he likes you, he told me so. As a matter of fact he's a likeable fellow is José. After all, he likes me too! And he's not so silent these days either."

"I can't help getting the impression he doesn't even like himself."

"Ah no, that's not the case by any means. They say if you like yourself without reservation, other people will like you too. José can sometimes measure out his meanness in dollops of generous proportions, but that's a case of putting on a show of his toughness. Iron-hard muscle? Why he's merely a cardboard cut-out, salsa without the spice, a softfruit salad. You have got to get used to him and his ways, that's the short end of it."

Bizcocho moved on. "The cross-eyed fellow, Cándido is it? How is he faring?" and the old ranchero was pleased to state that Cándido was okay sure enough, even though he did have some kind of warped mind and odd thinking. Which didn't stop the young man and his wife Laura from now having three daughters to boast of.

"Three muchachas you say? How the wheel of life turns round, my friend, and time steals your life bit by bit, like a pickpocket picking pesos. You look fit and chipper, Pancho, I must say."

"Ay well, I know I look old, but it's the only way to live a long life. There is old age and there is living long; I'd prefer living long."

Bizcocho laughed heartedly, not so much at Pancho's comment but because he felt he was in good company, which for him was a novelty and a welcome change. Although he was almost as old as the ranchero he had a youthful vitality about him, as well as an absurdly childish naivety.

"This is a very fine horse you have, muchacho," Bizcocho complimented the boy, drawing him into the conversation. "It was the first thing I noticed when you both came riding over. Bit of a racer I'd dare to vouch – is he?"

"He can be fairly fast," smiled Juan, pleased and proud of his Chapulín. He blushed when Pancho pointed out that the boy was being modest on the horse's account, for he could verify that the bay can run like the wind and run long and swiftly without hardly tiring – such stamina! "Well now, who's a fine handsome fellow, heh?" sang Bizcocho, talking now to the horse, leaning far over the pommel of the saddle.

The fist-beaten face of the wanderer beamed as he gazed around him, at sunparched rangeland, the occasional dust-drubbed tree, the blue-deep sky clear and bright. He saw it all with evident pleasure, while the horses' hooves cut through clumps of coarse wiregrass interspersed with small gatherings of dayflowers. "It's a Godly day friend Pancho. The land is resting peaceful like, and there's plenty of blue in the blue of that sky, wouldn't you say?"

"A darker depth of blue do you mean? Sí, we're high on the plateau here. Nearer the sun and the source of life. A brighter light we have in these parts. Even the dust has gold in it."

"Nature is not aware of its own beauty, heh? It doesn't know itself."

Bizcocho thought it all a regular joy to the eyes, that a day without a little joy was a day best forgotten. What he saw reminded him of Sonora, and he asked Pancho if he remembered his younger days in that particular region. The old ranchero could hardly forget those days of fun and laughs and no worries for the likes of himself and his old companion.

At last they reached the ranch and Bizcocho ate supper that evening with the rancheros, who made a hearty show of kindness toward him, even José. Pancho pressed him to stay on the ranch for a spell and to work again for a wage. The wandering traveller politely declined the offer, mentioning time speeding on when he worked regular hours, going much too fast for him to cope with. No, he would move on he said as soon as the sun showed its face the next day.

At one point during the course of their simple meal the wanderer of the wild set his topaz eyes on the simpleton Julian. They seemed able to communicate without speaking, like two animals of the same species. They had done exactly this sort of thing the last time Bizcocho passed through here. It was as though they readily understood each other in thought or by some form of instinct, without need of the words of man.

The following morning Bizcocho said his farewells to the host rancheros. Don Roberto's cook/housekeeper Tulia had kindly prepared some food for him to eat on his journeying. In point of fact she had done much more than that. She found a sturdy canvas backpack for him to carry, crammed it with food and other necessities as she saw fit, including spare shirt and pants that would suitably clothe him. Tulia even managed to root out a spare sombrero that was in far better shape than Bizcocho's disgraceful headgear. Tulia was a rose without thorns, Pancho averred, and the wanderer, surprised and grateful over the largesse, wholeheartedly agreed with his friend's sentiment.

At the last he spent a few moments with the stablehand Julian.

"Señor Bizcocho," smiled the youth, "where is it you go now?"

"West, Julian, or rather southwest, that's where I'm heading."

Julian thoughtfully clamped a stem of straw in his mouth, puffing at it as if it were a smoking-pipe. Soon, a pained expression came over his simple face. "Señor Bizcocho," he said earnestly, "don't go that way, the southwest. Go northeast, señor, far northeast where it will go well with you. You have seen many things, and done many things…"

Bizcocho smiled back at his wayward friend. "Sí, Julian, I think I understand. The saying has it : Life is doing it … and, well, dear death has done it." He may be a wanderer, he was thinking, forever moving from one place to the next, but he always knew where he was going, he was never lost.

A dumb pleading look filled the youth's face. "As I say, you have done many things, señor, but – but don't do this. Don't go southwest."

"Okay, Julian, if you say so, I'll go northeast. Does the future hold good for any of us? We shall never know because the future is always – well, always in the future where it belongs, heh?" and the traveller shook the youth's hand, quietly blessed him.

Bizcocho presently tramped off with his full backpack and smart sombrero, turning repeatedly to wave at everyone watching him leave. With a last backward bravado wave Bizcocho was soon enveloped in his own small cloud of dust, to disappear altogether behind mesquite and cactus in the distance.

The Wanderer of Chihuahua did not go northeast however, as Julian had strongly urged him to do, but went southwest as he had originally intended. From that time on he was never seen or heard of again.

48

Fire!

Gerardo was busy sorting out a tangled mess of reins and harnesses in the main stable. It was one early evening when a vicious strong wind was raging from the southwest, lifting dust and chaff. The wind soon increased in its intensity, straw debris and grit flying in the air. It whined and howled between the slatted boarding of the stable walls, stones and woodchips rattling against the timbers. As Gerardo worked in a rare moment of well-being he hummed tunelessly to himself.

The dog Salté, lying in the straw, suddenly sat up on his haunches, his ragged ears rising like radar scanners. He looked to right and left, up and down, and again side-swung his massive head to this side and that, bushy eyebrows raised in surprise − or it might even have been alarm. The canine beast began to whine too, like the wind whipping through gaps and cracks of the stable.

"I don't know how it is," voiced Pancho a little irritably, "but whenever you're happy Gerardo you make everyone else downright miserable."

"What do you mean? I was humming *La Carta Que Te Mande*. Do you know it?"

"Ah, I know it alright. A real charming song it is too, but sure done to death after you got hold of it. Uuy, it's a curious thing," the old ranchero rambled on, "but when you were making your 'noise' just now our Salté noticed straight off, and so did the young bay there. I was watching him, head going up, nostrils tightening, eyes rolling and ears pinned back flat − you could tell he wasn't liking it one little bit. The effect you have sometimes on our animals beggars belief. If you'd been nearer to that bay he would surely have nipped you one with his teeth. And if he could speak like us I expect he'd have already told you to shut it. I'll speak for him then and tell you kindly to shut it."

"The wind's strong as the devil out there," observed José, glancing out. "I mean it's coming on something wicked to what it was a while ago. I can't see across the corral for flying dust. Like smoke it is."

Nobody cared to comment.

"I don't know what to do with that chestnut colt," said Gerardo grimly. "He's so slow and lazy-like it seems to me. Have you noticed?"

"Hmm, he is a bit dreamy and lethargic with it is that one," agreed Pancho, "but I reckon I know how to fix his problem. I know how to fix *his* tune, Gerardo. If you go along to Tulia and ask her for some ginger – fresh stuff it is, she's sure to still have some."

"Ginger? Ginger?" queried Gerardo gratingly. "What's that?"

"Did you miss your schooling? It's a kind of spice from the Far East, looks like a root or a fat-fingered hand. Tulia gets it from a cousin of hers who works on a steamship on the China Sea route. He brings her back a bit of ginger every trip he makes."

"Once I've got the ginger, then what?" Gerardo made a grotesque face with easy plasticity.

"Why, you cut a piece off and peel it, score it a bit and shove it up the colt's back passage. That's what you do with it."

"You're joking me, is it?" said Gerardo suspiciously, the others tittering among themselves.

Gerardo pulled his rubber face, not at all a pretty sight, thought Pancho, but *pretty* repulsive. "No, amigo, straight up I tell you. Put a piece of the stuff up its backside and that'll soon liven him up and give him some 'go'. It's a damn fine remedy. The don told me of it ages ago. And by the by the Chinese have been using ginger for centuries. They maintain it makes you live longer, you know, if taken regularly."

"Taken regularly, is that so?" said the other, not entirely convinced.

"It's what the Chinese themselves say. You actually live longer on ginger." Gerardo wanted to know by how much you could live longer, meaning in the number of years. "Uuy, I couldn't tell you, Gerardo. The Bible says our natural span of life runs to threescore and ten, right? So maybe you might live fourscore or even longer."

"I don't know," responded Gerardo grudgingly. "Tomorrow I could get myself trampled to death by a stampeding herd of horses, so how will ginger help me there?"

Pancho gave him an exasperated look. "Tomorrow, hermano, if there was a stampeding herd of horses me and the boys would *throw* you under it. I'm talking about a *natural* lifespan without mishaps and accidents – or accidents on purpose."

"I don't know…" repeated the other, doubting Pancho's word. He thought it out a moment, then made his decision. "No, I'll take my chances and do without this ginger. I don't fancy spending the rest of my life packing pieces of ginger up my back-end."

Pancho roared off into loud guffaws. "Oh my!" he cried, trying to regain breath. "That's the remedy for a lethargic horse. *You eat it*, you dumb bean-brain! You put it in your food as the Chinese do."

This came as some relief to Gerardo. "Ah well, that's more like it," he grinned a tad sheepishly. He had visions of becoming the next Methuselah.

The old ranchero laid into him once more. "Why do you want to live so long for anyhow? You took a half day off last week and didn't know what to do with yourself. Bored to a standstill you were. Immortality for you would be just short of purgatory."

"But don't *you* want to grow old, Pancho?"

"He *is* old, you torn taco!" tossed in José maliciously.

"Sí, and I enjoy being old," smiled Pancho. "It's a damn sight better than the alternative – Now Gerardo, you go and get some ginger off Tulia, she'll let you have it if you ask her nicely – but don't smile at her, that only makes it worse; your 'worried' face is best for such. And tell her you want the fresh stuff, mind, not the powdered snuff rubbish. Then you can fix up your colt with it. Try some yourself by all means, only just think on about which end it should go in at. ¿Claro?"

At that moment Pancho stopped himself, head craned high and sniffing the air. "What's that smell?" he asked of everybody. "Like smoke I'm thinking."

"José just had a cigarro," said Emilio, "didn't you, José?"

"That was a while back," said the smoker somewhat mulishly and defensively, "when I put away them roans in the other stable." He spat contemptuously to make his point. Not fully satisfied he noisily hawked and spat again.

Pancho asked if the supper fire was out, Juan saying that he put that out some time ago, and put it out as a safety measure because of this contrary and fighting strong wind.

"Hold on!" gasped Pancho, eyes popping in alarm. "That's woodsmoke of a different sort I'll be bound. There's something afire, I'm certain of it. A fire! FIRE!"

49

Gutted

"Señor! Señor!" called Julian in an instant, dashing into the stable. "The roans' stable is on fire!"

"Right!" roared Pancho. "Come on you lot, move it!"

The men rushed as a crowd out of the stable, a riot of rancheros running pell-mell for the burning building.

"I closed the doors first, señor!" quavered Julian in a high-pitched frightened voice, running a fraction ahead of the old man who was bowling along like an angry bear. "The wind! The wind –"

"Was fanning the flames, eh?" puffed Pancho in his hurried trot.

"The wind was feeding the fire, señor, so I had to close the doors till help came."

"Bueno, Julian, you did the right thing."

"But the horses are still inside!"

"We'll soon have them out, muchacho, every last one of them – ¡Uuy! Don't you fret on that score – Lead them out, hermanos!" Pancho bellowed over at the men who had easily overtaken him.

José and Gerardo were into the thickly smoking stable in a flash, Julian flying in after them, releasing each wild rearing horse from its stall. Juan and Emilio waved their arms as the terrified animals clattered out from the smoke-choked stable, running to the safety of the nearest corral.

"Juanito!" boomed the old man. "To the bunkhouse! Buckets to the water-butt! And anything else that'll hold water. Start filling the lot!" and the boy shot off like a puma chasing prey. "You too, Emilio!" bawled Pancho.

Meanwhile the wind skirled and keened around the wooden buildings, making matters worse by fanning the flames already engulfing one end of the burning stable. Pancho quickly assessed the situation, realised the fire was getting dangerously out of control. At any rate the horses were out of the stable and safely gathered at the further side of the corral. He also took in the fact that the wind was blowing mostly from the direction of the remaining line of stables, which was something of a relief for him. Though the fire could easily spread he guessed from flying sparks shooting up from the blazing roof.

The men were beginning to see that there was little hope of saving the burning stable. It was paramount now to stop the other buildings from catching on fire. José jacked a pair of ladders up against the second stable, next to the one fully aflame. Juan in the meantime had lugged several buckets of water from the rear of the bunkhouse, ably assisted by Emilio. The fat man's face glistened with sweat from both the heat of the fire and from his herculean exertions carrying loaded buckets.

Cándido raced up the ladder like a monkey, with a full sloshing bucket which he passed on to José crouched near the guttering. José swung the metal pail in a wide sweep over the stable roof, dropped the bucket down to be grasped by Gerardo.

Gerardo galloped off to refill the pail from the water-butt, the only readily available source of water. Emilio helped like a Trojan with the refilling of buckets, hauling them over to the scene of the fire. Cándido continually flew up and down the ladder, passing near-full buckets to José.

Sparks were already landing on the second stable's roofing, smoking and smouldering in scattered spots on the vulnerable wooden roof. When José did not have water to throw about he cut along with amazing cat-like light-footedness across the sloping roof, stomping out small fires hungrily fed by the wind.

The doomed stable was by this time an inferno. Thick black smoke billowed up, blocking out the evening stars, flames flaring high into the wind-whipped sky. A terrific crashing of timbers as the main rafter beams fell into an orange-white holocaust. Sparks continued to fly, dancing in swirling smoke.

Pancho dipped a round billycan into a bucket and splashed water on the second stable's side wall nearest to the fire. The heat from the fire scorched his back and legs. Sparks landed on his clothing, and he too began to smoulder in spots on his person.

Julian took care of the frightened horses, leading them one by one with soft whisperings, squeezing them in among the other stables, away from the sight of smoke and flame.

"By God, this is hot work!" gasped Pancho, but he was actually enjoying the action and commotion all the same. He felt the heat too, which was not surprising, as his clothing was now afire. He was not aware of this danger and carried on sloshing water at the wooden wall before him – a human torch lighting up his own space.

It is a well-known fact in Mexico that God favours rogues and reprobates, as the old ranchero himself had once told doña María on the Ramos farm. This self-same point he unwittingly and quite unknowingly proved in the next moment. In a mighty sweat, choked with smoke and feeling extremely hot, the further dip of the billycan was extravagantly poured over his head in an effort to cool off. By this action Pancho instantly doused the growing flames devouring his denim shirt, which also extinguished his short career as a human torch. He showed mild surprise as hissing steam and smoke roiled about him. He had inadvertently though certainly saved his own skin, without knowing anything of it – not until later when he curiously examined his ruined shirt.

And the ruined stable burned itself into a great heap of charred beams and ashes. Hot ashes blew over the ground, setting ablaze dry scrub and gorsebrush. The rancheros concentrated on throwing their last precious supply of water over the black smouldering remains. The stink of damp ashes and charred wood tormented their nostrils.

Later, in the light of a rising half-moon looming above drifting smoke, Gerardo raked the ashes on a now defunct stable floor. Juan followed him with a can of water, ready to pour over obstinate red glowing coals under the ash mounds. His eyes smarted with smoke, face smudged with ash. Steam still hissed and smoke rose around him. The wind had died down only a short while ago, though ash continued floating down, like snowflakes.

It was near to an hour or so before dawn when Pancho decided that it was safe to retire for what remained of the night. The old man cast his eyes tiredly at the men teetering on the outside of the rectangle where the stable had stood. Their faces were streaked and smudged with black ash. They felt unutterably exhausted and more than ready for sleep.

"Well, hermanos," Pancho painfully rasped, throat sore with fire-smoke, "say what you will, but sometime soon – and I don't as yet know by what means – but we're going to have to find ourselves another stable to replace this one," pointing to a pile of fire rubble. His red-rimmed eyes scanned the dirty, disconsolate faces, finally resting on the firebrand José. "And it must be done," he went on darkly, "it must be done before the don gets back from his business trip in Guadalajara."

A heavy downpour of rain fell the following morning, too late to douse a flaming stable building, but late as it was did amply refill the water-butt by the bunkhouse.

SECOND INTERLUDE

Mexico got on with its life. With its fiestas and fairs and festivals, its celebrations and carnivals, firework displays and the *lotería*, its *charreadas* or rodeos. Within its crust it gave of its rich mineral veins and earthjuice; its oil and silver, its gold and zinc, its tin and copper and lead.

At a school in Monterrey a science teacher who was also required to teach music – even though he was tone-deaf – formed a school band. It was a crashing, thumping, discordant brass band; exuberant but essentially off-key. When the teacher felt that his pupils were competent enough, he marched them as a body into the streets of Monterrey. The young musicians were distracted by gathering onlookers, pouring out from their houses to titter among themselves at this outrageously catatonic, *furioso* din which was an offence to the ears.

The youngsters were all too aware of being laughed at and ridiculed; they blushed burningly at the humiliation of it. While the science teacher 'music master' serenely led them on along crowded thoroughfares.

Then something extraordinary happened. The children began to concentrate earnestly on their music and their instruments, ignoring altogether the teacher's worthless tuition. And soon gay martial airs resounded gloriously in the busy streets of this mighty industrial town, the people listening with pride, with respect, and with inspired uplifted hearts. The band had at last cohered into a pleasing harmonious ensemble. And all because the individual members had cared enough, committed themselves, tried of their utmost endeavours in a grand tradition of aspiring youth.

In a pueblito on the Rio Conchos, near the town of Delicías in the vast state of Chihuahua, a baby girl was christened, blessed by priests and parents, and feted by family and friends.

A wedding was underway somewhere in Tabasco. The modest adobe brick chapel, where the solemn ceremony was in progress, was filled to capacity with the bride and bridegroom's families, friends and curious bystanders. And the young man getting married, a simple country boy of nineteen summers blushed as much as the bride, but for a different reason, greatly astonished at all the attention he was receiving.

In the town of Gomez Palacio in the state of Durango an old ranchero had passed away and was being buried. The funeral was attended by his surviving wife and children, their sons and daughters, and their children – and a small knot of horsemen he had known and worked with. The old man had known that there is life in a single springtime leaf, sanctity in the earth's soil, and beauty in a flower or a child's smile.

When he was alive and robustly well, he had also been aware that man is substance and source of where he came from and where he will eventually go, like leaf and flower, unto dust and into the soil. And in the life of the earth his own life will be as long as the brief smile of a friend. The grand old patriarch would be long remembered, perhaps revered, and certainly honoured by his many progeny.

At various times of the day, usually early in the morning but at any time of any day, there is a clapping going on along the length and breadth of this horn-shaped country …

The sound of it came from nearly every home in every city and town and pueblo. In isolated homesteads on the slopes of the sierras, on the rugged central tableland down to the lowlands, came this long familiar clapping …

It was the sound of women *handclapping* tortillas!

Shaping them nice and round and flat, each one the size of a tea-plate.

Hundreds of thousands of brown hands slapping out pieces of maize dough. Up and down the entire country went on this homely handclapping. It was as if Mexico were applauding itself, and maybe rightly so, for this was a richly vibrant, dynamically contrasting, fun-filled, timeless, colourful country.

Part Nine

50

A Foundling

One hot day during a long fierce run of hot days, a curious event occurred. It was something unique in the experience of the rancheros. It began when José was out on a hardpan flat, riding his dappled grey colt, in search of a stray yearling which he imagined may have wandered this way. A desolate area of rock and shale, virtually no shade to speak of, the hardpan flat was unaccommodating and of little interest to man or beast. Yet José was drawn here, sensed that his stray was somewhere around the vicinity. A gut feeling told him to continue looking for a while – he tended to trust his gut feelings all in all.

Noontime was none too far off and José's temper was beginning to fray with scant patience left in him. He could scan around him in any direction, the distance distorted by heat haze. He might see mirage-like apparitions which could be taken for a horse, only to turn out as an unusual rock formation or even a cactus.

José was disappointed because his instincts had let him down this time. Why did he imagine he would find the stray in this inhospitable area staring emptily at him? But a strong intuition had lured him here, and now he regretted it.

He was about to turn around and ride on back to the grasslands when he thought he heard something, an unnatural kind of noise. Was it crying he could hear? He was near certain he heard crying, yet not altogether near certain; he could easily have just imagined it. But no, for there it was again. Seemed quite near too he guessed. An unmistakably human sound, no doubt of it this time.

There was a short gully or dry watercourse directly ahead of him and he nudged his mount forward. The noise had certainly come from that gully he knew – there it was once more, like someone crying, a child maybe.

He reached the lip of the gully and leaned over, peering down. It was a fairly deep gully and not very wide. There in the bottom, below a cut-bank and under the sparse shade of a stunted growth of scrub, was a straw hand-basket.

In the basket was a baby.

Its face was red and screwed tight with wailing, small fists clenched, chubby legs kicking out from swaddling clothes. José blinked twice in astonishment before his mind finally accepted what he saw. A high noon sun can easily play tricks if you are not careful, and he had seen enough mirages for one day. The now lusty bawling of the infant however irrevocably convinced him that this was indeed a reality. The poor creature was tormented by flies buzzing angrily about its exposed, baby-smelling wet face.

The ranchero looked about him once more before dismounting, but there was no one else to be seen. Stepping carefully into the gully, so as not to alarm the infant, he made gentle chuckling sounds in the manner of a hen approaching its chick. The baby saw him then, directly put a halt to its squalling and gazed at him with intense curiosity.

He stooped to lift the basket and the baby started again with louder cries of distress. José hastily lowered the basket, rubbed at his jaw, thinking hard. Being a father of two he came to a rightful decision. He bent once more and boldly gathered the child up in his arms. It stopped crying in an instant, gazed at him with what can only be described as mystification, which imitated exactly José's own look.

He climbed out of the gully, and with one arm cradling the babe he remounted his colt. There is nothing else for it, he reasoned to himself, but to take the baby to the ranch and to sort something out there.

Riding back at a gentle walk José had an expression of smugness on his hard swarthy face. His instincts had proved reliable after all, though obviously for quite a different reason. He had not found a stray yearling but an abandoned one-month or so baby boy. Or at any rate he assumed it was a boy; he had not bothered to check, only thinking so by the power of the little one's lungs.

Yes, the lone silent hombre was well satisfied with his 'catch' – by instinct alone no less. And the infant too remained remarkably quiet, perhaps enjoying the novelty of riding on a horse, gazing at the man with quizzical, black-button eyes.

51

Babycare I

"Why, he's a second Moses!" exclaimed Pancho a short while later. "Found in his basket, did you say, José, on the bank of a river?"

"Hell, no, Pancho, down in a dry gully. I found him in a very hot and dry gully. I don't reckon the little one liked it much."

The old ranchero nodded, either in agreement or merely acknowledging that he had heard the other's words; hard to tell by the closed look on his face. "It's a bit like a story from the Bible though, isn't it?" he felt forced to say. "Baby Moses found in the bulrushes …"

His mind then changed gear. "Well, what are we going to do with the little mite?" he asked the others. "Have you any ideas, Juanito?" he dropped on the boy hopefully. But Juan confessed that he hadn't any ideas at all; such matters were not mentioned in his study books.

"It needs a woman's touch to be sure," went on the old man, "but I'm loath to let Tulia get her hands on it, because she'll surely smother it to death with her love. So we'll keep this to ourselves for the present, eh?"

"It ought to have some milk at least," advised Emilio. "Who knows how long it was lying out there in the desert. Stands to reason it'll be hungry for milk."

"I don't know why we keep calling the poor babe 'it'. He's a boy to the bone, without a doubt."

"Then give him a shot of mezcal or something," suggested Cándido.

Pancho tightened his lips; he didn't seem pleased. "I'll give you a shot in a moment," he growled. "A bit of gunshot! When I say *boy* I mean a *baby* boy, you contrary-eyed cuckoo!"

"I can get some cow's milk off Tulia," gurgled Gerardo happily. "I've been there before now for milk when I had those stomach upsets. Tulia needn't know we've got a baby here. I'll tell her my guts are playing up again – Don't give it away yet, not till I can sort the little fellow out," he added somewhat gallantly, and went gallivanting off to the casa.

"The coming of this small one has sure made our Gerardo happy," observed Pancho, evidently pleased with the fact.

Then the weak-wit Julian appeared among the tight roundup of rancheros surrounding the infant. "Ayí, so you found the baby then, señor!" he smiled brilliantly.

"We found *a* baby, sí," said Pancho, giving the youth a curious look.

"I knew you would find him," continued Julian, flushed with a serene happiness.

"You mean you knew that we might possibly find a baby out in the desert at some time, is it, Julian? What are you actually trying to say, muchacho? What do *you* know about this abandoned niño, eh?"

"He was in my dream, señor," smiled Julian.

"A *he*, so you knew that much at least. Now what dream was this, Julian?"

"My dream of last night."

"Tell me about it."

"I dreamed it," said Julian in a thin voice, a little scared of the other's beetling brows.

"Sí, sí, but what exactly did you dream?"

"I dreamed that someone would find him."

"So you knew he would be missing, is that it?"

"No, señor. I dreamed of him out there alone." Julian pointed to the westward, where José had gone riding earlier on. "He was alright because I knew someone would find him."

The old ranchero put on an exasperated look. "If you knew the baby was out there in this terrible heat," he ground out slowly and distinctly so the simpleton would take it in, "why, oh why didn't you tell any one of us about it? Why, Julian?"

The sodden-wit dropped his head dejectedly and every vestige of his earlier happiness evaporated. He went on to explain : "Something told me to say nothing to anyone about it, or the dream wouldn't be the same dream. I knew he would be found, this baby, and he was, señor, just as I dreamed it."

"Okay, muy bien, muchacho," said old Pancho in a more conciliatory tone of voice, "but can you tell us anything else about him? Who his mother might be for instance, and why he was dumped out there in the wild?"

Julian gave a negative shake of his head. Then he brightened and asked, "Who found him, señor? Who found the little one?"

"José did, over on the hardpan flat. You know the place I think."

"Ayí, I thought it would be you, José," Julian smiled at the ranchero. "Looking for a stray, were you?" and the mystical sad-wit turned for the stable without waiting for an answer, leaving the men dumbfounded.

Pancho watched the retreating figure, and tilted his sombrero in order to scratch at his head. "I always did maintain," he said heavily, almost to himself, "that there is more to our Julian than meets the eye … but I'll never reckon what it might be. I will say this by and bye, if you know yourself through and through, you'll know the world."

He swung on José who still held the infant cradled in his arms. The baby's black-button eyes too were swinging, from face to face, following the voices with avid interest, as if it understood every word uttered. "Are you positive there was no one around that place, hermano?"

"Not a soul, Pancho, and I didn't even find the yearling either."

"Oh, we found your horse," clucked Cándido with glee. "Me and Gerardo. Your yearling was prancing around in that arroyo like I said, like I told you at the time, but you wouldn't listen."

"Okay, alright, so I was wrong," allowed the lone silent hombre, slightly miffed. Then he brightened of a sudden and said, "but I did find this little fellow, didn't I, you switch-eyed coyote!"

Cándido wafted over his amiable, charming smile. "So, José, do you reckon we can round up some more of these babes, the stray ones like?"

"José! Take it easy with the niño," Pancho warned him. "You're swinging him around as if he was a dead rat or something."

"Here, let me hold him for a spell," offered Emilio, and José passed the swaddled bundle on to the fat man who gently coddled it.

José hunkered down on his heels, elbows resting on knees. His eyes were down, sifting shreds of tobacco into a curved square of paper. He was out of the game now, let the others get on with it.

"Tickle his tummy, Emilio," said Cándido. "I used to like getting my tummy tickled when I was a niño, so my mamá told me."

"I liked having my toes tickled," said Emilio, nursing his small bundle.

Old Pancho put on his judicious mantle and said, "If your mamá had any sense, Cándido, she'd have tickled you to death."

"Tickled him to death," sniggered José, trying to roll himself a cigarro. "Oh, I like that one, Pancho! Tickled him to death, he-he-he!" scattering loose tobacco about his feet.

52

Babycare II

A 'baby debate' developed among the rancheros with old Pancho appointing himself as suitable for the chairmanship. "Now what do you suppose happened?" he began, face serious and concerned. "Was he put there and forgotten to be picked up? No, it can't be that," he answered himself. "Did they think – whoever left him there – did they imagine the baby would be found and taken care of? No, it can't be that either…"

The old man paused a moment to reflect or perhaps to collect the scattered confused thoughts racing about in his mind. "Hmm. Was he maybe put there to be picked up at a later time? But why should they do that? It just doesn't make any sense by my book. No, I reckon this poor fledgling fellow was for some reason or another deliberately abandoned. By its parents or more likely only by the mother. And if anyone should find him still alive, then good luck to him – and to the baby."

Pancho switched on his ferocious foul-tempered aspect, to strike terror into anyone bold enough to cross him. "Now what kind of a damned uncaring cruel sonofabitch would do such a thing?" he said heatedly. "To a helpless little creature like this! It's the sort of thing that makes you distrust humanity itself. It makes my blood boil and no mistake. ¡Uuy!"

"You know, the hardpan flat isn't all that far away from the highway," contributed Cándido, a sensible look on his face for once. "There's a track nearby which eventually leads to the highway. Whoever left the baby must have surely come from that way – And gotten away fast-like before José showed up."

"But why, for God's sake? Who could be mean enough to do such a thing as that?"

"Or desperate enough for some reason," said Juan. "But it's terrible, that baby could so easily have died."

"it's awful! Awful!" said Emilio hotly. "It's downright inhuman!"

"It's not a Mexican way either," said Pancho, "so maybe the mother is a foreigner, or whoever left the niño stranded like that. I'd string up the culprit, if I ever found the culprit, whoever it might be."

"Whoever abandoned him was not one of our kind of people," said Juan thoughtfully. "The mother of that baby is a rich person, I'd say. Certainly well-off. That little petticoat or whatever it is the baby's wearing is made of real silk. And the shawl thing is of the finest material I've ever seen. He's come from a very wealthy home, there's no doubting that."

"Ay caray and bless your head, Juanito, for what you keep in it," the old man complimented him. "Do you suppose then that this is an unwanted child? Well, that's obvious, what I mean is from maybe a mother who's not yet married. Just a young girl, say, who got herself in trouble."

"Something like that it would seem," agreed the boy. The others nodded.

"So where does it leave us? – Emilio! I hope you've washed your hands!" Pancho suddenly flung at the fat man.

The small creature in Emilio's arms was suckling contentedly on his fat forefinger.

"Well, here's Gerardo at last," said Cándido, "with the necessary tools too it looks like."

Old Pancho stared as Gerardo approached them. "A baby bottle with a teat on the end of it!" he exclaimed with delight. "So, Gerardo, Tulia knows we've got a baby, eh? What did she have to say about it, then? Coming over is she?"

"No, she is not coming over," grinned Gerardo, "and she doesn't know we've got a baby."

"Then how the devil did you manage to walk away with a baby's bottle and teat without her catching on?"

Gerardo genuflected. "If you promise not to tell, Pancho, and I'll have to whisper it in your ear." His grin widened as he put his head close to Pancho's own, cupped a hand by the old man's ear.

"Ho-ha-ha!" he roared a moment later. "¡Uuy! That's a real sweet gem! I'm sure we needn't hold it back from the boys, eh?" which galvanised Gerardo into a retreat to a safer distance.

"Go on, then," urged José warily, sensing he might be the butt of a joke, "tell us." He sucked hard on his cigarro, eyes slitted and watchful.

"He says – " Pancho had to control a bubbling amusement swarming up his chest – "Our Gerardo says, to put Tulia off the scent so to speak, he says he told her that he reckoned Cándido had been behaving like a baby of late, and wanted to show him up by presenting this baby bottle to him. With the milk and teat and all, ay caray!"

"What's so funny about that?" Cándido wanted to know.

Pancho wiped a hand over his jaw. "You tell him, Gerardo."

"Well, Tulia was right tickled by it," Gerardo carried on gleefully. "She laughed so much that tears came to her eyes – and she – she told me that she'd gone and wet her underdrawers!"

Cándido smiled a cynical, couldn't-care-less smile.

53

Babycare III

The rancheros crowded round Emilio, making infantile noises and pulling such faces as you would only normally see in a zoo; the naturally ugly Gerardo being the most outstanding of course.

"Here!" spluttered the fat man, the indignant surrogate father, "give him space to breath will you! And are we going to feed this baby or leave him to starve?"

"Pass him the bottle, Gerardo," purred Pancho.

Emilio fed the little foundling, who was in fact a chubby-built, robust baby boy. He smacked and gurgled at the bottle with a hearty appetite. "Like a ranchero on the mezcal," observed the fat man.

"Well soused and satisfied," fed in Cándido, eyes crosswise but contentedly sparkling.

"We should introduce him to tequila," suggested José. "I've still a drop I can let him have."

"Oh act your age, will you!"

"Only a suggestion."

"Tequila would sour the milk, don't you know. They don't mix."

Juan said that the baby must have been very hungry, the way he was guzzling at the bottle. "He'll want to sleep next I shouldn't wonder," said Pancho. "Gerardo, can you fix up a kind of wooden cot for him?"

"Gladly, gladly. Would you like nice smooth bevelled sides? I could also make it bow-shaped, you know, like a small rowing boat. Or I could – sí, I could maybe –"

"¡Újule! Any damn way, hombre, but we need one quick as quick."

Emilio continued feeding warm milk to the tiny tot, while Gerardo galumphed off to make a wood cot. The rancheros stood around the fat man as before, watching the infant with absorbing fascination. The baby seemed to have taken to the men, for he behaved admirably.

"We shall have to let Tulia know in the end," commented Cándido. "I mean, who's going to look after him when we're out there with the horses? Julian?"

"He will need a feed every three or four hours, I expect," added Emilio. "I think he likes his food, does this one," bending a beatific smile down on the child in his arms, dazzling it with his teeth.

"We ought to give him a name too," said Juan.

"How about *Moses*?" suggested Cándido. "On account of him being found in a basket on the river."

"In a gully, not a river, and how about naming him *José*?" returned José, throwing his cigarro butt in the dust and grinding it thoroughly with his boot-heel – He had no wish to start another conflagration. "After all it was me who found him, and *I* ought to give him a name to go by."

"Hasn't the poor thing gone through enough already without being saddled with your name?" said Cándido cuttingly. "First abandoned by his mother, then getting called José. What a start in life, he might as well be back in the desert and have done with it."

"Look, you – " began José menacingly.

"I have it!" Pancho put in adroitly. "We can call him Frontino José Arroyo.

"He was found in an arroyo." This met with Emilio's instant approval.

"Why Frontino?" asked José. "Or why not José Frontino?"

"Suit yourself," replied Pancho affably, "but Frontino was my father's name."

"Oh, I see ... Well, fine. Okay, then, shan't argue with that," José conceded.

Pancho was pleased at the outcome of the naming being settled. Cándido noted what tiny hands the infant had, chubby but very small indeed. He went on to ask Emilio if he could hold the baby boy for a moment.

"Later, hermano. I'm feeding the little fellow as you can see. Let's not disturb him, hey?"

"Handsome little mite, ain't he?" said Pancho. "Muy bonito. He'll have no problem with the señoritas when he's older."

"You know," said Cándido in serious, sober tones, which caught everyone's attention, "I'd heard that when Gerardo was very young his mamá entered him for a beautiful baby contest…"

The very idea of Gerardo, considered by the others as the ugliest man in the state, to have entered in a beautiful baby competition utterly stretched their imagination, bursting into gut-wrenching laughter.

"And he won it!"

Laughs again all round; even Gerardo, carrying an armful of timber, was grinning, though it looked more of a grimace on his rubbery, rough-featured face.

"The thing was," continued Cándido, "he'd been lying on his tummy in his cot, and all you could see was a round, blank, bare – bald, you might say – which was the back of his head. That 'smooth face' was the clincher though as far as the judges were concerned."

"Had he just been given a haircut then?" tittered José.

"No, from what I was told he hadn't a hair on his little round head. He was bald alright, and very rounded like a ball, like an ostrich egg lying in a baby's swaddling clothes – What's that stink?" Cándido crinkled his face. "Is it the niño?"

The fat man said he was afraid that the infant had messed himself, at both ends as it turned out. "You can still hold him for the present, amigo," Cándido generously backed down.

Juan wondered what could be used for nappies, as he could only think of bandages from the first aid packs. "We can use them, I suppose," said Emilio, "till we find something better suited – My! But he does smell a bit, doesn't he? The little rascal!"

Old Pancho seemed now to be watching on from a distance as it were. It sank into him heavily the realisation that whatever happened, sooner or later the baby would have to be given up and found a decent and proper home. It was not sensible or even feasible for the rancheros to keep him. It was not fair on the infant, he felt. So, at any rate he would not dare allow himself to become too strongly attached to the babe.

A short while later Gerardo was to be seen wandering about and muttering to himself; that the wood already examined would not suit, there must be some prime timber around here that would suit. But where was it? He couldn't put tabs on where exactly he had seen some wood that would suit. Stomping gauchely up and down and around various sheds and stables, thinking hard.

Then it came to him and he shot off someplace else, carpentry plans filling his head, and the type of timber he was after would most certainly suit.

Of course it was not long before Tulia found out about the presence of a baby on the ranch, because Julian had accidently let it slip out. From that time on it was old Tulia who took total responsibility for the baby's care.

Don Roberto's cook/housekeeper was in her element. Never married or having had any children herself, Tulia's long stifled maternal instincts came fully into play. She mostly kept the infant in a crib − handsomely crafted by Gerardo − in her large rambling kitchen. Where she devotedly and determinedly indulged her passion for fattening up what she thought a small scrap of an infant.

And, as it turned out, the most frequent visitor to the casa was the foundling's first surrogate father, none other than the not so lone and silent hombre − José.

54

Julian Upsets Juan

It was a blistering hot July holiday weekend and the rancheros had returned home to celebrate with their wives and children. Pancho and Juan had the hacienda to themselves, even don Roberto was away in Mexico City. The two almost had it to themselves; Tulia was still at the casa, and of course the stablehand Julian who had no home or family to go to.

Pancho pottered about the stables in his usual ambling, listing-walked way. He was in the satisfying process of inspecting a beautifully coloured palomino, which had arrived only the week before, when he heard a kind of moaning. It was emanating from the feed-barn he guessed. Deciding to investigate this strange sound he tramped through the thick corral dust.

He entered the dimness of the feed-barn and there sitting on a bale of straw was Juan. The boy had his knees tight together, elbows resting on them, and he was quietly weeping. The moaning Pancho had heard was in fact coming from Salté, in the dog's distress over his master's condition.

The ranchero kicked straw as he went quickly to the boy. He sat by his side, put a comforting arm around the shaking shoulders of his young charge.

"You're missing your mamá and papá, eh, muchacho?" he said, as tenderly as his rough gravelled voice would allow. "And your sisters too I reckon – Julia, Ruth, Cristina. I should have insisted you go home as the men have done – for they've surely missed their families these past months."

"No, P-Pancho, it's not that," choked out Juan, lifting his wet boy's face to the old grizzled ranchero's own. "It – it's Julian," he managed to stutter out.

"Julian?" echoed the old man in surprise. In some confusion he absently stroked the back of Salté, which at least shut the dog's moaning. "But surely our gentle Julian hasn't been doing you any harm, has he? Why, that young fellow hasn't a scrap of malice or violence in him, and never has. So what's with our Julian, then? How has he upset you like this?"

The boy put a sleeve to his eyes, pulled himself together as he felt a true ranchero type ought to. He turned to his revered friend and idol, saw kindness and empathy in those shallow-sea-blue eyes, and sighed heavily.

"I know Julian wouldn't harm anybody and hasn't harmed me at all," opened up Juan, his distress fast on the wane, voice waxing hard and strong. "But poor Julian, he's such an idiot – No, I don't mean that," he went on, sniffling a little. "I mean he is so – so simple, almost like a dumb animal at times."

Golden lances of sunlight cut through chinks in the feed-barn wall, shining on them both. He saw that the old man was about to say something, checked him with a half raised hand. "I spoke to him earlier on. I was trying to explain to him about Mark Twain's character *Huckleberry Finn* and his friendship with the black man, Jim. It was the bit about the French people that Huck and Jim were talking over. You know, where Huck's asking the black man whether a cat can talk like a cow, or a cow talk like a cat, because this Jim character couldn't understand a word of French, couldn't fathom why a Frenchman didn't speak English. I was attempting to put it over how Huck was trying in his turn to explain to Jim that it was natural for animals to use their own language – not a true spoken language – their instincts, and for different peoples to use theirs, which are spoken as anyone knows.

"You've read 'Huckleberry Finn', haven't you, Pancho?" asked the boy, giving another small though final sniffle.

"Well, no, can't say that I have – but don't worry because I do catch your meaning. The trouble was our Julian wasn't catching on at all, was he?"

"No, he sure wasn't," said the boy, breaking into a smile.

"Nice to see the smile, a smile can make a friend, can make your day. And our eyes are for seeing things with, not for making tears – So, that's what upset you, is it?"

"I felt so sorry for him. Sorry that he's missing out on so much in this marvellous world we live in. Most of it simply goes right by him and he isn't even aware that stuff is just passing him by…"

"Listen, my young friend," said Pancho in low tones, leaning toward the boy, "there are many poor ignorant people in the world, as you know. There are millions, tens of millions, who have never read Shakespeare, or even heard of him, and would be clueless if they had. I tell you, a great chunk of the world's population is near poverty stricken in that regard.

"There's none of us country people who's had proper schooling, except maybe for a few lucky ones, like don Roberto's boys. Take your own case as an example : You've hardly attended the school in the pueblo, because like most of the other kids you've had to work on the land, especially during harvest times, and this to help your family survive. Sure, your mamá has taught you a bit, bless her good heart and head. Your papá too has set you to bookwork and given you use of his library − best collection of books in this region, not counting don Roberto's, mind. Oh my! The don has some books, you wouldn't credit it.

"But you, my young star, you've mainly taught yourself. Look, you're very bright and clever, there's no doubt of that. You probably have more intelligence in that head of yours than all us rancheros put together − though maybe that's a backhanded compliment, for we're as daft as a stable of donkeys."

Pancho paused, put on his academic mantle, shabby and frayed though it was, and carried on, telling the boy that in life people start off on the same track, and branch out in different directions. In spite of that, they all in the end return to the same final destination. The boy's level of intelligence, he opined, was well on a par with a grown and reasonably educated city man. Moreover, if he wanted to relate to Julian and speak with him on the same footing, then he must lower his own sights accordingly.

Brain-wise, Julian was a moon, the old man affirmed, while Juan in comparison was a galaxy of stars. Yet there was still much they both had in common. The love of the land and what grows or lives on it. The understanding of horses and how to handle them.

"You know as well as me, amiguito, that when it comes to horses our Julian can beat us all hands down. There's not a thing he doesn't know concerning horses, or any livestock for that matter, and that's the truth of it."

There were stipples of light splashed on the straw-strewn barn floor, painting it silver and gold, eating away the corner shadows. The old man rubbed his jaw, chewed for a moment on his moustache, then lifted his craggy eyebrows.

"I know it's a roaster out there today, but let's take a short ride out, eh?

Go look over God's good Earth from our horses' backs. What do you say?"

"I'll saddle Macha for you," smiled Juan, bright-eyed, "as Chapulín is ready anyway," getting to his feet and springing into action.

"¡Bueno!" grinned Pancho happily. "We can head south and take a look at don Roberto's longhorns – By the bye, where is our Julian?"

"Over at the casa I think, spending time with Tulia – and the baby!"

"Ay, Tulia is almost a mother to him … To them both – Let's roll then!"

As they led their mounts out from the shade of the stable, heat and harsh light jumped on them, and a dust-devil whirled crazily before them.

55

Julian's History

Moments later Pancho and Juan were riding their mounts at an unhurried easy canter. Past rocky ridges and grassy knolls, over a spring-fed stream, on into a wide grass plain. The old man sniffed appreciatively at the dry fragrance of summer-beige grass. He saw the dominance of the grass, the multitudinous armies of fine-pointed spears, the golden hair of the land, as he imagined it. Home and shelter and sustenance for birds, beasts and insects. The drysoil lay immobile, silent in its depth and earthcrust darkness. Scudding clouds overhead threw their cloud shadow over the land, glided along the grassy terrain, folding over the distant foothills.

They presently found the herd of cattle, well spread about the plain, placidly grazing under a broiling sun. As the horses' hooves threshed through the grass, at every step ahead of them a small cloud of white butterflies rose and fluttered away. The two reined their mounts to a halt, leaned forward in the saddle and gazed at the pool-eyed cattle.

"You know, Juanito," said the old man a short while later, "We are all animals in a sense."

Man was a higher form of creature, he maintained, but an animal type all the same. Civilised life had taken away most of man's animal instincts. Man plays out his life on the stage of life, as that Shakespeare fellow had once put it, he said to the boy, but the bard had put it in better language than his own.

He didn't really think somehow that people were any better off than their ancient ancestors – or savage natives still living in the forests and jungles far down to the south of this country.

He was getting to his point. "Our Julian is closer to those kind of people. Closer to Earth and to nature and its many animals. He's nearer to being an animal, in the sense I'm speaking of, than you and me could ever be. And that's not a bad thing at all by my reasoning, hmm…"

Old Pancho ran spatula fingers over the pommel of his saddle, felt its hot leather, and carried on : "You could say that Julian is a deer in the forest, a bird on the wing, a puppy dog chasing its own tail. His brain is small and poorly developed, or rather possibly damaged, and all his common sense is in his heart. Julian has no need of our civilised world, and probably not even aware that it exists, as we know it does. Don Roberto's success as a landowner and businessman makes him a life rich and fulfilling, but not as much as Julian's own life as he himself sees it …

"So you don't have to pity him, amiguito, or feel sorry for him in any way. Instead, you may feel a little envious of him, as I do sometimes. Feel glad and happy for him, as he is that way most of the time – pure and innocent and simple."

The ranchero listened to a hot-dry whine of working insects in the air, watched the movement of a ground-wind sifting its way through rolling pastureland. In the air was a fluting of small summer birds, sweet as ripe berries in their callings, soft as spring water, reminding the old man of many past summers just like this one. And, above it all, windscattered clouds filled the skyspace, racing above their own shifting shadows.

He turned to the boy. "I don't think I ever told you how we came by Julian, did I?" No, the youngster hadn't been told; he only knew that Julian had been here a number of years, at least since he could remember. "Well, a good few years ago I found Julian myself near the town of Fresnillo."

What a pathetic sight he had been too, Pancho told the boy in grave tones. A scruffy, neglected, bedraggled urchin boy with an idiot grin on his poor thin face. His parents had apparently died when he was but six or seven years old. He had no brothers or sisters as the old man could make out. The child's uncle had taken him in and supposedly taken care of him. But the uncle had ill-used the boy and worked him almost to death – Pancho had found this out a long time later.

One time, after a cruel beating to within an inch of his young life, Julian had the sense and courage to run away. He began to roam the countryside like a tramp or hobo. He lived on what he could find, seeds and berries and handouts given by anyone he could humbly scrounge from. This he did for nearly two years, a poor simple soul with no home or friends to call his own.

"I found him near Fresnillo, lying in a ditch by the roadside, with one big swollen broken ankle. I took him into town and had a doctor look at his ankle, and the doc fixed him good enough. He told me that he thought the boy was mentally retarded, a wandering waif who'd been hanging about the streets of the town a great deal. After that I figured the poor rascal would need a proper home, but not there in that town, or in any town. No, I could see he was a creature suitable only for the country, and that was where he ought to be …

"So I brought him back to don Roberto's land, and the don didn't mind in the least. The muchacho could work for him, he said, have a decent wage and wholesome food, and shelter as well.

"More importantly, at that time, he needed to be among folk who'd care for his welfare, look after him, and treat him decently as a human being. Tulia comes to mind on that score. She gave him a kind of loving attention he had never before experienced – bless her for that.

"And you know, Juanny, he hardly looked inside the old bunkhouse, let alone sleep in it. No-o, right from the start Julian slept in the stables, from that day to this. And I for one had never seen a more happy or contented young buck as Julian."

"He took to the horses, then?" quietly asked Juan.

"He took to them straight away, as a fledgling bird takes to the air, and has lived with them these many years past. He has this amazing, intuitive understanding of horses. Better than any horseman I know – there I go repeating myself like the proverbial parrot…"

"What about that uncle of his, what happened to him?"

"Ah, sí, that one. I heard a long time later that the cruel swine came to some sticky end. He got his just deserts by all accounts. Julian doesn't know this by the bye, so we can keep that bit of knowledge in wraps – Whew! But it's hot I'll warrant. We can ride on back now, Juanito. ¡Ay que bueno, muchacho, vamónos!"

They rode through the hot wind-scoured grassland under a relentless scorching sun.

And the long summer days burned on. The deep blue of the sky never diminished, nor the brightness of light, on this Mexican highland plateau.

Part Ten

56

Stable Plan

"Has anyone given some thought as to how we're going to replace that stable José kindly burned down for us?" asked Pancho one day a week or so after the conflagration incident. He looked at the men in turn, finished with his eyes resting on José. "We need a stable up on that bare spot before the don gets back from Guadalajara. Any ideas forthcoming? How about you, José?" casting a 'lawyer-for-the-prosecution' look at the firebrand.

There was nothing of pyrophobia in José, he simply loved fire and could hardly resist from setting about making it. However, these days he had to curb such dangerous urges.

"Well, I did think of something, sí," responded the unwitting arsonist, raising a hand to scratch his ear. "You know them night goods trains that stop at the junction to take on water? There's one that comes through about once a month, and all it carries is timber. Loads of timber. Building timber. Enough to knock up a row of stables."

Pancho glanced his way with narrowed eyes. "What exactly are you suggesting, hombre?"

"I thought maybe we could raid it like on the next run, which is due this week as it happens. Always stops at the junction, to take on water like. We need only take enough for our stable, maybe a much bigger one. It's mostly government stuff anyhow, so no one will be out of pocket. It seemed like a good idea when it first came to me," José ended lamely, seeing the other's dark looks.

The old man did not reply at once, but stared at José with incredulity. "No, hombre, it won't do," he said emphatically. "¡Újule! We'll be serving time in a federal penitentiary with the key thrown away. We wouldn't ever again see the light of day. No, it's not on. What a damned reckless risky business! Anyone else got any bright ideas? Good sensible law-abiding practical ideas?" His eyes swivelled round once more.

"You know, old don Fernando is breeding pigs now in a big way," obliquely offered Emilio.

"Sí, and Tulia's runner beans are coming up lovely this year," the old man returned with heavy sarcasm. "Ay caray, hombre, have you been sleeping or what?"

"Of course he's been sleeping," slipped in Cándido, "what else could you expect?"

"If you'll let me finish what I was about to tell you," said the fat man aggrievedly. "Since don Fernando has been breeding his pigs he hasn't as many horses as he used to have on his ranch. I know for a fact that one of his stables is standing empty and has been for a year."

"So you're suggesting we pick it up and walk off with it, is that it?" Pancho reposted in a voice like thunder, and becoming more sarcastic by the minute.

"I just think – I simply reckon he'll sell it to us if offered a fair price." Emilio showed his projecting upper front teeth in a wide smile.

Old Pancho considered this for a moment, then said, "Don Fernando? No, I don't think so. Even if he charged us the earth, which he would – and make no mistake about it, we've got to find ourselves a stable soon, or we're out on our backsides. Well, this stable, how do we shift it from don Fernando's place to here? One stable the size of two houses…"

"That's no problem," said Gerardo, bright-eyed with enthusiasm. "I know the stable Emilio's talking of. Clapboard it is, like the one burned down. We just dismangle it, bring its timber over in the big waggon, and then we resemble it!" Gerardo looked greatly pleased with himself.

"I think I know what he's saying," Juan smiled, shooting a quick amused glance sidewise at Pancho.

"I do too, just about," replied old Pancho, pulling back a grin. "Could it be done I wonder? No, I don't suppose it can, any more than knowing the limit of infinity."

"Sure it could," put in Cándido, "and we'd have it for nothing as well."

"How is that then?"

"I'll *win* it off him."

"How? Not cards! Not playing poker surely?"

Cándido smiled his charming 'winning' smile.

"Oh no, muchacho, it won't do!" rebelled Pancho. "Don Fernando is a good friend of mine and I won't have him cheated at cards by you card-sharpers, oh no!"

"It's alright, I won't cheat the old fellow. But I'm hot at poker when I get the chance of a game, José too. Fernando likes his card-playing anyhow, especially poker – you know that."

Pancho pondered, the idea seeped through to him with lukewarm enthusiasm. In all honesty he thought this notion fanciful in the extreme.

"It's the only way," José brought in the big guns, "the only way to get ourselves a stable in double quick time, and time is against us. I mean, how else could we do it in the time left to us?"

For a project such as this, the dissembling and rebuilding of a stable from scratch as it were, Gerardo considered himself an adept; and perhaps rightly so, because he was uncannily skilful in anything related to carpentry, which was his chief passion and earlier trade long before he fell into ranching and horse-training.

"I can do the dismangling," Gerardo garbled. "If you remember me once saying, I started out as a carpenter when I was a boy. Served my full apprenticeship, I did – got a certificate to prove it. I'm certified, I am!"

"Why, that's true enough," Pancho conceded, referring to the carpentry and not the qualification, warming slightly to the idea. "You are fairly good at working with wood. Hmm … But maybe you've done enough *dismangling* for the present."

"Me and José can ride over tomorrow, as it's a holiday," said Cándido, flashing his squint eyes, "and I can guarantee you'll have a stable for the use of by nightfall. What do you say, Pancho?"

"Okay, okay, it suits I guess," agreed the old ranchero at last, "as long as there's no damn cheating, eh?"

"No cheating, amigo, my solemn promise on it."

"You sure don't look solemn."

"You've got my word on it," said Cándido, working hard at appearing solemn.

"Will we have the time I'm wondering…" Pancho was back vacillating. "Sí, I suppose so. If you make time you can save time, and there's time enough for that. Alright then, hermanos, that's what we'll do – And don't spare the horses, the waggon horses. ¡Ay que caray, muy bien!"

He wandered over to the bald patch where a stable once stood not so long ago, and where another will hopefully cover that empty spot.

57

Building the Stable I

The next day Cándido and José set off for don Fernando's ranch. They took the largest waggon, drawn by two powerful bay horses. Gerardo went along with them. He had insisted on it, not to play in the card game but to look over the coveted stable.

The men played through the daylong hours – Cándido, José, don Fernando, and one of his rancheros. Gerardo spent his time fruitfully poring over every plank and boarding of the stable in question; a long rectangular, high-walled building with low-angled roofing. Each single piece of wood, including that on the roof, was marked by him with a special sort of coding, using chalk.

When evening drew on and the dusk smoked in bluely and darkly, Gerardo had marked every piece of timber of which the stable was made, even the inside stalls. It was then when the men came out from the bunkhouse where they had been playing all these long hours past.

Cándido and José were grinning with happy triumphant faces.

"It's ours, amigo, doors and all!" exulted Cándido.

"Right!" returned Gerardo, galvanised into a business-like state. "We're going to need some lighting rigged here while we strip down the building," he added importantly.

With surcharged energy Gerardo bustled about, carrying an air of responsibility rather lightly on his shoulders.

Don Fernando's men graciously assisted them in dismantling the stable, no hard feelings apparent on their part. It took several hours, short breaks occasionally taken for a snort or two of mezcal, compliments of José. Gerardo went charging about, toing and froing between one stack of timber and another.

The job was done in record time, everyone agreed. Gerardo insisted on collecting every nail, tack and staple, diligently and carefully drawing the nails from the timber pieces, so as to be used again when rebuilding. The timber was stacked in the waggon under Gerardo's fussy directions. Flailing his arms and shouting out orders, such was his authority that several of don Fernando's men assumed he must be the ranch foreman at don Roberto's.

The poker-players and the carpenter returned to the hacienda just as the sky turned peach-pink with a new dawn. They rolled into the corral grounds, cracking whips, whooping it up with waving sombreros and wild wolf-calls. This was probably on account of the mezcal they had consumed during the early hours, and of course the euphoria from their victory at the gaming table.

Pancho allowed them three hours only to sleep it off, then roused them unmercifully to begin work at once on re-erecting the peripatetic stable on the site of the old one. He gave top priority to the project because he felt that time was against them. Don Roberto was due to return at any time over the next few days.

Gerardo was put in sole charge. He stood with legs manfully planted wide apart, hands resting on his hips, looking for all the world like a general viewing a battleground. His plans were made – mostly filed away in his head – and there in front of him were his materials and his tools and his expectant assistants. He strode about exuding self-importance, barking out orders, much to the amusement of his fellow rancheros.

First off, as he saw it, deep square holes had to be dug for the positioning of corner and doorway supporting beams. The heavy timber pieces were placed in concrete, measured out exactly perpendicular, and allowed to set, major roof beams and crossbeams already positioned, forming the basic skeletal structure, thus stabilising the whole. Pancho was bemused by, as he saw it, the sheer clunkiness of Gerardo's procedures. All of this took a day and a night, allowing the concrete to set hard.

At one point, in utter exasperation, Gerardo pushed his sombrero far forward and scratched the back of his head. He thought his helpers at times a disruption and a danger, and was beginning to believe that they were about as useful as a bucket with no bottom to it. He pressed and plugged and pegged on with his carpentry calculations, with his wholly incompetent helpers, and – because of their gross incompetence – with not a few nervous bouts of hypochondria.

However, the structure held itself firm, and so things were doing fine so far.

Gerardo had his assistants straightening out the original nails, as there were few new ones to spare. In hammering straight the used nails José managed to hit his thumb at least three times, cursing roundly at each 'self-inflicted' hammer blow. His language was as blue as his swelling thumb, the thumbnail turning black. Pancho asked him whether he knew which nail he was supposed to hit, cruel and unsympathetic words which did not go down well with the injured ranchero.

"Oh leave off that!" grunted Gerardo with an impatient flip of his hand. José's injured thumb was already swollen and turning a horrible purple-black. A thickly bandaged thumb pulled him out from this task, Gerardo setting him onto something less dangerous – or suicidal. He instructed José in the laying out of boards and planks spread over the entire corral grounds, for the front, side, and end elevations of the building. Beyond the corral Gerardo had him lining up ready the required timbers for the roof and internal structures such as the horse-stalls. Juan assisted him in this task, and soon found that he himself was now doing all the work. José skived off as much as he could get away with, still muttering vile curses not fit for a boy's ears – not that Juan minded as he'd heard it all before.

Gerardo was storming about like a bad-tempered cop in a traffic jam. He had set his teeth and his mind into the work of building a stable; or rather gritted his teeth at the wholesale ineptitude of his co-workers.

A time later he began to feel fairly satisfied in his tortured mind that things were actually progressing, his carpentry instincts telling him that it was so.

This was going to be no botched job. No indeed, not while he was in charge of proceedings and with his reputation to maintain. He grimaced as a twinge tugged hurtfully in his stomach. He sighed a martyr's sigh …

58

Buiilding the Stable II

On the following day the men seemed in better condition to tackle the labour-intensive work of building. They carried on with a will and an extraordinarily and surprising co-ordination. At least it began that way.

The first major task of the morning was the positioning and nailing down of the secondary horizontal and roof cross-beams, using a spirit-level for greater accuracy which Gerardo – as chief builder and architect – managed to accomplish with some skill and aplomb. Recognising his talent at last the rancheros took his orders more readily and without question. Needless to note however, there was still a great deal of joking around and a bit of silly horseplay going on, which both Gerardo and Pancho tried to curb. Despite these minor setbacks the building was slowly taking shape.

Gerardo was examining the joists of a window-frame he had made in some masterly fashion. He had intended all along to have a window on the west side of the 'new' stable. Pancho, too, carefully appraised the finished product, declared it well and neatly made and duly praised the carpenter, who drank in the compliment as though it were an elixir. To the old man it seemed that Gerardo rose six inches in stature. Even his lumpy, ugly face was somehow transformed to something hinting at near-handsomeness.

A time later the builder was bent over almost double and precariously balanced, fiddly fingers delving in a toolbox, determined to find something he knew was somewhere in that toolbox. For Cándido, who was right behind him, an opportunity he saw here was irresistible. All he need do was to give a gentle push with his foot against Gerardo's backside.

The carpenter went sprawling, kicking over his toolbox. The culprit, with a concerned expression stitched to his face, acted as if he had accidently backed into the other. He even held a plank in both hands, surely evidence enough of his pure-white innocence. Gerardo growled, but at least the item he'd been searching for, a smaller spirit-level, was there directly at his feet.

The work continued afresh. The hours rolled on into afternoon. Gerardo was by now at the stage of becoming somewhat obsessed over his coded and numbered sequence of clapboards. He was exasperatingly upset when he discovered Salté peeing on one of the planks, erasing the number that had been chalked on it.

"That damned dog!" he complained angrily to Pancho. "He's this very moment pissed on my board. Not just anywhere on my board, oh no, he has to do it right on the number. Don't know where the hell I am now, thanks to that mutt."

"Look, amigo," the old man attempted to sooth him, "what difference does it make anyhow? This planking is all of the same size, isn't it?"

Gerardo ground his teeth and growled, "You don't understand. I want the stable exactly how it was on don Fernando's ranch. The whole thing fitted perfectly."

"Sí, I grant you that, but surely you can still do that without an exact board here and an exact board somewhere else – they're all the same size, the same thickness too. I don't get it, hermano."

Gerardo glimpsed a little patience on the horizon and plucked a patient look for the benefit of his friend. "I know what you're saying, I know where you're at, but when this stable was first built it fitted snug-tight with every piece in its place."

He took a pencil from behind his ear, used it to scratch his ear, and went on : "Over time a line of boards at one spot warped this way and others warped another way, see? They still weaved and knit in any one section, if you follow me, and so in putting it all back together, well, it has to be right. Each board fitting in with its old neighbour. The structure is stable then."

"The structure is *a* stable then, hmm," returned Pancho, face set deadpan.

"Oh it will be stable, you can count on it. Only at the moment I don't know where I am with this middle section," and Gerardo wandered off to the rear of the half-completed stable, muttering away to himself.

The old ranchero, purely out of habit, gazed up at the sky, saw a wide-winged buzzard sailing silently in the far deep blue heights. Then he glanced down at the instigator, who sat with his tail thumping the dust, a fawning grin directed at him.

"Salté," he addressed the dog slyly, "what was that number you pissed on, eh? Tell me, perro." He was surprised when the animal gave two short sharp barks, then continued grinning at him. Satisfied, Pancho turned and headed over to the rear of the stable.

"Oye, Gerardo, it's number two," he informed the builder, holding his not-giving-anything-away deadpan look.

"What is? What're you on about?"

"The clapboard you're so concerned over, the one which got its number washed off – pissed off, you'd say – Anyway, it's number two."

"How do you know?"

"What's his name just told me."

"Who?"

"Why – what's his name? – At any rate it's number two."

"No, it can't be, because I – Ahh, wait a moment, let me check that middle lot again…"

The carpenter rummaged through his pile of timber, checked the boards recently nailed on to his mid-section, muttering and calculating, and once more checking off chalked numbers on the clapboards.

"You know, Pancho," he said at last, "what's his name could very well be right, I think it is a number two."

"Who's that, then?" asked the other, keeping a straight face.

"Who's what?" Gerardo was getting confused.

"What's his name."

"I don't know, but I reckon he's right."

"Well, there you have it, amigo."

Gerardo's day brightened of a sudden. He bustled and chivvied importantly around the stable, in much the manner of a great architect surveying his new creation.

It might only be a modest second-hand stable but in his eyes it could be a magnificent cathedral.

In clapboard.

59

Building the Stable III

Cándido pushed a ladder up to a near-finished side of the skeletal building. He was about to duck beneath it when he was checked mid-stride by a sharp cry from Pancho.

"You must never walk under a ladder, muchacho," he warned. "It's bad luck and disrespectful too I'll have you know."

"Ah, amigo, that's old women's talk."

"No it isn't, far from it. You see how the ladder and the wall and the ground make a triangle? Well, that's a symbol of the Holy Trinity. You walk through that triangle and you're breaking the symbolism. Not only that but you're making a pact of friendship with the Devil himself. *Por favor,* for all our sakes, don't ever walk under a leaning ladder – and that means this one as well. ¿Claro?"

"Okay, if you say so," smiled the young man, stepping with exaggerated carefulness around the ladder, as if it were going to bite him.

Emilio, yawning like an alligator, felt he had done sufficient labour for the present and was desperate to get his head down somewhere to sleep awhile. He realised the safest and quietest place was inside the unfinished stable. This was because all the activity of building – noisy and chaotic in the manner of most Mexican enterprises involving more than two men – was being done on the outside at this time. So he stole inside and sat on the floor, back against the newly nailed-down planking, sombrero tilted low over his eyes.

On the outside meanwhile Julian – who was reluctantly shanghaied into giving his fullest assistance – the youth headed for one end of the stable carrying a long plank balanced on his shoulder.

"No, Julian!" called Gerardo frantically, "the other side there, muchacho!"

Julian turned to the speaker, his long plank sweeping ninety degrees, the rear end of which missed José's face by a whisker, swiping the cigarro he was smoking clear from his lips. José swore at him, and the simpleton turned in the opposite direction to apologise. The plank swung up and round with him, the end of it hitting Cándido on the rump.

As Cándido was already up a ladder and placing a plank in position on top of another using both hands, he quite naturally lost his balance. He had nothing to hang onto, except the top plank which was loose and resting on five or six other planks also resting loosely one atop the other, ready to be nailed down. The ineluctable laws of physics would not allow that top plank to support the dead weight of a hanging body.

It collapsed instantly, clapping concertina-style against the one below it, then dropping to the ground on the other side – the inside. Cándido's hands fell on the top edge of each succeeding plank as they snapped shut one upon the other, and fell below. For Cándido it must have seemed a sensation similar to that of falling down a flight of stairs, hitting each step.

At last – in a mere millisecond as it happened – his fall was finally broken when his hands gripped the first of the planks which had already been nailed secure. He clung to this plank for sheer life, calling pitifully to the others for help.

Fate seems invariably capable of dealing a blow to those who least expect it, and it was unfortunate that Emilio should choose the particular spot he did to take unsanctioned repose, because it was directly under the path of the falling planks. The first one fell on his head, mashing his sombrero and waking him both, the second broke in two on his astonished upturned face, and the remainder buried him like a wooden tent.

On the other side – the outside – Cándido was still bawling for assistance. He could not hang on much longer, and could not understand why no one came rushing to save him. The fact was, unknown to him but blatantly obvious to the others, he was hanging a 'cliff-edge' six inches only from the ground.

"Come on, hermano," said Pancho, grinning, "we can't have you hanging about here all day."

"*Adíos*, amigo," smirked José.

"Damn you lot!" spat out Cándido.

And he let go.

His reattachment to the planet Earth was so speedily and unexpectedly accomplished, he instinctively bent his knees and rolled over the ground, much like a landing paratrooper. He was so successful as a human ball that he bowled along directly in the path of Julian who tripped over him. Julian was so startled he threw his long plank in the air, before keeling over Cándido's compressed form. The plank too, obeying the laws of gravity, came down hard, breaking in two across Cándido's arched back.

This arresting piece of drama played out to its natural conclusion when Emilio suddenly blundered from out the stable, carrying a face full of fury. The anger was because he assumed someone had deliberately thrown planks down on him. He tripped over Julian who was getting to his feet, and fell heavily over the recumbent Cándido before him. It was only at this late stage that Cándido suffered from his fall off the ladder.

Apart from these occasional mishaps, the work on rebuilding the stable was, all the same, in Master Builder Gerardo's opinion, coming along just as he had planned it. Hands on hips and a pencil stuck strategically behind each ear, he strutted around and dished out his commands like a Mexican Isambard Kingdom Brunel.

60

Uncle's Shed in Querétaro

The stable was up and running – so to speak – and looking as if it had never moved an inch, well before don Roberto returned from his business trip to Guadalajara. It had taken the rancheros two full days, allowing the first day for the foundation and supporting timbers to set hard in their concrete bases.

Cándido, José and Gerardo had hardly slept in over fifty hours, a fact of a feat which vastly impressed Emilio, who fully understood the value of sleep and rest, regarding the men's mammoth sleep-denial as one without equal. In celebration he had himself an extra snooze, knowing full well that he could never have done what his compatriots had achieved.

The men stood around the freshly erected building, tired and weary but pleased with themselves, and overtly admiring their handiwork. Gerardo was of course singularly proud of his achievement. He had good reason to be, considering the poor quality of skill in those who had helped him. All the same, he allowed gratuitously, they had done a fair enough job of it which he very much appreciated.

And was not he himself deserving of praise? "I did my utmost here, if I may so say. It is my best work and I admit it with all due honesty," gratulated Gerardo generously. He stood tall and confident, an idea forming in his mind of building next a new and larger bunkhouse, or perhaps a wooden house for each ranchero, with covered verandas and a bath-house to boot. Secretly, in that he dare not disclose such a thought to the others, he daydreamed of building, entirely from scratch and on his own, a magnificent soaring mansion house. In clapboard and stable planks. There seemed no end to his building ambitions – the Christopher

Wren of Mexico. Be that as it may, there was one slight problem as he saw it.

Where would he get such an amount of clapboard?

"My uncle in Querétaro once built himself a garden-shed," Cándido confided to his companions. "This was before they put up the new houses at the back of his place. There was a fair bit of land, you see. It wasn't his but he used it all the same to grow vegetables and suchlike. When he thought he could get away with it, knowing what Aunty was like, he also grew a little marijuana as well, which he liked to smoke in his pipe."

So Cándido's uncle built himself a wooden garden-shed, and was immensely proud of it once the structure was complete. Cándido's listeners sat or squatted where they were, knowing without question that there was more to come.

"When it was finished he just had to drag our Aunty out of the house to take a look at it. Aunty walked right round it before saying anything. 'Well?' my uncle starts up. 'What do you think to it?' 'It's very nice,' says Aunty, 'but what's it supposed to be?' 'What's it supposed to be!' said my uncle. 'It's a garden-shed. That's what it's supposed to be. What did you think it was?' And my Aunty, after a short pause and eyeing uncle in a wary kind of way, she says, 'Oh, I thought it was a big box to keep things in.'

"'A box!' said my uncle. 'To keep things in! What put that in your head?' 'Well,' says Aunty, 'it looks to me like a box with a fancy roof on it. I mean, it doesn't have a door, does it?' 'Doesn't have a door!' said my uncle. 'Here, woman,' he said, and he takes Aunty by the hand and they traipse round the shed.

"My uncle's rabbiting on, 'A window this side, look … blank on this side, as you can see … another window here on this side … blank on this – .' My uncle walks on his own round the shed again, muttering away to himself. He can't believe it but sure enough he'd forgotten to put in the door."

So Cándido's uncle is ripping out the planking and starts again working on his door. After a deal of effort sawing and fitting, measuring and fixing up straight, he at last has his door. But he soon encounters a further problem – which he ought to have foreseen. His door can't open out but only open in. He finds it quite impossible to store anything in the shed because the in-swinging door is in the way and taking all the space. Uncle had fixed his hinges on the wrong side.

He put away his marijuana-filled pipe he'd been smoking, suspecting it had much to do with these recurrent faults. He sets to once more – with a clearer head as heretofore – and corrects the hinges, enabling the door to open out instead of in, thus giving himself space for storage. And as Cándido earlier stated, his uncle was fair proud of his shed, now that it was a proper working garden-shed.

Gerardo regarded the young tale-teller sceptically. "Is that the end of it, then?" he hazarded.

Cándido somewhat candidly glanced about him, then carried on to finalise his story. "Not exactly, no," he confessed, lips curling with the beginning of a smile. "You see, the same thing happened as what did here with the stable. It got burnt to the ground."

"There you have it," said José with a satisfied smirk. "It could happen to anyone, like I said."

"How did the shed catch afire in the first place?" pressed Pancho.

"Ah well," the young man extended his smile, "my uncle always used to smoke his pipe in the shed, because Aunty wouldn't allow it in the house. She said it stank the place out – like a Chinese brothel or something –"

"Would your aunty *know* of such places?" Pancho asked.

"What places?"

"What you just said, about Chinese brothels. It's hard to imagine your aunty –"

"Oh, *I* said that! Not Aunty."

Pancho turned his face to Juan at his side and said judicially, "Are you taking all this in, muchacho? If you are I'd prefer you disregard it, every bit of it," the boy suppressing a curling of his lips.

"Anyway, uncle's pipe smelled like a sewer," Cándido continued. "Small wonder, the rubbish he used to stuff in it, mixed with a bit of his home-grown marijuana. I guess he must have tapped his pipe out over some rags or something on the floor, and the shed caught on fire.

"All the people in the street came out to watch it burning. It was a lovely blaze, my uncle said."

"So now he has no garden-shed," said Gerardo.

"He has no garden, because like I said they built them new houses at the back. In my uncle's yard now you couldn't hardly swing a cat."

61

Weatherwise

The divisions of the day, the fore and noon and after noon, seemed as one prolonged daylight bright suspension of time. As the hot days dragged on the sun-heat burned the earth-crust, drawing out its summer fill.

On some afternoons, late almost toward evening, a short refreshing shower of rain would fall on this high central plateau land, darkened rainclouds breaking the monotonous blue of sky. And the rain would wash stone and rock, green the grass again and rid it of the ubiquitous dust and grit.

The dust was laid, at least for a while.

Short-lived summer wildflowers then made an appearance, even on stony tracts of land. Peppering the ground, dots and pops of colour peeping out from nook and crevice in the rocky wastelands. A flush of flowers in the rock cracks; reds and yellows, blue and lilac and orange. And small white ones. Odd ones here, clusters there, adding a vivacity to the vast sienna and cinnamon landscape. Such miniscule wildflowers with tiny, tightly embraced petals, so compact and close to the ground that the wind never caught them, and because of this they kept their coy and secret scents to themselves.

After the rain showers had passed over there was a scent of damp earth which came up sharp and strong and invigorating. It was as if the land were thankful to be quenching its thirst and losing its dry harshness. This rain darkly stained the earth. It was a life-sustaining stain, giving growth to plant and flower.

Out of this miracle came the voices of birds, calling anew and flitting from one wet branch of – say, a beefwood tree – and on to another in a joyful flight of freedom.

The rain was good for the land, if it rained often enough, and the land benefited greatly from it. It increased the power and potential of growing things. The summer-weary soil was rejuvenated and became more actively productive. Especially in its nourishment of plants and other land-grown foods, which in their turn nourished the people and the animals of the country regions.

Part Eleven

Part Eleven

62

A Horse Named Emperor

The rancheros of don Roberto were taking a midday break, lounging indolently about the stables and corral fencing. The wooden slatted walls of the stables creaked under the burden of a hot noon sun, the men amiably and irreverently discussing religion.

"What I don't understand in the New Testament," said Pancho, combing his moustache with blunt fingers, "is the parable of the good Samaritan. I mean, that Samaritan finds a naked man in the desert and straight off he's clothing the fellow, feeding him and setting him up for life so to speak."

The old ranchero rubbed a hand over his jaw and gazed at his listeners. His eye lines crinkled with amusement and tiny particles of dust ran down his swarthy cheeks.

"Now if I were to wander in the wilds of Guanajuato and I came across a Samaritan type, I'd soon be ripping off my heavies and shorties, no word of a lie on that score. He would come across me and take pity on this poor old ranchero fellow with nothing on his back, and maybe fix me up in a nice new suit and sombrero. Thanks to him I'd have a good solid meal in my belly, a snort or two of best tequila, and perhaps a life pension to round things off. Because the good Samaritan would be certain to see me secure and straight for the rest of my natural. Don't you think?"

He dropped a hand, capped his knee, began to rub it. "But if I were to find a fellow out there completely stark-naked with his tackle dangling in front of him, well, I'd think twice about going anywhere near the likes of him. I'd take him for a lunatic, and being generally a sensible sort I'd steer well clear of him. That's what I would do, without a doubt, ay caray. On the other hand though, there's the possibility he might be some eccentric wealthy dude, like the emperor with no clothes."

"I don't remember there being an emperor with no clothes in the Bible," said Gerardo gloomily, swiping at the fly-thick air around him.

"No, hermano, I dare say you don't, for it's from a kid's story."

"Do you remember that first black stallion don Roberto had?" said José, having just rolled himself a prosperous-looking fat cigarro with none of his usual tight, skimping of tobacco. "He was called *Emperor*."

"Sí, José, the don loved that horse," returned Pancho. "He took the animal to Guadalajara that time when *el presidente* was visiting the town. The don was in the parade riding his stallion *Emperor* with *los charros del norte*. His youngest boy Jorge was there in the crowds, for they had a splendid fiesta on as well. A real fine day it was for a parade such as that. There they were, coming along *Calzada Independencia*. 'Here's the emperor coming!' shouts Jorge, and some hombre behind him says, 'You mean el presidente don't you?' And Jorge says, 'Sí, he's riding along too!'"

The old man automatically and instinctively waved a hand in front of him to scatter a cloud of whining insects. "Ay que caray, it was a shame Emperor broke his forelegs in a fall and had to be destroyed. Don Roberto asked me to do the shooting of the poor beast, because he couldn't bring himself to do it. No-o, he could not do it no-how." Pancho clicked his tongue.

José studied the ash-tipped end of his cigarro, practically admiring it. He glanced up and said, "Didn't he have the horse buried with honours?"

"Sí, he certainly did do that, but first off he had wanted him stuffed and mounted –"

"Mounted?" Cándido cut in. "Can you mount a dead horse?"

"Mounted on a stand or pedestal, you cactus thorn!" Pancho blew back hotly. "The thing was, when that gross fool of a taxidermist had done with the job poor Emperor looked more like a damned pregnant camel. The don then wanted me to shoot the taxidermist.

"Sí, it upset the don terribly. He couldn't get over it for a long while. Right up until I found *Velvet Night* for him to be exact. Now there was a real strong stud stallion for you. Within a month or two he had laid all the mares we had, then started nosing around the mare donkeys, would you believe!"

"No, I wouldn't believe," said Cándido contrarily.

"I'd believe Pancho any time," gruffed Gerardo, "than I would you, you flea-eyed tall-storyteller!"

"No doubt of it though," Pancho swung back round, "that *Velvet Night* was some rare rampant beast," he concluded good-humouredly, the weathered lines on his face dancing as he spoke.

"Wait a moment though," he tacked, straightening up, "I have a 'paper clipping somewhere of that time in Guadalajara with a picture of the don in front of the municipal building, standing besides – Oye, Julian!" he called over to the young stablehand. "Run to the bunkhouse if you will, muchacho, and fetch me that saddlebag of mine, it's hanging over the bean-sack."

Julian dutifully trotted off. "Sí, hermanos," Pancho continued, "it's a picture of don Roberto standing with *el presidente de México* himself."

Julian returned moments later carrying Pancho's dusty leather saddlebag, and the old ranchero groped about in the bag, muttering softly. "Aha, here it is!" he cried. "I thought I had it somewhere in safekeeping." He unfolded a tattered newspaper cutting. "Here you are then – look at this, Julian, you see it?" Pancho passed the paper on to the poor-wit.

The youth's eyes widened in surprise. He had rarely seen a picture or photograph. "Why!" he shrilled in delight and wonder, "if it isn't the very likeness of his honour the boss man. Look at that! Isn't it so much like our don Roberto? The same clothes and everything. I remember him wearing a fancy jacket like this one. The very likeness of our don Roberto on this little piece of paper!"

"It is him, you dunghead!" José threw at him. "Now pass it over so we can all have a look at it, you *burrito*!"

Julian still held the paper. "Don Roberto himself…" he murmured in wonder. Holding the paper out to expose the picture to the others, he then in all innocence put a question to them : "And who is this hombre with the boss man?"

Pancho considered this the finest All-Time First Prize gaffe, and it set the others to fall about in great gusts of laughter. Julian was simply pleased that he had said something that must have been clever indeed.

63

Likes and Dislikes

*I*n the suncrushed corral under a blue-wide sky the dog Salté dropped
to his haunches and turned over onto his back. He rubbed and rolled
his backbone in warm silky aromatic dust, pushed and kicked out his
paws in canine ecstasy. Then he just as suddenly stopped, smothered in fine
dust, eyes blinking as he checked to see if anyone might be watching him.
Satisfied that the coast was clear – and it was clear also to him that he could
do exactly what he wanted to do – he continued on rolling about like an
overgrown puppy, enjoying his dust-bath.

The big hound soon tired of it after a spell and got to his feet, looking
as if he had been dipped in a huge ash-can. He shook himself with vigour,
enveloped in the smoky dust-storm he had created. He lowered his muzzle
and sneezed, and sneezed again.

Salté next trotted purposely to a certain spot which somehow activated
his doggy instincts. He began to paddle with his forelegs and kicked dust
with his powerful hind-legs, dog-certain that a bone was buried here. But
maybe not, maybe he had miscalculated, for he found nothing and soon
gave that up.

There was something far more fulfilling to take up, because of a sudden
he pointed his nose, catching the scent of a rat near the stables. His dish-rag
ears rose in an instant. He was about to take the appropriate offensive action,
when he realised that he had really over-exerted his physical capacities by all
that energetic rolling in the dust. He glanced around once more to confirm
the belief of still being unobserved by his master. Salté nonchalantly made
off to the shade of a beefwood tree to snatch himself a sly little sleep. A dust-
devil scuttled over the ground behind him.

At the main stable entrance the boy Juan prepared a cook-fire in order to heat a pan of beans, while the rancheros carried on loping hungrily about the stable, looking in on the horses in their stalls.

"He looks happy enough," José commented enviously, indicating a chestnut bay, "chewing away he is at that straw."

"He's not exactly chewing, amigo," said Pancho. "That's what cows do. No, he's grinding, he is. They grind their grub is what horses do." He moved on to another stall. "You see the mare there, the red dun? Isn't she muy bonita? A real lady is that one and no mistake, hmm."

"Don't smile at it, Emilio," cracked Cándido. "If she sees your horsey teeth she'll think you're trying it on with her."

"Well, I don't mind admitting," drawled Pancho drolly, "I'd go to bed with that lovely mare." He turned to Cándido, winking. "Only we're not married, you see, so it wouldn't be proper, would it?" letting loose a gusty bellow of laughter.

"The horse is a wonder of creation, to be sure," old Pancho pattered on, after collecting himself together. "The most noble of all God's creatures. But I like any animal I suppose. Mind you, there is one particular specimen I just can't tolerate not one bit."

"Oh," voiced Gerardo, "and what would that be then?"

"I'm ashamed to say it but it's the Chihuahua dog, the dog from our own country. A cousin of mine had one for a time and I couldn't take to it no matter what. Every time I saw the damn thing I always felt like booting it up the backside, the fish-eyed skinny creature. But I never did, kick it one I mean, because one kick up its rear-end would send it straight to doggie heaven in no time you could mention. Ah well, that's my only animal dislike I reckon…"

Salté, droopy-eyed with sleep, came loping past him. "But I like you, even though you're in need of a shave," referring to the dog's muzzle thickly coated with dust. Salté settled himself at Juan's feet, falling off again into sleep.

"I don't like rats and snakes and scorpions – " began Gerardo.

"Well, if you ask me – " cut in José.

" – And I haven't finished yet. I don't like mosquitoes either, nor coyotes, wolves, cats, vultures, spiders, frogs, worms, and hogs."

"What do you like?" asked Cándido.

"Well, apart from the horse which I like for many reasons, I care a bit for the opossum."

"I thought that would come up," said José. "How is your pet opossum getting along these days?"

"Oh, real fine!" gurgled Gerardo happily. "When I first got it I'd let her out at night, you know, in the hope she'd meet a mate and carry young."

"That was up until," said Pancho dryly, "up until you finally found out that *it* was a *he*."

"Ah sí, I couldn't see for myself at first, on account of all that hair on her – on him."

"I don't like snakes and scorpions either," said José. "And I don't care much for tempered horses."

"*Tempered?*" queried Cándido.

"Bad-tempered, ill-tempered horses. I don't like them. And specially when they bit you or try to bite you."

"Aha!" said Pancho. "No one gets bitten oftener than José, be it horse or dog. They must like the taste of you, hermano."

"I don't mind a horse biting me," admitted Gerardo, "and I've been bitten often enough. It goes with the job I suppose."

"I don't like Emilio's fleas," said Cándido, "when they jump off him onto me. Bite as soon as they land they do."

"You're wasting your breath, tormentor," Pancho warned him. "Emilio's fast asleep."

"No, I'm not," came a sleepy, starch-structured voice.

"I wouldn't like a snake bite me," said Gerardo. "A snake-bite can be real nasty, real dangerous."

"Nasty and dangerous to be sure," grinned Cándido cheekily, "for the snake."

"I'll bite you, you crook-eyed coyote!"

"Say, what's a love-bite?" wanted to know Emilio, popping up into the land of the living. "What exactly does it mean? Does anyone know?"

"And I thought you were in dozyland. Anyway, it means nothing at all, just stuff and nonsense that kids get up to. By the bye, I advise you all not to bite Cándido – you don't know where he's been."

"As I think on it the animal I detest the most," José carried on where he had left off, searching in his pocket for tobacco, "is the mule."

"Whatever it is you want from a mule," Pancho barged in, "all you'll get is obstinacy."

"Which is mainly why I can't stand them," José regained his ground, and also found his tobacco pouch, untying the string that held it closed. "A damned stubborn creature is the mule. I'd never own a mule, not if you gave me one for free. I just don't like mules." He began to pour tobacco shreds into a cigarro paper, none too carefully, as he was now fuming.

"The thing is, José," pursued Pancho, "mules don't seem to like you. I've seen one or two give you a good kick with a hind-hoof."

"But that was accidental, like," retorted José, scattering loose tobacco over the floor. "They didn't mean to kick me."

"Oh I think they did," laughed the old man. "You could see that glint in their eyes every time, as if to say, 'I'm going to floor this son-of-a-bitch!'"

José was so incensed he failed to pay heed to his tobacco pouch which emptied out to be lost in straw.

Salté was growling in his sleep; ears, haunches and tail twitching and trembling.

"He's dreaming, I suppose," guessed Gerardo.

"Chasing jackrabbits," suggested José.

"I never thought that dogs could dream," wedged in Emilio, "at least not like humans can."

"Should be the other way around," Pancho put over, "for I often heard you growling in your sleep, with your feet twitching like two dancing shoes. Sí, you sleep exactly like a hound – only, a dog smells better."

"He does dream a lot – Salté I mean," said Juan, making a small contribution to the inane chatter, "and that's because he's one mighty lazy, dopey hound-dog."

"You love him for it though," Pancho returned. "Come on, admit it."

"A friend for life," smiled the boy. Then he offhandedly but fondly cuffed the beast's shaggy head, to which there was no response whatsoever.

Cándido caught on a thought, and said, "My uncle in Querétaro once had a dog –"

"We don't wish to know about it," Gerardo objected.

"– It was a big dog, bigger than Salté here. In fact it was *massive*, too big for my uncle's tiny house. Aunty was afraid of it, for it was taller than her, even when it was sitting. 'Why do you want such a huge brute?' she asked my uncle. And he told her that it was an excellent guard-dog."

To give the beast a degree of credibility Cándido's uncle named it 'Killer'. However, as so often happens with uncle's notions, it turned out that the name proved a misnomer. One night near the end of the first week's residence at uncle's, 'Killer' showed how unfit he was for his role. An intruder dropped into uncle's cramped back-yard and began helping himself to pots of fresh-grown marijuana. 'Killer' bounded into the yard and threw himself at the burglar. With lion-size paws on the man's shoulders, he sweetly slopped his face with friendly licks. Wrenching the dog from him the man gathered up his gains and speedily scarpered from the yard.

"Wasn't much of a guard-dog then, was it?" tittered José with naked malice.

"Well, I have to say it was actually," Cándido contradicted the other, and began to explain why : "The following week – a Saturday, it was, shopping day – my uncle and Aunty were returning from the market. And they couldn't get in their own house, because Killer wouldn't let them. He was barking and baying fit to shake the whole neighbourhood, growling and snarling and snapping his jaws the moment Aunty went near her front door. This went on for hours. In the end a next-door neighbour was so fed up with the awful racket that he came round with a hunting rifle and shot the hound dead. Aunty was only relieved that she was now able to enter her home. But my uncle moped for a month.

"Lost his guard-dog and lost three large pots of finest prime quality marijuana."

64

A Peaceful Sunday

I t was a Sunday. Quiet and peaceful as a Sunday should be. The men and the boy Juan had attended an early service at the nearby pueblo chapel, and were now mooching around the corral and stables, doing nothing in particular. Emilio was missing from this roundup of rancheros, visiting his family.

A bold, brazen sun created a bright dazzling light across the sky, making gold-dust of dirt dust, and the horsemen crinkled their eyes as the harsh sunlight hit them. A dust-devil suddenly whirligigged its way across the corral ground, and as suddenly completely vanished.

Cándido, bored out of his skull, slumped indolently against the corral fencing, picking his nose with careful introspective attention. The sun began to heat the corral fencing, the saddles of the mounts, the boarded stable walls, giving off that peculiarly pleasant summery fragrance of hot wood and leather.

Pancho was absorbed in chewing on a thick callus on the pad of his thumb, like a dog gnawing contentedly on a bone. He absently, as was always the case, gazed up at the sky, seeing yet not seeing but taking it in all the same. Not a cloud to be seen in the broad belt of blue above the rim of distant hills. And a persistent nagging wind hugged the ground as though it were loath to rise any higher, sweeping and scouring everything in its path.

All at once another sense sprouted alive in the old ranchero, his nose twitching like an insect's antennae.

"What's he doing?" he asked at large. "What's he up to?"

"Who? José?" responded Cándido, still leaning languidly against warm fencing. "He's burning rubbish. Can't you see he's burning rubbish?"

"Don't try to tangle with me, you twist-eyed tamale! I mean what kind of rubbish and why him of all people – the devil's own stoker."

The old man was well aware that when it came to starting fires there was no denying José's culpability. He considered him a born-and-bred arsonist, a dedicated firebrand.

"Well," continued Cándido coldly, "didn't you tell him to sort out the saddle-room and throw out the stuff we no longer used or need?"

"I grant you that but I didn't tell him to burn it," gruffed Pancho.

Cándido stared at the old ranchero with a cold glint in his eye, and said, "He did a fine job of burning that stable not so long ago. It kind of qualifies him for such a job, don't you think?"

Pancho ignored this and shouted over to José to put out that damn fire or maybe someone else will get himself scorched.

Then young Julian came trotting by, stumble-footedly and leading by its halter a fine, powerful bay horse.

"That's it, lead him on, Julian," commanded Pancho lightly. "Wait, muchacho! Hold a moment! What's that scab I see on his pastern? Sí, right there! Clean him up, there's a good fellow. Rub in some of that liniment first to soften it up a bit, then clean him up smartly," giving the bay a fond thump on the withers, and with a look at the simpleton which plainly said that it be done immediately. Julian obediently led the flawed beast back to the stable for immediate 'treatment'.

Coming out from the stable was Juan, leading his own special bay, Chapulín, already saddled and ready for a run somewhere. The boy swung easily and lithely into the saddle, and Chapulín gave a little side skip as he took Juan's weight on the near stirrup. The horse pawed and scraped the ground with his hoof, eager or impatient to be off. Juan gave him a gentle nudge, all it needed to set the bay off at a trot.

"Be back in time for beans and tortillas!" Pancho bawled over at the fast retreating rider.

"Keep Salté here!" called back Juan.

"Here, Salté!" ordered Gerardo in his best dog-training voice. "You're going nowhere, you lumping mutt."

The dog philosophically settled down to cleansing himself of fleas with tongue and teeth – much too hot anyway to be gallivanting around. Gerardo looked on in some bemusement. At one point the animal, showing all its teeth, appeared as a ferocious wolf, the next it appeared positively goofy and silly. What an ugly beast was Gerardo's unkindly thought. What a great scruff-coated ugly looking beast it is. And at this damning appraisal Gerardo pulled such a grimace of distaste that he was no better looking than the dog itself.

"Here, José, help me shift this bale," pleaded Cándido, coming alive from the doldrums at last. "Two men could do this very well, whereas half a man couldn't do it one whit."

"What do you mean, '*half a man*'? Do you mean a boy?"

"No, half a man, just as I say."

"How the devil do you figure that? Half a man!"

"Well, my Laura, she says I'm always telling her that I'm the better half … so one half of me at least –"

And he stopped himself there.

"You're right about one thing," poked in Pancho with a grin, "when you said that half a man couldn't do it at all – whichever half you might be."

"Ah-ha! That backfired on him," José snickered maliciously.

The old man was long accustomed to Cándido's proclivity for expressing the absurd, but he was not always forced to accept it. "You talk too much," he told him. "I don't mind you opening your mouth to let the flies in but not for rubbishy nonsense to fly out."

"Silly stupid dog!" muttered José under his breath.

"Speaking of which," said the old ranchero, glancing over Cándido's way, "whatever happened to that brute of a hound you owned?"

"He's well gone," Cándido carelessly tossed back, regaining some of his carefree confidence which nearly went astray. "He near tore off the arm of a man in San Stefan and the policia ordered him to be put down."

"Why should the man be put down," smirked José, "when he only near lost an arm?"

"The dog was put down, you rabbit dropping!"

"So, did you shoot it then?" asked the other mock-conciliatorily.

"No, I didn't shoot it. What do you take me for – Zapata! Like any civilised person would do in the circumstances, I took him to the vet who put him down for me."

"Probably shot it," mused José *sotto voce*.

"José, didn't you once own a mule?" side-tracked Pancho. He knew that José hated mules with an uncompromising passion.

"No, that was my brother-in-law. He once asked me to shoe his mule." He glared around at everyone. "You ever tried to shoe a mule?"

"I haven't, no," returned Cándido, "but I did once manage to get the socks on."

"Oh listen to this flit-eyed fool!"

"Don't be taken in by his foolishness, amigo," put in Pancho. "He's fairly got his head on straight – for a Querétaro man."

"I'm no Querétaro man," Cándido contradicted him. "That's my uncle. My uncle's from Querétaro. I'm originally from San Stefan."

"Oh, a townie!" sneered José, sticking in his piece. "And I thought you were born out there in some arroyo."

Gerardo grunted, for attention. "Wherever it was," he opened up lugubriously, "it sure was bad news for this world we live in."

"And you, José, you come from where is it, San Juan?" Cándido said cuttingly and ignoring Gerardo's volley of invective. "That's got to be the smallest pueblito in all Mexico. Why, it's so damn small that when you set fire to the place that time you could see the flames from two metres away."

"Don't knock José's knack for setting things afire, for it's a talent to be envied," said Pancho affably, neatly snipping the tension between these two fireball fool-hardies. "Anyway, ay que caray," he went on, "it doesn't matter a damn where you come from or where you were born, it's where you're at now that counts."

"I hardly know where I'm at these days," grumped Gerardo.

"I know how you feel, hermano," Pancho interrupted him. "You find it difficult to get to where you're going, especially when you don't know where you're going – or why."

"But I do know this," continued Gerardo in a grudging tone, "I know I came from an unhappy and luckless family … My old mamá must have spent half her life in bed poorly. And the old man – best damned carpenter in the whole State, bless his memory – he made such beautiful cabinets and the like for mayors and senators, and those uppity swine mostwise never paid him for his work."

"Ay well, hermano," said Pancho, putting on his philosopher's cap, "disappointment is like medicine, it comes in doses and can leave a bitter taste. But adversity like university can teach you a lot, I always say. Don't get so riled up, amigo, there is no virtue in anger; it's a waste of emotion. A good temper will help you keep your friends, believe me, and a sensible attitude is as good as money in the bank."

Later, in the afternoon, when there didn't seem much on in the way of work – it was Sunday after all – José shot off riding his trusty colt for what was for him a customary lone ride toward far reaches of the ranchlands. The lone silent hombre …

Less than an hour later and at least two short of his usual time away, he came riding back, in true José-mode, thundering in in a wild and reckless manner. In a storm of dust he came to an abrupt halt before the men sitting outside the main stable.

He held aloft a white flimsy garment. "I found this blouse, a señorita's blouse!" he exulted, like a cavalryman who had taken the enemy's colours.

"José! You didn't … ?" began Cándido.

"Molest some helpless young lady? No, I did not!" retorted the other, with an emphatic spit in the dust.

"Where'd you find it?" quietly asked Pancho. "If you didn't take it off someone."

"Over by the long ridge, on the west side."

"You're always finding things, aren't you?"

The old man was alluding here to José's recent remarkable find and rescue of a real live baby boy.

"Well, Pancho, what do you make of that?" asked Cándido. "How come some señorita – or señora – get to lose her blouse? She didn't just throw it away because, as you can see for yourself, it's a brand new thing. Quality there too I'd say without contradiction."

José had meanwhile surrendered the garment to the inquisitive fingers of Gerardo and Juan. They all wondered how something so patently new and no doubt costly had ended up abandoned out on the wilds of the long ridge.

It occurred to young Juan that here was a mystery which may have dark and sinister undertones, which appealed to his boyish sensibilities. He voiced his concern to Pancho who reluctantly agreed that it smacked of a possible suspicious incident of some kind.

At present, without enlightenment or any reasonable conjecture worth favouring, there was nothing that could be done. Except that the old man advised José to take the item of clothing to Tulia for safekeeping. Don Roberto's housekeeper would know how to store and preserve it.

"Won't Tulia be tempted to wear it herself?" said Gerardo.

"¡Carambas!" Pancho exploded. "Tulia's as big as that sow she keeps.

That little scrap of a blouse wouldn't even make a decent bobcap for our Tulia!"

"Maybe we should inform the *rurales*," suggested Cándido. "We don't know what could have happened."

"Oh listen to this one! We can keep them out of it," snapped the old man. He had no time for the local rural police. "They're a worthless bunch of thieving rogues."

"Is that why we never see them around these parts?"

"Don Roberto thinks as I do. He warned them long ago to stay off his land. There's nothing here to interest the likes of those crooked no-gooders."

Juan could not help but point out that whoever the blouse belonged to was of a small size, obviously a child.

"It's a kiddie's garment to be sure," agreed Pancho. "Now what – ?"

Something else attracted the old ranchero's roving hawk eye. "Is that one of Tulia's?" he asked, pointing to a chicken brazenly beaking and chipping away at a broken piece of taco at Gerardo's feet. "Well of course I know it is – Julian! JULIAN! Ahh, there you are, muchacho. Take that bird back where it belongs – and check the hen-coop for holes. It escaped somehow."

"Don't you care for chickens?" Cándido asked cheekily, as Julian scooped up the feathered offender and went trippingly off to Tulia's hen-house.

The old man certainly did care for chickens, but not one liable at any moment to be flattened by a horse's stomping hoof.

Gerardo was now fussily fidgeting and groping about in a scruffy sackcloth tool-bag, his very own personal property. He glanced up, ugly face creased with concern. "Anyone seen my hoof pick?" he asked at large.

"Anyone seen my rubber hammer?" said Cándido, deadpan-faced.

"Are you trying to be funny?"

"No, amigo, I'm deadly serious. I can't find my rubber hammer. Must have misplaced it somehow."

"A *rubber* hammer! Of all things, a damn rubber hammer! Anyhow, what would you want with a *rubber* hammer?"

"You were once a carpenter, weren't you? So you really ought to know."

"No, I don't know. Never heard of such a foolish thing as a rubber hammer. What use is a damn rubber hammer? Why would you want a *rubber* hammer, for crying out loud!"

Deadpan-face said, "Well, it's a lot quieter when you're hammering things."

Gerardo turned on José who was openly sniggering. "I know he's only fooling. *You* know he's damn well fooling! We *all* know he's just a crazy cross-eyed idiot!"

"The answer then," said José, trying to keep a straight face, "is to lock him up in Tulia's chicken coop."

"What, and have all the hens eggless for a month!" threw out Pancho.

"I'll tell you something though," went on Gerardo, in a lighter mood, "If I only had my own steel-head *ball pein* hammer, for I can't find that anywhere either."

"What would you do with it if you happen to find it?" enquired Juan.

"I was thinking of knocking up a little foot-locker," returned the carpenter ranchero, "to keep my stuff in – and not lose things."

"You disappoint me," said Pancho. "I was hoping you'd use it to hammer some home truths into Cándido here. Hammer some sense into him is all I ask, hmm…"

By sundown Emilio had returned, arriving when the men were noisily devouring a late meal of mashed black beans and tortillas.

Pancho thought that the fat man was looking decidedly down-in-the-dumps. Too despondent by half. "You look like you lost a bag of gold and found a bag of nuts."

"As a matter of fact I did lose something," Emilio answered morosely. "I bought something from the market yesterday and lost the damn thing on my way home."

"What was it?"

"A birthday present for my Lupita who'll be seven next week Wednesday."

The men exchanged knowing looks.

"What exactly did you get for her?" asked Cándido.

"Like I said, a nice birthday gift, and I lost the damn thing somehow on my way home."

"You still haven't told us what exactly you bought and lost."

"Why, it was a lovely little white blouse. Just the right size, said the woman at the market stall, for a seven-year-old muchacha – What's so funny?" as the men exchanged broad brassy grins.

"Well, what's so damn funny about it? I couldn't help losing it, and that's all there is to it." Emilio was breaking into a fit of fury.

The old man made a decision. "José, cut along to Tulia's would you amigo, and ask Tulia – and mind you ask her sweetly – ask her for a lovely little white blouse that would suit a seven-year-old muchacha."

"I don't know why you're all grinning like a bunch of monkeys – Ask Tulia! Ask Tulia? What the hell makes you think Tulia would have such a thing, hey? She has no kids, never has had. Ask Tulia – Pah! You're all mad."

"You never know, Emilio, but good things can happen when you least expect it."

"Well, I don't expect anything from Tulia except beans and tortillas." The unhappy soul set himself to rest on a bed of straw.

"I wouldn't go to sleep just yet…"

"Why not, it looks like you've eaten all the beans." There was no stopping the fat man as he settled into a comfortable reclining position.

Pancho, his mind now elsewhere, was over generous in scattering chopped hot peppers on his food. Soon, tears rolled down his sunset-red cheeks.

Gerardo found his hoof pick. He had been sitting on it all this time. And Cándido magically produced the other's treasured steel-head *ball pein* hammer. He had earlier deliberately hidden it.

While José, along with Juan, sloped off on their 'mission of mercy'.

"I have heard," Juan was saying, with a boyish grin, "that there is such a thing as a *glass* hammer. Cándido once told me about it."

"That could only have come from Cándido. A glass hammer can't be of much use, can it?"

"Well, you can see what you're hitting when you're hitting it. It's limited of course to one use, and if you're desperate enough to want to see what you are hitting when you're hitting it."

José was tickled enough to reach for his tobacco pouch and roll himself a bonus cigarro.

65

Hair-Dryers and Missing Spurs

Young Juan was once again in charge of the supper beans. They simmered in an iron pot held on a trivet over the cook-fire. The boy listened to the inconsequential babble and banter of the rancheros.

Cándido was feeling in top form and ready to make his unique contribution to the pre-supper patter.

"My uncle in Querétaro once bought himself a mule," he opened up, "along with a cart. For his job you see as a travelling salesman. He was the only travelling salesman in the town who went round on a mule and cart."

"How're the beans, Juanito?"

"Coming on."

"So, soon be coming off. ¡Bueno!"

"What was he selling then, your uncle?" asked José, rolling a skimped, pin-thick cigarro – he was running out of tobacco.

"Oh, he's sold all sorts of things in his time," continued Cándido. "When he had the mule and cart he was selling those new-fangled electric hair-dryers. Imagine it, hair-dryers in this dry country, and with half the houses in town that didn't have electricity. But you've got to give him his due, my uncle, he'll try anything to make an honest peso."

The rancheros were sat on bales of straw or squatted on the floor, prepared for more to come, as they well knew.

"I remember him telling me of going to a real fancy house on *Piña Suarez* which was certain to have electric power. He's trying mighty hard to flog a hair-dryer to the lady of the house, and more than ready to give a demonstration of its usefulness. 'No!' said the lady of the house, attempting to back off from him, 'You needn't bother showing me, I don't want one, thank you very much,' she said. My uncle being really pushy as a salesman, probably because he hadn't sold a single item in two solid weeks – anyway, he wouldn't take no for an answer. Seeing a plug outlet he sets to and switches on this hair-dryer, turning it to maximum power. He aims it at the poor woman's head. The thing was he didn't know that she was wearing a hairpiece – you know, a wig – and it takes off in the air like a flying fruit-bat. And the gardener has to be called for to eject my uncle off the premises."

"You and your crazy stories," said Gerardo, shaking his head and pulling a grotesque grimace on his ugly face.

"Wait a moment though, I'm not finished yet," grinned Cándido, conscious of the chuckling going on around him. "When he got home on some other day and the mule is tied up in the backyard, he decided to wash it down, because the beast was stinking like a sewer rat. After he washed it he thought he'd dry it down with one of the hair-dryers. So he unties the mule and leads it into the kitchen. This is when Aunty is out, it goes without saying – she'd never allow such a filthy smelly animal in her kitchen. Anyhow, my uncle plugs in the hair-dryer, set again to maximum power.

"Well, have you ever heard an electric hair-dryer when it's full on? The mule was spooked. It back-kicked and upended the kitchen table, scattering stuff around and smashing a lot of Aunty's best crockery. The mule in its fright galloped madly up the yard, flattened the yard-gate, and shot up the street and disappeared. My uncle never saw it again. Not that it mattered much, because the following week he got the push for consistently poor sales.

"And then there was another time when my uncle –"

He was almost off into stride once more but Emilio suddenly spun round on him. The normally easy-going good-natured fat man was furious over something. He was being put to the acid test, and he was not going to put up with it.

"I'm not going to put up with this!" he exploded with searing fire-hazardous wrath.

"What?"

"Where are my spurs, Cándido? My new spurs!" he blasted into the young man angrily. "You've got my spurs. You've gone and taken them!"

"I haven't got your spurs," the other responded truculently. "What would I want with your damn spurs when I've got my own spurs?"

"Yours are only fit for the scrap heap, mine are brand new! Where have you hidden them, you thieving vulture!"

"I wouldn't bother if I were you, Emilio," advised José. His thin cigarro was stuck to his lips as if glued there, and when he spoke it jolted about like a conductor's baton. "You won't get it out of him, not in a month of fiestas."

"That's right," agreed Gerardo, "wild horses wouldn't drag it out of him, neither the spurs nor a confessional."

"Confession, hermano," the old man corrected him.

"Sí, that's what I just said."

The two antagonists squared off and faced each other.

"Just watch yourself!"

"I am watching myself, so what?"

"So watch yourself then, because I'm warning you."

"You're doing what?"

"You heard me."

Cándido now felt compelled to bring out higher calibre ammunition: "Why, you broad-ended lout! Fat goof-toothed lazy layabout! You bed-bug!" he hurled back at him.

Emilio bristled at this slanderous slime thrown at him. Not to be outdone he retorted, "And you're a cock-eyed cockerel!"

The other was stung to further fitting insults : "Horse-mouthed domino-toothed sad-sack!"

Emilio was scorching furious. "Say that again!" he roared. "I'm warning you. Just say that again," clenching his fists and teeth, anger glowing dully on his fat face.

"I don't count my melons twice."

"No, but you take other people's spurs. Where are my damn spurs?" he asked again huffily.

"I'd leave off it," Pancho cautioned, as Emilio lunged forward to grab the other by his collar, "he's not going to spill the beans," he added offhandedly. At that precise moment Cándido stepped back to avoid the fat man, booted feet landing in the cook-fire, kicking over the pot of beans Juan was heating. "On the other hand, though…" now added Pancho adroitly.

This caused a laugh to erupt from José. "That's a *numero uno* for a dead certainty. He's not going to spill the beans, and he spills the beans – the beans in the pot!" The laughter caused his cigarro to come unstuck from his lip to fly into the fire, which effectively cut short his amusement.

Emilio did not consider it funny, reiterating the fact that his brand new spurs were still missing.

"There's not a bean for our meal, either," said Pancho. "Juanito, scoop them back in the pot," he lightly commanded. "They'll wash off alright if you add more water." He glanced around at the others. "Well, otherwise we will have no supper, will we?"

66

The Mechanical Horse

The fracas soon simmered down due to lack of steam, and José reminded Cándido that he was about to say more about his uncle. Gerardo was of the opinion that Cándido was just as crazy as his uncle evidently showed, even though the ugly man's ears perked up to an alert-and-listening position.

"Well," began Cándido, more than ready to give a command performance of his strange storytelling skills, "did I tell you about the time my uncle made a metal horse?"

"A metal horse! Such madness!" gestured Gerardo, throwing up his arms. "There's no end to these mad stories." But this was only a gesture; he really meant that Cándido should continue on, which he did.

"You must hear this," he told the others, his cheeks creasing in a smile. "My uncle is something of an inventor, or at any rate he always fancied himself as an inventor. He was the only one who thought so, mind, no one else did – Aunty least of all.

"Anyhow, he put his mind to an idea and built a mechanical horse. It was specifically meant for fat people who needed to lose weight."

"How was that then?" wanted to know José.

"If you'll kindly keep quiet a moment, I'm coming to that. This mechanical beast bucked and swung about, and you needed to use every muscle in your body to stay in control of it. Steam came out of it as well, to help melt down excess fat. The idea was, as my uncle explained to me, was that the mechanical horse was meant to tone your muscles and get rid of unwanted fat on a person –"

"Emilio ought to have a ride on one of them," said José.

"When I said quiet I meant shut your mouth, see?" Cándido then carried on : "It was a weight-reducing machine, but a novelty one looking exactly like a horse, with a saddle and all that."

The listeners had at first been shuffling their feet and fidgeting about, thinking of food. Supper was now temporarily forgotten as they listened more intently to Cándido's ludicrous tale, even believing in what they were being told. There was no reason not to, because most of his unusual stories no matter how farfetched were in fact as true as he said they were.

Once the 'mechanical horse' was built, tested, and found to be in good working order, as Cándido's uncle assumed at the time, he had it hoisted onto the back of a truck and taken to the municipal building in town. He wanted to interest the town's mayor in it, and for two sound reasons. Firstly, the mayor himself was a fat bear of a man, grossly overweight and carrying a huge 'rolling hills' stomach. Secondly, and perhaps more importantly, the mayor wasn't short of a peso or two, in fact he was a wealthy man. The inventor uncle had hopes of getting the mayor to help finance the production of copies of this amazing weight-reducing machine.

Cándido's listeners sat forward with strained looks, ears cocked like jackrabbits, hanging on his every word. That is, except for Emilio who wandered around mooching and mumbling, still in search of his missing spurs.

"So the 'horse' was set up in the mayor's spacious private office. And it was unfortunate – as you'll later realise when I tell you – that so many of the town's dignitaries should be present at this first trial demonstration. But the mayor had insisted on it – there are many ways of showing off your wealth, if you have it, and this costly machine was just the ticket. The mayor, as keen as a stud horse starting on its rounds, he strips down and dons a vest and sports shorts, and a couple of the officials help him to mount this metal contraption, his feet securely strapped in the stirrups – just like a real horse.

"Off it goes, this mechanical horse, bucking and pitching, kicking the lid off as the cowboys say, and steaming like a locomotive going flat out. The fat mayor, not being a horseman by anyone's standard, was a little bit shy and self-conscious at first. What with everyone staring on and all. But he soon found that he needed all his concentration to stay saddled."

Cándido raised his arms and shrugged a 'there-you-have-it' kind of shrug. "Well of course it being one of my uncle's inventions, something had to go wrong somewhere, and something did – several things as a matter of fact, one after another. First of all a spring goes near the croup of the 'horse', and a long flat metal bar suddenly slams up and sticks to the mayor's fat sweaty back. A bolt goes next by the horse's 'mane' and another bar shoots upright, holding the mayor tight by the stomach and chest. So it's like he's locked in a vice.

"The look on the mayor's face by this time, as everybody there couldn't help but notice, was a priceless picture of shock and surprise, fit for the front page of all the dailies. Then the left stirrup goes haywire and jacks upward real vicious-like, taking the mayor's chubby leg with it. Not to be outshined the right stirrup drops down and back. It's as if the poor fellow has jack-knifed and turned into human scissors, opened as far as they can go."

The storyteller wiped a hand across his mouth to suppress a developing smile. "The machine is heating up meanwhile, steam billowing up and filling the office. There's also a nasty smell of burning coming from the metal horse, and sure enough there's smoke escaping from the mayor's shorts. At this stage you'd think it couldn't possibly get any worse. Well, you'd be wrong. Something gives way on the saddle and the mayor finds that his private parts are trapped between two steaming hot pipes clamped tight on him.

"My uncle dares to take a quick look at the unfortunate fatty on his 'horse'. The mayor's eyes are popping and watering at the same time, and his hair is standing spike-like as if he'd taken an electric shock or something. He probably had. A few of the dignitaries have to leave the room, lest they suddenly burst out laughing. The steam and smoke is already hiding some smirks.

"Well, the legs of the mechanical horse finally buckle under and the whole machine falls apart into many pieces, with nuts and bolts bouncing and flying about and little metal cogwheels rolling across the office floor. One or two office greasers help the poor mayor to his feet. Soon after a dark-suited 'heavy' comes along and throws my uncle over the balcony into the street below. The 'heavy' then asks permission of his honour to jump over the balcony after the mad inventor and break an arm and a leg, if they're not already broken as a result of the fall.

"'No, leave him be,' says the mayor, 'it's alright, leave the man alone and let him go. I've just weighed myself, and I've lost half a kilo already!'"

The rancheros jounced around with merriment over this tale. Except for Emilio who, still grumbling to himself, went to sit on a nearby bale of straw.

No sooner had he lowered his bulk on the bale when he shot off as though he had by mistake sat on a hot iron stove, a piercing scream on his lips.

"Good God in Heaven! Oh, my saints!" exclaimed Gerardo, aghast. "What the hell happened there?"

The men stared over at Emilio running in circles like a scalded cat.

"If you want my opinion," offered Pancho pithily, "I reckon our Emilio has at last found his missing spurs."

67

Juan and Pancho

These were busy, interesting, happy times for young Juan. The men too seemed more at ease and content among themselves, in spite of occasional spats and fallouts. They were not visiting their wives and children as often as before, and this was perhaps because of the boy's presence. He somehow made their days of work lighter and shorter, with time flying on in hurried flurries. The weeks contracted and sped on by, and the rancheros evidently seemed not to miss their own families. They had their own family here on don Roberto's hacienda, this close-knit male community, each dependent on another in the daily working schedules.

These were indeed memorable good times for the boy. There was one overriding reason for it which Juan appreciated more than anything else in the world. The rancheros never treated him as a child. On the ranch he was doing manly things and was as much a man as any of the horsemen. They knew this, had sensed it from the beginning, and abided by it throughout his time spent with them.

In some respects young Juan was superior to the men, although this sense of superiority was never openly displayed or even hinted at or used as an advantageous wedge in their everyday affairs. The matter of one-upmanship lay of course in the boy's sharp, quick intelligence and his knowledge of many things quite outside the experience of the simple horsemen.

They teased the boy and rough-played with him, as they did constantly with one another. But to a man they admired his book-learning, almost in awe of it. More easily appreciated was his ability to swiftly pick up on anything to do with the horse training techniques and related skills. The boy could ride and ride well, having superb control of his mount – his own horse Chapulín. He could do any menial chore, get on with it cheerfully and enthusiastically. They found him personable, possessed a wickedly clever sense of humour, habitually keen to work at any kind of task, and always friendly with everyone.

There would come a time at odd intervals when the men felt it necessary to be on their own. Whoever it might be, when feeling pressured by the demands of the job, or by some imperative urge, would of a sudden simply walk or ride away for a spell. José certainly did it often enough, to strengthen as it were his self-imposed role as 'the lone silent hombre'. And Pancho in particular often did this, to 'recharge his batteries' as he put it.

He would go in search of his own remote spot and sit on an outcrop of rock, or remain in the saddle of his favourite mount, the white, raw-boned mare Macha. The old ranchero would listen to the near silence of the land. For him there would be a sense of timelessness when a solitary fly whirred and buzzed nearby. A ground wind might be blowing, stirring up the dust. He might be lucky enough to see and hear a predator bird cruising in a wind-flow and calling haunting lonely notes. It was to him a sound akin to a man's spirit out there in that splendid sun-ravaged isolation he loved so earnestly.

If the old man remained out there long enough he could eventually be aware of his own soul – as his notion took him – running through him and the land and past time. He would then feel utterly relaxed and at peace and at one with the earth. Still as stone in the silence. That was old Pancho.

An icon of the landscape.

THIRD INTERLUDE

Mexico's population was increasing day by day. A baby boom was bursting over the land. Even in these hot and lazy summer months the country was expanding – people-wise. Every few minutes of each day a new-born child came into existence, into Mexico's history, its economics, its everyday growing life. Out on the high and arid central plateau, the humid jungle lowlands, the northern desert wastes, and the flat and swampy coastlands; in any of these regions of the country at some time or other babies were coming into their world.

Only this morning, as the sun was beginning to rise high, burning toward its diurnal noon zenith, a heavily pregnant woman stopped her hoeing in a field outside of a town in Guanajuato. She trod along a dry-ridged furrow to the shade of a mesquite tree at the edge of the field. And there, within a short time, she gave birth to a boy. She was assisted by other female fieldhands. They tied and cut the babe's umbilical cord, threw a bloodied placenta to nearby scavenging dogs, and cleaned up the mother, who now had a total of four offspring. The amateur midwives wrapped the minutes-old infant in a spare rebozo (or scarf), strapping him to his mother's back. That done, they all returned to the harsh sun-glare and continued their work in the field.

In the town itself two more babies were born in the space of half an hour between them. Born within the white, clean, clinical walls of a hospital maternity room, to middle-class mothers.

And as this same day approached its noon hour a girl named Quichita, resident of the small town of San Juan del Rio, became a mother for the first time. Quichita was seventeen years old, and her carefree teenage was now already over and done with.

On the stroke of high noon a new-born baby's cry could be heard in the hut of a rug-weaver in Chiapas. Another future pair of hands to weave a rug, to help the family make ends meet.

And in a little of afternoon in a pueblito near San Blas on the southwest coast, a certain señor Gustavo Limon, a fisherman who worked the shallow waters around the Island group called Isla Tres Marías, became a father for the sixth time. A baby boy. Another fisherman in the making perhaps, if, by the time the boy grew up, any fish were left to be caught in the soon to be polluted waters of the Pacific Ocean.

So it went on all over this colourful, vibrant, fecund country; a girl born here and a boy born another place. And the various regions continued their growth from day to week to month.

Yet, among these newborn babes there could never be another Emiliano Zapata or a Pancho Villa. There could not ever be another Francisco Madero or Victoriano Huerta or Venustiano Carranza. As there could never be another *Grito de Dolores* or a *Porfiriato*, because times had changed in Mexico since the revolutionary days when the century was young.

Would it be possible however to see another David Siqueros or a Diego Rivera to paint beautiful murals? Or a Carlos Fuentes to write a novel? Or maybe a Carlos Chavez to write a symphony?

Assuredly, among the babies born each day, there would certainly be a baker or a potter, a basket-weaver or a metal-worker, a *vaquero* or a mariachi player. Or even an idiot; because it is said in the countryside that there is one born every day.

Part Twelve

Part Twelve

68

Gerardo's Ingrowing Toenail

There were no two ways about it. Gerardo was in pain. And when Gerardo was in pain the World was compelled to pause and take due notice. The ranchero could hardly walk on his left foot. He limped heavily in to the stable, feeling and looking very sorry for himself.

"Ay que caray," commented Pancho, "here's our Gerardo then, the one-winged wonder, with a face as sad and long as a weeping willow. ¿Que paso, hombre?"

"It's my foot," said the sufferer.

"That's why you're hopping about, is it? Because of your foot. What's wrong with your foot?"

"It's my big toe."

"Ah, the details are coming out now, are they? Or are they?"

"I've got an ingrowing toenail."

"In growing where?" asked Cándido.

Gerardo could not have been more at his grouchiest, no doubt because of the pain he was evidently enduring. "Up my armpit, where do you think! You cripple-eyed coyote!"

"Oye, you're the crippled one!" returned Cándido captiously.

"*Con calma*, my friend," Pancho soothed the sufferer. "After all it is indeed you that's crippled, not wandering-eyes here. Well, so much for tight-fitting boots; like tight-fitting pantalones, they're not good for your health."

"Why don't you cut the nail?" suggested Cándido, trying a smooth and gentle approach.

"Oh I've tried that time after time," gasped Gerardo, hopping on one foot, "and it's gotten worse of late."

"Painful things are ingrowing toenails," Pancho commiserated with him.

"Damn right they are. Do you know, it's like a long nail being driven into my – " And Gerardo stopped himself, realising what he had said. Cándido turned to hide a smile.

"I know what you mean, compadre," said Pancho, almost sweetly. "Look, why don't you get some hot water on the go? We'll put some salt and vinegar in it –"

"Don't forget the onions and chillies," cut in Cándido, "to make a nice tasty soup of it."

" – and you soak your bad foot in it," finished Pancho.

"What was that, east-and-west eyes?" Gerardo asked of his tormentor.

"I was only saying," the young man adroitly side-tracked, warily smiling, "I knew a man who had an ingrowing toenail. He was from Aguascaliente way."

" Sí?" responded Gerardo guardedly. "Another of your daft stories is it?"

"No, hermano, straight up, a perfectly true tale I can assure you."

Gerardo stared back at him, hard-eyed and tight-lipped. "He was fixed by some miraculous cure no doubt, is that what you're going to say?" he asked, biting at the bait.

"No, not exactly. The fellow did have an ingrowing toenail problem for a long while. Real bad he was with it, poor hombre – just like you."

"Then the problem was somehow solved, I take it."

"Well, I suppose it was in a way, sí, you're right there."

"So what happened to him?" Gerardo smelled a rat at last and was poised ready to pounce on the other if he as much as put a smile on his face.

Cándido sagely backed a few paces. "It was quite simple really. You see, he had no need to worry over it anymore, no need whatever."

"And why was that?"

"The fellow was put out of his misery by suddenly dying of a heart attack."

Gerardo filled his lungs. "I'll kill him, Pancho!" roared the dupe furiously. "So help me God I'll kill the crooked-eyed son-of-a-moron!"

"Pull in your reins there," said the old ranchero. He turned on the younger man. "Don't go away, you – ¡Oye, Cándido! You get back here and fill up a pan and put it on the fire. ¡Rapído!

"Now, Gerardo, you sit yourself there, hermano, and let's get your boot off … Ah, there you see, we'll soon have you walking properly, instead of hopping about like a one-legged cockerel."

Thus coddled and comforted Gerardo was greatly mollified and beginning to appreciate the old man's solicitude and warming compassion.

"By the by, how's our José Frontino Arroyo getting on?" asked Pancho, referring to the foundling baby now in the smothering care of don Roberto's housekeeper Tulia. His blue eyes swung on José.

The swarthy-faced ranchero had just lit up a thin, meanly-made cigarro. "I saw him again this morning," he said wheezily, cigarette smoke getting the better of him. "The little fellow is putting on some weight, thanks to Tulia spoiling him with all kinds of tasty bits. I don't mind that," José added possessively in fatherly tones.

"Ay que bueno, that's good to hear," said Pancho, satisfied, as the other squirted a jet of tobacco-stained spittle between his teeth, the gobbet hitting the ground in a soft spurt of dust.

The massive dog Salté made his appearance. He splayed himself out in front of his master, shaggy head resting on his paws, with one ear stiffly erect like radar antennae, the other flopped down and 'sleeping'. His wolf-grey eyes were focused on Gerardo. A bout of pain had exhausted the hapless ranchero, as he yawned widely, fit to accommodate a tortilla sideways.

Pancho nudged the boy Juan at his side. "Just look at him," he whispered, indicating the dog.

Salté, intently watching Gerardo, also began to yawn, a long wide languid stretching of jaws and jowl, generally making a sloppy, slovenly spectacle of it. Juan crowned him one with the spade of his backhand. Salté slunk away a pace or two, a dejected tail tucked shamefully between his hind-legs.

Then a field-mouse darted directly across his vision, not two metres in front of him − such brazen audacity. The dog's head shot up sharply, both ears erect and alert. He saw a mouse-tail vanishing in straw. He glanced at his owner − Juan was occupied in a conversation with the old man − and the canine instinct must have come to a hound of his lazy lolloping propensities: Why be a hero all the time? Who cares?

He laid himself down again before his master, his floppy-eared head dropped, and one tired droopy eye closed, then the other.

Gerardo had one boot and sock off, judicially examining his ingrowing toenail.

69

Mamá and the Girls I

L ater, the rancheros sat disconsolately around the useless fire, useless because there was nothing to cook on it or even anything to heat up. It was Gerardo's turn to soak the beans the day before, but a preoccupation with his ingrowing toenail had made him forget the task. All they had to eat was a pile of tortillas Tulia had made, and a handful of chillies.

Old Pancho debated with himself on whether to send someone over to the casa or not and bring back some eggs. He decided the men could do without a meal for once, to teach them a lesson. It would do no harm to them to fast a little he reasoned and they could look forward with greater appreciation to tomorrow's meal.

Salté, who had peaceably dozed and dreamed this last quarter hour by Juan's feet, of a sudden poked up his massive head. His nose began working, twitching and sniffing the air. His ears rose like hoisted flags. Then in the next instant he went bounding off, breaking into a mad gallop.

"Uuy, Juanito, your Salté has found himself a bitch I'm thinking," said Pancho. "He's smelled out a bitch somewhere."

"Smelled a rat more like," said José, carving a stick with his knife, "but look at him go."

"It'll be that small pack of coyotes he'll be after, over by the hillock," guessed Gerardo.

"Something has caught his interest, that's for sure," said Cándido. "That's the most energy he's shown this week."

"Hey, what's happening?" yawned Emilio, coming out of one of his mini-comas. José advised him to go back to his dreamland as he was not missing anything. "Supper ready yet?" asked the fat man. "That's what I'm missing."

"What supper?"

"Look, compadres," said Pancho suddenly. "That's why Salté shot off like a bullet, we've got company it would appear," pointing at a trio of figures in the distance, tramping to them in their own little dustcloud. Salté ran energetically around the three like a sheepdog rounding up sheep.

"It's mamá!" cried Juan jubilantly, "with Rutí and Julia. My, look at the stuff they're carrying, as much as you could load on a burro. Come on Cándido, let's give them a hand." The pair went haring off to the approaching females.

As they came nearer there were boisterous cries of '¡Ahua!' from the men, accompanied by piercing wolf whistles. Doña María and the girls flushed with pleasure at this warm welcome given them by the rancheros, flushed also by their exertions in travelling with such prodigious loads.

"The whistles were for me I expect were they?" said mamá, puffing like a steam train as she wavered slightly with her baggage toward the campfire. "Or maybe for my beautiful daughters?"

"Ah, the beautiful mother I'd say, María," coughed out Pancho, grinning from ear to ear like a wedge of melon, vastly pleased at seeing them, "you can depend on it."

"What about me, then?" piped Julia, standing with slim arms akimbo like a common fishwife.

"One or two for you as well, my lovely rose," cooed Pancho, scooping the child up in his arms and hugging her. She tinkled out her small girl's laughter, her breath like the scent of peaches, fresh and clean and fruity.

He saw on her face a look as sweet as July cherries, innocent as incense.

She clambered up around his neck, straddling his chunky shoulders, and smacked him on the back, crying "Yaah! Yaah!" And the old ranchero trotted around the fire with her, to the amusement of his compatriots.

"My '¡Ahua!' was for you, doña María," Gerardo greeted her. He coughed deprecatingly into his hand. His rubbery, lumpish face shaped itself into something that might resemble a shy smile.

"My whistle, doña María, was for Cándido," said Emilio with delicious satisfaction, showing his buck teeth in a wide smile. "On account of that lovely kiss-curl of his. Look at the kiss-curl, hermanos, doesn't it suit him?"

"What kiss-curl? I haven't got a kiss-curl!" cried Cándido, hurriedly pushing unruly hair under his sombrero and grinning like an idiot.

"On the subject of *whistles*, muchacho," Pancho's eyes pounced on him.

"Don't worry," the young man assured him, "it's in hand, believe it, so you can stop your fretting."

"Well, you look in very good health, María," the old ranchero's attention switched back to mamá. "Like a lovely pumpkin at harvest time."

"Oh I'm fairing up you might say, but what about you, Pancho, how are you?"

"Like the year my precious I have my seasons and it's springtime to be sure, after seeing you and the muchachas. Now, what's all this gear you've brought?" he asked with a wave at the bags and baskets stacked in a pile, and knowing full well what it might be. "Are we preparing for a siege or what is it? You needn't be shy with me, as you're aware, so do tell."

"A change of shirt and socks for Juan, that's what I have here," said mamá with a closed expression on her plump, homely face. "Plus some food we've brought for you and your ranchero rogues. I don't know why I bothered, you positively don't deserve it, spending every bit of your time out here and not visiting us even once. Ha!"

"Busy hands and busy days, and no rest for the wicked and we're wicked enough," Pancho offered by way of an excuse.

"¡Uuy! Look at this!" said José excitedly, dropping his whittled stick. "A chicken, a whole roasted chicken! And what's this, muchacha," – addressing Ruth – " is it a bag of corncakes you're trying to hide from us? The Lord be Holy, I've never seen so much good grub."

Salté nudged and snouted among the bags too, and received a hard clout on the head from his master.

"Hey, look at what we've got here!" squealed Emilio with equal excitement, holding in his fat fist a large jar of pickled green chillies he managed to filch from a basket.

"There're tamales in here!" gloated Gerardo. "Still warm they are. You feel this –"

"Hands off!" snapped mamá, swiping at him. "They're for later. Now, who would like some chicken *sopa* with rice and coriander? It's in a pot and only needs a rewarm on the fire – Ha! Look at that candle flame!" as her full figure jounced near toward the campfire. "You call that a fire, you bunch of forget-me-nots!"

Pancho explained that they allowed the fire to go down, as there was no food to cook or heat up.

"Ha!" was the most that mamá could say to that. She immediately took control and made her own kitchen out of the campfire site, ordering the girls to collect wood, water, and a bench. The rancheros looked on, having being told to stay out of the way or else they would know about it.

"Ay que caray, that's women for you," sighed Pancho philosophically, eyes rising to gaze for a moment at the electric-blue of the early evening sky.

The horsemen were naturally overjoyed at this unexpected intrusion on their strictly male environ. And such superb timing, as they looked forward with salivating eagerness to the prospect of eating a supper after all. It would be a veritable feast and a welcome special change.

The females got on with it in customary flair, order and expertise which mesmerised the watching males. The westering sun shone fully on their happy faces, setting them aflame with warm, rich colours.

70

Mamá and the Girls II

A short while later, as the sun was fast sinking, a merry group indeed was ranged around a roaring campfire, enjoying the treat of a banquet-style feast, their conversation of a different turn than the norm. The rancheros were refreshingly polite and civilised with one another. They had of a sudden acquired a remarkable sense of the correct social proprieties, took to it too with bounce and buoyancy.

A bench was hauled out from the bunkhouse for the fairer sex to sit upon with a degree of decorum. The men had washed, one after the other, slyly and surreptitiously, by creeping up to the water-butt behind the bunkhouse, each thinking himself the only one to have done so.

Rust-gold dust danced in the evening light as the party ate and chatted. They were not unlike an extended family celebrating a reunion, nattering many to the dozen and continually interrupting one another, each so eager to say his piece. The men often broke into gales of laughter over the smallest thing, as though this female company were an entertainment specially laid on for their delectation.

"Ah, this food, María," sang Pancho. "¡Ay que rico! Fit for the gods – and rancheros too."

"Would you like some chillies?" offered Ruth shyly, slightly intimidated by this roundup of rough-visaged males facing her. "They're very hot, these ones are."

"Gracias, Rutí, I think I will indulge, as they say. You know, muchacha, I reckon God made chillies hot so pulque wouldn't get wasted, if you catch my drift."

"Speaking of which," wormed in José, "pass the pulque, Pancho – If you please," he added, making a modestly polite bow.

"Oh look at that!" suddenly cried Julia in high glee, pointing across the way.

Two well-fed fat-breasted sparrows were sitting on a post, so close together that their full-balled bodies touched.

"¡Ay que bonita!" enthused Ruth.

Salté too saw the feathered twosome; he opened his jaws out wide, long tongue slavering and, to Pancho watching him, appeared to be making a silent laugh.

He might well have found amusement, for the two birds in perfect unison cockily bobbed their little heads to right and to left, right and left again. Then four beady eyes stared forward at the group around the fire. They bobbed a swift glance at each other, ruffled their chubby chests, and with uncanny timing flew as a co-ordinated team off the post and away.

"Your Juanito has been entertaining us grandly, doña María," Gerardo opened up with uncharacteristic gaiety, "with his harmonica playing and his storytelling." A mosquito whined incessantly near his ear and he made a frantic swipe at it. His ear stung with the force of his slap.

"Picking up bad habits as well I shouldn't wonder," mamá responded with mock severity. "Goodness knows what stories he's heard from you ruffians. That wouldn't bother your conscience, Pancho, I don't suppose."

He gave her a roguish grin. "They say a good conscience gives an ease of mind. Mine is easy I dare to say, by and large."

"Phaw!"

"Conscience is the guiding light for us to see by," Pancho rumbled on amiably.

"Well, devils in the chapel!" declared mamá.

"Familiarity breeds germs."

"Ha! That's how you put it, hey? Piffle!"

He allowed the comment to drift away with the dust.

A hint of a smile curled about mamá's lips. "But what I really want to know is, what have you been feeding my boy on? He's shot up like a beanstalk."

This was safer ground. "Well, you know us, María," grinned the old man with a side-wink at his side-kicks, "you know we're always at it pulling one another's leg. But with Juanito here we pulled both his legs, arms as well. So, as you can see for yourself it's gone and stretched him some."

"Ha!" mamá popped out, dismissing the old ranchero's humour with the contempt she thought it deserved.

Salté had in the meantime been stalking everyone in the circle, hoping for a hand-out which never materialised. He curled himself at Juan's feet in what he supposed an irresistible fur-stroking puppy-dog attitude which could only be rewarded with tasty titbits of food. This coy stance of hope began to wear thin after a while, when not much seemed to come of his ploy. He settled into a sulk for a time – this hound was famous for his funks and sulks – then tried another rather radical approach by sitting erect and putting out a paw like a brazen beggar. A sharp blow to his scruffy head put him firmly back in 'sulk mode', fortified by resentment and a gross sense of unfairness.

"It was good you came when you did, doña María," said Cándido, changing the subject, "what with the food and everything. Because a certain dumbhead – My apologies!" – He directed at the 'dumbhead' – "This certain person forgot to soak the beans when he should have, and we've had nothing to eat all day."

"Tulia usually soaks them for me over at the casa," grumbled Gerardo, "but she forgot this time."

"In any case it was your responsibility, hombre," Cándido chided him somewhat lightly; there was no mistaking his dredged up benignity.

"Maybe Gerardo has a sixth sense and knew María was on her way here today," Pancho smiled on the luckless ranchero. "The day is ending well at any rate I must own. Good food in our bellies and the female company better still, eh?" turning to mamá with a cavalier swoop. "You know, I can live for a week on a pretty señora's smile."

"Ha!" she shot back, her stock response to such flowery flattery.

"But surely, my desert blossom," pressed Pancho in the same vein, "you honestly didn't walk all the way here with that heap of goods and chattels, did you? You three weak females?"

"Who's weak? Not us! No, of course we didn't walk that distance. Walking all that way, the very idea." Mamá presented an inscrutable face, meaning a witticism was looming. "We caught an autobus, didn't we, muchachas? They run every hour on the hour right by our farm. You get on at the pig-pens, pay your peso, and woof! you're here in no time."

Pancho slapped his thigh and roared with laughter. "Did you hear that then, hermanos? She's a regular Coco is this one, I'll be bound."

"We got a lift," mamá admitted, "on don Vicente's cart."

Pancho, nearly losing his way, asked if don Vicente was driving. Of course he was, who else, was the reply. The old man then stated that don Vicente was a lecherous old goat. Mamá stated that don Vicente had always treated her with the utmost courtesy. That comment was allowed to lie.

"And how are you getting back, *mi amor*?" asked the ranchero oilily.

"Don Vicente will pick us up again tomorrow morning –"

"Him again! The old goat, that he is."

"Wait a moment, I'm not finished. Don Vicente will get us over at la casa where he dropped us earlier on. The muchachas and myself are staying over at don Roberto's tonight. In the main guest-room no less, or so Tulia told me, and she's the housekeeper so she should know.

"So you can dim those lights, Francisco Ramírez, which are turned full on in those wicked eyes of yours."

"As the saying has it, María, a man is as innocent as he is until he isn't."

"I wouldn't put *you* down as an innocent."

"No, you'd just put me down, as you do," and old Pancho rolled off again into thunderous laughter.

71

Mamá and the Girls III

"One other thing," said mamá, when the old man's outburst subsided, having brought tears to his eyes, "which one of you sinners is going to chaperone me and my muchachas back to the casa tonight?"

"I WILL!" came the all-male *basso profundo* choir of eager rancheros in masterly synchronization.

"I'll go with you, mamá," said Juan quietly, conscious of his family duties. And at the same time at last throwing some food scraps to the panting slavering starving beast at his feet.

"¡Tambien!" mamá said, satisfied, "and before we do, here is another small surprise for you worthless *desperados*," lifting out from a string bag at her feet a quart bottle of best gold tequila. Again the male voice choir sounded off and sang their praises and approbation.

"Where's the salt?" asked José eagerly.

"Lemons too we need," added Gerardo, eyes glittering with a rare happiness, which quite improved his looks.

"We've got limes here," said Juan, "which will do just the same."

The rancheros continued babbling animatedly among themselves, eyes glinting with anticipation, rubbing hands together, ready to pounce on the horsemen's favourite spirit and belly-warmer. Mamá produced a shotglass but the men preferred to drink from the neck of the bottle as custom required.

"¡Salut! María!" the old man toasted that worthy lady, the first to take a swig, passing the bottle next to Juan on his right.

The boy glanced at his mother with a pleading 'Don't-dare-say-anything' sort of look. He tipped the bottle to his mouth and gulped a choking throat-searing swallow. With tears in his eyes he passed the bottle on to the next man, pleased with himself as he sucked on a half-lime. He threw a grateful glance over mamá's way, who did not mind in the least; a boy among men is compelled to act like a man was her thought on the matter.

"Not to put a damp rag on it," she said, eyeing Pancho, "but has my Juanito been doing his studying while he's been here living among you lot of rascals?"

"Oh, assuredly, María," replied the old man in all honesty. "Why, only yesterday, when we were riding by the arroyo, the muchacho was so engrossed – I take it that's the word – so engrossed in his book he nearly fell in the arroyo. Chapulín pulled up in the nick of time. A sensible horse is Chapulín – Oye, José, don't hog the bottle, hombre, and pass it on por favor."

"Well, that's some assurance I suppose," was mamá's comment. "But then again I know my boy. He'll always do what's best."

An appalling realisation gripped young Juan. 'What if mamá were to – Oh, mamá, please don't do it!' was the boy's tortured thought. But it was too late as his mother rounded on him and pressed him tight to her bosom, not caring to notice the young one's hotly blushing cheeks.

"Emilio is as bad," Cándido complained. "Pass it over, you pig, your big teeth are swimming in it – Sorry, would you please pass it over, Emilio?"

The sun was setting, and even the dust appeared to be settling down at last, there being no wind to speak of to stir and drive it.

"And how are things on the farm, my precious desert flower?" asked Pancho conversationally.

"Everything is fine," mamá returned. "Antonio sends his regards to you all."

"¡GRACIAS, DOÑA MARÍA!" the men chorused in unison.

"We've got four new kittens," little Julia broke a temporary bout of girly shyness; like her sister feeling somewhat overpowered by the manly rancheros. "From the black one, *Nightstar.*"

"Ay, trust Nightstar," said Pancho, smiling benignly, "she's forever out at night looking for a bit of –"

"Such nice company we have here, hey, Pancho?" Cándido sliced in neatly.

"Eh? Ah sí, amigo – Gracias, Gerardo," as the bottle was passed once again to the old ranchero. "Ah, there's a star falling, my friends," he went on cheerily, glancing up at the new nightsky. "Which means that some poor soul, someone somewhere, has given up the ghost and is winging it this very moment to the heavens – Ay que rico, María, these tamales are the best you've ever done I'm bound to say. ¡Excellente!"

"Why, thank you, Francisco. The muchachas did say I was to make them specially for you."

"The muchachas are like you mi amor and know exactly what I fancy…"

A ripple of laughter rolled round the campfire.

"Not quite, you scoundrel, but enough for the present at their tender age."

"I know what you mean, María," countered Pancho, still holding the bottle of tequila in his fist.

"And I know what you know, or think you know, what I mean too."

"Ah well, we know where we are then," returned the other, giving in without a fight. "The saying has it, the only way to get rid of temptation is to fall for it."

"Ha! You're full of yourself, so you are, Señor Ramírez."

"What are you two rabbiting on about?" asked Cándido with a grin.

"Never you mind, young man," mamá tossed at him.

"Let's have that bottle, Pancho – if you please," interjected José.

"Ay, María, he's young yet and not had time to get his brains in proper ticking order." The old man glanced amiably over Cándido's way. "You keep a tight rein on that tongue of yours, young fellow, it runs off too freely – Isn't that so, mi amor? – I'll thank you, Cándido, to be as quiet as a mouse in house slippers, and then we'll get some peace around here – Now, what were we saying, María, my dove?"

"Never mind me," replied mamá dismissively, wishing to change the subject. "There is something very important that comes to me right now and I want some answers…"

Old Pancho quickly scanned the faces of his compatriots, searching for a hint of guilt or anything else that requires 'some answers'.

Doña María dived in deeply. "What about this baby you found on its own in the desert? Tell me about it. Who found the babe? Did he see anyone running off? Have you found out who the parents might be? What's going to happen to the poor little infant? Are you keeping him out here? Among you rough rogues?"

"Easy, easy," grinned the old man. "So you've met our José Frontino, eh? Healthy little fellow wouldn't you say?"

"You're not going to keep the child and raise him as a ranchero, are you?"

"Well, María, we have given some thought to the matter, and as much as we'd like to keep the little one among us…" Pancho paused a moment, eyeing mamá with a careful scrutiny.

"¿Sí?" she prompted him.

"We had a meeting – Didn't we hold a meeting, hermanos? – and gave this matter some serious thought."

"So what was the outcome of your meeting and your serious thoughts?"

Pancho jumped in on this. "We decided that little José Frontino should have a proper mamá and papá, if such could be found not too far away from us; suitable people as parents, mind, so hopefully little José can then live a normal, decent, happy life."

"And may God grant it. That's very good thinking, that is." Mamá presented an approving smile to the men around her, and they responded by beaming back with wide-stretched mouths. Then they stared down at the toes of their boots with affected interest. "By the by," went on mamá, "who's been playing father to him?"

"I HAVE!" lustily sang the all-male choir.

"I reckon our José here takes credit for that and should be accorded that title," said Pancho expansively. "José it was who found the niño out on the hardpan flat. Hmm. We had a vote on it, you know, and José was given two votes on account of him finding the little fellow in the first place – and saving the little one's life because of it.

"We decided that José Frontino should have proper parents as he deserves. What do you say, María?"

"Oh, your decision was the right one, an excellent one, I'm sure of that," said mamá warmly.

"We were wondering, María…"

"I'm certain you were and I know what you mean, what you're getting at," mused mamá. "Let me just think on this one…"

She gazed long and hard at the vast starry space of sky … at the countless, the eternal stars …

The men stared at her as though she were the revered Lady of Guadalupe.

72

Mamá and the Girls: Finale

*D*oña María was being careful in her deliberations. She creased her brow in concentration, chin in one small plump hand, giving serious consideration to the ranchero's decision in finding adoptive parents for the foundling, even at one point conferring with her own two female offspring. Pancho said he could tell doña María was thinking very hard because he was sure he saw steam coming from her ears – a comment everyone ignored.

Mamá chewed her lower lip as though having anxious thoughts; but she wasn't having anxious thoughts, she was simply thinking hard about this present predicament.

Gerardo crouched before the fire, like some monstrous toad, such was the ugly and grotesque expression he had quite inadvertently put on his face. Now fairly glassy-eyed and groggy with tequila, he grinned over at the two girls. They blanched and gulped; they thought he looked at that moment so positively hideous in aspect. He straightened his face, making a more amenable sight for young female eyes.

At last, mamá's face lit up of a sudden and she snapped her fingers. "Of course! Should have realised straight away but just wasn't thinking right. I have the very thing," leaning forward in her eagerness to enlighten the men, who also bent their frames as if they were about to cook up a conspiracy.

"Well?" prodded Pancho.

Mamá smiled a superior smile. "You know Joaquin and Cornelia Díaz who live in the pueblo?"

"¡Sí! ¡Sí!" the men nodded acknowledgement of the fact.

"I don't know if you heard this but Cornelia was told she could never have another baby. The news near broke her heart, poor thing. I know, for they both badly wanted a baby brother for their little girl − I forget her name, but the important thing is, there would be no question of those two not accepting this baby you found. Adopting a child, in other words. Cornelia will be thrilled to pieces I'm sure of it, and it'll make a whole woman of her again. They're such a nice pair too, Cornelia and Joaquin. I know them well and −"

"Say no more!" declared Pancho portentously. He directed his gaze at each ranchero in turn. "It couldn't be better I'm thinking, hermanos. It's settled, eh? I know Joaquin Díaz myself and a fine young man he is, without a doubt."

"I know Joaquin too," said Cándido. "We went to school together − when there was school, our *maestro* went missing half the time."

"So you are all in agreement then?" smiled mamá happily.

"¡SÍ, DOÑA MARÍA!" they responded most emphatically.

"¡Ay que caray!" burst out the old man. "That was speedily done and to everyone's satisfaction. One minute our José Frontino has no relations and the next he has a mamá *and* a papá."

He turned to doña María and added, with a wink at his compatriots, "Little José also has *six* godfathers. You didn't know that, did you? Your Juanito is one of them."

"¡Chihuahuas!" cried mamá, exploding with joy.

"There is something else, my dove, which only we rancheros know about." The men were in on this and were now grinning for all their worth, nodding assent before doña María. "You see, we knew that José Frontino wouldn't be without a mother and father for long. We also knew that whoever they might be they'd certainly be of our own kind. Which is to say, poor but honest, simple but God-fearing. After all, only the poor will help the poor, and why it is that a poor man's door is always open. Thanks to your choice, María, that young couple from the pueblo suit the bill just so."

"I say the same," said Cándido.

"And me," threw in the others.

Then the chatter languished, the men exchanging odd looks, and mamá wondered why. She looked to Pancho who put a forefinger to the side of his nose, massaged his nose and sniffed the air, as if he had more of import to relate. He had.

"We all also agreed," he opened up, straightening his frame and sitting almost at military attention, "agreed to take out of our own wages each month a small sum of money – just a small sum, mind. This would be put in a kind of trust fund and kept for the time when José Frontino would need it, for a proper education or something like as much." He shifted slightly in his seat, almost slouching now, somewhat discomforted. "Well, that was what we agreed on…" he ended quietly.

Mamá was rendered perfectly speechless, her mouth fell open with the impact of what she had just heard. Wide eyes gazed with unconcealed astonishment, not unmixed with admiration, as though looking upon a string of living saints. Finding her voice a moment later she said, "Well, I'll skin a cat! You are the nicest people I could ever hope to meet in a lifetime. I've always thought so anyway, and this proves why. From my heart I bless each one of you."

The horsemen dropped their heads and coloured plum-red with embarrassment. One hand went up to pull at an ear, and a hand searched out a nose in order to scratch it; another found solace in rubbing vigorously at a neck, while another pair of hands wrestled agitatedly one with the other.

"I'm off to the pueblo tomorrow," announced mamá in hushed tones, to do honour to the occasion, "and I'll speak to Cornelia and Joaquin. I'll put the proposal to them gently-like so as not to give them too great a shock. I will also mention you being the child's godfathers, but shall keep silent for the present about the trust fund – that can wait for another time and only when you say so. We must get this done as quickly as possible for the baby's sake. The sooner that baby boy has a mamá and papá to speak of, the better I shall feel over the matter."

"He can't speak yet," said Cándido.

"You know what I mean," she laughed. "The important thing is for that little infant to quickly bond with the adoptive parents."

"Pass the bottle, Pancho," José skimmed over, "or have you adopted it? Bonded with it? This calls for a celebration drink."

"And pass it over this side for a change," said Gerardo glowingly.

"Right! First, a toast to our foundling, our little godchild," grinned Pancho, waving the bottle about. "To José Frontino Arroyo-Díaz! ¡Salud!" and each man in turn had a swig.

There was a pause in the conversation. The starry night was so compellingly beautiful, a perfect Mexican summer night. Everyone seemed to be aware and touched by it, felt the mystery and magic of it. Even the normally insensitive José was inwardly moved, but careful not to allow his feelings to show a face to the others.

"Ay que caray, such splendid magnificence," old Pancho exalted. "Such a multitude – look at that array! – enough to make you star-blind, uuy."

"Ha! So you are starstruck, is it?" teased doña María, "you old romantic!"

"The stars tell us a story, María, a story as long as the universe is infinite. See now! Did you see that? Another falling star, another soul on the way to Heaven."

"I sometimes see stars in the daytime," declared Cándido. As there was no response he went on : "When that bay colt decides to give me a kick. I see stars then."

"I knew I'd trained it right," grinned Pancho.

Later, when the saddle-horses settled themselves quietly for the night, the nocturnal birds and furry animals looking for their own supper, and the bottle of tequila near empty, the rancheros sang *corridos*, the popular Mexican folk ballads, accompanied by Juan on his harmonica. The younglings Julia and Ruth had long since fallen fast asleep, exhausted after their trek across open country; Julia curled on the old man's lap, Ruth nestled by mamá's feet before the fire.

Pancho hummed contentedly to himself, gazing at the occasional shooting star in the depths of the darkness, enjoying the warm silk air of a black satin night, the star-sequined velvet sky, the vast broadclothed earth.

Juan escorted his mother and his sisters to the casa of don Roberto as promised. Cándido went with them, carrying Julia asleep in his arms. The rancheros finally rolled into their sleeping positions and settled down for the night, replete with good food and drink – and lovely female company.

Someone broke wind, a long low rumble, causing another to snigger under his *sarape*. The campfire eventually consumed itself and silently died a death. A soft nightwind flowed freely over the open ranchlands beyond the corrals and stables.

The long night hours slowly turned, and the land crackled with the lowering temperature, and the vast canopy of stars shone brilliantly in the illimitable nightsky.

Part Thirteen

73

Juan Lost

Juan was on his own and a long way from the ranch. It was one of those hot dusty tiring days of high summer when every movement of body seemed to require a pushing effort. There was himself, there was his mount Chapulín; and there was something wrong. The boy's normally fresh sun-flushed face an entirely different colour today.

He had felt it coming only within the last half hour or so. He began to feel nauseous, his face turned to a turgid, pale mud-green, the cheeks indrawn. He desperately needed to open his bowels. He dismounted carefully, holding himself in, the sickness too welling up in his throat.

There was a short shallow gully a few paces away and he walked to it mincingly with short steps, hardly allowing his legs to open. Once in the gully he made rapid motions of arms and body.

Chapulín, having taken himself to grazing nearby, caught the stench smoking from the gully. The bay clopped upwind of it, snorting and shaking his mane.

Moments later Juan staggered from out the gully, his face deathly grey. He called weakly for Chapulín, and the horse came to him, hooves clipping and crushing soft rock. Juan smelled his horse-sweat and immediately vomited, for the second time in as many minutes.

The boy's chest and stomach were racked with a hot, cutting pain, and he seemed to be gasping for air. He wiped sour froth from his mouth with a sleeve. Then he bent slightly in an effort to ease stabbing pains, gripped his kneecaps with both hands.

A return to the ranch as soon as he could was what mattered now, he realised. It was late morning, a harsh glaring sun climbing to the meridian. The heat from it was too intolerable to bear in his present condition.

He grabbed a hold of Chapulín by the cinch – missing the halter – and tentatively raised a foot to the stirrup. In the high stretching of his leg once again felt that imperative urge to empty his bowels. He rushed back into the gully.

This time he crawled from out the gully on hands and knees, a long skein of spittle dangling from his chin. Juan felt in a real bad way. His face was now ashen, the eyes dark-ringed and deep in their cavities.

Ever so slowly and exhaustingly the boy managed to mount Chapulín, who nickered nervously, sensing something wrong. Juan felt in a cold sweat which sent him shivering through his whole frame. While the sun beat down fierily on his head and shoulders.

He plodded on, hardly knowing in which direction he was going, relying entirely on his mount. Thick salty tears gummed and filmed over his eyes, and the searing bright light bouncing from the surrounding land appeared as a dark cave to his defective vision. The heat shimmer flowed like lava ahead of him, distorting the shapes of things in surreal, mysterious ways.

He rode slowly still under a clear deep blue sky, with dazzling, eye-aching sunlight, breeze-swept dust and a hazy horizon. His eyeballs swelled painfully as though some unknown pressure was acting on them.

A short while later Juan thought he saw some buildings a distance in front of him. He nudged his horse on. How could he have arrived at the ranch so soon? the main thought running in his fevered mind. There was indeed a line of buildings in a wide hollow ahead, lying strangely low to the ground and ill-defined in the shimmering air. The stables surely, thought the boy, hope surging in him.

He was mistaken; they were pig-pens.

Juan halted his horse at one end of the row of various sized pig-pens. So here he was, he thought with dismay, not even on don Roberto's land but at the edge of don Fernando's ranch. The pens had only recently been erected, built not of adobe brick but of large concrete blocks. With roofing of corrugated galvanised iron, shining like molten silver in the sunlight. The pens contained straw strewn over each floor; there were no pigs at all, no indication that the pens had ever been used.

It was shelter at any rate and Juan needed to get from under the sun's malevolent glare. The silence around him was like a far screaming in his ears. Not a breath of wind here in the hollow of the land. The air was still and silent and hot.

He slid from the saddle, left Chapulín to fend for himself, and went down on his knees to enter the low end pen. The horse dropped his head and began to crop coarse yellow grass growing sparsely about this area.

Juan gave a thankful sigh of relief, once he found himself in the shade. He soon discovered however that it was becoming baking hot in the pen, the sun heating the iron roof as a flame would heat a frying-pan. The boy felt beyond caring at this point. He was left terribly weak, tired, and thirsty.

Dreadfully thirsty.

The energy required in order to retrieve a water-canteen strapped to his mount could not possibly be mustered at present. He would have to do without it until later. He lay in a heap in the straw on the concrete floor. And fell into a troubled heat-exhausted, fever-weakened sleep.

74

Juan's Suffering

A time passed, the sun now well beyond the meridian. It seemed like a baker's oven in the pen where Juan lay fitfully dozing. The air was charged with a frenzy of flies whining high-pitched and monotonous. The boy sweated copiously and insects surrounded his moist eyes like cattle at a watering-hole. He no longer had the strength or inclination to brush them away – he saw it as a pointless exercise anyway, for there was no way to be rid of them.

Time moved slowly on. The sun burned down on the metal roof. Within the pen wooden cross-beams clicked with a sound like jumping grasshoppers with the burden of heat.

His face pallid and streaked with salty sweat, cheeks tight and drawn, the boy bore his suffering in silence. The heat, the flies, his sick fevered condition, all speedily sapped his strength and spirit.

The paler light of early evening came sweeping in. Juan had not moved an inch from his original position. He was awake but dare not make a stir. His stomach and bowels rumbled ominously, and he gasped for water. Flies probed at cracks in his dry lips, attracted to the vomit sourness of his breath, buzzing heavily and tormenting him.

He heard a sound and sensed some movement outside the pen, tried to raise himself and open his gummy eyelids. The chestnut bay thrust in his head to draw straw from the floor.

"Chapulín…" croaked Juan weakly, gazing near-blindly at the long equine head blocking light at the entrance. "Go home, boy … Go, Chapulín, let them find you … back to the ranch. Away, boy!" he urged lowly, pain pulsating on his fevered brow.

The horse withdrew his head, wandered the length of the empty pens, snatching at dry fragrant straw. Prepared to wait any period of time for his young master.

Juan felt a spasm, his bowels churning once more. He crawled to the pen entrance like a wounded animal, reached only as far as the threshold. But it was too late. He had done it. It was a mere smear of moisture from his now seriously dehydrated body, but he imagined he had filled his pants. Panting a little he crawled back into the gloom of the pen, face burning with shame. What would the men think of him when they found out? He agonised over this for the next hour or two. He tried a couple of times to be sick, but could only retch dryly, sorely. The emotion of shame and the effort of trying to be sick tired him as much as the severe bout of diarrhoea he was evidently suffering from.

The boy once again slipped away into a fitful sleep, one hand resting under his clammy, dust-smudged face.

The darkness of night descended like a drop-curtain. The lonely line of empty pig-pens a remote entity under the black galactic void of the night sky.

The next morning found the boy still under the iron roofing of the small pig-pen. The heat came on and built up and burned the metal roofing as before.

Soon, the number of flies increased, drawn to a fetid stink within the tight enclosure. The flies whined and war'd incessantly. Juan dozed on, dehydrated and delirious.

He was no longer in command of himself or his body motions. If he did not take water soon he would in all probability be dead by nightfall.

The boy rested with his head on one arm.

With an effort he licked the salty sweat on his arm, and it was like a meal to him.

So he searched the length of his arm with weary greedy eyes, and he licked his arm as a dog would lick its paw.

Until eventually, and perhaps fortuitously, he lost consciousness.

75

Juan Found

Yelled the voice of a rider, "He's in here, Pancho!"

It was José who had called. With him were Cándido and the old ranchero, one of two search parties which had been out since first light of dawn.

As José dismounted, Chapulín came trotting up from the opposite end of the pig-pens, whinnying with pleasure. José ducked his head in the end pen, into an almost deafening din of summer flies in the hot dry smelly air. He immediately checked the boy's pulse, withdrew uneasily from the opening.

"Alive?" bawled Pancho, storming toward him. "Is he alive?"

"Barely, I'd say…" José was shocked at the condition of the boy, and saddened too; he was experiencing new and cutting emotions. He could not look at Pancho.

"Here, let me through!" and the old man was inside in a flash. The stench and heat hit him like a hammer blow. Swarms of black flies made a quick escape.

A moment later he was cradling the boy in his arms as if he were a baby, rocking him to and fro. "Ay que caray … Ay que caray…" he murmured in a lost and desolate voice.

"Here," said José, poking in his swarthy face, "the canteen."

Pancho took the water-canteen from him, its top already off, tipped the neck to the boy's cracked salt-crystal lips. Juan feebly gasped.

"God! But he's far gone," bemoaned the old ranchero, appalled at the physical change in the boy.

"How is he?"

Cándido's face appeared at the entrance, alert and serious. The old man glanced bleakly over at him.

"Amigo," he said softly, "this is okay to wet his whistle with," indicating the canteen, "but it won't do for him to drink I'm thinking. Not yet at any rate. Slow and easy is the game here. Did you notice the cactus round at the back?"

"Why sí, I did, Pancho," grimly smiled the young man, understanding at once. "You want that I should tap it?"

"Fill your canteen, Cándido, if you can. Only, don't be so long over it. This muchacho is hanging on a hairsbreadth. About all done in…"

Pancho gingerly washed the boy's wan face, using water from José's canteen. Then he tenderly wiped his face dry with his own bandanna. Juan came round by slow degrees, dreamily eyeing the old ranchero as a suckling pup would eye its mother. Pancho warded off a cloud of maddened insects with a flapping hand.

"P-Pancho…" hoarsely whispered the boy in the old ranchero's arm embrace.

"Shush, mi amiguito. I know exactly what happened. Me and the others caught the 'runs' as well – Montezuma's revenge they call it. Gerardo was taken real bad with it. That's why we were so late in getting started looking for you." To the boy in his arms his voice sounded kind of hollow in the tin and concrete cubicle they were occupying, but familiar and friendly all the same. "It was that damned old chicken we had to break our fast. I said it was a bit suspect at the time, but we carried on and ate the damned stuff anyway. Uuy, did it have us running!"

Pancho stroked the boy's hair as he spoke to him, without any conscious thought of it, as he would unthinkingly caress the flank of a horse, gently and with fondness.

"And that was only yesterday morning," he went on in a rasping whisper. "You look as though you haven't eaten in a week, ay caray. Anyhow Tulia will soon fatten you up again with some good *fresh* food – and lots of fruit; I'll make sure she gives you loads of fruit, which is fine for a troubled stomach. We'll build you up again to how you were before. Hmm…"

Juan tried to speak but the old man gently shushed him, his thick fingers stroking the fever-stained face of his charge. Hearing familiar voices gave a pleasant jolt to the boy, and he in turn gave in to his condition and fainted. In this blessed spell of oblivion his fevered, weakened body was getting a chance to recover a little.

He is young and resilient and will pull through, thought Pancho, and would soon be his strong self again.

The boy regained consciousness.

"Pancho?" and Juan gave him a helpless little-boy-eyed look.

"It's okay, I know what you want to say, don't worry on it, mi amiguito," and there was a pronounced protective affection in his tone of voice.

"But I have to tell you, because you ought to know. I've messed my pants, that's what I've done." There, it was out now. "I just had to tell you."

"Like I said, Juanny, it is alright."

"So you already know?" breathed the boy.

"A rough guess you might say." The old man forced a grin, as he held the boy in an ageless, manly tender-heartedness.

"I'm so sorry about it. I've let you down, I've brought shame on the rancheros."

"No, nothing like as such, I can assure you. It doesn't bother me one tiny bit and there's nothing to be ashamed of." Pancho paused, a humorous twinkling showing in his blue eyes. "I'll tell you why you've nothing to fret yourself over or be ashamed of. Listen, yesterday both Gerardo and Emilio did exactly the same thing, mucked their pants they did – would you credit it! They had it bad as well, though maybe not as bad as you though I guess."

The old ranchero decided to go one further. "Do you know what?" he continued, leaning confidentially in a little. "José laughed so much he mucked his pants too, because he'd no control. We all had it, you see, the 'runs', that 'Montezuma's revenge'. But for God's sake don't tell José I told you. He'd put a knife to me and no mistake – might even set fire to me."

He stopped himself a moment, the mirth gone from his eyes. They now appeared inward looking, as though he were searching out his soul, solemn and almost glazed over.

"I'll tell you something else too, Juanny," he carried on at last. "You can thank our Julian for us coming out this way and finding you. He pleaded with me to ride to this spot. This is where I would find you, he told me. All that *non*-sense in his damaged brainbox, yet I'd back him on his instincts any time – even though I refused at first to take him at his word, none of us did. But Julian was right all along. Here we are."

He lifted his head, called out, "How's it going, Cándido?"

"About nearly there, a moment longer."

Pancho dropped his head. "Gerardo and Emilio took off to the northern grasslands, because they thought you had said you'd be heading that way yesterday morning. Me and the others first checked one or two likely places, then decided to ride out this way, as our Julian had directed – Ah, here's Cándido coming – Oye, José! You there?" he called out harshly.

"He's away," Cándido told him, showing himself at the pen entrance. "This is about half-full and should do I reckon," he continued, passing his canteen to the old man.

"Gone to tell the others that we've found our young ranchero?"

"Sí – Hola, Juanito! You look chipper."

Cándido wanted to say something amusing to lift the spirits of his poorly friend, but decided not; it simply didn't seem appropriate. He was inwardly stunned at the boy's appearance.

"Well now my brave young ranchero," said Pancho, putting the canteen to Juan's lips, "you get this down your neck, and you'll be a new man in no time worth mentioning. There's stuff in this cactus juice that'll kill off those tiny beasts playing havoc with your guts. This is the very pap of old Mother Earth herself…"

And in that straw-strewn pig-pen, the boy tenderly cradled in the old man's arms began to suckle the cool life-giving sustenance, drawn from the bosom of *México*.

76

A Priest Calls

One day reaching toward dusk Pancho and the simpleton stablehand Julian were together grooming a black stallion, a horse scheduled for rail-freight to Mexico City first thing on the following day. The rancheros and young Juan were out on the range, so it was quiet at present.

Julian had a blade of grass in his mouth and he sucked and chewed on it as if it were a sugar-barley stick. Pancho hummed softly to himself, as the pair of them diligently brushed away with currycombs at the already sleek coat of the stallion.

Then Julian suddenly hissed, "¡Señor!" and the other looked at him askance. "There's someone coming. Look!"

The old man glanced the way of Julian's pointing finger. He saw in the near distance, silhouetted against the light of the dying sun, a figure heading straight toward them.

It showed itself more clearly now as a short, tubby man wearing the black garb of a priest. His robes were covered in travel dust, and his sandalled feet slapped up dust around bare ankles. On his back was strapped an old army knapsack, probably containing the man's worldly possessions; at least Pancho surmised as much, for the man looked poor as a chapel candle.

The priest stepped with quick short strides, his garments flapping, alongside the corral fencing, boldly let himself in through the open gate at the side. He might have known this place; he might have owned it, from a familiar air of having done all this before many times over. He was however a total stranger.

Pancho strode forward to meet him.

"*Buenas tardes, padre*, welcome!" he greeted the man cheerily. "What brings you to these wild parts?"

"Buenas tardes, my friends," the priest returned, a cherubic smile on his dusty face. "God be with you. And a pleasure it is to meet you, friend, a pleasure indeed." They warmly shook hands, eyes swiftly appraising on both sides.

"Have you travelled far, padre? You look as if you have, if I might so say." Old Pancho gazed at him with keen attention. He turned to the fail-wit. "Oye, Julian, bring out a bale for our padre to rest on, there's a good fellow – Quick now, muchacho! – From where, did you say, padre?" pursuing his present interest.

"From Guadalajara, the city itself," smiled the priest, wiping his brow with a grubby pocket handkerchief. On a rounded head, untidy and dust-spotted, he had short, thick, basalt-black hair, stiffly upstanding like the bristles on a hard scrubbing brush.

"You haven't walked it from Guadalajara I take it?" grinned the old ranchero good-humouredly, hands on his hips, gazing down on the short fat man.

"No, no, bless you," chuckled the other. It was the response of a cheerful man of a permanent optimistic bent, no matter how hard the going, no matter what life threw at you. "I came by autobus and train and autobus again. I got off at the highway back there," indicating the direction with a nod of his head. "From there of course I had the fortuitous use of my own two legs – the feet wearing more than the legs," and he sighed happily.

"Where is it you go, padre, if you don't mind an old man's pokey nose at other's business?"

"No, no, I don't mind in the least – Oh, thank you, young man. Bless you, I am most grateful indeed," as Julian dropped a bale of straw before the priest, then sidled back to attend to the stallion.

"Who is that young man?" enquired the priest, still not answering the ranchero's question. "He has a light of God in those eyes of his, and I am rarely mistaken in such matters."

"Ah, he's our Julian, padre, a stable-boy here. He's not quite a full peso, a little short of the nuts and bolts up here, you understand," putting a thick finger to the side of his skull. "A fine worker all the same and a good muchacho, I'm also bound to say – Here, sit yourself, padre."

The priest lowered his portly bulk on the straw bale, put away his handkerchief, smiling benevolently and expectantly at the old ranchero before him.

Pancho returned the look. "You were saying, padre?" he tried again. "You're off to where is it, then?"

"Oh yes, the leprosarium at San Juan. I believe it lies in the next valley due east of here, or so I was informed."

"Why," said Pancho with a surprised laugh, "I thought that place had closed down years ago."

"There are still a few poor souls living in the place, so I've been led to believe," smiled the priest, his fat cheeks filling out. "I am invariably the one called upon for these kind of tasks," he continued chattily, "a fallen stitch from the fabric of life, that is me, you could say."

"Then you'll be relieving old Father Antonio, is it?"

"I shall be taking over his duties, certainly," said the priest, suddenly losing his smile. "Father Antonio passed away two weeks ago this day."

"Ah … I'm sorry to hear it, padre, I didn't know you see. Though he was getting on in years and not too chipper health-wise. As it is said, padre, death is the ultimate result of birth."

"Yes, quite, that is it exactly," returned the other.

"Ay well, we all fall eventually, like leaves of autumn; only, leaves generally do it more gracefully, hmm." The priest agreed with this odd sentiment with a nod of his round head. "Well, padre, if you ran all the way to San Juan it'll be dark before you reach even halfway there." The ranchero leaned down toward the little plump man. "I'll tell you what I can do for you, padre, with your permission. You can take one of our saddle-ponies and I'll ride with you. Take you directly to the leprosarium. I know exactly where it lies. It's not in San Juan itself but a fair way near."

"That is very kind of you, my good fellow," responded the tubby priest, showing a smile of relief. "I shall most certainly like to take you up on your generous offer, for I'll not reach the place tonight in walking there, will I?"

"Not even if you run," reiterated Pancho, "and I'm forgetting my manners. If you'll forgive me, padre, one moment – Oye, Julian!" he shouted over to the young simpleton. "Just canter over to the casa if you will and ask Tulia to spare us a handsome half of watermelon, if she kindly would – And oye, listen on muchacho, some of her own baked *bolillos*, ask her nicely, and it won't go amiss if she can see fit to slipping in a slice or two of ham, uuy. Hmm … with maybe chilli pickle and cheese to keep it company. I fancy that should fit the bill and suit the occasion too. Off you go then!"

Julian dutifully trotted off to the casa, chased by his own trail of dust.

77

Father Felipe

Pancho affably chattered away to the priest. "You know, padre, the thought has just occurred to me," waving a finger in the air like a magic wand, "you could stay at the casa this night. Gladly welcome to it I can tell you. Don Roberto is away in San Luis Potosi on business, and you can take the special guest-room he always has ready. The don's housekeeper Tulia would be right pleased to have a man of the cloth sleeping in the house; she'd feel safer while the don's away. We can head for San Juan at first light. How does that strike you, padre, what do you say, eh?" The old ranchero's smile was warm and sincere.

"That is most kind indeed," enthused the chubby cleric. "God will thank you for this generous show of hospitality. He must have guided me here to this place."

"Ah, you're welcome, padre," Pancho pattered on, "and we can have a supper of sorts soon when young Julian shows his face."

The old man held himself in check a moment, slightly disconcerted by the priest's eyes which were fastened staring hard at him.

"Is anything the matter, padre?" he asked. "Are you comfortable enough? We can eat shortly as I say."

"Oh, I am abundantly comfortable and I thank you for your care and solicitude, my good fellow," the other smiled again. He produced a breviary from the folds of his cassock, short fat fingers fidgeting with it.

"So Julian is the name of that young man?" he continued, the smile still there on his rounded features. "Such godliness I see in him. And this is the horse ranch of the famous don Roberto, I take it?"

"That's correct, padre. You've heard of our don, then?"

"I have indeed," returned the priest smilingly. "I have heard of him, and also of one who is simple and takes the name of Julian."

"The very same," said Pancho, a little taken aback, "and he's fetching our supper even as we speak. He won't be long. I expect you're starving hungry, is it?"

"Yes, yes, I did have a modest refreshment around noon today, but nothing of note – nothing of substance – I am afraid to say. Or rather my stomach is trying to tell me." The little fat man broke into a throaty chuckle.

Then he became serious again, started once more to stare at the old ranchero. Pancho turned his face from the penetrating eyes, feeling uncomfortable. He was about to spit but stopped himself in time, out of respect for the man-of-the-cloth.

"I don't suppose, but would you – " began the priest in earnest tones, "would you be the horseman Francisco Ramírez?"

"The very same!" laughed the old ranchero, again taken aback with surprise. "How did you know that, padre?"

"I was simply making connections," the priest brought back his benevolent smile. "The rancher don Roberto and a simple soul named Julian. The same Julian I have now set eyes on, with a spirituality that could only come from the man who saved his life?"

"Saved his life?"

"Yes, when he was but a boy. The man I have heard much of – " His eyes bored into Pancho's own, albeit benignly. " – Standing here before me, I do believe. Bless my fortune in finding this place, and it is an honour to meet you, señor Francisco Ramírez!"

"Ay que caray, I suppose I do have something of a reputation, padre," grinned Pancho deprecatingly, "but nothing clever in it, I can assure you. It's more a case for notoriety than anything I'm bound to admit – Ah, here's Julian with the grub – Take it round to the fire, muchacho!" he roared over. "We'll be along directly."

He turned back to the priest, made something of a courtly bow and said, "Now that the light's failing, padre, why don't we go round the other side of this stable. There's a champion campfire burning, or should be by now, and a bench there for you to sit on. Just follow me, if you would."

"Thank you, Francisco, but please, call me Father Felipe, for such is my name and calling."

"Muy bien, Father Felipe it is," acknowledged the old man, and he led the priest to the usual fire site.

"It appears very quiet here," observed Father Felipe.

"Ay well, my compañeros are with the horse herd which is out grazing for the night. They'll be sleeping on the range tonight. It should keep them away from mischief – There you go, Father Felipe, you sit yourself down. The food's here ready for us, bless the muchacho."

As the two ate and chatted in the friendliest of terms Pancho could not help feeling something of wonderment over the simple food he was eating. It was so remarkably, incredibly delicious; he couldn't remember anything tasting so good. It was like manna from heaven, or so he imagined it. He was so taken up with it that he even dared to mention it to the priest.

"The housekeeper of don Roberto's must truly be a treasure," replied Father Felipe, an enigmatic smile playing about his mouth.

Presently Julian trotted up to them, stumbling over something outside of the firelight. "You want I should see to the cow then, señor?" he asked diffidently in his high girl's voice, casting a shy smile over at the priest.

"Ah sí, by all means, Julian, you go on, muchacho, do what you think best," said Pancho, replete with the finest richest food he had ever tasted in his entire life. In fact he still could not overcome the mystery and marvel of it.

"Do you have a sick cow?" quietly enquired Father Felipe.

"Why, sí, that we do," replied Pancho in astonishment.

"Would you mind if I take a look at it? I'd be very interested in seeing the animal."

"No, no, I don't mind a bit. It's in the cow-barn. Come, I'll show you where," Pancho went on, getting to his feet. His face still registered some astonishment.

Father Felipe rose too and they walked in starlight to the cow-barn. The beast was indeed quite sick. Lying stiffly on its side, a pained, bewildered look on its face, tongue thickened and protruding from a foaming mouth.

"We don't know what's ailing her," allowed Pancho, hopelessness in his voice. "It'll probably be dead by morning, I'm thinking."

Julian stepped back to make space for the priest, who squatted down close to the recumbent animal. He placed a hand gently on the beast's upper chest, his other hand stroking its neck. The old man and Julian exchanged looks of incredulity as Father Felipe softly prayed, his hand not moving from the cow's chest. This unusual affair went on for a deal of time, then he rose stiffly to his feet.

"If your young Julian could direct me to the casa?" he smiled tiredly at Pancho. "I shall of a certainty sleep well tonight. I shall indeed…"

That night the old ranchero lay under his sleeping blanket beneath a galaxy of ice-blue stars, gazing at them in bemusement. He was thinking what a singular character was his new friend Father Felipe.

He also thought about the marvellously scrumptious food he had eaten for supper. His taste-buds must have suddenly gone haywire, he conjectured. Before finally dropping off into sleep his eyes wandered for a last view of the deepdark silent starspace. Those stars! How mysterious they can be when you're susceptible to it, he was musing, and life too if it comes to that.

Early the following morning he escorted Father Felipe to the San Juan Leprosarium, less than an hour's ride away. When he returned later the same morning, the old man happened to glance over into the small field behind don Roberto's house.

He was utterly astounded at what he saw. There in the centre of the field, as large as life and hungry as a jackrabbit, was the supposed sick cow. She was placidly grazing over succulent grass, apparently in the very best of health.

FOURTH INTERLUDE

It is the minutiae of everyday life which generally goes unrecorded, and ordinary or poor people in particular are sadly neglected in this regard. One need only pick up a newspaper to learn that a president said such-and-such a thing, or a military bigwig stated something or other, and a state governor announced something else. A politician said something clever, though it benefited the populace not one whit. One might ponder the results if a roving, questing eye were to range the length and breadth of Mexico's geography to see what the poor and ordinary people were actually doing ...

Two eleven-year-old boys went hurrying home in a small town in Guerrero, having attended their first Confirmation class. In their hands they clutched transfer prints of biblical characters and a small cheap album to stick them in, given by their local priest. The following day the boys' mothers were flouncing and filliping about the *Mercado*, boasting of their sons who had been to their very first Confirmation class – a matter of moment!

In a pueblito in Michoacan a happy little girl named Rosalia Ortiz was celebrating her birthday with a party. Every youngster in the pueblito, some fifty or more, from toddlers to teenagers, had been invited. And every family contributed in the way of gifts and food and balloons, which has always been the way of the Mexican poor.

When a large cream sponge cake with burning candles was ceremoniously put before Rosalia, she was encouraged to blow out the candles. Leaning forward she blew hard, snuffing out the candle flames. Then someone pushed her face into the top cream layer, as tradition demanded, amid cheers and shrieks from the many children around her, and Rosalia didn't even cry but laughed with the others. The cake was then cut by the little girl's mother, to be shared out among the festive mob of young ones.

In a crowded street in a northwest district of Mexico D.F. a man was stabbed to death. This was done in broad daylight. While in another district further west and almost at the same time, a father of four was also stabbed, though luckily it was not fatal, inflicted by a rampaging madman drunk on raw alcohol, the poor man's hard liquor.

Señora Margarita Alvarez was the pride and wonder of her tiny village in Jalisco, for two easily identifiable reasons. She weighed all of one-hundred and sixty kilograms which was a great weight indeed; and was the mother of thirteen children – a remarkable record for one aged only 37 years.

There she sat, this señora Margarita Alvarez, on a stool in front of her hut, thighs spread like a plain, plucking feathers off a freshly killed chicken. Between the rolling hills of her calves a toddler offspring sat burbling merrily, white chicken feathers sticking like a decoration to his thick mop of greasy hair.

The poor people of Mexico, all over the country, were working and playing and praying, selling and singing, cooking and conniving, gossiping and gesticulating, living their life on Earth.

They fashioned exquisite things in silver and gold, in glass and jade and stone. They made mats and rugs and shawls, baskets and belts.

They hand-wove exotically coloured cloth of wool and cotton from the material grown or reared on the land.

They carved wood and sculpted basalt, tooled intricate filigree in many kinds of metal. Embroidered traditional patterns and colours on various textiles, painted decorative motifs in startlingly vivid colour on *amatl*, or bark paper, and cut and shaped beautiful paper flowers.

And the people worked the land. They dug and ploughed, sowed and planted, nurtured and cultivated and harvested – they grew good things in the earth, and knew this to be so.

The poor people worked, not so much with their minds but with their hands; clever, knowing, skilled, intelligent hands. The use of their hands was a power and a force that shaped their life and livelihood, guided by soul and heart, ever constant, as constant as their poverty.

They knew what the real grit of life is and lived it fully in both work and in play.

They coursed through the country's bloodstream.

Part Fourteen

78

Corral Capers

T he summer morning sun was up and active, its conflagration of light filling the day, routing shadow, baking the earthcrust. Two of Tulia's hens wandered over into the corral – forbidden territory! – back-kicking dung and cornstraw, beaking and tocking at the spice-dry ground.

The rancheros were sitting on the dust-capped corral fencing or lounging against the windscoured stable wall. Julian tripped out from the stable, scattering the hens, leading a saddled sorrel which was to be sold to a farmer later in the day. He passed the halter to young Juan.

The boy spoke gently to the horse, stroking his long sleek neck, and he felt the hot mealy breath of the animal against his face. He placed a booted foot in the stirrup, leapt easily and smoothly into the saddle. He led off at a hurried walk, riding the full circuit of the corral grounds, his face relaxed with self-assurance.

"Keep your heels down, Juanito," advised Pancho from his perch on the fencing. "That's it, you've got it this side of perfect, try to stay that way. What was I saying to you before? Persistence and perseverance makes for perfection. Well done, amiguito!"

His merry blue eyes then fell on the demi-wit. "Fetch the mares out now, Julian, so we can take a good look at them," he gravelled huskily in his morning voice.

Julian looked down at the ground as he walked, carefully placing his feet in hoof-prints stamped on the thick-dust ground. It appeared as if he were prancing across the corral-yard like a two-legged horse. So intent was he that he walked into wood. The men nearly fell off the fencing with their laughter.

"The stable doors are in two halves, Julian," said Pancho good-humouredly, "and you did close that half yourself if you remember."

"Sí, señor," grinned the simple youth, rubbing at his forehead.

Meanwhile Juan broke the sorrel into a canter, and José lifted the gate-latch to let rider and horse out to greater freedom of movement. Juan gave his mount free rein and off he galloped in a flurry of dust, loose stones flying.

"Handsome one, isn't he?" observed Gerardo, fanning and flapping his hands after inadvertently touching some stinging spurge-nettle growing by one of the stables.

"Who, our Juanito?" said Emilio.

"The damned horse I mean. By God's grace I'll have a mount like that one of these days," Gerardo added more genially. He jounced and hopped about in hopes of easing the nettle stings.

Above the men a long cavalry of separate cloud rode silently across the plain of blue. It had an outrider or scout, a lone cloud a small distance ahead of the main force, and a rear-guard of two clouds dragging along behind the main mass. Pancho glanced up and eyed the angle of the sun, guessed it would be about mid-forenoon.

Julian appeared with a string of sorrel mares, young frisky animals prancing and curvetting about the corral, as though with a need to show off their vigour and youth.

"You know," said Cándido, crossed-eyes gazing on the beasts, "those mares there remind me of the horses used in a circus I went to once in Gomez Palacio. It was at that circus when a clown took me off my seat in the front row and stood me in the centre of the ring. Then he pulled a gun on me and fired –"

"He missed, obviously," said José maliciously. "How sad."

"Another mad tale on its way I imagine," guessed Gerardo.

"No, listen, hombre. It was a water-pistol, see, and he shot water over my face and the crowds roared. I roared as well. Cried my eyes out in fright I did. I was only a muchacho at the time."

"You still are," Pancho pointed out.

"Ah well, now I'm an old and wise muchacho, but then I was good and innocent, like."

"You! Good and innocent! Oh-oh-oh!" Gerardo guffawed with glee.

"What's up with him? He's actually laughing, our Gerardo."

"Let him laugh," lipped Pancho, "it'll do him some good."

Still chuckling to himself Gerardo put a hand into his vest pocket.

His most treasured possession was a family heirloom that had been passed down to him as the senior of his siblings. It was a pocket-watch, but a cheap one of hardly any value except as a heirloom, and only being of sentimental worth to its present owner.

He would occasionally tug it out from his vest pocket and click it open – he liked that clicking sound when opened or shut. Not so much to check the time but to remind himself that he was head of his family, now that both parents had long gone to meet their Maker.

Whenever he opened its lid, with that pleasant clicking accompaniment, Cándido would be in there like a shot and ask for the time, giving a sideways shifty glance at Pancho. The old man would take quick cognizance of the sun's angle.

"What time is it, Gerardo?"

"Fifteen after three," the old man would cut in.

"It's a quarter-past three," Gerardo would reply, closing the lid.

Now, Gerardo pulled out his pocket-watch. Cándido signalled Pancho with a telling wink.

"What time is it, Gerardo?"

"Ten-thirty," popped in Pancho, after a swift gauge of the sun's position. "Maybe twenty-five after ten."

"It's twenty-five minutes past ten," obliged Gerardo.

"Sí," the old ranchero winked back at Cándido, "the sun is my watch – and my compass too."

Gerardo snapped the lid of his time-keeper with a satisfied air. He did so like the sound of its clean metallic click as the top was snapped shut.

79

Circus Freaks

T he horsemen continued sitting about the corral fencing, doing nothing in particular except chuntering away like market women. José, rolling himself a cigarro, asked the others if they remembered the time when a circus train was passing through. "It stopped at our junction to take on water."

"Ah, sí," smiled Pancho, recalling the time, "the whole train full of circus people, six or seven flatcars with caged animals strapped on – And those dancing dwarfs, do you remember those dancing dwarfs?"

Cándido mentioned that two clowns escaped. "How's that?" asked someone.

"It was an act put on for the folk at the rail junction. Dressed as convicts they were, complete with ball-and-chain. Trying to escape, pretending like. They kept getting tangled with the balls-and-chains. It was very funny to watch – especially for free."

Gerardo thought that the dwarfs were good, having him in stitches with their silly antics. Emilio was of a different opinion and didn't think it was fair.

"What wasn't fair?" asked someone.

"Well, exploiting those poor people, those – those freaks. You know, dwarfs and hunchbacks and bearded ladies."

"They're not real, those beards on the ladies. They're wearing hair-pieces that's all, theatrical false beards," explained Cándido.

"Well, I know different," replied Emilio. "My own grand-mamá had a beard, or near enough. You wouldn't believe the amount of hair she had on her chin – a damn sight more than grandpapá."

"Uuy, that's only a bit of hair, hermano," laughed Pancho. "I have it myself growing out of my ears and nostrils. Grows fast too, too fast for my liking. It's there overnight, like damn mushrooms. All part of growing old I suppose."

José's thought processes, jumping as they usually do, went off at a tangent quite remote from the present conversation. "My papá was lame most of his life," he said, his cigarro wisping smoke as he spoke, "on account of twisting his foot when he was a kid. Limped for the rest of his life he did."

"I knew a man," said Cándido, "a man from Celaya – you knew him, Pancho – and he had the biggest ears you'd ever see on a human being. Flag-Ears Arturo they called him, with ears as big as an Indian elephant."

"Don't you mean an African elephant?" the old man interrupted him. "That's the one with large ears."

"Sí, that's what I mean, though they weren't exactly *that* big, but big enough for a hombre. And this poor Arturo, well, you wouldn't credit it. When he was a kid his mamá would never let him ride a bike or a horse, lest he take off into the air and do himself an injury."

"Why did they call him 'flag-ears' and not 'big-ears'?" asked someone.

"Ah, I can explain that easily enough. On National Day they would paint Arturo's ears green, white and red, stick a flag in his hands, and put him in the parade. From a distance he looked like a lot of flags flying."

"The stories this one comes out with," declared Gerardo, glowering. "I mean – Away with you, Salté! There's nothing here for you, perro. Damned beast is sniffing at my crotch again."

"Well take good care, hermano," grinned Pancho, "for he's not yet had any breakfast."

Gerardo picked some soft rubbery foreign matter from his nose and looked at it with studied interest. Satisfied that it was not worth eating, he rubbed it lightly between thumb and forefinger to form a dry pellet – dry enough to flick at the dog.

"Has anyone ever seen the matchbox-seller who hangs out at the main autobus station in Mexico City?" This surprise enquiry came from Cándido. "You know, at *Terminal del Norte*?"

"The legless one, you mean?" said José.

"That's him. He gets around on a square wooden tray with chair castors at the corners, and he pushes himself along, like."

A whiff of cheap tobacco smoke assailed Pancho's nose, and he turned abruptly, giving José a nasty, condemnatory look, which had no effect whatsoever on the habitual and uncaring smoker.

"I wouldn't mind being legless for a spell," mused José, on an altogether different tack. "I haven't had a decent snort of liquor in an age – or at any rate that's how it seems." He spat in the dust to show how serious he considered this dilemma.

"Maybe that poor legless fellow should join a circus," suggested Emilio with heavy sarcasm.

"Maybe you should too," Cándido threw back. "People would pay good money to see teeth like yours."

"And go dizzy looking at you, you cross-eyed wonder."

"Well, Emilio, you may think it's unfair," said Pancho slowly, "this so-called exploiting of folk's disabilities, but you can look at it another way you know. Now take José here, and his long silences, he could easily be taken for a deaf-mute by any stranger who didn't know him…"

"What was that?" muttered José, wary-eyed and about to bristle up.

"You see, he's halfway there already – No, what I mean to say is this…"

He told how the circus freaks, as the other called them, lived and worked together in the same environment. Thus they did not stand out as much as they would if they were among normal people. Moreover, the old man went on, if they could take advantage of their physical defects and make a living out of it in the bargain, then they could hardly call themselves disabled or disadvantaged in the first place. That was the old ranchero's opinion on the matter, giving the others food for thought.

No, he confirmed resolutely, people should really feel sorry for the blind and the deaf and the lame; those who were starving or grieving over a lost one, or very young and motherless. There are plenty of those kind around all over the country, he informed the fat man. Each of these poor souls is on his own in this world, which is the pity of it.

He reminded Emilio – and it went for everyone, he stressed to the others – it is said that before you are born you are nothing, and after you die you become the same. Nothing.

"And if you're nothing in between, then who's fault is that? Think on it. You won't make footprints on the path of life if you sit on your arse all the time. In life you need to set out your own identity, you've got to make your own kind of splash. And doing it is better than talking about it. Those poor so-called freaks would know what I'm aiming at – They're real fine, Julian!"

he called to the young stablehand. "Lead them out to graze, there's a good fellow – Open the gate, José, por favor."

Pancho had done his bit and said his piece. "Well, I'm off to see Tulia to scrounge some eggs for us if I can. Now, hermanos, you'll promise not to laugh at the way I walk, eh? Don't think I'm freakish or anything like that and I'll thank you for it. ¡Hasta luego!" he ended, dropping from the fencing.

Unfortunately, the collar of his camisa snagged on a nail and he was left dangling there like a heavy bearskin coat on a hook.

"What're you hanging about for?" smirked José, and began to roll himself a fresh extra fat cigarro in celebration of the satisfaction at seeing his antagonist 'in stays' as it were.

The shirt collar ripped free. Unperturbed, or at least feigning unconcern amid the raucous laughter sounding off around him, Pancho was off. Squaring his broad shoulder he went gimping and stumping listingly toward the casa, wide backside swinging to left and right. But he was inwardly perturbed about the sudden disappearance of his precious dignity.

80

Uncle's Parrot

It was a fine and windless evening, Venus rising and etched sharply in the fading apple-green sky. The rancheros had already finished supper and there appeared to be few of the pestiferous mosquitoes about to annoy them. They sat in the usual semi-circle round the woodfire, quietly and companionably indulging in inconsequential small-talk.

"Did anyone see the lame coyote today limping through the arroyo?"

"Shoot it dead, did you, José?" asked someone.

"No, I didn't. I never shoot at anything that's lame. My old papá was lame nearly all his life, as I've said before –"

"At least ten times. So you didn't shoot your papá, then? He being lame and all," said someone. It could have been Cándido.

" – Anyway, it was so quiet and peaceful in the arroyo and I didn't want to spoil it."

José opened his tobacco pouch and felt about in it, wondering if there was enough to make a cigarro. He was short of tobacco again.

"My uncle in Querétaro once fancied having a coyote as a pet," said Cándido, "to improve his *macho* image he told me. But Aunty soon put him straight on that score. As far as she was concerned, she said to him, he could damn well go whistle for a coyote. He wasn't getting one and that was that. The next day he bought himself a red-and-yellow parrot from the Mercado."

"Speaking of whistles…" butted in Pancho.

"I know, I know," grinned Cándido, raising hands in mock surrender, "I'm still working on it. You'll have your whistle all in good time, I promise you."

"Could your uncle's parrot whistle?" José wanted to know, rolling himself a rather meagre cigarro, having managed to collect bits of tobacco and fluff from his pouch. He felt like one deprived of the necessities of life.

"Not as I know of," replied Cándido reflectively, "but it sure was one queer parrot I can tell you. You see, it once belonged to an American sailor who got rid of it in Vera Cruz or someplace."

"Why was it queer, then?" pursued José, lighting his sad specimen of a cigarro from a burning stick plucked from the fire. "I mean, it had to be a queer one in any case, it being your uncle's parrot, but how exactly was it queer?"

"José," interjected old Pancho, "throw some more sticks on that sorry little fire, I know you like to feed it well. Fire up the heating machine, said the scientist to his assistant."

"Well," continued Cándido, "it only spoke English words you see, like *'Pretty Polly'* and *'Close the hatches'*."

"*Close-the-hatches*'? What's that supposed to mean?"

"Only the saints know, and any Yankee sailor. Sí. And there was a time when Aunty was washing her hair at the kitchen sink, which was where the parrot was kept in its cage –"

"In the kitchen sink?" queried someone with a knowing smile, though it was more of a smirk so probably it was José.

"In the kitchen is what I meant. So Aunty is busy rinsing her hair, when in comes the local priest, unexpected like. *'Screw you, mate!'* says the parrot. *'¿Que que?'* says Aunty, soapsuds in her eyes. *Jig-a-jig! Jig-a-jig! Only two dollars!'* says the parrot.

"Aunty wipes her face on a towel and sees the priest standing there. Well, Aunty sometimes takes in American art students to help pay the rent, and understands a fair bit of English. The trouble was, so did the priest, and he thought Aunty had spoken to him. And Aunty thought the priest had spoken to her. They looked at one another in a total embarrassed silence. The priest makes a hurried excuse and is out of the house in a flash, and never called again. Aunty thought it prudent to start going to a different church from that time on."

Pancho, who also understood some English, appreciated Cándido's tale although he suspected its veracity. His attention was turned to the sombre face Gerardo was showing. "What's wrong with you, hombre?" he laid into him. "You've got a face as long as a horse collar."

José kindly commented that Gerardo's face was made that way, and returned to puffing contentedly on his thin cigarro.

"I don't know," began Gerardo, tugging absently at the lobe of one ear, "it's just that – well, I've found I don't piss like I used to."

"Where's our Juanito?" sidestepped the old man.

"Over by the tree there," said José, "catching the last of the light." He blew a perfect smoke-ring and sat admiring it.

"Ah, studying I expect. Go on, Gerardo, you were saying?"

"I used to piss like a fountain," complained the hapless ranchero, "but now I only dribble, sort of."

Pancho let him know that the condition was only a sign of growing old.

"I'm two years older than you, Gerardo," said José, "and I don't dribble."

"You do when you're eating," quipped the old man.

"I pee like a waterspout," boasted Cándido.

"No wonder," said Pancho, "you're still a young man, and besides, you've a wife close by to adjust your plumbing gear now and then."

"Now and then is too true," the younger man returned ruefully.

The old ranchero saw Gerardo's problem as one of his own making, telling him he didn't sleep right, didn't eat right or drink enough water, didn't take proper care of himself. He told him that he himself would often visit Tulia's kitchen in order to scrounge what he could in the way of fruit and fresh greens, all of which he ate in their raw state.

"Ayí, there's your answer then," said Cándido. "What you must do, amigo, is go out there with the horses and start grazing. Then you'll soon be pissing over walls again like you used to."

"Sí," agreed José with some excitement, as he was about to drop a witty remark. "How do you think Emilio got those big teeth of his? Through eating grass like a horse." He giggled like a girl, over-done by his own witticism.

"Are you the same, Pancho?" asked Gerardo eagerly. "You being older than any of us here."

"No way, hombre. I can piss right up to the heavens, in a manner of speaking. Well, you've seen me often enough haven't you?"

"What's happening?" wheezed Emilio, suddenly torn from sweet gentle slumber on a 'sofa' of straw bales. He raised himself into a sitting position; snooze-stiffened, rumpled and scruffy-looking with straw scattered over his fat form, a quizzical, irritable expression on his sleep-puffed face. "Well, what's happening?" he repeated.

"Nothing's happening, you lazy lolling lout."

"You were saying, Pancho … ?"

"I hope the parrot's listening to this…" said someone.

81

Pancho Dwells on Life

"We can thank the Lord for one thing at any rate," said Pancho a moment later.

He went on to explain how man doesn't grow old as fast as animals. A dog or a horse went from middle-age to old-age in only a few years. A sixteen-year-old dog was well in its dotage and that was the way of it. A man grows old at a much slower pace. From first feeling old to actually reaching a state of old-age took a long time.

"From twenty-five to thirty-five years, I guess. Two lifetimes of a dog."

Cándido expressed great satisfaction in the notion of living two lifetimes.

"What!" exclaimed Gerardo, aghast at such an idea. "You mean living seven-score years instead of threescore and ten?"

"That's about the size of it and it'll do for me."

All very well to say that, Pancho interposed at that point, reminding the young man of a general fact of life. He was not guaranteed to live one full life, never mind two. He could get himself killed at any time or any place. It was possible he might not even see this day out, though the sun was already down.

"Think on this my friend. Out there in the big world, in our own country and in countries far and wide, there are people dying every minute of sickness or old age. Getting shot or falling down a shaft or off a cliff.

Getting hit by a truck or autobus. In a plane crash, a train crash, lost in a landslide, drowned in a flood, starved to death, trampled to death, beaten to death – ah, there's no end of it."

No, the old man reiterated, a full life was not a guarantee of life. Far from it. Cándido could get himself kicked by a horse on the morrow, a blow that would send him to eternity. He could be swallowed up by the Earth, in an earthquake for instance.

"'Thou shalt be visited of the Lord of hosts with thunder, and with earthquake …'" Pancho quoted.

He spotted the boy coming towards them, taking loose-limbed panther-like steps, the gait of youth. "Oye, Juanito, you've come to join us at last, eh? The light is failing, as it must. Sit by me, here you go – Shove yourself over, Cándido, and make proper space for our young scholar. Here, muchacho, that's it. We're discussing old age, which mightn't interest you."

"It's a shame we have to grow old, isn't it?" stealed in Emilio, giving the men a myopic stare, having recently clawed himself out – and still not fully recovered – from a deep doze. "I'm thirty-six, and it would be good to stay thirty-six for the rest of my life. But why do we age so?"

The fat man threw a glance over at Pancho for a possible answer. The old ranchero did not say anything but looked up at a vast unclouded nightsky stretched irreducibly across the starry heavens; awesome and majestic, solemn and remote, silent and unknown.

"Have you noticed how a flower grows?" he opened up, head back to eye level.

He described how a flower first sprouts up, little green shoots bursting open, the stem growing taller and firmer and fuller. Then that beautiful miracle of colour suddenly materialising on some sunny day, its scent emanating fresh and strong.

He mentioned that flowers were around long before man and monkey.

So too were insects, and the two went together naturally. In fact one couldn't do without the other, for a very special reason.

He asked his listeners to think a moment – they duly complied by putting on serious, scholastic countenances, which caused Juan to inwardly smile. Why was the flower so colourful and beautiful? he asked them, but it was a rhetorical question and so they remained mute, still retaining their studious looks. Millions of years before man came along to admire them, he continued. It was entirely for the insects' benefit, he said simply. Insects can easily pick up the scent of a flower from great distances. The flower part of a plant, he expounded further, was a kind of colour code, a guide so to speak, in the mass of green where you found grass and trees and bush. Insects saw this colour differently from man, and were attracted to it. Attracted to the nectar in the centre of a flower-head.

"It's the nectar these little buzzing rascals are after. Once they're in their own flower cantina – as I see it, as you'd see it – supping for all they're worth, their wings or bodies are picking up pollen. They move on to another 'cantina' – just as we'd do when we're in town – and pollinate another flower.

"So the flower lives on in later generations, as you live on in your sons and daughters. You follow my drift? Of course you do."

The men knew exactly what happens next, Pancho put to them, because it is seen every year. '… The grass withereth and the flower fadeth …' as the Old Testament states. Why should the flower fade and die? Why can't it live longer? Did the men know that? No, by their silence they didn't know that, so old Pancho told them.

The flower dies because it has served its purpose in life, done its duty, need not live on any longer. It must make room in the land for other later flowers from future seasons.

The old man glanced beyond the group. Saw that the distant mountains were now purple-hued and darkening; and the raw earth colours of the landscape faded out as night came on.

"So, Emilio, you marry and have kids, and your kids have a bit or maybe a lot of you in them. Over life's slow time they grow up and you grow old. Old enough if you're lucky enough to see your children's children. When you eventually experience that, you'll easily understand the life of a flower, and the life of man. In your old age you find yourself well satisfied with what's come your way. You think like an older man, not a thirty-six-year old, which isn't natural anyhow, now is it?"

Gerardo wanted to know how the matter stood if you didn't marry.

"Well, that's fine too, for life is infinitely varied and there're lots of things to do. We can each fit in somewhere, even though it's sometimes a round peg in a square hole."

"Shouldn't that be a square peg in a round hole?" queried Cándido.

"Look you, squint-eye, is your name Cándido or Bandido? What's the damned difference I'd like to know?"

"Well, as they say," smiled the young man charmingly, "a rose is a rose is a rose…"

"And an idiot is a fool is a Cándido."

"Why is a peg put in a hole in the first place?" asked José innocently.

"To fill the hole space I shouldn't wonder. Now will you clam up, the lot of you, and take a look at that sky? Drink it in, hermanos, if you're thirsty for a true sight of beauty. Ay que caray and what a night sky it is to be sure. A full moon will be up in an hour or so − Hope your Salté doesn't notice it, though," nudging the boy in the ribs, "else he'll be at his usual frantic baying, the great hairy beast."

And the men fell silent, including Pancho, gazing at the star-peppered sky on this softwind murmured summer night.

Part Fifteen

Part Fifteen

82

Training Horses

It was one hot and trying Saturday morning, and for old Pancho nothing seemed to be going right. The corral grounds, the horses, the stable walls, all awash with sunlight; harsh, glaring and sharp-edged. It made the men squint and blink, and they craved for shade and some surcease.

"Where's Gerardo?" asked Pancho bad temperedly.

"He's in there I think saddling that roan," said Cándido coolly, and trying to stay cool, temper-wise at least.

"Stop gritting your teeth, damn it!" flowed out like a flash-flood from the stable, as Gerardo was apparently holding the bit of a bridle, having problems with his mount.

"But I said the bay!" bawled Pancho, boiling up.

Then Gerardo, smelling of dung and dust and rotted straw, emerged with a white-muzzled chestnut bay. He gave the old man a soft putty grin. He stepped out splay-footed as he led the horse out. The mount appeared to be mimicking him.

With pursed lips Pancho studied the scene. "For the love of grace and wisdom, don't have him spraddled out like that," he shouted at him brassily. "Tuck its legs in a bit, or it'll fall flat on its arse."

Gerardo paused, dithering and wondering what he should do next. He fussily altered the stirrup length to exactly how he thought it should be. He mounted the animal.

"Now swing him round," commanded Pancho in a cracked, pot-simmering voice. He swung round himself, slamming into a post, which bent and nearly broke the brim of his sombrero. This only fired up his temper to a higher degree, his dignity also dented. "No, that way, hombre! Look where you're going!"

José, leaning against the corral fencing, said nothing during this concerto of confusing contradictions, quietly enjoying a freshly rolled cigarro and once again playing his role of the lone, silent hombre.

Young Juan made his appearance on a bay mare. Seeing the boy's cheerful smile, Pancho's normal sense of mildness and equanimity was fully restored. He set the boy off.

"Turn him tight, Juanito, watch your heels and don't grip so hard on them reins. Give a bit, easy now, and there you have it, muchacho!" hollered the now happy old ranchero, as Juan rode the bay in circuits about the corral enclosure. A horse he had quite taken to, a lovely chestnut, flecked with a cream-white mane and tail of bronze-gold.

"That'll do it, you've done real fine," said the ranchero, looking over with a critical eye. "Grab the halter, Emilio – Break your trot, Juanito, a running walk now, that will do it. Easy there, she's had enough I reckon. José! José, you're ready with the yearling, eh? Away you go then, hombre. ¡Andale!"

José took hold of a short-tailed dark bay yearling and vaulted into the saddle like a circus performer. He was away at once.

The boy sidled up to the old ranchero, slapping dust from his leather chaps, a confident grin spread over his young eager features.

"She's a pacer is that one," Pancho smiled on the boy. "Mettlesome with it, to be sure. Hardy legs, fine fetlocks, good all round is that one. High-spirited too I might add, as I like them, you can safely bet on that." He hawked and turned, spat in the burning dust at his feet. "You can take this one as well if you fancy it, when José stops showing off with her."

"A big animal for a yearling," Juan observed, experience teaching him something every day.

"Ah sí, such a large one as you say, yet so fragile too, you understand. Not delicate like, no-o ... fragile like I said, meaning breakable." The old man felt at his moustache, began stroking it reflectively. "You see a niño take a fall on his backside and he near bounces back up again. Even you, a young one like yourself, could take a fall and not break a thing."

Pancho laughed, continued on : "It might put a flush on your face, but no bones broken – unless it was a bad fall, mind. But if I were to take a tumble at my time of life, I'd be sure to break a leg, maybe even two – though I can tell you in confidence that it wouldn't be any more than that

– legs, I'm meaning," winking a merry blue eye at the boy. "It would be on account of my size and weight and height – and age too I guess."

He scratched the back of his neck, then put hands on his hips. "Now the roan mare José is circusing about on, she's sixteen hands tall. She's full in the flanks but tight in her belly, as you can see for yourself. Were she to take a bad fall I reckon it would be the end of her, hmm …

"But you can try the chestnut colt first. If he wants to jump over the cactus like he sometimes does, then let him rip, but don't force it. Well, shall we saddle him up?"

An hour later on this sweltering Saturday morning the rancheros were still at it, trying out various manoeuvres with trained and semi-trained mounts. Pancho stood in the centre of the corral, tugging absently at his moustache. A dust-devil twisted across the trampled ground in front of him. In the corral Juan sat tight on a chestnut stallion, a slightly nervous expression on the faces of both rider and horse.

"Is he tameable you might ask. Well, he assuredly is," Pancho was telling the boy in quiet tones. "There are few horses that aren't. They're foals all their lives, as dogs are always puppies – or at any rate acting that way, you know, playful like and in need of attention, and of praise in particular. Like kids they are."

The old ranchero slashed his riding-crop at a clump of mouse-ear chickweed defiantly standing in the middle of the well-trodden ground. Its hairy leaves scattered and fell into the dust. When he realised what he had done he threw a shamefaced grin at Juan.

"What you need to know here, you know it by doing it. Making a good start has a job already half done. You can make a mistake and make it again, but any more would be a disaster. So you're knowing by doing. As simple as that.

"You need to dominate him by putting the fear of God or man in him," he went on in a harsh gravelled voice. "He needs to be submissive without being dependent on you all the time. You must like him, Juanito, which I know you do, and he must samewise like you. To develop a mutual trust, you understand. Once that's achieved he'll be willing to do lots of things purely in order to please you and make you happy, making himself happy in the bargain – Oye, José, is Gerardo on the black stallion yet?" he yelled over beyond the makeshift fencing.

"Sí, taking him up the hill-slope as you asked him to."

"Bueno, gracias – Now, Juanito, not too much fear, mind, or it'll work against you. A remembered punishment will last longer in his horsy mind than a remembered reward or praise."

He didn't need to inform the boy, but he did anyway, that it worked both ways, and it was best to strike a balance between the two. The important thing, he stressed, was to be effective as soon as possible, train them hard and as quickly as they could. Moreover this was possible, he pointed out, by using different training methods as the boy had seen that day, instead of one long and dull repetitive way, which helps the horse along without boring him.

"Then, if things work out as we want them to, we can make him more willing to go along with our orders and commands."

During the ranchero's monologue Juan was getting to know his mount, pulling him this way and that, walking and trotting him, with an occasional stroke of the neck and words of praise, or a sharp slap and deeply-dug heel in his side.

"You're doing okay mi amiguito, like you've known each other your whole life through. He knows now who's the boss, don't you feel? Try the tight wheeling action again…"

Later in the day the rancheros with a herd of horses moved out on to open country, setting up a temporary corral. And the training continued.

So it went on. After a stretch of time Juan dismounted a sorrel he'd tried a few tricks with, and joined Pancho. The two of them looked out over the windcut grasslands, observing Gerardo who was now taking a black stallion up and down a small hill in the mid-distance.

This animal had a reputation for bucking, and was near enough cured of it but not entirely. When horse and rider ascended the hill Gerardo deliberately induced the animal to buck, which in its bloody-mindedness it refused to comply. Indeed, it was difficult to buck traversing a steep slope. At least the horse knew it.

Pancho wondered if Gerardo knew it.

83

Juan Takes a Fall

Old Pancho was engrossed in gazing at the sky, at grey and blue-grey rain-promising cloud cover curdling above the plain. He hoped that it would rain, and turned his attention earthward. Two bay stallions hung about a dungpile, tossing their manes and pawing the ground, snorting and posturing at each other.

"Why are those two almost fighting over that dung?" asked Juan.

The ranchero observed the horses in question, studying their erratic and aggressive behaviour. "It's a question of who shitted first, me or you? That's what they're on about."

The boy laughed, and said, "Why's that then?"

"Have you heard of the saying, 'He who laughs last laughs the longest'? It's something like that I suppose. The one who drops his dung last is the dominant male – the one there with the longer tail."

"Ah, the other is backing off and trotting away, with a sulky look on his face, though in all probability it'll be a submissive look."

Juan laughed again. "Sulky look! Submissive look! How can you tell that on a horse's face?"

"Oh, there are certain signs," admitted the old ranchero enigmatically, and trying to control a widening grin. "¡Újule! Damn these midges, there must be some water lying around someplace."

"You're right too. Over that way, you can see the sun flashing off it."

"Ah sí, there it is." Pancho felt inordinately pleased at his prediction of water lying nearby. "I wondered where these damned midges had come from."

A young jackrabbit skittered on ahead of them, lost itself in tall grass. A lone prowling hawk high above kept an eye on it, waiting for it to move and come out into more open ground. The midges spun about in maddened spiralings, living out their day.

Gerardo came riding hard toward the corral, and the wind tore at the stallion's black mane.

"How is he then, amigo?" asked Pancho, when the other came to a sudden halt in a flurry of dust, the mount blowing noisily through its lips.

"He's learning, I reckon," grinned Gerardo, swiftly dismounting. He lifted his sombrero and shook a shower of dust from his matted hair. "God, it gets in everywhere!" he griped.

"I know, damned midges, a nuisance."

"I think he means – " began Juan, and stopped. The stallion snorted and backed at the sight of him, the only one who had not yet ridden him.

"Are you going to try him, Juanito?" challenged the old ranchero. "Everyone else has. He's probably put behind his pitching habit, or at any rate learnt not to by this time. But you never know though. Up you come, muchacho, I'll hold him – Bueno, off you go!"

The boy however first leaned forward, talking quietly to the animal and assuring him, stroking his black neck sleek with sweat. He cantered him away.

"Take him up the rise, Juanito!" called over Pancho, in a voice fit to wake the deceased. He carefully watched the movements of the animal's ears, neck and tail. Juan broke him into a full gallop toward the hill-slope.

"That damned beast is going to pitch, I just know it," muttered Pancho, yet there were no indications of this in the horse's behaviour; simply a gut feeling he couldn't shake away.

The steed ran fast and well, and was almost at the summit of the hill, its hooves kicking up dust and loose rock.

Then it happened. It had to happen. The stallion slyly and suddenly halted in his tracks and viciously bucked, sending Juan flying over his head. It was a long way to the ground and the boy fell awkwardly and heavily. One arm was pinned under him as his chest and arm hit sharp rock. A long gash opened up along the inside of his arm, bleeding profusely. The boy sat where he had fallen, too stunned to notice his injured arm.

All the rancheros, instantly alert to the crisis, came running. Then the pain got to Juan and with a vengeance. His young pale face tightened. He looked up at the men around him with surprise and shock.

"Get a hold of that damned horse, Gerardo!" stormed Pancho. "Here, muchacho, let's look at the cut." His normally gruff, gravelled voice became gentle, a soft rasping sound.

The wound was not deep but clean cut and a good hand long. Blood poured down the boy's arm as he held it up, gazing at his injury with a solemn detachment, as though it belonged to someone else.

Pancho took the boy's wrist and lifted the arm vertically, giving Cándido a swift significant glance which was instantly and correctly interpreted. The young ranchero held the upper reach of the boy's arm tight in his hand-grip, while the old ranchero swabbed at the long gash with his bandanna, after first shaking it of its dust.

"Uuy, muchacho," he said in a bantering tone, "you've more blood in you than a town abattoir – Hold his arm well up, amigo," he directed the other quietly. "Real tight over that big vein."

Old Pancho stepped back, turned, and began undoing his flies.

"A fine time for that!" exclaimed José, watching with astonishment as the old man pissed on in the dust at his feet.

"Shut it, José," hissed Cándido. "He knows what he's doing."

Pancho hunkered down on his heels, and with two fingers stirred his urine into the dirt, making a creamy foaming mud-pack. He scooped it up with one spatula paw, then straightened himself. He plastered the mud mixture liberally over the bleeding wound, completely covering the cut and effectively stanching the flow of blood. It looked worse than it actually was.

"You can ease off the pressure bit by bit, Cándido," he advised the young man, "but keep that arm raised for the present. Have you got your hip-flask handy, José?"

"Sí," grinned the other somewhat sheepishly, understanding the entire performance at last, "though it's in my saddlebag somewhere. I'll just be a moment…"

"Muy bien. We'll let our young ranchero war hero here have a slug or two. José's tequila or mezcal is grand stuff for replacing lost blood, I always find," his attention fully on the patient who was coming out from his initial shock and getting some colour back into his cheeks. "You see, Juanito, with us rancheros, what runs in us is half-blood, the other half being good quality grade drinking liquor.

"And that piss-and-earth poultice will fix you better than any bandage will, at least for the time being."

The horsemen stood around the boy, concealing their concern by cracking silly jokes and assuring him in their rough simple way, as men will when one among them is bravely wounded and in need of some succour.

Flies greedily gathered and gorged on the quickly blackening blood spattered on the ground. A dust-devil was up on its hindmost, swirling around like a Spanish dancer, then fast disappearing.

The men soon rode back to the hacienda, leaving the herd to graze.

Gerardo took the troublesome black stallion, Juan returned to his faithful mount Chapulín.

And the rain-filled clouds that had followed them, opened up in a burst. Rain sluiced down the men and the horses in a quick heavy downpour. It cooled and cleared the air, settled the dust for a while. The clouds moved on and the sun came out in a blinding glare. In the fresh humid air flies raged and pestered man and beast.

Back at the hacienda Tulia made a monumental fuss over Juan's wound, carefully washing it, applying antiseptic lotion, cleaning it properly and expertly bandaging his arm. It gave the old woman infinite satisfaction to fret over and pamper a wet and bedraggled boy with a bleeding arm. Long suppressed maternal instincts came to the fore as she slavishly attended to him.

It had also been noted by the men that through his ordeal the boy had remained stoic and passed a painful boundary with honour. In their eyes he had become one of them – a true ranchero type. The boy had this day 'earned his spurs', and no one was more proud and pleased about it than old Pancho.

84

Midday Happy Hour

Another Sunday, and don Roberto's rancheros were returning from a service at a small chapel in a nearby pueblo. They rode in dust-laden wind-touched air under a dry and searing southern sky, which summoned up summer scents of grass and wild herbs.

They presently stabled the horses, after a walk and feed, then roamed aimlessly about the corral yards, waiting for Tulia to send them their midday food.

Pancho strode purposely across the dusty sunlit yard, as if on an errand of importance, Cándido close behind him. Of a sudden the old man stopped dead in his tracks and gazed upward with a fixed expression.

If someone were to stare intently up at the sky, any noticing passerby would naturally be curious to know what the other was staring at. The passerby would no doubt in turn also stare intently up at the sky. Even though the sky may be clear and blue and quite empty. Which was the case here.

Cándido almost collided with the old ranchero, who turned, flashing a wink at him. "You see it?" he said quietly.

"Sí," grinned the young man, catching on, and he too began to stare fixedly at the wide blue blank expanse of sky. Behind them a dust-devil leapt up, fanatically dervishing across the corral.

José and Gerardo soon caught up with them, craning their necks and searching blindingly to east and west with puzzled wandering eyes.

"What is it?" asked Gerardo. "What are you looking at?"

"There!" said Pancho, vaguely pointing an arm.

"I can't see anything," said José.

"I can," declared Cándido. "Plain as a cactus in the desert. There, you see?"

"No, I don't see. What can you see? What the hell is it, then?" blew José irritably. "You two must have damned good eyesight is all I can say. Do you see anything, Gerardo?"

"What is it?" repeated Gerardo. "What is it I'm supposed to see?"

"Oh, it's plain enough for God's sake!" said Cándido with feeling.

Gerardo stopped craning his neck, which was beginning to stiffen up, and eyed the young ranchero with open suspicion and some hostility. "It's a trick!" he exclaimed at last, correctly reading Cándido's face.

"No-o, it's not a trick," drawled Pancho slowly. "It's the sky."

"Is that what you two were gawping at?" José almost shouted. "The damned empty sky!" He sniffed and hawked and spat his contempt.

"I said it was a trick," said Gerardo, aggrieved.

"And I said it's the sky," returned Pancho affably. "Which it is."

The pair of dupes huffed, went on to the haybarn, scuffing their boots and angrily kicking at loose stones in the dust.

Juan joined the old ranchero, Salté making an appearance and at his heels. They too headed for the cool sanctuary of the barn, the earth dazed by the near-noon light and heat.

"Where's our Julian?" said Pancho. "Ah, there you are."

He found the soft-wit deep in the gloom of the barn, stacking huge bales of straw and working with a frenetic energy.

"Mind where you're going, Julian, and be careful of that –"

Thock!

" – that there rake. Emilio was looking for it earlier on, he'll be pleased you've found it for him," smiled the old man, and plumped himself down on a bale of cornstraw.

"Sí, señor," bleated Julian, rubbing at his nose.

"He does so much graft around here," noted Juan, not altogether happy.

Pancho smiled on the boy. "As they say, it's better to be on your feet and working than sitting in the lap of luxury doing nothing."

He went on enumerating the many tasks the stablehand took on; fetching and carrying, saddling the horses for the men, collecting fodder, grooming and feeding the livestock, cleaning out the stables, attending the calving and foaling, as well as roping and breaking in the horses.

"But you're not hard done by, are you, muchacho?"

"No, señor," Julian responded, smiling ingenuously, "because the men do all the real hard work. They're the ones who have to train the horses," and with that profound statement over with, he picked a strand of straw and stuck it in his mouth.

"So you see, Juanito," grinned the old ranchero, "he's not at all hard done by, by his own admission – Oye, Julian, have you picked up the feed yet from the rail depot? Better set on it straight away. ¡Andale!" He affectionately slapped the youth on his back, at the same time whispering in his ear that he needn't go until after the midday meal was over.

Julian trotted off to harness a horse and waggon in readiness for a trip to the local rail depot, a duty he always enjoyed, chewing contentedly on his piece of straw.

"No, give it no mind, Juanito. He thrives on work, does our Julian, and good honest work never harms anyone. Now, shall we take a – Ah, look there, Gerardo is doing some sort of a dance. Uuy, amigo, are you practicing for the next festival, is it?"

"Damned cockroach!" grated Gerardo, "but I've killed it dead for sure."

"Why, was it bothering you? Offended you in some way, eh? Interfering with your life, was it? A life is to be lived, hombre, not snuffed out for no good reason."

"I can't stand the damned things," Gerardo gritted.

"You stood on that one hard enough."

"There was a big one scuttling about Tulia's kitchen the other day," said José, "when I went round to scrounge one of those watermelons she'd bought from don Luis." His dark swarthy face turned on an evil smile. "I put a boot-heel right on it, crushed the son-of-a-bitch flat, for I can't tolerate cockroaches either."

"So you've told us before – and a time before that."

"A strange thing though, Pancho, you'd never imagine it, but the roach's blood was purple. *Purple!* How could that be you ask yourself. Never seen the like in all my born days. Purple blood…"

"A right royal roach," said Pancho.

"But how was that?" asked Gerardo, gloomily thinking about it. "How come it had purple blood? Sounds like the work of the Devil to me."

The old man said he knew why and began to explain how very simple the matter really was. Last Michaelmas Tulia had bought herself some fancy candles. They were the coloured type, and she had chosen purple candles.

So it stands to reason and as plain as day, he concluded, that the cockroach José had stomped on had been feasting on Tulia's coloured candles.

"So that's all there was to it," said Gerardo, a trace of disappointment evident in his voice.

It being in his nature to elaborate further if the opportunity was there, Pancho went on by declaring that when mankind has used the bounty on this beneficent Earth to the utmost limit, when man has warred and famine-fed himself into extinction, along with most of the creatures of soil and sea and sky … there will be two species left to survive. One will be the rat, the other the cockroach. He believed there were none as clever as those two for surviving.

He made a downward sweep of his moustache with one hand. The dog Salté trotted to him, to lick his hand. "Who's a big soft hairy mammoth hound, then?" he said fondly, knuckling the animal's huge skull. Such attention was bliss, the beast couldn't get enough of it.

The men had mixed feelings towards Juan's canine companion. Salté was loved and hated with equal measure. One time, the hound itself fell in love with José, of all people, who could barely tolerate him. The dog had begun to follow him everywhere, clung to him like a burr. He was stuck fast to the ranchero like glue.

"Away, perro, damn you!" responded the recipient of this dogged devotion.

Less than a week later, when José changed his camisa, Salté dropped him cold. And the reason why was because Salté's affections were in fact false and not for José, but for a toffee that had melted in the pocket of the ranchero's shirt.

Now, the great canine was basking in the old man's pampering. A fly alighted on his cold moist muzzle, causing him to sneeze.

And the hot noon air thrummed with winged insects where sunshine poured in between the slatted wood wall of the barn.

At least the dog was happy this noon hour.

Pancho stirred himself. "Anyone got a bone?"

85

Juan's Hair-Cutting Skills

Later, after a Sunday midday meal prepared by Tulia, the boy Juan was kept busy cutting the rancheros' hair. He was not exactly adept at cutting hair, merely the only one who had volunteered to do the necessary chore. The men had allowed their hair to grow an inordinate length over these summer months.

Gerardo's hair – he had already had his haircut by Juan – could be seen as two wide, hard-bristle appendages, one each side above the ear and beneath the brim of his sombrero, looking like stiff ear-flaps or the clipped wings of a bird of prey.

It was now Emilio's turn to have his hair cut and he sat heavily on a bench-seat taken from the bunkhouse. With a pair of blunt, rusty scissors Juan set to his task of attacking Emilio's lank, beetle-black head of growth. The young barber industriously clipped and scissored away at the thick black thatch of matted hair, wedges and tufts of it falling to the floor.

"You might have washed it first, Emilio," the boy lightly admonished him, as he laboriously cropped away, lopping off great greasy hanks from the bale of black.

"Ayí sí, Juanito, but I forgot," ruefully admitted the fat man, watching curiously as swashes of thick hair fell like chunks of felt at his feet.

"You fell asleep, you mean," bantered Cándido.

"He stinks as well," said José, not unkindly but as a point of fact.

"Ay sí," agreed Pancho, "he hums so much at times even his own shadow is loath to follow him."

"Look at the bull neck on him," goaded Gerardo, now that the neck was exposed. "You get fatter every day. How do you do it?"

"I fill him up at his backside with a bicycle-pump," quipped the old man.

"It's the massive amount of sleep he gets," offered Cándido, "storing his energy."

"Will you leave off about my sleeping habits? We all need sleep, you know," the fat one added aggrievedly, peeping from under Juan's shears with unfriendly eyes.

"You need it for life itself," chipped in José, "like we need air."

"I'm not fat either … just well-built."

"Like a brick mansion. It has to be the food that's given him such a generous girth, and nothing else," Pancho pointed out, chaffing him unmercifully.

A silence followed, everybody collecting up a second wind. Eyes were focused on the salon maestro. Juan dipped a hand into a wooden basin belonging to Tulia, lifting out a heavy dollop of yellow cooking fat. He spread it on his hands and then liberally piled it on to Emilio's hair, massaging it into his scalp. He combed the hair out, as he would currycomb a horse's mane, stepped back to admire his handiwork. Emilio's hair was so black, sleeked down and shiny, so plastered and lacquered with cooking fat, so neatly cut bare about the neck, that it looked less like a head of hair but rather more resembled a thick metallic helmet shaped to his skull.

Cándido immediately took him for a character from a horror comic he had read recently, the fat man appearing quite grotesque. It reminded Pancho of an oil-slick or a drowned crow or something similarly hideous and frightful on his head.

"Oh, *wapo!*" commented the old man. "You didn't look as good as that on your wedding day, amigo. Uuy, you do look wapo to be sure. Doesn't he look real handsome, hermanos?"

"You think so?" said the fat man, flattered beyond measure over this recognition of his new image, and grinning so widely that his big buck teeth seemed ready to jump out.

"Well, maybe you should have just a little bit more off the top," said Pancho judiciously, "then you'd look a fair film star type without a doubt."

"You think so?" repeated Emilio, revelling in this gross over-the-top flattery.

"Uuy, there's no sure steady love as self-love, is there? Our Emilio is getting as vain as an advertisement. Get back to work on him, Juanito, and while you're at it I'll tell you a tale about young Julian. I shouldn't run the rascal down I know, but never mind, it won't do any harm to him I don't suppose…"

The men edged forward, eager to hear anything that concerned the simpleton, for it was certain to be entertaining.

"There was a time I remember," began Pancho, in his slow, storytelling tone of voice, "when don Roberto was away in Mexico City on some business or other."

The old ranchero leaned forward, fully into his narrative which went something on the following lines : Don Roberto phoned his casa in order to check on a matter or two. Only, there was no one in the house; no one that is until Julian happened to walk in at the moment when the phone rang. The simple fellow had never used a telephone in his life, and he approached it as though it were a vicious dog with rabies, as Pancho expressed it. The lame-wit gingerly lifted the receiver – (The old man put a fist to his ear in imitation of someone using a telephone) – and said :

"¡Hola! Hello!" at the top of his voice.

"Hello, this is Roberto in Mexico City."

"¡Hola!" yelled Julian again. "*Perdónome* – excuse me – but don Roberto is in Mexico City," he shouted into the phone.

"This *is* don Roberto speaking!" the don shouted back, "*in* Mexico City."

Julian looked wildly about, then at the phone, said : "Don Roberto? Are you really in Mexico City?" asked the youth, his voice high-pitched with surprise.

"Sí, damn it!" flared the don.

"Well, I could have sworn you were right here in the same room, Boss. As if you were right here in front of me."

(Pancho paused a moment, watching Juan slashing and snipping away at Emilio's thick-gloss top, then went on.)

"I presume this is Julian on the line?" said the don.

"¡Ayí!" exclaimed Julian in further surprise. "You're all that way down south in Mexico City, Boss, and you knew it was me here in your casa. How did you know it was me, Boss?" Still shrieking down the phone.

"Because, Julian, I know your voice. Now will you stop your yelling and try to speak normally, and just listen to me a moment. I want you to tell Pancho to hold on to those two roan geldings. He's not to let them go, as I've decided to keep them. Can you tell him that?"

"I can hear you okay, Boss, from all that way in Mexico City. But I know señor Pancho is over by the corral stables, and he wouldn't hear me even if I shouted."

"I mean tell him when you see him, Julian, tell him when you *next* see him." The don was getting near rattled.

"There's another thing," he said to the slow-wit, "I'll be back earlier than planned. You tell José — when you next *see* José — tell him to take the bay and trap to the railroad depot tomorrow at 3.30 in the afternoon."

"I'll tell José, Boss, but even if he's slow as a snail hitching the bay and takes it walking over, he's going to be at the railroad depot tomorrow well before 3.30."

"I mean," said the don, trying not to bawl into his receiver, "I mean for him to be there *by* 3.30. Have you got that?"

"I understand, Boss."

"Is Tulia there?"

"No, Boss, Tulia is out somewhere, with the chickens I think, Boss."

"Well now, you can put the phone back on the hook. You can put the phone down now, Julian."

A long moment passed. Julian still held the receiver to his ear.

"Hello, Julian, you're still there?"

"Hello, Boss, are you still in Mexico City?"

"I am indeed," said the don, gritting his teeth, "and it's as well I'm here and not there, otherwise I'd be thrashing you!"

And the don angrily slammed down the phone at his end.

"A good five minutes later," Pancho said, concluding his story — in fact a true one — "Julian is still talking to a dead phone, according to Tulia, who had heard the whole charade. 'Hello! Hello!' he's saying. 'Have you moved from Mexico City, Boss, because I can't hear you anymore? Hello!'"

The old man bellowed heartily. He had pieced together this tale from Tulia and the don. When he managed to regain his composure he wanted to know whose turn it was next for a haircut.

"Yours, Pancho," said José. "We're all done."

"Surely not. Have you cut José's mop, muchacho? It looks much the same as before to me."

"I had what is called a neat trim," said José primly, "and a trim is as good as a crop, only finer."

"Oh it is, is it? Well, alright then," conceded the old ranchero. "I'll have a trim too, an all-round trim, mind. And do inside my ears, will you, Juanito? There's more hair in my ears than what I've got under my armpits, I'm sure. Eyebrows as well, you can trim them two bushes down for me, I reckon."

Pancho sat himself squarely on a bale of straw smoking with dust.

He paused a moment, a finger in the air, thinking of something.

"Do I need to take off my sombrero, or will you manage?" he wanted to know.

Part Sixteen

86

Flights of Fancy

"Look at that Paloma in the sky," said Pancho late one afternoon. "Do you see it? To the left of the stables … Ay caray, flying so gracefully so freely. You couldn't be any more free than that, uuy. I expect that's how the expression came to be, you know, 'As free as a bird'. It must be fine to have that sort of freedom, eh? They say when you're single you're free as a bird, but when you're wedded you get your wings clipped – Isn't that so, Gerardo? … He's not answering me. Ay well, there's wisdom even in a foolish man's silence. In fact, Gerardo's silences are his best parts, I could easily listen to them."

Gerardo said not a word. Cándido was faintly amused when he saw that Gerardo had a dark dollop of horse-muck sticking on the end of his nose. How did it get there? he wondered. Should he tell him? No, he should not. Couldn't he see it, for the love of sweet sanity! Couldn't he smell it?

Cándido gave a significant superior sniff. So much, he thought, for not seeing things further than the end of one's nose …

"What must it be like to fly?" speculated Emilio, remarkably wide awake and chipper for a change. "In one of them aeroplanes I mean. Has anyone here ever flown in an aeroplane?" but no one answered him. The men were absorbed in scratching themselves, picking a nose, or searching for lice in their clothing.

Then Cándido had it in mind to say something. "The highest I've ever been I think is about three metres, when I climbed a ladder to look at a bird's nest on the stable eave."

"And what the hell has that got to do with flying?" grated Gerardo irritably, breaking his silence.

"Well, I fell off the ladder, didn't I?" continued Cándido. "Then I went *flying*, by God!"

"You're always falling off ladders," said José.

"¡Ay que caray!" exclaimed Pancho. "You could so easily have broken your neck."

"So easily," said José, smirking, "but still wouldn't do it."

"I was just coming to that," retorted Pancho caustically.

Cándido smiled his fetching smile. "I was lucky I guess, I landed on my feet like a cat."

"Well, there you have it then," punched in Pancho.

"That's typical," grumped Gerardo. "If he fell in cattleshit he'd get up smelling of lavender."

"Speaking of which," said Cándido, glancing at the other's mucky nose, "well, no matter, it's of no moment…"

Said Pancho : "We're high up here, as you know, on this plateau where we live and work. We're a few thousand metres above sea level. That's high for you."

"That's as maybe," countered Cándido, "but it doesn't constitute flying though, does it?" for which the old man returned him a pitying look.

"When you think on it," mused Pancho, deciding it would be safer all round to return to the original topic of interest, "an aeroplane is only a big metal bird in the sky, which is what the jungle Indians think. As a passenger you'd sit somewhere in its ribcage. But it's longer of course, like a giant cigar tube. That's all it is, with engines and wings on it."

"What are they like inside then?" asked Gerardo, scratching vigorously at an armpit. "Are all the people squashed together like beans in a pod, like cattle in a truck?"

"No, no, hombre, there's plenty of room on those aeroplanes. People pay good money you know to travel in an aeroplane."

"It'll have seats in it, then?" pursued Gerardo.

"Of course it'll have seats in it, you bone-brain jackrabbit!" José spat at him. "Every big aeroplane has seats in it. Plenty of stools and benches to sit on, and little round windows as well to look through and see the whole world like a giant ball below you."

"Expensive business though, flying in an aeroplane, like Pancho says," commented Cándido. "They'll have sofas and settees for you to sit on, but that's only in first class, I suppose. It must come pretty expensive for such comfort."

"That's not the end of it," Pancho went on, "because I've heard that some of them big aeroplanes have a little cantina on board –"

"A cantina!" gasped Gerardo.

"He's having you on, amigo," said José.

"No, I'm not. It's as true as I sit here. What I mean is they have a small bar on board. They have women up in them too, who take good care of you during a flight to wherever you're going. They give you a little pillow to rest your head, and they buy you drinks, or so I'm led to understand – by my book I reckon it's the other way around, *you* buy *them* drinks. And as I say they take good care of you. They wear a uniform of sorts, these aeroplane women. They even cook and serve food for you. How about that then, eh?"

"What, beans and tortillas and suchlike?" queried Gerardo, a hand down one of his boots, scratching intently at a flea bite on his shin, and still sporting the blob of dung on the end of his nose.

"Well, you have to understand, amigo, a lot of these aeroplanes go on long journeys, or flights as they call them," explained the old man, wearing his mantle of worldly wisdom. "International flights is the term used by them. And I'll hazard a guess that you get *international* foods on board of them."

He expanded further. "For instance, if you're flying to say Washington or maybe Chicago, the uniformed women on board would fix up burgers and hot-dogs for you, as is well known – or ought to be. If you're heading for Peking in China, you'd get Chop Suey dished up, which you have to eat with two little sticks. You fly to London in England and it's beef and pudding. You go on to Paris in France and they'll serve you frogs' legs done in a sauce."

"It doesn't seem right to me," moaned Emilio. "I mean, these aeroplanes fly very high in the sky and are so much nearer to the Good Lord Himself. And there you are, buying drinks for women you don't know and stuffing your face with disgusting foreign food like *choppie-suey* and frogs' legs. It just doesn't seem right."

"We're as near to God here on the ground," gravelled Pancho, "as them aeroplane passengers thousands of metres up in the heavens. I dare say we're as near to Him as vespers is to suppertime and sunset. God is all around and even within us, and you ought to know that, you heathen."

"Sí, I was forgetting," returned the fat man contritely, "so maybe I'd better shut up and get a little sleep … or I'll never go to Heaven."

"The road is open to it," smiled Cándido. "I'll show you the way if you like."

"There's no one sure road to Heaven," Pancho pontificated, "you can get there by any route you fancy."

"Is it really true," began Gerardo grimly, "that the Frenchies eat frogs' legs?"

"The French eat horsemeat too," young Juan tossed in, joining them.

"Horse meat!" cried José, appalled. "Why, the uncivilised swine, so they are!"

"There's no end to the kinds of meat that folk will eat," said Pancho. "Man will eat bear and fox and mule and camel ... And the Chinese, you wouldn't credit it, they eat dogs. They eat that lovely looking Chow dog. The Japanese next door to them, they eat caterpillars. Which isn't so bad come to think on it, considering we've the maguey worm sitting in many a bottle of mezcal or tequila."

"Grasshoppers as well, we eat in our own country," Juan pointed out, "crisp-fried and tasty they say, but I wouldn't know myself."

"I would," said José, "get offered them often enough by the village women."

"In America, in the southern states at least," added Pancho, "they eat the meat of rattlesnake and the opossum –"

"The opossum!" glowered Gerardo in outrage, thinking of his own pet opossum. "Them damn gringos will eat anything."

"Well, over here too, the opossum is sometimes cooked and eaten," Pancho warned the other.

"I'd just like to see them get a hold of my little baby, ¡carambas!"

Gerardo swiped an indignant hand at his nose, dislodging the lump of dung, which fell on the toe of José's recently polished left boot. The swarthy ranchero gave the ugly one a look hard enough to crush him.

"Been picking your nose again, Gerardo?" cheeped Cándido.

"There're all manner of things that man will chuck down his gullet," the old man continued on remorselessly. "Pigeon's feet and larks' tongues, spiders and beetles, fish lips and bull's testicles – and guess what, flowers as well."

"Flowers, you say?" yawned Emilio, who had nearly dropped into a temporary stupor.

"Doesn't doña María herself sometimes cook flowers for us? You know, the large petal ones which she stuffs with something or other. ¡Ay que rico! And the gringos use flowers in their cookery, flower buds and flower-heads. Some kind of tea is made from a flower, dried it is – what's its name now? – ah sí, wild chamomile, that's it. Marigolds are used to colour butter, and some flowers are candied in sugar, like violet petals. Well, as the good Bible tells us : 'Man did eat angels' food : he sent them meat to the full'."

"Ay, hermanos," said Cándido, grinning widely, "will we be ready for our tortillas and *frijoles* tonight?"

"I fancy Cándido's liver," suggested Gerardo, "his cheek I get every day," which raised a good hearty laugh from the old man.

87

Pablo's False Teeth

One evening, after a supper of black beans and tortillas with fiery hot chillies, Pancho put salt on his forefinger and began rubbing at his teeth to clean them. Next, he took a thin sliver of wood from the pocket of his leather vest, where he always kept it, and picked at his teeth.

José watched him with slight irritability. "Why are you always poking that little stick in your mouth?" he asked shortly. "It'll all go down eventually and get digested."

"The thing is, hermano, that's not the case one whit," responded the old ranchero, and felt compelled to tell the other why. "Food gets lodged between your teeth and it sits there to rot. Leave it long enough and pretty soon your teeth rot too. Look – " as Pancho bared his teeth, " – an old man like me and still with all my grinders."

He glanced stable-ward as a white dove alighted on the gable end. It flared its wings and stretched out its neck and looked around, then snuggled down and began to preen the moonwhite down on its breast.

Without anyone being consciously aware of it – except perhaps the old ranchero – dusk and dust together fell swiftly and silently. It began to draw chilly, as it will in these upland parts. Young Juan considered it his personal calling to hunt out a pile of ponchos usually stored in the saddle-room.

As soon as the cold touched him he was up like a jungle cat to fetch the ponchos and dish them out to the horsemen. Salté tried to follow him but a 'Stay!' command rooted him to the spot, a hurt and unmistakably sullen expression on his canine face. The men put on the proffered ponchos, grunts of satisfaction skimming Juan's way.

They fell silent for a spell, at ease and comfortable in their quietude, sometimes gazing up at a shell-pink evening sky, as the red-flushed face of the setting sun began to sink into the jagged shoulders of the distant mountains.

A saddle-horse tethered nearby loudly broke wind, abruptly breaking the silence, and that triggered them back into conversation.

"Do you remember old Pablo and his teeth?" Gerardo opened up.

"Uuy, I remember our Pablo sure enough," said Pancho. "He lost all his teeth before he reached his middle-age, every single one of them. Black they were, because of his habit of chewing tobacco. They dropped out one tooth after another till there were none left. I heard that he bought himself a second-hand pair of chompers in some tienda or the mercado in Dolores Hidalgo. From the very first they fitted him loosely, as he was always ready to admit. Wouldn't change them though, he liked their shape and whiteness. I say *white* by Pablo's standards, they were as yellow as an age-old mule's."

Old Pancho's eyes were momentarily diverted. A barn mouse peeped its whiskered face from a corner of a stook of straw, casting around with an inquisitive nose, until a movement made by José sent it straight back where it had come from.

"He could talk the door off a barn, could Pablo, and never stopped his gabbing," Gerardo went on. "And sometimes he'd be talking so fast his false teeth would fly out. They hit me in the face one time," he added, as a mosquito droned about his ear and he slapped his hand hard at it, stinging his own ear with the force of the slap.

"And our Pablo would say, 'Where's ... mmm ... my mm-teeth?'" Pancho mimicked, putting away his toothpick.

"Talk you to death, he could," continued Gerardo, nursing a sore ear, "until he died of a sudden and –"

"He was killed by his own bull," said Cándido. "Kicked and cracked his skull, was what I heard."

Said José, "One kick was all it took, and off he went to join his Maker..."

"Ay que caray, and bless his soul in Heaven," said Pancho with a sigh. "And just think, Pablo would have the Good Lord's Ear to bend for all eternity."

"Where is he now?" asked Cándido.

"Oh, you reckon he has visiting rights to us still alive?"

"No, I mean where is he buried?"

"He lies now in the cemetery at Dolores Hidalgo," the old man told him. He paused a moment, gazing significantly at the others. "About a week after he'd been dead and buried it was rumoured that a strange sound was coming from Pablo's grave. Of course," he went on with a closed, deadpan face, "of course there are the sceptics who say it was just the wind blowing the loose urn by his headstone. That's as maybe, but the common belief was that it was Pablo's false teeth still clacking away in his grave – like castanets dropping on a tiled floor."

And the evening shadows lengthened and bats began flitting in and out of the nearby stables, and the first silent stars appeared and gazed down winkingly on the rancheros ranged about the woodfire, and there they talked on peaceably under a summer starlit sky.

88

Dominoes and a Doctor

A Saturday afternoon. That morning the rancheros had seen off a cavey of trained remounts at the local railroad depot, the horses destined for Mexico City and some army cavalry squadron.

The men milled about in the main stable, relieved to be in shade and away from a horrendous scorching sun.

"Glad to be rid of that rough roan," grumped Gerardo. "He was giving me sleepless nights with his damn tricky ways."

"I'm sure going to miss that light bay," mooned Cándido. "He had eyes like an impala. A real handsome creature he was and so easy to work."

"Well," began Pancho, "that's enough of your love life. We're all in need of some light entertainment. Get the dominoes out, Gerardo. José, set up the board if you will," as he clumped and crashed his way through cornstraw, raising waves of dust and chaff.

He kicked bales into place to form a table and seating. "Sit next to me, Juanito?" He regarded the boy as his personal lucky mascot. Juan was also a representative of A Crowd of Spectators, not a player. Emilio also was only there to watch – and to whistle on any cheaters. The fat man set himself comfortably on a line of bales, lying leaning on one elbow like some well-fed Eastern potentate.

The box of dominoes was found. Gerardo had spent two months handcrafting the dominoes and box, with that typical flair and skill of the Mexican artisan, fashioning the pieces from sweet scented cedarwood.

José placed a square sheet of plywood on a large bale, and four players arranged themselves in their apparently accustomed places : Cándido and Pancho on one side, José and Gerardo opposite them.

"My turn it is for first drop," said José, giving the others a dark, inscrutable look.

"Me to shuffle, I believe," said Gerardo, lovingly sliding dominoes out from their scented box. Their clicking together was a pleasing sound to the men's ears. It reminded them of earlier countless convivial games.

Pancho caught the pleasant smell of cedarwood, in competition with the rich heady whiff of fresh dung and the sharp pungency of horse-piss.

The game began.

The old man held all his dominoes in one large paw and held close to his chest, away from Cándido on his left; the other players had theirs standing landscape-wise in an arc before them.

José slammed down a double-five. "Got rid of you, you bastard!"

PANCHO : "Don't blaspheme, José, not on a Sunday."

JOSÉ : "I won't, but today is Saturday."

CÁNDIDO : "Say, I've got a real lousy lot here. Can I call for a reshuffle?"

PANCHO : "We've each got seven dominoes and we each picked blindly –"

JOSÉ : "It's you to go, Pancho."

PANCHO : "A weed is a plant just as a flower is a plant. We think we're all unequal but we're really the same."

JOSÉ : "It's your go, Pancho!"

PANCHO : "How is that then?"

GERARDO : "I just dropped a five-one."

PANCHO : "Ahh ... Hmm…"

He put down a five-four.

CÁNDIDO : "Thank you, hermano," getting shot of his double-four.

José followed up with a four-two, Gerardo slyly off-loaded a double-one. Pancho suspected that something interesting was developing here and triumphantly blocked with a one-two. He leaned to the boy on his right, giving him a crafty sideways look, as if to say 'Let him try and sort that one out!'

Cándido smiled a warm, engaging smile and smilingly clapped down a two-six. José chased that with a double-two, enabling Gerardo to happily dump his 'big, heavy' double-six.

"It's your turn, Pancho."

But the old ranchero's ears were tuned to two sparrows merrily chirping a duet in the rafters. One sparrow chased the other, both twittering with the joy of life; alighting on a stall-top, flitting to the broad back of a bay, now on to a saddle hooked to the wall, then out swiftly into the bright sunlight beyond the stable doors.

"Pancho! It's you to drop. Are we here for the day!"

PANCHO : "Ahh, it's me, is it? Right, I can get shut of this six-three."

CÁNDIDO : "Which leaves me with little choice – here's a three-five."

JOSÉ : "We'll let it stay with my two-three."

GERARDO : "Still with the game, muchachos, I've got a three-one."

CÁNDIDO : "*I've got a three one!*" (Mimicking the other)

Pancho's keen hawk-eye caught on a mouse that skittered across an opening between two bales of straw, losing itself in dark shadow. The sparrows returned, dipping in and out of the stable eaves, in and out in a flash, like a whiplash. Like they owned the place, though the old man knew that it was indeed their domain for this summer season.

"Pancho, are you knocking? Can't you go?"

PANCHO : "Oh I can go alright, just about. How's this five-two?"

CÁNDIDO : "Phew! Just made it, one-four. Your move, José. You to go, José. Don't *you* start daydreaming."

JOSÉ : "You know I can't go, damn you to hell!"

PANCHO : "Will you stop your cursing on the Lord's day."

GERARDO : "It's Saturday today. Saturday!"

CÁNDIDO : "So you're knocking, José. Gerardo?"

GERARDO : "Still in with a chance. Four-six."

PANCHO : "Me too, barely. Blank-two."

CÁNDIDO : "Muy bien. Thank you. A slot for my double-blank."

JOSÉ : "I'll cut that with a blank-one."

GERARDO : "How about a one-six, hey? (Gloatingly) A sweet one-six. Six . . six. Got a six, Pancho?"

PANCHO : "How can I have a six when they're all on the board. Damn you!"

JOSÉ : "No swearing por favor, not on a *Saturday*."

"Not quite all on the board, amigo," Cándido smiled a little smugly, putting in place a six-three.

"Ah! Gracias for that," said José, slapping down his five-blank.

"And I thank you, friend," grinned Gerardo, placing his last domino, a blank-four. "End of game, muchachos, end of game!"

"Saddle-stitched!" said Pancho, pursing his lips. "I'm left with a blank-three here."

"I have a blank-six," said Cándido, with a face that appeared as if it had not pulled a smile in a month.

"I win, compadres," said Gerardo, so pleased with himself one might think he had made a huge lottery win.

"When you crafted these dominoes," rasped Pancho, "did you make extra blanks?"

Young Juan turned the dominoes over face-down for the next game, having failed as Pancho's lucky mascot.

"Your shuffle again, Gerardo, and you to start."

"What's that whistling?" asked José of a sudden. "Someone's whistling. Can you hear someone whistling?"

"It's only Emilio," Cándido enlightened him.

The fat man was now on his back and fast asleep with his mouth wide open. With every exhaling breath he whistled through his large buck teeth.

"Your go again, Pancho," José reminded the old man. "Make Cándido sweat a bit, why don't you?"

"I know what you're up to," countered Cándido. "I can read you like a book."

"Oh?" said Pancho perkily. "You can read José like a book, eh? And what chapter are you up to?"

"I mean I know his every move."

"Nice drop that, Gerardo. Can't you go, Pancho?"

Said Pancho, "It's impossible to read another man's thoughts, but I suppose you can often make good and accurate guesses. So, what's his next move, eh, tell me that, you wonky-eyed wizard!"

"What I mean to say is I reckon I know him better than he knows himself."

"Do you know *your* self?"

"Of course I do. Don't you?"

"Know yourself and you know the world," parried Pancho.

"And what's that supposed to mean?"

"It means you're a fool and a fake, but at least you already know that because you know yourself — Ahh! Is that you, Julian? Have you bedded them stalls like I told you to?"

"Sí, señor," piped the poor-wit, tripping in on the proceedings.

"Nice and deep?"

"Sí."

"It's your turn, Cándido, wake up, hombre."

"Good fresh dry straw?"

"Sí, señor."

"Bueno. Now, muchacho, go to my saddlebag nailed to the wall – you know where it is. You'll find some sweeties. You can have one – No, make that two. And bring two for Juanito."

"That's four! Gracias, señor."

"'That's four' he says," grinned the old man. "We'll yet make a scholar of him, by all-that's-good."

"What in thunder!" exclaimed someone.

The game was as good as over. An unusual visitation … an encroachment on the ranchero's simple, old-worldly existence was upon them. Dominoes forgotten, the rancheros tumbled out into the harsh light of day.

From a cloud of dust and noise like distant gunfire a rusty, battered old jalopy came chugging and steaming toward the group by the stables, its exhaust backfiring at intervals, startling and spooking the horses within the corral.

"What the devil's that?" said José in astonishment. "Who is that?"

"Don't you know?" grinned Pancho. "That'll be don Marcos."

"Oh … him. Of course, I remember now."

The decrepit crate, smothered in thick dust, came to a choking, grinding halt. Out jumped a tall figure, equally endowed with a generous covering of dust, waving and smiling at the rancheros. He was Doctor Marcos Luis Gómez, who'd long enjoyed a kind of business acquaintance with don Roberto – and with Pancho.

He was attired in a severe city black suit, now grey with dust, which he slapped from himself and not making much difference. He strode with long jaunty steps toward the men.

"¡Hola, Marcos!" the old man greeted him with warmth. "You've been to don Roberto's, I take it, eh?"

"Just passed by the hacienda, Francisco. But I did see the don on his front porch and he kindly waved to me – in that regal way of his, you know. I always find him a courteous gentleman."

"A true *caballero*, our don Roberto. So, compadre, what brings you out to the wilds?"

"On my way to San Stefan."

"Ahh, to get fresh medical supplies, no doubt, eh?"

"No, my friend, I intend to pay a call on my mother-in-law, doña Esperanza."

"Hmm. That's a treat for sure. I know Esperanza very well. When you consider the disposition of that notable lady, sour lemons come to mind. But she is your wife's mother, and here am I openly insulting her – and you, compadre. My apologies. My mouth moves before my brain does."

"No apologies needed, Francisco. Doña Esperanza is a sour old bitch at the best of times, with a voice that can cut through steel, and the whole world knows it."

Doctor Gómez however was duty-bound to make the visit, he informed the rancheros, to sort out a certain embarrassing domestic matter on his wife's account, the details of which he couldn't possibly divulge before this present company.

"Now, if you will excuse me, honourable caballeros, while I have a word or two with Gerardo," who all this time had pulled and tugged at the doctor's sleeve in order to attract his attention.

"This way, Doctor Gómez, if you please," pressed Gerardo in urgent tones, leading the medical man away from the others, who were all looking on with knowing, amused grins on their faces.

"Well, Gerardo, how are we?" which was asked somewhere behind the stables.

"Fair to middling I'd say, Doctor, fair to middling."

"We are cheerful enough today at any rate, which is a good sign. We're happy and healthy, are we not?"

"Apart from an odd twinge of late, Doctor."

"An odd twinge you say. Explain yourself more fully my good fellow, I beg of you."

"Well, I sometimes feel a kind of twinging pain here in my –" Gerardo pointed. "Here in my groin. It comes and goes like."

"Let us see your tongue … Say 'Argh!'"

Gerardo emitted a noise which reminded the doctor of a death rattle.

"Good, splendid! We are enormously pleased. Yes, we are doing very well indeed. And are our bowels behaving as they should? Properly regulated are we? My dear fellow, we can now put away our tongue. Thank you."

"Usually regular, Doctor, except when I'm not regular which is fairly regular. You see, I was constipated for a bit last month."

"Constipated, were we? For how long exactly did we suffer this bout of inconvenience?"

"Around seven or eight days or thereabouts. I lost count. Then I drank a spill of water from some stagnant pool and I was no longer constipated. I had diarrhoea for four full days."

This was all grist for the mill as far as señor Gómez was concerned, as he listened with Hippocratic solicitude. However, Gerardo was no near finished yet as he bent the good doctor's ear, rabbiting on about his many recent ailments, real or imagined. Tirelessly and relentlessly and monotonously.

"Well, we shall see what the future holds for us, but we are in fine fettle today," said the now exasperated doctor, attempting to cut short the consultation, as he was forced to do on previous occasions.

The good Gómez at last gave up on him.

"You are suffering from hypochondria, you know that, don't you?"

"Ahh!" breathed out Gerardo with evident satisfaction, "I knew there was something other than my aches and groin pains."

"Well, I must make haste for San Stefan, pressing business you know," making off purposely back to his waiting vehicle.

The tall – now less jaunty – figure of the doctor waved somewhat wearily to the group of still grinning rancheros, and boarded his old, tank-sized jalopy. The vintage engine coughed and noisily fired up, gears crashed heavily, and the machine jump-started into a forward motion. It roared away like some wounded prehistoric beast.

Gerardo, plainly gratified, had allowed his exhausted interlocutor to finally escape his clutches. Gerardo stood with stomach drawn in in a stance of stony hardiness, chest out like a puff-adder.

"I like your open four-seater!" he shouted at the rolling dust-cloud, with all the manly, full-throated bellow of a Class A healthy specimen of humanity.

The particularity here must now be explained, because the reason the rancheros had looked on with those knowing, amused grins was over the simple fact that Doctor Marcos Luis Gómez … was in fact a fully trained bona fide veterinary surgeon. And in his professional capacity he considered Gerardo to be as sound as a strapping Siberian stallion.

FIFTH INTERLUDE

It is the minutiae of everyday life which generally goes unrecorded, and animals in particular are sadly neglected in this respect. One might ponder the question, that if animals were as clever as humans would they write a history of their own various species? And of the small and inconsequential things of everyday life? ...

In a cornfield near the town of Celaya a large male rat was scuttering along a furrow, his whiskered nose to the earth. He stopped in his tracks, nose up and twitching. He could not see too well but was able to discern something ahead of him. It was one of those two-legged creatures. A dangerous species of animal.

The rat sensed no immediate danger or fear however because the other creature was stationary. It dropped its leg skins and squatted in a furrow. No, there was nothing to fear here, instinct told the rat. In point of fact the other creature, also a male, was quite vulnerable, particularly as his lower skin was shed around his hocks. He busied about the furrow with utter complacency and satisfaction. Then he snatched a handful of leaves and wiped his tail end. Up came the skin again.

The rat watched carefully and curiously as the creature kicked earth over his droppings. The soil halted the hot stink of dung, and in time would undergo a change of chemical composition and enrich the soil for the growth of plants and things.

The man-creature moved on, in an opposite direction, the rat still cautiously watching him with black beady eyes. Then the rat continued on his way too, in his daylong, lifelong search for sustenance.

In a place called Emancipación in the state of Zacatecas a man beat his own donkey to death with a heavy hardwood stick. The donkey had been his only means of transportation, his beast of burden, his sole means of livelihood. The unfortunate animal had merely acted temporarily recalcitrant – because it was half-starved – and brutally killed for it. The man later got drunk on mezcal; after that, he could no longer afford to drink.

And somewhere on the high road between Fresnillo and Sain Alto, in the same state, a donkey was hit by a speeding truck, and died in terrible agony of its injuries.

While in a small pueblo near Camacho, also in Zacatecas, a man gave his best donkey to his son-in-law, newly married a week ago. And the son-in-law was overjoyed with the generous gift and deeply grateful. He made sure that his beast was always well fed and watered, and carried no burden beyond its capacity. In short, the animal was greatly taken care of, and prove of lasting value to its new owner.

Three mares dropped their foals on a ranch in Chihuahua, within half an hour of one another. In a high pine forest in Oaxaca a lone hunter's rifle jammed as he sighted a white-tailed deer, and the creature ran deeper into the forest and safety.

While in a brooding blue-green woodland area of Campeche a sleek fawn-coloured jaguar mated with another of the same colouring. A rare and notable event for such a rare species of cat, once revered almost as a god by the ancient Olmec Indians of 3,000 years ago.

Somewhere in the Sierra de los Alamitos in Coahuila a groundling mouse searched about for titbits of food. She was an old mouse, had borne seven litters in her long mouselife, and was purblind with old age. Her fur was patchy, scabby and sore, because of constant scratching, an unwilling host to sand fleas.

Now tottering about the terrain, it was a poor and miserable existence for her. She peered listlessly and myopically up above, but there was nothing there except the vast deep blue of the Coahuilan desert sky. She wandered aimlessly on and out in the open.

Moments later a hawk swooped down and snatched her with its crampon talons, took her into the rarefied air. Her neck was broken, but that was not how she had died. The moment the hawk had hit her, she frighted, and her old heart blessedly failed her.

No more would she bear litters of young, or ever go hungry again, or feel any more pain and discomfort.

And the sand fleas jumped instinctively and unhesitatingly into the down feathers of the predator hawk.

Part Seventeen

89

The Annual Race

Near mid-August and many fiestas were underway at this time up and down the country. There even seemed a carnival atmosphere prevailing on the ranchlands.

It was the time of the racing. The rancheros were out on a favoured section of the range which bordered the tiny pueblito of San Juan. Don Roberto's regular cowmen were in the vicinity, organising their own races. There were also crowds of spectators, drawn from the simple adobe huts of San Juan. Others arrived from further afield.

A fair number of the onlookers were women, their heads blue-wrapped with traditional rebozos. Scores of unruly kids ran about playing their own games and shrieking with laughter. Many of the boys pretended to be race horses 'galloping' on two legs, neighing and snorting for a realistic effect. While some little girls staidly and shyly clutched at their mothers' homespun skirts, watching the boys with slight contempt.

Pancho saw two boys in the crowd, bunching up a small drove of brown-coated goats. He ordered José to clear them off to the hill-slopes, or at least away from the racing tracks. And there were not a few old men, retired ranchero types, small and gnarled and wiry, with tattered straw sombreros tilting cockily over dark wrinkled faces; ready to observe and pass judgement over every procedure with attentive professional interest. And making small bets among themselves, exchanging in low value centavos.

Pancho's men had earlier soaped and greased and polished for the event. Horse-saddles shone like new, and so did the boots and spurs. They were sportily clad in almost new tightly fitted ranchero striped pantalones. Denim shirts and leather vests brushed down, inside bands of their sombreros washed of sweat and grime and dust. Tulia's cooking fat generously rubbed into thick black hair and combed through with a currycomb.

Emilio had enjoyed an early night of sleep. Gerardo, apparently free of aches and ailments, dressed at his most spiffiest, gussied up and prinked with a bright crimson silk bandanna, as though he were a mariachi player. His compadres were amused at the idea of Gerardo masquerading as a foppish poseur.

"Who's a pretty boy, then?" Cándido teased him.

The rancheros were about ready for the first race.

To be more truthful however it was not so much a race but rather a test of skill in horse control and co-ordination. The idea was to gallop full out over a flat stretch of ground and halt exactly over a chosen spot where a centavo coin was placed.

"I'm putting the centavos three paces apart," announced Pancho, the self-appointed steward, organiser and judge; and as a racing official he ought properly to wear a badge so stating, if such a thing existed – which didn't in this case. The men agreed however by the rules they had themselves drawn up.

"Here will do nicely – and over here … Whoever goes first will set off from that cactus there," he went on, pointing his arm. "From that direction you should catch a glint of the sun on your centavo," glancing at possible contenders.

He looked around him questioningly. "Hmm … Now, who's the challenger?"

"I am," said José darkly, and speculative eyes turned his way.

Pancho paused a moment in order to persuade the others that he was inclined to give this matter some serious consideration.

"Bueno, fair enough, and who are you challenging, amigo?" he asked presently.

The other pointed to Cándido. "He'll do," he said, slyly grinning.

"Okay, Cándido, is it?"

"Fine with me," charmingly smiled the younger man.

"Fair enough, and that's good enough," said Pancho officiously. Then, forgetting his dignified mantle of officialdom, he turned and spat in the dust. "As you see, José," he carried on urbanely, "your centavo is placed one pace in front of Cándido's, so you set off one pace ahead of him by the cactus, just as the rules state, okay? Muy bien. One last thing, riders don't touch on the track – instantly disqualified if you do – so keep yourselves well apart. Three paces apart to be exact, eh? And you call the start as well, José, in your own time of course.

"That's it, I guess – wouldn't you say, Gerardo?" addressing his assistant steward.

"I guess so," guessed Gerardo agreeably.

With his smart, spiffy apparel, including the snazzy red silk bandanna, his usually unkempt hair greased and slicked down; in spite of all these improvements made upon his person, there was nothing to infringe on his innate ugliness. All the same, thought Pancho kindly, quite a transformation from the limp, scruffy, crumpled figure that Gerardo normally portrayed.

"Who's a pretty boy then!" again voiced Cándido cooingly.

"Well off you go, hermanos – ¡Pronto!" ordered the old ranchero with officious curtness.

José and Cándido cantered easily on to the allotted position by a solitary cactus plant some eight hundred paces away, a cloud of dust following in their wake. The watching crowds, many not knowing exactly what was going on, began to cheer the relatively slow moving cloud of dust behind each rider.

"José is damned fast on a horse," said Gerardo. "We all know that."

"Cándido can shift too when he wants to," countered Juan, rooting for his friend.

"The one essential element in this," put in Emilio, "is to stop dead where the centavo lies. You can ride as fast as you like but for scoring crucial points it's stopping where that centavo is which counts."

"Do you know what Herodotus said about horses in his *Histories?*" the old man asked of anyone who might be listening.

"No," said Gerardo, "not unless you tell us."

"He said that the ancient Massagetae barbarians worshipped the sun and used to offer the horse as a sacrifice."

"A horse as sacrifice!" exploded Gerardo, utterly appalled at the notion. "The damned barbarians!"

"Well, that's what they were, barbarians, as I've only just told you. But do you know why they sacrificed horses?"

"No, unless you're going to tell us."

"Because it was considered the fastest of all the mortal creatures and the only one fit for sacrifice to the speediest of the gods – that sun in the sky."

"Well, as I say, José is fast on –"

"THEY'RE OFF!"

90

José Wins a Race

José and Cándido. José full in the lead, having an extra pace at the start-off. Dashing along the dusty track, the horses whiplashed on left and right flanks, eyes rolling and bulging, dust spewing up behind them. And the crowds seething with excitable chatter; shouting and whooping with energy.

A hundred paces into the run now and the two riders were neck-and-neck. They were grinning or grimacing, one could not tell which. But certainly they were gritting their teeth as the dust spumed up around them. The horses ran free-reined, whips spitting at them like snake venom. On they raced, galloping flat out.

"Come on, you burros!" shouted Emilio, his buck teeth shining in the clear sunlight.

Gerardo placed two fingers in his mouth and blew a long piercing whistle.

"Go it, go, Cándido!" bawled the boy, trying to outshout the others.

Pancho watched the riders, gauging the distance left to them, counting the seconds in his head.

Less than two-hundred paces to go, the pair of racers still running neck-and-neck. The sun picked out a gleam of sweat on the wind-whipped horses, hooves hammering thunderously over the land.

José began to take the front by a head.

The dust clouded high and the sound of the hooves increased as they ran between lines of spectators waving and shouting and stamping their feet. The folk of San Juan cheered madly for José, who comes from their pueblo, urging the rider on. And on came the two of them, heads low, faces intent and strained, wildly digging spurs in the horses' flanks.

Ten short paces to go. The crucial stage of this race, the vital element of correct timing and control. A deep roar erupted from the crowds.

"WHOA!"

José stopped dead with his mount, Cándido one full second behind him. The two horses reared their heads. Pancho rushed to them.

"Hold still! Hold still, damn it!" he called out, eyeing the position of each man's centavo. "A hand in front of yours, José," he told the challenger. "Cándido, you're half a pace too short, my friend."

People started to collect around the two mounted men, chattering with excitement, looking on the riders as if they were film stars. Among the men a few side bets may have been made here.

"José is the winner!" declared Gerardo gustily.

"Hush your lip, you," growled Pancho, "that's my job as steward – José wins this first race!" he grinned.

José began to show off, taking the reins and moving his feet, pushing his dappled grey colt in a tight 180-degree turn one way and then the other as he screwed and sidled his mount. The crowds backed off, smiling uncertainly.

"Okay, José, you're still the challenger," said the old man, "so who's your next victim going to be?"

"Gerardo!"

"Oh no, I'm out of it this year," said Gerardo, putting on an agonised look, "on account of my back. I still haven't got over that muscle strain. You can count me out, por favor." So the chronic hypochondriac was not free of aches and pains after all.

"¡Újule, hombre!" snapped Pancho in near disgust, giving Gerardo a dirty look.

"Emilio, then," declared the challenger.

"Ah no, not for me," returned the fat man apologetically. "I could never win or even come near, not with José, and everybody knows it, surely. It wouldn't be a fair race, would it? Where is the competition? Challenge someone else, hombre. We want to see some real action anyway, don't we?"

A surrounding crowd of old men, mostly retired rancheros, mumbled their disapproval. Pancho felt he was being made to look embarrassed. He was embarrassed. He glared at the two fall-outs with utter disfavour.

Then José's dark eyes fell on the boy.

"Juanito!" he cried.

"That's fine with me," smiled Juan, emulating his friend Cándido. He swiftly leapt into the saddle on Chapulín.

The boy turned his mount and the bay side-stepped with neat precision, first one way then the next, as if executing a dance routine. The clever, comical movements proved a crowd-pleaser, causing them to roar with delight and amusement.

José lordly walked his colt back to the starting point, Juan casually following at the same pace.

"How are the vaqueros doing over there?" asked Gerardo, indicating the other racing teams from the cowmen.

"They say Victor has won twice so far," Emilio told him.

Said Pancho, "Those wins, they go with his name."

"Never mind those *cow*boys," said Cándido. "Any bets on Juanito winning this one?"

Said Pancho, "Didn't know you were a betting man, hermano."

"He won't beat José," predicted Emilio. "He's only a kid."

Said Pancho, "One mean fast smart kid."

"Fifty-fifty chance I'd say," gambled Gerardo.

"It'll be close, I reckon," proffered Pancho, "but the boy will have the style, I know that much. And Chapulín is a swift and strong beast too."

"You reckon?" said Cándido. "Well, I say he'll beat José outright. José must be tired by now. Any bets, then? Come on. No bets?"

"Look, he's only a kid," repeated Emilio.

"So? That's to his advantage : lighter weight, quicker reflexes – these things count you know."

"And Chapulín," put in Pancho, "is like an extension of the muchacho himself."

"That's what I say –"

"THEY'RE AWAY!"

91

José Runs Again...

The distant drumming got gradually louder as the racing pair came on, tearing along the track. Juan overtook José after the first six seconds, stayed ahead for the entire race. The boy never used his whip. He was low in the saddle, his head near to Chapulín's own, urging the bay on with fierce murmurings and soft clicking sounds. They were as one body, as the old ranchero had stated, with one purpose and a single goal. Chapulín stretched his neck, stretched the whole length of himself, and flew across the ground effortlessly it seemed to everyone watching.

The grace and speed of the chestnut bay was a wonder to behold. Running with the wind, dark mane streaming, hard muscles cording and flexing, hooves hitting lightly on the earth. Pancho watched in awe and admiration. So too did the retired rancheros, recognising quality and skill when they saw it. And the crowds madly cheered.

José, face tight with taut nerves of concentration, lashed at his mount's foam-flecked flanks and crupper. The end was near.

"WHOA!"

The old ranchero dashed to them, quickly assessed the halted positions. He pursed his lips in deliberation. "About a hand short this time, José," he announced in a neutral tone of voice. "Juanito is short as well, by two hands at least, muchacho. A close one. That's damned good, my boy. Well, José wins again."

"Well done, hermano," grinned Gerardo, "and you too, Juanito. That was fine riding, a treat to see."

"It was too," agreed Cándido. "Superb stuff. Good work, amigo."

Juan felt proud and pleased with his efforts, and thanked the men in turn. He let José know how impressive was his own effort, which José gallantly acknowledged with a genuine smile of gratitude and thanks.

There was a pause in the proceedings, then …

"Pancho!"

"Uuy, what is it now?"

"I'm challenging you," said José, "that's what it is now." He looked arrogant and haughty, switched his mount from one side to the other, arched forward over the pommel of his saddle.

"Do you not want a break first?" asked Gerardo. "You are entitled to one, you know."

"I'm okay," José let him know in an easy, casual tone. Adrenaline coursed through him and he was not going to stop now. He grinned, adding, "I'm only just getting into my stride."

Gerardo cast a critical eye on the sweat and foam soaked dappled grey colt. "Your mount looks all done in," he grated disapprovingly.

"He's okay. Like me, ready for more."

"Go on, Pancho, you show him then," encouraged Emilio.

"I can be steward," gloated Gerardo.

"Would you like a stool to mount your Macha, old man?" Cándido cocked a crossed eye and gave a wide smile at Pancho.

"Don't ever laugh at the old, muchacho, just hope you get there yourself."

The ranchero swung youthfully up into the saddle, trotted off to the cactus starting point without so much as a backward glance. José trailed behind him.

Gerardo began to breathe heavily – or it may have been a sigh – looking interestedly around him, soaking up the atmosphere with satisfaction. Some people were staring at him, he noticed, probably taking him for the race official, which of course he was, albeit temporarily. Or they were perhaps admiring his bright crimson silk bandanna – or they may simply have stared at his striking, uncompromising ugliness. He self-consciously adjusted his bandanna.

"This will be one hell of a race," said Cándido, "for old Pancho always has lots of tricks up his sleeve."

"Tricks? Are you implying some form of cheating? Are you saying he won't be abiding by our rules?" wanted to know Gerardo, conscious of his status as temporary steward.

"I mean he's a man of long experience, that's what I mean."

"Will he be able to beat José, though? That's the thing," said Emilio.

"He wiped him out completely last year, remember? Beat him soundly."

"Ah, but he's got his age against him now," gainsaid Gerardo.

"Hellfire, they're *both* a year older, and José is no spring bantam neither," Cándido threw back. "I tell you I'm betting on Pancho myself."

"Me, too," said Juan with feeling. "My bet is on Pancho."

"Look, he's an old man," pushed Emilio.

"So? That's to his advantage : longer experience, careful strategies…"

"Careful strategies!" scoffed the fat man.

"It's hard to tell, I suppose," began Gerardo. "But then, as Steward I'm not supposed to make any comment, for or against –"

"OFF THEY GO!"

92

... and Again

José was well in the lead along the first hundred and fifty paces, then the old ranchero suddenly caught up with him. Only two seconds ago Pancho was at least a horse-length behind his competitor, next he was right there with him, stayed with him like a leech. They ran together for the rest of the race.

Macha was fleet and sure of foot, running splendidly. Like the boy, Pancho was as one with his mount; and like Juan he too had no need of the whip. He rode hard and tight, low in the saddle, giving Macha her head. His sombrero was wind-squared at the front as he raced on, going at such a pace that his denim shirt ballooned out at his back.

"Go for it! Go on!" everyone shouted lustily, each plugging for a chosen favourite.

On the final stretch the riders were dangerously close to each other and could collide at any moment, or so it appeared to the spectators looking on. If they did come into a collision the race would automatically be scrubbed and declared void; and only if they survived crashing into one another.

Yet each rider ran true in his own narrow stretch of track, a testimony to their horsemanship skills. They had the full and undivided attention of everybody. The campesino spectators, normally morose and taciturn, were gleefully jumping about with great excitement, waving and roaring to the thrill of the race. Even the old retired rancheros were momentarily 'young' again, skipping on booted feet, agitated in a vigour of movement.

"WHOA!"

Gerardo was there in an instant, strained back muscles quite forgotten, to measure with his own eyes the end result of the riders' sudden jarring halt.

"José! Half a hand below – short, that is," he shot out with splendid aplomb and authority. "And Pancho … Damn it but I can't see where the centavo is."

The old ranchero, irrepressible as his nature intended, with devil-may-care nonchalance, leaned over to one side of his saddle and spat in the dust.

"Lift her right foreleg," he commanded, smiling with utter self-assurance and complacency. He stood in his stirrups, in his fist the reins held taut as a bowstring. "The right I said, not the left, see it?"

"Well, I'll be a – " Gerardo was stuck for speech. When he lifted Macha's foreleg, there was the little centavo shining boldly dead centre of her hoof-print.

"My God, Pancho wins this one!" called Cándido happily.

"Hold on, you, that's for me to say," Gerardo told him. He stood erect and raised an arm, loudly declared, "Francisco Ramírez is the winner! Absolutely spot on the target, couldn't be bettered."

"There's no ranchero like an old ranchero," said Emilio with significance, as if it were a famous quote.

"Well done, Pancho!" the boy enthusiastically congratulated his dear friend and mentor.

"That's a win two years in a row," glowed Gerardo, impressed.

"Three times in five years, I believe," smiled Cándido, "just to keep the record straight."

"It was a damn good race and all," conceded José graciously.

"Ay que caray, amigo," Pancho sang pleasantly, "you do belt on with that colt of yours," warmly slapping the loser's back.

The fact of the matter was, Pancho had anticipated the race this year, feeling it might possibly be his last, and had secretly trained for it. But then, so had José practiced on the sly. As it turned out however he was no match for the old maestro – There is no ranchero like an old ranchero, as Emilio had so fittingly put it.

Having no further interest in racing José thought it time for a well deserved smoke, but managed to find only a very small stub end of a cigarro in his vest pocket. When he came to light it he almost set aflame the clusters of hair growing out from his nostrils.

An old retired ranchero, perhaps taking pity on him, ambled forward and offered the racing man a full fat commercially made cigarette. The oldie had in fact won a bit of money betting on José's first two races.

Moments later Cándido said, "Uh-oh, what's this? One of the *cow*boys is riding over this way."

"Who is it?" asked Emilio.

93

A Challenge

Presently a thickset coarse-faced man with craggy brows rode forward, reining in his mount before Pancho. He was one of don Roberto's cowmen, a hacienda foreman. No doubt he had organised the races among his own men, some of whom slowly brought their mounts forward, eager looks on their faces.

"We've got a challenger for you, Pancho," said the foreman in friendly tones.

"Ah, Manuel. A *vaquero*, eh?" The old man looked pleased, and a little curious too.

"Not exactly, compadre," said the other pleasantly. "He's a young contender from the pueblito, wanting to try out his wings as it were."

"Bueno. Let's see him. Where is he?"

Manuel turned in his saddle. "Have him come forward, hermanos."

The men manoeuvred their mounts to one side, allowing passageway for the contending rider to show himself.

Pancho immediately expressed astonishment when he saw him. He was a mere muchacho. He could not be any more than fourteen or fifteen years, the old man guessed. Mounted on a well-formed strawberry roan colt. Where had that animal come from? he wondered. The boy shyly nudged his horse to the front of the pack of riders.

He was small and lithe, a little dark-haired Adonis. Large coffee-brown eyes gazed steadily and expectantly at the old ranchero. Pancho was debating a slight problem in his mind. The roan was bare-backed, it had no saddle.

"No saddle, I see," addressing the foreman Manuel.

"He always rides without one," returned Manuel.

"There are certain rules, as you know, amigo."

"I know that, Pancho, but is this so important − for just this once? He rides so well without a saddle, like an Indian − but he's no Indian. He only wants a chance. You'll let the lad run, compadre?" the other pleaded hopefully, as if he had read the old man's thoughts. "He'd like to take you on, and he can ride, I can assure of that − otherwise how could I allow it?"

Pancho was yet to accede to this unusual request. He looked steadfastly at the boy.

"What's your name, muchacho?"

"Jesús, señor. Jesús Sierro."

"From San Juan, is it?"

"Sí, señor." The boy guided the roan nearer to this famed ranchero whom he'd had the audacity to dare him with a challenge. Or someone had put him up to it, mused Pancho to himself. If the muchacho was at all apprehensive, it did not show on his face. His features in fact still bore the keen expectancy as before.

Pancho took a closer inspection of the boy. He noticed at once livid sores on his upper lip and both his ears. Scar tissue and excrescences covered the young one's neck and the backs of his hands.

So, he was from the leprosarium, that much was evident.

"You know the rules, Jesús Sierro?" The old man's tone was more curt than courteous.

"Sí, señor," the boy nodded eagerly. He turned to smile at the foreman Manuel. His challenge was accepted it seemed, and he glanced gratefully at the coarse-faced cowman as if it were all his doing.

"We vaqueros have been racing a longer run," Manuel spoke directly to the old ranchero. "Any chance of increasing the length of your run − say, from the mesquite there?" indicating a thorny shrub-like tree some seven or eight hundred paces further on from the cactus starting point.

Easily doubles the run. "Alright with me," readily agreed Pancho. "But tell me, Manuel, who set the muchacho up for this? Because someone sure did. Was it you, by any chance?"

"No, no!" laughed the cowman. "If you must know, it was that new priest at the lepers' place. Father Felipe, is it? It was his idea."

So, Father Felipe was behind it. I wonder what the canny padre is up to here? thought Pancho.

"He said the boy ought to give it a try," Manuel told him, "and to challenge the best of them."

"Ah, did he now?"

"His very words, compadre."

"Ah … hmm." Pancho obviously had nothing further to say.

He motioned Macha round, with a nod of acknowledgement at Manuel, and cantered away to the new starting place where the lone mesquite tree stood. The crowd of horsemen broke away, Jesús Sierro followed the old ranchero, holding on to the roan's thick mane.

"He's a damned leper!" voiced José in disgust moments later.

"Who is?" asked Gerardo, a little confused.

"That kid. He must be from the leper colony. This shouldn't be allowed, you know."

Said Cándido, "Oh, stop your clack, you old aunty."

Enquired Gerardo, "He's got leprosy, you say?"

"No, he's got pimples on his cheeks," José snapped back.

Gerardo gesticulated. "He's diseased then. We'll all get it. Our faces will drop off!"

"In your case is that so bad?" cut in Cándido at that juncture. "Hellfire, Gerardo, it's not contagious, you know."

"I always thought leprosy was contagious."

"You thought wrong. It's not contagious, it's been proved."

"Well, I don't intend going anywhere near him. I catch things easily, I do."

The rancheros continued squabbling as Pancho and the boy held their mounts ready by the mesquite tree in the near distance. The two riders appeared to be in conference, heads close together.

He has no saddle either, said someone, probably Gerardo. Drop off as well, did it? Cándido laced into him. What chance had he against Pancho? Someone else said. We'll soon find out, won't we? The rules state, a proper saddle cinched secure.

"Oh, shut it. Leave off."

"THERE THEY GO!"

94

Jesús Sierro

A sudden dustcloud formed where the two riders shot off. For the first several hundred paces they rode close as though harnessed together, running a fair fast speed. Along either side of the ill-defined racetrack people shouted and waved them on.

Jesús Sierro felt sheer exhilaration in this all-out mad gallop, the wind hard in his face. He gripped the roan's mane in clenched fists, knees clamped tight to the horse's flanks. He was conscious of a tremendous speed and a sense of freedom it gave him, as though he were in flight. It was good for once to be away from the hateful miserable existence he had to endure within the thick-walled confines of the old leprosarium. This was more like it, he exulted, running hard and fast with the famous Francisco Ramírez. A great moment indeed for the boy, an experience to be long remembered.

There on each side of him, instead of being shunned as a leper, the folk cheered and waved sombreros and rebozos, the vision blurred by speed and wind tears, voices lost in a thunder of hooves.

Pancho hardly gave his young challenger a glance. It was more than he could do to concentrate on his riding and to keep up with his racing adversary. This muchacho is a damned natural, he soon realised. Better than Juan, better than his own rancheros. And, it had to come out, even better than himself. There was no doubt of it, this kid was an expert and flawless horseman. He rode like an Indian brave of the old American West, with an apparent ease and verve which astonished the now struggling old man. Yet Jesús Sierro was but a boy. Some kind of prodigy all the same.

The mare and the roan colt sped on, hooves flying, hitting dust and gravel on the stone-hard ground. They pelted along head by head as before, a long line of raised dust boiling up behind them. The spectators roared and urged them on to a greater speed.

When they reached three-quarter the length of their extensive run, something quite unexpected happened. It was then that a child on his own decided to toddle across the path of the onrushing riders. In a nearby crowd a woman screamed.

Pancho and the boy, instantly alerted to the danger, saw the little figure barely yards ahead of them, and took quick evasive action only just in time. They veered sharply away from one another and the child, rode over rough ground beyond the stretch of racing track, where a collection of onlookers backed in an instinctive way. A thick dustcloud whipped about the toddler as the two riders galloped on past him, left enveloped in a fog of dust. He began to wail.

Only seconds later Macha's hooves hit large loose rocks. The level ground was gone, here was treacherous rock and stone. She lost her grip on solid earth, slipped on one hoof, going too fast to correct her balance. Macha was over on her side an instant later, rider half under her. She rolled once, ending on her chest, rear legs splayed. The ranchero rolled too, like a large chunky ball, till his momentum spent itself.

Tense seconds ticked away. Pancho, disoriented and somewhat confused, shook his head, blinked dust out of his eyes. People began crowding round him. His first conscious action was to put a hand to his head. Yes, thankfully, his sombrero was still firmly stuck where it should be. There was hope yet for his swiftly diminishing dignity – that all-important pride which meant so much to him.

He sat up, felt himself all over, to discover no bones broken. He was however badly bruised, including his precious ego. The old man got shakily to his feet, head down as he slapped dust from himself to hide his acute embarrassment. Just about *everybody* was there it seemed to him.

Then he immediately dismissed *everybody* as of no consequence and thought instead of his mare. Is Macha alright?

A wall-eyed retired ranchero brought his mount to him, courteously passed over the reins. Pancho thanked the man, then checked over Macha's legs and ribs. He suspected a strained tendon on the right hind-leg. Otherwise she was okay too, he realised with a mighty flood of relief.

Cándido and Juan rode into view, scattering the milling crowd. They leapt from their mounts and rushed to the old man.

"Are you okay?" they asked in unison, with expressions of deep concern. "I'm okay."

"You're sure of that?"

"I'm fine, just fine. Don't fuss," he answered them, gazing about with a bewildered and abstracted air. "Did the kid reach his centavo?" he wanted to know.

"Reach it!" exclaimed Cándido. "Why, the kid won it hands down. He stopped dead on that damned centavo. Gerardo will verify it. It was simply unbelievable. The roan's left fore-hoof rested squarely on the coin."

"Amazing as well how he stayed on the horse's back," said Juan breathlessly, "when he halted so suddenly like that. With no saddle! It was brilliantly done."

The old man rubbed his jaw. Still shaken up a bit he tried to collect himself, to relax and forget his present humiliation. But no one seemed to be aware, to know or care what he was going through. The folk regarded him as they had always done, with warmth and affection.

He glanced around him again, saw Jesús Sierro on his strawberry roan colt there in front of him. The boy put a hand to one scabrous, leprous ear, picking at it in his present nervous agitation. The old ranchero's fall had somehow spoilt his magnificent victory.

"Are you alright, señor Ramírez?" he inquired timidly.

Pancho stared at him for what seemed a long time. "Dismount, young fellow," he ordered him rather curtly. The boy obeyed. "Here, muchacho, come here."

Jesús Sierro stepped forward with hesitant steps to face the greatly renowned horseman Francisco Ramírez. His huge brown eyes gazed apprehensively into the blue eyes of the old man. He had done no wrong, he knew, except beat this famous ranchero at his own game. But he had nevertheless won the race fair and square.

Did the boy feel superior perhaps for having beaten him? Pancho's mind processed this thought. No, that was pride there in his look, surely? And there was pride behind the expression of concern. The boy should be proud all the same for what was a singular achievement. He had run against and beaten one of the best horsemen in the state.

Pancho took in the unsightly sores marring what was a truly handsome, noble countenance. A leper! What a waste of a superlative and peerless horseman. How far he could have gone, this natural born rider. The world would have been his but for the terrible stigma of his physical condition.

The old man felt utter admiration for the way the young rider had conducted himself, from their first meeting less than an hour ago to this present moment. He was massively humbled in this boy's presence.

And another thought suddenly struck him. Father Felipe had a remarkable way with him of picking out God's children.

He took a short step forward, smiling broadly, and embraced the diminutive figure of the leper boy. Jesús Sierro.

95

Eyes and Things

Supper was over. It was a fine clear evening, the stars beginning to show themselves in a fading, lemon-green, moonless sky. Only the mosquitoes bothered the men sitting and loafing around the campfire. Emilio leaned his broad fat back against a bale of straw, and within moments he dropped in a deep contented sleep. José lit a cigarro – a fat one on account of having a goodly supply of tobacco at present – lit it from a smouldering twig of wood snatched from the fire. He pulled in the smoke with evident satisfaction.

Pancho glared at him. He was in the mood now to say what had niggled him for a long stretch of time. "Why do you smoke that donkey dung, José?" he lobbed over at him chidingly.

"This is quality tobacco, I'll have you know. Got it only yesterday."

"It can't be good for you. Most of the time it has you coughing up your lungs."

He told the others around him that he didn't understand this smoking business. It wasn't natural was his opinion on it. The Good Lord did not intend for man to deliberately put harmful smoke into his lungs.

"Imagine this. I'm an innocent fresh from the ancient times and I meet up with José here. I'd watch him fascinated as he rubbed old dry leaves in his hands, roll the mess in a slip of scroll, stick it in his mouth, then set fire to it. Now I ask you, where's the sense in that, eh?"

"I enjoy my smokes," pushed José. He coughed, and went on : "They calm me, like."

"Sure they do, and I hear you every morning coughing your insides out. A very enjoyable business it must be. I'll tell you that Walter Raleigh fellow has a lot to answer for."

"I thought it was Cortes who introduced tobacco to the world," said Gerardo. He slapped a hand at a mosquito tormenting the back of his neck. Looking at the blot of blood – his own – on the palm of his hand, he said with relief, "Well I got that one alright, the little devil."

"Wait a moment," said Pancho, "we're at cross purposes here. Let's ask our educated one –"

"Fire away," smiled Cándido.

"Not you, you half-star brandy, I mean our young Juanito. Who started all this, muchacho?"

"You damn well started it!" cried José heatedly. "When you howled on about me smoking my cigarro. Can't have a decent smoke in peace here."

Pancho ignored the outburst. "Who started this tobacco business, Juanito?" he asked again, glancing paternal-eyed at the boy.

"If you really want to know," said Juan, grinning, "I think it was a man called Morris, from Marlboro country."

"He's kidding us," said Cándido. "Juanito's been with us lot so long the craziness is catching."

"Cándido's catching on too, is it?" chuckled the old man. He leaned to one side and tipped Juan a wink. Then he glanced over the way, his eyes now magnetised to a manganese-violet sky. "You were saying, Juanito?" turning back to the boy.

"It all started here in the Americas," Juan went on in more serious tones, "and was smoked at Indian religious ceremonies. Raleigh took the tobacco plant to Europe –"

"There! What did I just say?" butted in Pancho.

" – The smoking habit then returned to the Americas. Strange, it was only last week when I read about it."

"Well, let's not have any more cross purposes," said José with a sly grin, which meant he had a witticism to throw out, "or our cross-eyed Cándido will want to know why, heh-heh!"

"That's alright, hombre," said the young man, unoffended. "With these eyes of mine I can see where you're going and where you've been as well – *Heh! Heh!*"

Pancho came out with his easy taunting patter : "I do like Cándido's sensible ways, that I do. He elevates your soul, doesn't he just. He has no mind to speak of – or has he? At any rate it's of no matter. If I may so say."

The young man compressed his lips in a show of contempt, then decided to let it ride and changed the subject : "Do you remember Benito who used to be don Roberto's houseboy? House*boy*! Why, he was old, real old – older than you, Pancho."

"No one's older than me," growled the mature gentleman; and, suspecting that he was only joking, Cándido dared to show a patronizing smile.

There was a pregnant kind of silence, everyone glancing at one another. Pancho broke it. "Well?" he continued in the same churlishly growling tone. "What about Benito?"

"Ah, sí," kick-started Cándido. "Old Benito, he used to sleep – fast asleep, mind – with one eye wide open."

"Imagine that," responded José, "sleeping with one of your eyes open. That's pretty weird I'd say, not natural like." He spat in the dust at his feet for emphasize.

"Hmm, well," Pancho piped in, softening his voice somewhat, "Benito always was one to keep an eye on things – even when he's sleeping."

Cándido said, "What about Francisco here?"

Said José, "Who? Oh, Pancho. What about him?"

"Tells me he always knows my every move because he has eyes at the back of his head."

To which José wittily replied, "Can't see where he's going but knows where he's been."

Cándido carried on : "Remember that little señorita from José's pueblo? Pretty thing she was, quite bonita. Only, she had a glass eye –"

"A *glass* eye?" Gerardo was intrigued.

"A glass eye. Brown it was, like her real other one. Even had little flecks in it like a real eye and not a marble. You wouldn't know which eye was the real one when you looked at her."

"And so," interposed Juan, "she married a handsome caballero and lived happily ever after?"

"No, Juanny, didn't she die of some fever that summer when a few went down with it? In your pueblo, José?"

"Sí, I remember, and her name was Panfila. A pretty señorita…"

To this the men instinctively gazed upward, at the dry dusty darkness of the young night, the black-flooded star-speckled nightsky.

"And there's The Evil Eye," said Gerardo.

Said Cándido, "What about it?"

"Well, they say old señora Isabel has the evil eye."

"What exactly is an evil eye?" asked Juan.

"Señora Isabel can give you the evil eye. She only has to stare at you, it is said, and you would wither away like a dead leaf."

"Why," Pancho put in, "our José here could give you one of those."

"That's right," Cándido confirmed. "What you'd call a 'withering' look. Give us one now, José, why don't you?"

José gave him his regular aggressive 'to-hell-with-you' look, which the other candidly considered withering enough.

"Speaking of eyes," Gerardo was off again, "when I was a kid in Dolores I knew a muchacho who had one of his eyes pushed right out from its socket, and his grandmamá gave it a wash and slipped it back in again for him."

"That must have hurt," twitted José.

"No, she never felt a thing," cracked Cándido.

"I wasn't asking you," snarled José, "you squint-eyed comedian."

"Isn't a human eyeball attached to a strand of sinew or something?" asked Juan.

"That's right, and she washed that as well, Juanny," returned Gerardo.

Said Cándido, "In soap and hot water?"

"No, no, you foul-eyed fool! She washed the eye in goat's milk. Sí, she knew what she was about, that old grandmamá. And before she got it sorted, the kid's eyeball bounced up and down just like a yo-yo."

"I once met a man in San Stefan," began Pancho, "when I was there after the feast of Candelaria – forgot which year it was, but some time back – and this fellow had two different coloured eyes. One was brown and the other was blue."

"Well you've got *two* blue eyes which is damned queer for a Mexican," observed José.

"I remember reading somewhere," said Juan, "about Alexander the Great having one green eye and one black."

"Well," smiled Cándido, "José's wife sometimes gives him a black eye – doesn't she, José?"

"I'll black yours for you if you don't shut it," the other retorted. José could always verbally knock other folk down but could never take a dose of it himself without feeling offended.

"Now Pancho Villa, he had green eyes you know, hazel-green they were," offered the old ranchero.

"Hell, you didn't remember that detail, did you?" said Gerardo, scratching for all his worth at another mosquito bite on his wrist.

"No, you're right, hermano, I didn't know of it personally, but a cousin of mine did because he was one of Villa's *dorados*."

"I reckon you are Pancho Villa," said Cándido, "a reincarnation. You've got all his traits and even look like him."

"That's exactly what I once said," put in Juan. "But Villa was an outlaw and an illiterate peasant –"

"Who here isn't?" José broke in.

" – He was a hard man and very brutal at times. I've read a lot now about Pancho Villa. When he was alive they say he was a one for the señoritas. He could easily charm the ladies and they in turn were fascinated by him by all accounts."

"I need say no more," said Cándido. "You can't get closer than that. But I'll tell you what really convinces me that he's Pancho Villa's reincarnation, and it's those black spots he has low on his chest – Show them your black spots, Pancho."

Gerardo wanted to know what that bit of information was supposed to indicate.

"Didn't you know? He was gunned down by government forces, wasn't he? Shot to death in the chest by those *federale* bastards."

At this, Pancho puffed out his chest, pulling a mean villainous face at the men around him.

"Sí, I'm convinced I suppose," agreed Gerardo, glancing over at the historic bandit lookalike.

Cándido continued on: "I mean to say, look at that broad forehead. Look at his moustache, look at his general build, and the way he rides a horse – not to mention that special knack he has of attracting the womenfolk. Oh, he's Pancho Villa alright, you mark my words."

"And I'm Coco the Clown," said José.

"We already know that, hombre," voiced Emilio of a sudden, having come out of a momentary coma.

José chose to ignore the fat one. "There was a man in Durango I once knew," he began, "who only had one eye. He was born with just one eye, the other completely sealed over. They used to call him Cyclops –"

"What!" exclaimed Pancho. "You mean to say his eye was set in the middle of his forehead?"

"No, no, he had one left eye."

"He had one eye left," quipped Cándido.

"But they mostly called him 'One-Eye'," went on José, "and never used his proper name, whatever it was. Folk would say, 'Hey you, One-Eye! Come over here.' My old man was lame most of his life and he used to get called too. Some people have no respect for another's misfortune."

"Hey you, dunghead!" mimicked Emilio. "Come over here."

"If I did," responded José menacingly, "I'd smash in your buck teeth, you horse's mouth."

"You mean you'll try," challenged the fat man. "Don't be too much of an optimist on that score."

This little sally prompted Pancho to tell him that an optimist was the fellow who approached a bull with a milk-pail.

He then dipped a wet finger in a dish of rock-salt, put finger to his mouth to suck, as though it were sweet powdered sherbet. The salt made him thirsty and he sipped from a tin mug of water, all the while wafting a hand at the evening mosquitoes.

"I wish we could get rid of these damn mosquitoes, they're slowly eating us away," Cándido complained.

"I wish I could get rid of this boil on the back of my neck," moaned Emilio. "It hurts like hell."

"Ah, you poor pecan," Pancho teased him. "It's the lousy food you manage to find to eat," he said unsympathetically. "Too many sweet things, too much grease, too many fatstuffs. Not to mention a lack of washing. You should wash more often, hombre, and not forget your neck."

"My sister's got a pimple, a big red one, right on the tip of her nose," Gerardo informed the group.

"I remember old Grandmamá Ruben," said José, "Who had a wart on the end of her chin. It had one thick black hair growing from it, right in the .middle. Looking at that wart was like seeing the back-end of a mouse."

"To get rid of a wart, so they say," began Pancho, "you need to –"

"Lop it off with a machete," cut in Cándido.

"No, you foolish little muchacho, listen. You need a potato and you peel the potato. Cut the potato in half and rub the flat side over the wart three to six times a day. If you do that every day for five years it'll go away – poof! – just like that."

The men watched as fresh wood thrown on the fire began to flare, sparks spitting into the smoky air. The smoke caused the mosquitoes to make a strategic withdrawal.

Said Gerardo, "You know that fellow who comes to visit don Roberto now and then? The bald one with a head shaped like an egg? Well, when the don once caught me calling the fellow 'egghead' he put me to cleaning out his pig-pens."

"When the don puts you to work in his pig-pens," said Pancho, "you can be sure you're in the dog-house."

"I knew a man who had three hands," tossed in Cándido, a bland and innocent expression on his face.

"How was that, then?" Gerardo guffawed. "A man with three hands. What next? Never heard such damned nonsense. Another of your stupid stories I'll wager."

"Met him in town one day at the autobus station. He was struggling with a load of baggage –"

"And you said, 'Do you want a hand?'" Juan anticipated him.

"Ah!" shot out Pancho. "So you knew him as well, did you, Juanito?" which set the rancheros off in fits of laughter.

It was quite dark now, the sky blinking with starglitter. Emilio yawned widely, showing his large teeth in the firelight. Gerardo, on seeing him, yawned too. José, happening to glance in his direction, felt a compulsion to follow suit. He in turn was observed by Cándido who could not help but yawn as well, immediately following José's example. Emilio's eyes were on Cándido and he repeated himself – full circle. Pancho and young Juan saw the entire thing, exchanging knowing looks and chuckling.

"What's the joke?" asked Gerardo glumly.

Pancho white-lied. "I was just saying to Juanito here how certain things in life can be contagious."

"Ah, like diseases you mean?"

"Other things as well," José poked in. "You buy yourself a nice new saddle for your mount and the next minute everybody wants one."

Cándido then opened up. "When my uncle in Querétaro was down with a bad cold a few winters back, he was off work for a week. When he was better and back at his job, everyone in his street were laid up with colds. That's contagion for you."

"They say," began Emilio innocently, "they say that yawning can be contagious."

At this remark Pancho and the boy instantly burst out laughing, and the fat man could not understand why he was so popular all of a sudden.

The woodfire eventually burned itself out and the men retired after another long summer day. Each lay on his back gazing at the blackness of the sky, at the broad straight stardust trail of the Milky Way, at the silent salt-crystal stars.

They dropped off one by one, sleeping through the slow turning of shadow-dark night.

Part Eighteen

96

Father Felipe Returns

"We've got ourselves a visitor, it looks like."

It was Gerardo who had spoken. It was near noon and the rancheros were finishing off a series of training manoeuvres with a batch of chestnut bays, inside and around the main corral.

Everyone stopped what they were doing, gawping over to where Gerardo had pointed. They saw a roly-poly figure of a man astride an extremely decrepit donkey clipping ponderously towards them. The stranger's black garb billowed about him as a hot wind blew gustily against his front, a cloud of dust streaking away behind man and beast.

"Why, it's Father Felipe," said Pancho, "come to visit us heathens and sinners."

"Who's he when he's at home?" asked Cándido cautiously.

"Father Felipe runs the leprosarium over by San Juan."

"Helping old Father Antonio, is he?" Gerardo wanted to know.

"The old priest went on to meet his Maker. Didn't you know? A few weeks ago it was – Father Felipe! ¡Buenos dias! ¿Que paso? Welcome! God be with you, padre, as surely He must. It's good to see you again," as the old ranchero stumped forward to meet the short and portly priest.

"Good morning, Francisco – Gentlemen, a good day to you," said Father Felipe, awkwardly dismounting from the donkey with as much dignity as he could muster under the circumstances. "I trust all is well with you, Francisco? A pleasure to see you too my very dear fellow. In such robust health as well I believe. No more aches from your fall at the races?" His cherubic face beamed at the old man.

"Ah, you know about that, eh?" Pancho rubbed at his jaw with slight embarrassment.

"These are your stalwart fellow *caballeros*, I presume," the priest nodding agreeably to each of the men in turn.

Pancho introduced him to his hardy compatriots one by one. José was quietly respectful as he took the priest's small podgy hand and shook it. Gerardo genuflected in his greeting, looking as stiff and solemn as a chapel statue. For some unknown reason Emilio appeared awestruck and full of reverence. Cándido became cordial and polite, though faintly amused at the sight of this little tubby man.

"We were just about to break off, Father Felipe," said Pancho, his blue eyes merry and bright. "Going to eat soon in point of fact, so your timing is perfect. You will join us in a bite to eat I hope? Nothing fancy, for we're simple folk, and there's always plenty to go round, our Tulia will see to that."

"Your generous hospitality is appreciated and welcomed by yours humbly, Francisco. I accept without hesitation and thank you heartily for it," beamed the priest happily, who had indeed timed it perfectly as he had planned.

"Sit yourself, Father, por favor – Oye, Gerardo, go chase up Julian if you will, for we're sorely starving today, I shouldn't wonder. I know I could easily eat my leather vest, hmm."

"You're forgetting something, Pancho," said José. "Julian has taken the don in his trap to the railroad depot."

"Ah sí, it must have slipped my mind, as these things do."

"You're getting old, that's what it is," Cándido cruelly commented.

"Sí, muchacho," smiled the old ranchero, unoffended, "the longer the life you lead the harder it is to live it, ay caray."

Gerardo gallantly came to the rescue, volunteering to go himself.

"I'll help you," came a young voice from the stable entranceway.

"Who is that, Francisco?" politely inquired the priest, watching a youthful figure loping off with Gerardo.

"Our Juanito, Father Felipe. Juan Ramos, son of don Antonio who owns a farm by San Angelo way."

"Oh, very good. So Julian is not with you I take it?"

The old man saw a bit of disappointment there in the priest's face. "No, Father, I'm afraid not. As José says, he's away on an errand." He deftly changed the subject. "So you've got yourself some transportation, I see," grinning mischievously as he pointed at the pathetic, aged donkey. "Did the villagers saddle you with that? And probably fleeced you too for what looks to me like a big grey bag of bones."

"Oh, but he is strong and sturdy, and not to say totally reliable, I can assure you," the priest continued smiling at everyone before him. "The animal does in fact belong to our small colony. Which I am happy to say is growing larger by and by. I now have some twenty poor souls to administer to."

"Speaking of which, Father, how is that young fellow getting along? Jesús Sierro."

Father Felipe crossed one short fat leg over the other, and managed to hold it so; crossed legs like that an unusual sight for the rancheros, who stared at him as if he had just dropped in from another planet.

"Yes, Jesús. Kind of you to enquire and I'm pleased you have. Actually, I have rather startling news to relate concerning that boy," as he leaned forward slightly, chubby hands resting on fat knees, his whole frame now precariously balanced on the bale he was sat on.

"He's alright, isn't he, Father?"

"Oh absolutely. Very much so, I'm glad to say. That's the whole point of it, you see. Since the day of the horse racing a lot of people have taken an interest in Jesús."

The men too leaned forward on their bales of straw in a hushed expectant manner.

Father Felipe went on. "You see, the entire matter revolves around the boy's exemplary riding skills – his racing skills to be exact. In no time at all it seemed certain bigwigs from Mexico City got wind of it and travelled up to pay us a call. They wanted to meet the boy and see him in action as it were. I was taken fairly aback, I do assure you."

"Riding on that strawberry roan, maybe?"

"Just so, Francisco."

"Where did he get that horse, might I ask?"

"It was on loan to him from don Luis. You know don Luis?"

"Sí, the food marketing man. A very rich fellow as we understand."

"Exactly so my friend. That is where the horse came from. Well now, there was a most extraordinary occurrence only two days after the important visitors returned to Mexico City."

Father Felipe, in some apparent need of religious support, uncrossed his legs and delved into the folds of his cassock and brought out his breviary.

His soft podgy fingers fondled the little leather book in his lap, in much the same manner as a blind person feeling an object he cannot identify.

"An American fellow showed up in my office at the leprosarium. He was from San Antonio, Texas, so he informed me, and he too wanted to see Jesús ride. Do you know, he spent the entire day with us and we talked for hours in my office.

"This American fellow had a great deal to say…"

The rancheros were hooked. They glanced at one another and then back to the priest, like a gathering of acolytes before an oracle. They seemed to sense that something of perhaps a religious nature was about to unfold.

Their countrywise intuitive feelings were not far off the mark …

97

Good News

*T*he rancheros listened raptly as Father Felipe disclosed how there might possibly be a chance of recovery from the boy's present medical state, so the American had so stated and strongly believed. After all, Jesús was only in the early stages of leprosy, the priest emphasised. The Texan stranger wanted to see what could be done about it.

He stayed overnight at the leprosarium, using Father Felipe's own living quarters. It was already agreed that the American, a wealthy rancher and owner of several famous race horses, should take total responsibility for the boy's welfare, and perhaps his future too.

On the following day he left for Mexico City to sort out a visa, and then later flew back to the United States, taking Jesús Sierro with him. The boy was placed in a special isolation ward of a hospital in Houston, Texas.

"Which is really why I came along to see you today, Francisco," smiled the priest, "as I knew that you would be interested. Well hear this my friend. I received a long-distance telephone call early this morning. Very good news, you'll be pleased to learn. Jesús is apparently quite settled in and happy where he is. It seems from what the doctors say there is every hope of the boy making a full recovery. *A full recovery!*"

Father Felipe slapped his knees with marked enthusiasm, face shining red with pleasure. The men put on pleased and satisfied smiles on their faces, nodding gleefully at one another as if it had been all their doing.

Father Felipe continued. "It has been reported and passed on that Jesús is already responding favourably to the specialist treatment he is receiving there in the Houston hospital. Isn't that rather wonderful?" – The horsemen readily agreed with vigorous nods and wide grins – "It will of course take some time to make headway, I was informed by the kindly Texan rancher – a great deal of time it would appear. Be that as it may, the essential matter is that the boy is definitely going to be alright. He should, if things work out as predicted, become a normal healthy boy."

The priest blinked at Pancho with moist, emotive eyes. "I wanted you to know that, Francisco," he concluded, lifting out a grubby handkerchief so as to wipe his nose.

"This is great news," said the old ranchero, delighted over the outcome, "and you couldn't have brought me anything better." The men too again nodded and smiled at the priest and at one another.

"I knew that you would be pleased," sighed Father Felipe, cherubic cheeks happily gleaming.

"But tell me, Father, how on earth did these people find out about the boy in the first place? I mean those characters from Mexico City and this Texan hombre."

"I couldn't honestly say how it all came about, Francisco. Perhaps because of Jesús's recent reputation as a racing horseman – though still a boy. The news of such spectacular displays as he has shown are quickly known and bandied about, wouldn't you say?" Father Felipe put on his enigmatic smile which the old man was now beginning to recognise.

Pancho gave some thought to the talented leper boy who had thumped a dent in his own reputation. Maybe he would go far, as he had once felt he ought to. At any rate events of moment were already set in motion, for Jesús was already in the United States, where he would certainly gain from the best possible medical treatment.

Maybe he *will* have the world at his feet. One thing was a surety, old Pancho realised at once. Jesús Sierro would not be returning to the San Juan Leprosarium.

"The stars are shining even now," he declared with delight, "and it's nigh on noon."

"Stars shining?" said Cándido cockily. "Where?"

"Only we can't see them till night-time falls. The sun gets in the way you see – or don't you see?"

"I see – my mistake."

"Learning from a mistake is as good as learning from a teacher, and maybe that's taught you a lesson. You didn't catch my drift, did you? What

I was meaning to imply is this : The stars are out there and shining for that muchacho, Jesús Sierro."

Pancho leaned to one side, clapped the priest affectionately on the back. "Another thing, Father Felipe, after you left us to go to your new post, our cow – Tulia's cow, that is – made a remarkable turnaround and is no longer ailing. No, far from it, I never knew what it was she was down with, but stranger still, how she recovered from it so miraculously quick. I reckon you intervened on our behalf through the good offices of the Lord. Now then, I've said my piece, hmm. What say you?"

"Oh no, Francisco," laughed the priest, his chubby jowls shaking, "it was simply the loving care and attention of that young man of yours, Julian. I said the last time he has a look of godliness about him. A pity he's not here, for I would dearly wish to speak to him. I would indeed…"

98

Good Food

Ashort while later the roundup of rancheros and their guest were tucking into Tulia's food. Curiously for Pancho, he again experienced the sensation of eating the most marvellous, the most exquisite and mouth-watering food he had ever tasted. The others watched him with interest as he stuffed and filled his face.

At one point, between luscious bites of a meat tamale, he enquired, "How is it, hermanos?"

"How is what?" wanted to know Cándido.

"The grub, muchacho, the food. How do you find it?"

Cándido shrugged noncommittally and turned to the others, as if to say 'Just humour him'.

José thought it was okay, nothing out of the ordinary, Gerardo said it was fine, while Emilio considered it not bad.

"Cándido?"

"Look, Pancho, it's alright. We get these tamales every week, the beans every day and it's the same as usual. Nothing special. What's the matter with you? Is yours off or something?"

The old ranchero then turned to the priest. "How is the food, Father Felipe? How do you find it?" he asked in earnest.

"Oh, very tasty indeed," the black-garbed man gave his enigmatic smile. "Your housekeeper is to be highly commended."

"Don Roberto's housekeeper," Pancho corrected him. "Does anyone mind me finishing off this plate?"

"Help yourself," offered Cándido, "we've had enough."

"Hope you enjoyed it … as I am," piling the remains of food onto his plate and setting to with gusto, like he hadn't eaten in a month.

"Looks like we've got more company coming in," observed José, indicating a moving dustcloud in the southeast.

"Why, it's Julian with the pony and trap, I'll be bound," said Pancho in evident surprise. "Sí, it is Julian. He didn't waste any time getting back, by God – Excuse me, Father, a slip of the tongue you understand, my apologies."

Then Julian was in the yard, enveloped in fine travel dust. He leapt from the buckboard seat, passed the reins to young Juan, who had got up to help him.

"Father Felipe!" shrilled the simpleton, excitement in his high-pitched tone. "I came as quick as I could, Father!"

Pancho glanced quizzically at the priest, who returned the same look. "You knew Father Felipe was coming today, muchacho?" queried the old man, his brows meeting.

"Sí, señor, I knew last night."

"I didn't know I was coming myself last night," admitted the priest in a whisper to Pancho.

"Last night, eh? How was that then, Julian?"

"He spoke to me – Didn't you, Father Felipe? – in my dream last night." The simple youth smiled ingenuously at the disconcerted priest.

Father Felipe rose from his seat, laid a hand on Pancho's shoulder. "Let me speak to him on our own, Francisco, if you don't mind. He intrigues me, as I know I keep telling you, but he is truly a creature of God, of that I have no doubts."

He walked away, Julian chattering gaily by his side.

The men were silent a few moments, then Gerardo decided to say something : "A good man there, Pancho, don't you think? A damn sight better than that doddering old Father Antonio."

"I agree," said Emilio, "a real fine man. I like him."

"Sí, sí…" muttered Pancho, momentarily bemused.

He stared over at the retreating figure of Father Felipe, his cassock ballooning in the wind, head bent intently toward the simple young soul at his side.

"Sí, truly a man of God…"

And the long summer sun stormed and seared fierily on, and hot winds scoured the earth and raised the ubiquitous dust.

99

Juan's Leaving

The golden wash of sun-hot summer days passed, one after another, everlasting in their light and heat and aridness. The land raked by burning winds and dust and grit, under a deep-blue empty naked sky. Sun-frazzled flowers fading away, their season done.

Juan's time with the rancheros was now also at an end. It was late August and the boy was ready to return to the Ramos homestead. On his last day, after a morning of work with the men around the hard, hoof-hammered corral grounds, he and Pancho took one final ride together over the now-familiar terrain of the rangelands.

On they rode at an easy canter in companionable silence through peppergrass and tansy. Clouds and their shadows on the land swept along soundlessly. In the near distance before them the last flowering horsemint gave a lilac hue to patches of the rolling corn-yellow grassland. Then they were into dustdrift sandy scrubland, the fine sand wind-patterned corrugations.

The two reined in their mounts to a halt.

"It looks like a sea," observed Juan in quiet tones, "with the tide coming in slow-like…" as he gazed about him, clear-eyed, keen-eyed, as the young are.

It was a few moments before old Pancho answered him. "Do you know, Juanito – and I don't mind admitting this to you," he said slowly in his familiar rasping gravelled voice, "but I have never seen the sea, for all my years on this good Earth."

He spoke nothing less than the truth. He would dearly love to see a seashore. Not the gently shelving sandy sort but a high cliff-faced seashore, where the land sheared away and dropped to rocks and crashing waves.

He told the boy he had seen what he imagined looked like seas. Seas of sand in Sonora and Chihuahua. And the great ocean of blue in the sky on a cloudless day. If he did see a small cloud or two, he could readily imagine them as old Spanish galleons sailing the blue ocean.

It is said that all the seas of the world are salty, he went on. Cannot be drunk or used for anything of worth, that vast mass of water covering – what? – three-quarters of the Earth's surface. All the same he had tasted sand in the deserts of this land of Mexico, and in parts the sand too tasted of salt. Wasn't that something? he said smiling.

He would like to visit the coast one day – east or west, he wasn't fussed as it made no difference to him – just to watch and listen to the waves. But then, he had somehow reckoned that he had heard them before. In the grassland areas of the northern states when a ground wind was blowing. Or in woodland when the wind was up, he heard the pounding surf and heard the lashing of waves.

The old ranchero paused, breathed in the peppery scent of dust in the air, the musky odour of sundried shortgrass. What did it matter in not actually seeing the sea, he reasoned in husky tones. He had seen other wonders of nature during his life of inland travelling. Ridden the sands and plains – and yes, eaten dust as well.

He once rode from Monterrey to Nuevo Laredo during a wintertime when the entire region was covered in snow. Something you'd hardly credit, he mused on. He had once climbed the Sierra Madre to see a whole world far below him. He had walked amid fields of growing corn and new spring grass, and small seas of wildflowers …

"No, mi amiguito, I have never seen the sea but I reckon I've already been there somehow…"

He glanced up and noticed white wisps and feathering of cloud floating freely in the vast blue dome of the sky.

"Well, shall we head on back?" he said with a sigh. "You'll have your gear to pack, I expect, your books and things."

They wheeled the horses Macha and Chapulín and trotted homeward through wind-flung dust.

Later, by the stables on the hacienda, Juan quietly packed his saddlebags and was soon ready to leave. He swung the book-heavy load onto Chapulín's back. The bay nudged his nose into Juan's shoulder, as if to say 'What's this great load you're giving me, then!'

The men came round one by one to say farewell, grasping and gently holding the boy's hand in true Mexican manner. Even the hound Salté got a rub and a pat on the head from every one of them.

The rancheros were truly sorry the boy was leaving them. He had enlivened their lonely existence on the ranch for a while. For a time they had felt and thought as they had during their own younger days, thanks to Juan's unwitting influence on them. Because of this they were grateful. They each hugged the boy and, quite unashamedly, somehow managed to wet their eyes in the process.

After the childlike Julian had said his goodbye, giving his young friend a long clinging embrace, he went alone to one of the stables. There he sobbed his simple heart out, as though he were never to see his friend again.

The old man stood uncertainly at the main stable entrance, scratching his nose, then his neck, and back to his nose; all the while affectionately regarding his young charge. "So, you'll be off, then?" he said unnecessarily, and for once not knowing what to do with his hands. "God go with you, my young star," he added thickly. He gave the boy a Mexican *abrazo*, completely enfolding him in his long powerful arms.

As they held tight in this farewell embrace, each must have recollected many interesting and sometimes extraordinary events the summer months had thrown up with such abundance and diversity. They had lived through a short but happily memorable measure of time that could never be repeated, no matter how often Juan returned to the ranch in future summers. For the boy certainly it had proved an upward learning curve toward maturity, and set him irrevocably on the path to true manhood.

Tulia's chickens were out and about again, back-kicking and pecking at the barren ground. Salté eyed them with total disinterestedness. He had better things to do at present than waste time and precious energy in chasing a few scrawny fowl.

They were to be on their way then, horse, young rider and faithful dog. Salté now appeared eager to be off for home – for he had cannily sensed that they were heading for home – and even Chapulín was nickering with pleasure and anticipation; all three now ready for the journey to the Ramos farmstead.

A moment later Juan was about to swing up into the saddle, but hesitated. He turned and flung his arms once more around the old ranchero. They held each other a precious moment longer. Then the boy hoisted himself onto Chapulín with a determined air.

He gave a last brave though glittered-eyed smile at his old mentor, heeled his horse on, and off went the bay at a smart round trot. Salté as usual bounded on ahead of horse and rider, his large ears flapping like two scruffy dust-rags. Later, he'd have his nose to the ground, ready to sniff out a thousand odours, snatching at faint soughing scents only his hound-dog nose could discern.

The rancheros stopped what they had been doing and ambled over to a discreet distance behind the old man, each with his own thoughts, none of them saying a single word, as if they were deaf mutes.

Pancho watched horse and rider and canine friend disappear distortedly into the heat shimmer in the mid-distance. Affecting composure, but with little effect, he brusquely waved away a fly from a dampened cheek. About him Tulia's chickens ravaged the earth with grubbing claws and clicking beaks.

A dust-devil whisked across the sun-bleached corral ground.

"Well, the muchacho has gone," the old ranchero said aloud, though he was only addressing himself.

At any rate there was no one near him to heed the words; moments earlier the men had wandered off, listlessly and aimlessly.

Pancho brushed with his sleeve at moisture that was beginning to blur his vision. He turned abruptly and gimped into the shade of the stable.

100

Funerals, Weddings and Dreams

*I*n the evening of the same day Juan had left them the rancheros sat subdued over their supper, with the sundown shadows creeping out their length and adding to the almost morbid atmosphere. It was a long while after they had eaten before anyone felt the temerity to speak.

Then Cándido snapped into the morose silence. "Well, compañeros, next week the film people come."

"Those Hollywood hombres, is it?" voiced Gerardo.

"That's it, to make a movie with the don's longhorns."

"Pretty soon," put in Pancho, "the cattlemen will be out rounding up the entire herd. Don Roberto told me himself he'll want those steers taken to Montezuma's Canyon."

"You mean we're going to help them?" asked José, lighting up a rat's-tail thin cigarro – he was short on tobacco once again.

"That's the size of it, sí," Pancho told him.

"Well then, who's the trail-boss?" José wanted to know.

"Trail-boss!" crowed Cándido. "We're only going as far as Montezuma's."

"All the same," pursued José, "we need a man in charge who knows what he's doing."

"It's been taken care of," grinned the old ranchero a little smugly.

"Manuel's the foreman," said Gerardo. "He'll do it, surely?"

Pancho enlightened the other by stating that Manuel had taken off home with back trouble, due to a fall.

"So who's it to be? Not you, Pancho!" grumped Gerardo.

"Why not, hombre, I've worked with cattle most of my life. I was working with cattle in Sonora before you were even born." The old man put some uplift into his voice tone. "And by the by, guess who else is coming next week? No, you'll never guess, I can warrant it."

"Who is it, then?" enquired Emilio, suddenly roused from a quick doze.

"That young nephew of his, that's who. Diego he's called."

"Don't know him," said someone.

"You will when next week comes along, because we have to take charge of him, the don says."

"What, and take the herd to the canyon?" asked someone.

"He's coming with us, by all accounts, so that's that."

"Can he ride a horse?" asked José, then drew hungrily on his poor excuse of a cigarette.

"He fancies himself as a *charro*, so I've been informed."

"Hell, one of them! That's all we need." José spat angrily on the fire, as if the fire was to blame.

The rancheros once more fell silent for a spell, in a mood verging on despair. Pancho felt he had to break the dreary uncomfortable quietness. "¡Újule! We are a merry lot I must say. Like we've just come back from a funeral or something."

"Funerals, weddings, I hate them," returned Gerardo grouchily. "I didn't even want to go to my own wedding, only I was forced into it. My Teresa's old man insisted on it, seeing as I'd put her in the family way."

"What about your own funeral," charmingly smiled Cándido, "you'll attend that with a bit more enthusiasm, I hope?"

"I'll be at your damn funeral first, that's for sure," Gerardo glared at him.

"What if you die before me, then? Which is more likely, the way you're going."

"I'll be there, one way or another, you can count on it, and I'll haunt you to your grave, you queer-eyed colt."

"You haunt me now and I'm not even half-dead or anywhere near."

"I used to think there could be no such thing as being half-dead, until Emilio came to work with us." José smiled a wicked smile; he was evidently relishing a witticism which he was about to unleash on the others. "He's always half-dead on his feet, hee-hee!"

"Hey, what was that?" said the fat man, now fully awake after his doze.

Pancho returned to the original topic of discussion. "The best wedding I ever went to was don Carlo's in June of last year – or was it the year before? You were at that one, Gerardo, weren't you?"

"Sí, I was there alright," gritted Gerardo, remembering, "and it was the year before. It was going quite smoothly until that damned half-blind drunkard Alfonso showed up."

"You're right there," agreed Pancho. "You could say he was always *blind* drunk. He could drink me under the table, in spite of his very poor eyesight – though maybe that has nothing to do with it."

Gerardo didn't know why the man was invited in the first place, because he always caused trouble wherever he went. As the man had such poor sight Gerardo assumed that he would stay at home and not venture out for any reason.

The fact was, as Pancho reaffirmed, Alfonso hadn't been invited to don Carlo's wedding but showed up anyway. He simply barged in, stumbling half-blind and fully-drunk which was his usual way. At the reception he had stepped on the bride's dainty little foot with his iron-shod boots. The poor bride went purple in the face and hopped about on one foot. A big girl she was too, Pancho reckoned. She lost her balance and toppled into some bushes, base over tip. Bent right over with her face in thick foliage and wide posterior in the air.

"She was wearing red under-drawers, as I recall – in fact I remember it well," said Gerardo. "Talk about a red flag before a bull. None of us dare make a move to help her, lest the view be spoilt, for she was showing all the fruit she had," eyes aglitter at the keen remembrance of the spectacle. "We was memorised by it."

"You were what?" butted in Cándido.

"I said we was memorised by it, are you deaf?"

"Oh, I thought you said mesmerized."

"There you go, you did hear me."

Pancho pressed on, telling how Alfonso stood before the priest, mistaking him for the bridegroom. He shook the cleric's hand, congratulated him and hoped he was fit enough to carry himself with honour through the coming nuptials.

"Then the half-blind silly old fart started kissing the bride's grandmother, believing she was the bride. Kissed the toothless old crone full on the mouth, and she never had so much attention in fifty years or more."

"Such is life when your sight is shot to pieces," sighed Pancho.

Said Gerardo, "I'll not be going to any more damned weddings anywise. If anyone should invite me I'll tell them they can go whistle."

"That reminds me," said Cándido, fishing in his pants pocket, "I have something for you, Pancho."

"Ah sí, and what's that, then?" The young man handed over to him an exquisitely carved wooden whistle. "¡Ay que bueno!" beamed the old ranchero, highly satisfied and touched at the gesture. "So you didn't let me down after all, muchacho, which means more to me than anything I can think of," fondling the whistle in his great paws. "A real handsome job of work it is too. I shall treasure this little piece of craftsmanship. Gracias, amigo, muchas gracias."

"Give it a blow," urged Gerardo.

"You whistle up the wind. I'll blow this when the right time comes along and not before." The old man winked a merry blue eye at everyone. "I never imagined you'd finish it, Cándido, I honestly didn't, not in my wildest dreams."

"Speaking of dreams," said the younger man, a genuine look of sincerity on his handsome features, "I oftentimes dream at night and they're not usually pleasant dreams either. Not exactly nightmares I have, you will appreciate, but nasty, disturbing sort of dreams.

"But since Juanito stayed with us my dreams became real nice and happy, like. It got so I looked forward to hitting the hay each night when he was here. I kind of hope it continues the same, now that he's gone…"

A dead silence ensued.

"Don't look at me like that, Gerardo, I'm only telling you what's the truth and what I thinks on it."

"I was waiting for your funny bit, something weird and crazy, as you usually do. Ah, well…"

"It's the strangest thing, you know, the dreams we sometimes dream," mused Pancho reflectively, rolling his fingers over the smooth polished wood of his whistle. "You remember the other night when it was so still? The horses were quiet right through the night, not a fidget among them.

"There were not even the normal night noises you hear. And the fire too was quiet, just glowed, and finally went out. Not a breath of wind all night. Well, that was the night I had my dream…"

The old ranchero had dreamed of someone he once knew – must be a long way back, he told the others. It could have been near forty years or more since he had last seen this fellow, had never given him a single thought in all the time since then. And there he was before his eyes, as clear to him as the rancheros gathered here around him. He awakened then suddenly. Thinking, why had he dreamed of the man he'd known so long ago?

After a moment he considered a nagging point. Why had he even asked himself the question when he well knew the answer to it? The fellow he had known died the moment during which he dreamed of him. He was as certain of this as he was of the morning rise of the sun. The man's soul was passing on, and his soul passed over Pancho, as a way of a final farewell to an old friend from their Sonora days way back in the past.

"Ah well, when the past is past it is past, past consideration, past redemption, and there is no way you can change it either. So there you have it."

There was a momentary silence, then Cándido spoke : "But you have no proof that he died, this friend of yours. What you dream about is from your subconscious and has nothing to do with the real world."

"I would like to think it was so," smiled Pancho a little sadly, "but I've had two or three such dreams in recent times. And there is at least one which confirms my belief in what had really happened – the proof you were speaking of."

The old man began to explain. It happened a year or so ago when he had a dream much like the one of the other night. He saw a face in this dream. It was unmistakably Rodrigo Ríaz, a friend he had known when they were both boys. He recognised his boyhood friend in the dream.

About a month later, when speaking to young Juan's mamá, doña María Ramos, she told him of a letter she had received the week before from her sister in Mexico City. Doña María's sister had put a particular question in her letter : Had Francisco Ramírez ever known of a man named Rodrigo Ríaz? This Rodrigo had apparently been asking about Pancho, on his deathbed as it turned out. It was evident that he died that same night he appeared in Pancho's dream.

"Sí, strange it is, this matter of dreams and what we dream of. It is said that dreams tell us who and what we really are, and understanding our own dreams help us to understand ourselves. But who of us fully understands all his dreams?" moralized the old man.

"But that's the way of it I guess." He pulled at his moustache, rubbed his jaw, said not another word. His compatriots too remained silent.

But no longer were their spirits sapped and stultified; they were feeling uplifted, little by little.

The crimson of the setting sun consumed the blue of sky. Twilight-shadowed the land, and night came on. The men slept dreamfully under a starfired silent nightsky.

SIXTH INTERLUDE

There came a time in Mexico's recent history when there was a movement astir all over the land. It began slowly and gradually and insidiously. The country people were leaving the countryside. They were leaving the toil and hardship and poverty of rural life, to try their luck in the cities. In Mexico City, and Guadalajara and Monterrey. But mostly they headed for *Ciudad de México* – Mexico City. Emptying the land and filling the city to overflowing. For a considerably lengthy period the people continued to be poor.

More came in every day. Coming in droves, and driven by desires, by hopes of chance and luck or opportunity – anything but the grinding, backbreaking toil of their rural days. On still they poured into the great and growing metropolis. A decade later this influx of humanity would increase fivefold, then tenfold, and double again.

And these people who left the open land behind, had forsaken the land, and in the city streets they were for a long time a lost entity with no proper or stable identity. Shanties were cropping up all around the *Distrito Federal*. The poor people lived in makeshift dwellings of cardboard and canvas, between high-rise buildings and on any spare ground that could be found.

It took some time for the mighty megalopolis to absorb them and sustain them with gainful employment. Among these labourers of the land were others who had been affected by the nation's drift toward modernization. These were the saddlers and the harness-makers, the blacksmiths and the farriers. The new modern Mexico had little need of these near-obsolete trades. So these craftsmen of old worked as mechanics in auto workshops, or took up semi-skilled work in tin and steel and chemicals.

The mass of migrants eventually found work in factories and mills, in workshops and offices and on new and vast construction sites. They trickled in to foundries and sweatshops and warehouses. And they became shoeshine boys and street vendors. They became motor mechanics and waiters and taxi-drivers. They became peddlers and cooks, washwomen and house-servants to the rich. And they worked in smoke and steam, in gas and fumes and bad light, in confined spaces and dark places.

The people from the land hammered and hewed and hefted, and they stamped and sewed and spun. These people cut and baked and welded, and they mounted and forged and pressed. They drove and wove and blew, and they washed and scrubbed and dyed. They dug and packed and moulded, and they oiled and ironed and smelted. They drilled and dredged, riveted, pounded, and blasted.

And these people, originally from the countryside, dirtied their hands, not in earth's honest soil but in oil and grease and carbon dust; in printer's ink and paint, and all manner of corrosive, eye-stinging, dangerous chemical compounds. They walked, not on good green grass but on asphalt and concrete and macadam. They trod on metal grids and steel pylons and iron girders. Their feet scrunched on gravel and cinders and garbage-strewn waste ground …

On Mexico's main thoroughfare, the long, broad avenue named *Paseo de la Reforma* – built by the order of Maximilian to please his wife, the Empress Carlota – 13-year-old Chico Mendez was doing extremely well for himself. He had arrived in the city only a month ago with his family; his parents and younger brother and two sisters. Luckily, they had relatives to go to at first and so never wandered the streets homeless.

Chico earned his living selling cartons of tissues to motorists on the busy boulevard. He had picked a good strategic 'beat' between the last two set of traffic lights at the top end of this wide tree-lined avenue – near the monolithic *Officina de Gobernacíon* building.

With his engaging fulsome looks and cheerful smile Chico sold out his stock several times a day, the motorists unable to resist the boy's natural charm.

A few blocks further down, 42-year-old and jobless Alberto Sanchez Reyes tramped sullenly by the streaming, honking, vehicular traffic, amid the acrid stink of exhaust fumes. Alberto was daydreaming, dreaming of the pueblo he had left six long weeks ago. And he panted and pined for the smell of sweet straw and clear fresh country air.

Most of these people who had come from the land forgot the smell of the land. They could no longer remember the homely odour of a stable or a chicken-house or pig-pen. They forgot the timeless pungency of manure and pleasant fragrance of cornstraw. They could not recall the spice of earthdust or the sweet earth scent after a rainfall. Could no longer imagine the lush dark green of alfalfa, the riotous colour of wildflowers, the rich golden yellow of ripened corn. Lost to them the majesty of a hawk in flight, the vast deep blue of a clear summer sky, the sheer mysterious beauty of distant mountains in dawnlight.

They had left the land behind them, these people of the land, given up tradition and heritage, forsaken the bounty of land for good and forever.

BOOK III

Summer's End

Part Nineteen

101

The Herd Moves Off

T he sun slowly passed its zenith and burned down over don Roberto's six-hundred head of long-horned cattle as they shuffled through dust and wild spear-head grass on the hacienda grazing plain. The longhorns massed and milled about in confusion. Many of them had earlier consumed poor quality feed and were breaking wind with monotonous regularity. The foul obnoxious stink they exuded mingled with the odours of cattle-sweat and freshly dropped dung. In the closing in on one another, attracting a swarm of whining insects, they generated a tremendous heat, the rising thermals smoked with dust.

"Spread these beasts out a bit, hermanos," ordered Pancho. "It's getting like the meat market at Nuevo Las Casas Grandes. Move them out, boys, room enough out there, by God!"

The cattle moved on with the moil of many hooves in the dust, over ground of flinty stone and wildrock, of cactus and slatestone, into a thick yellow haze of tree-high dust.

Old Pancho rode his white mare Macha. His cracked saddle-leather features were set in a faint smile of satisfaction as he looked over the serried rabble of cattle. He wheeled his mount, signalled to his point man Cándido who saw the gesture and at once turned his horse, a spirited strongly built chestnut gelding. He rode up to the old ranchero in a smother of dust.

Pancho shaded an eye with one hand and regarded the angle of the early afternoon sun as it balanced over the scorched brown earth. "May as well get them on the move," he grated in his raw, rough toned voice, resting a large square fist on the saddle-bow. "Where's José, by the by?"

"With the drag, I think, last I saw," smiled the young man.

"Is he now? Que bueno. Okay, let's get them on. ¡Vamónos! ¡Rapído!"

"Ayí yah! Aghh-ha!" Cándido yelled with enthusiastic energy, cracking his whip smartly in the air.

The great herd began to move in a sloppy irregular chain through the dust, bawling and lowing, tails switching at flies. The lead steers, hooves crunching soft sandstone, trotted to their usual place at the point. A rust-brown beast separated from the rest and lumbered into a patch of scrub as if looking for something to eat. A few longhorns began to follow it.

"Ya-yarrh!" cried Cándido, cracking his whip and heading off the wandering animals, a scum of dust rising from the ground. A cowman rode up to assist him, went on at a fast canter, redirecting the beasts.

There was a deep drumming on the sun-inflamed land as the herd got properly under way. Pancho neck-reined Macha, stood in his stirrups and inhaled the hot steaming breath of the cattle, the smouldering heat and the pungent, nose-tingling dust. It reminded him so much of his earlier days in Sonora. This was the kind of life he knew and loved best and felt wholly in his element.

He gazed over beyond the herd, beyond the swelter of dry fine peppery dust, at a fair stretch of heat shimmer rippling oilily at the foot of bald rugged hills in the far distance. He positioned himself some few paces from the edge of the herd on its right flank. His ears took in as if it were music the continual din of thumping hooves and bellowing of cattle. Scorching dust caked the mucus in his nose. Using two fingers he blew and cleared his nose.

José appeared on his favourite dappled grey colt, riding to him at a swift trot. Dust fumed about him. His weather-beaten features cracked open in a grin. He too liked working with cattle – for a change.

"I thought you were riding drag," the old horseman barked at him.

"Someone already there," replied José succinctly, reining in his horse. "You don't seriously expect an old hand like me to ride drag, do you?" he asked somewhat pompously, tobacco-stained teeth showing darkly in his swarthy face.

"Well, why not? It suits you I reckon," Pancho chaffed him.

"*Carajo*, I thank you very much for that," the other shot out mulishly. He turned in the saddle and spat, raising a tiny spume of dust. He looked put out, drew a deep breath and slowly expelled it.

With an affable wag of his head the old man soothed him. "Don't get your back up so, amigo, relax. You're right, it's not for you to be eating the dust. Ride over to the *mesa* if you will and collect the strays." José put on a puzzled expression. "By the dry watercourse, a few usually end up around there." Pancho winked a roguish eye at him. "Off you go, amigo. ¡Andale!"

José nodded and spurred on the colt.

"Don't tire that mount of yours!" Pancho shouted after him. "Ay que caray," he muttered to himself, "he wears horses out as Casanova wears out women."

He lifted his sombrero and ran fingers through his thatch of ginger hair. Sweat stood out on his brow, hot dust pecked sneezingly at his nostrils. Tilting the brim of his sombrero low over his eyes against the pulsing sunglare, he gazed absently into the large eyes of a young roan.

"What are you looking at, eh?" the old ranchero said jocularly to the roan. "I suppose if a cat can look at a king you can look at me, is it?" The animal stared back dolefully.

Pancho nudged his mount forward with a gentle pressure of his knees and moved on with the rumble of the herd, the lead steers lost, enveloped in a shimmering heat-haze. Again, he was made aware of the powerful smell of cattle on the move, mingled with a spicy scent of dust.

The sun was hard as bronze in the sky and burning unrelentingly.

102

Diego

At the precise moment Pancho was wondering who exactly was riding in the drag – or rear – of the herd, another rider hove in sight on a wiry short-legged pony. It was Diego, a teenager and the nephew of don Roberto. He was a light-skinned stringy youth, wild and unkempt in appearance. His face bore a pronounced mean look, of a kind one would perhaps associate with a hardened city delinquent. His eyes were jet-black, flinty and malignant; the eyes of a prairie bird of prey.

Riding at a fast though inexperienced lope toward the old ranchero, he whistled tunelessly to the tinny blare of sound coming from a transistor radio strapped to his saddle-horn.

Pancho gently reined in his horse and incuriously regarded the youth. A troublesome individual if he ever saw one, he surmised. "Well, it's Diego then, and where did you sprout from, eh?"

The youth stared back at him unblinkingly with an insolent expression on his thin, pinched features. Diego had been raised in a city environment – the great sprawling metropolis that is Mexico D.F. – and was by all accounts a product of where he came from, a typical *ladino* – a city-bred lout. He held his own views on the peasants of the country, felt contempt for them, hated their insular pueblo life. He felt only disgust for what he considered a slower pace of life, insufferable traditionalisms, and the stupidly reserved, suspicious, halting nature of anyone who lived outside of big cities.

Diego had yet to comprehend the enormous difference that existed between the stolid, taciturn tillers of the land and the roving, high-hearted, free-spirited rancheros. The horsemen were an entirely different breed, and the youth in his ignorance had unwittingly lumped them all into one category, which would sooner or later perhaps become his downfall.

"I'm riding drag," he snarled at the old man.

"Ah, is that it?" Pancho said in a neutral tone. "Then maybe you'd better get yourself back there, muchacho."

It was Pancho's responsibility to move the herd, and in such a circumstance as this he rightly took his position seriously. It was a natural sense of duty drawn from civil conscientiousness and not in the least affected.

He could not say why but Pancho had taken an immediate dislike and mistrust of this youth from the big city. Moreover, he was determined that the job in hand was not to be jeopardised in any way by this city-bred wolverine. And it irritated him in seeing the other's erroneous sense of power over him, simply because of being don Roberto's own kin.

"You'd better move," the old ranchero warned him.

"In my own good time, alright?" Diego threw out challengingly, a scornful glitter in his eyes.

At that he stepped from the saddle, apparently to urinate. He unzipped the flies of sun-faded jeans and directed a golden jet at a rock. The rock hissed and steamed. Pancho bided his time, eyeing the youth with only the faintest cursoriness of attention. As he waited he scratched at sweatsalt on the back of his neck, nose sniffing the scent of the earth.

Then he spotted what he recognised as a Colt .22 pistol tucked in a holster belt buckled around the youth's slim hips. So the muchacho is armed, he thought not without some foreboding.

"A *pistolero*, eh?" he grunted with heavy sarcasm. "*Por la Santísma*, I hope you don't intend using that thing around here," he remarked evenly, pointing to the offensive weapon. There was a storm warning in his eyes.

"I don't see that it's any business of yours," Diego insolently hurled at him.

"None of my business you say? That's what you think is it? Why, I'll give you a smart punch where it really hurts, you skinny goat!" Pancho fumed, voice rising. He was already falling out with this city sewer rat which he took him to be.

Diego did not so much as spare him a glance. He casually zipped his jeans, slapped dust from his thin shanks and, with a slight show of self-consciousness, he snugged down his gunbelt.

The old ranchero's temper was rising with the afternoon heat. "Did you hear me?" he roared. "¡Chingado, muchacho! I'm asking did you hear what I said?" loud voice throttling the air.

"I heard," replied the youth, turning a surly face towards him. "Don't worry old man I won't be firing it."

"Damn right you won't. You could spook the entire herd." Pancho's tone expressed nothing but distrust. There was no telling what this young city slicker would do out in the country, giving him a grizzled look of distaste.

Diego sullenly − and inexpertly, as the old man saw − remounted the pony. He shot Pancho a glance of acid hatred, pulled his mount round violently and galloped off, leaving a billowing trail of dust behind him.

The old horseman dropped the matter from his mind, soon regaining his characteristic good humour and amiability. He took hold of Macha and sent her on forward, riding at a canter alongside the fringe of the herd. Forward through hot sienna dust, over dry grass tufts, stones and dung, in the fierce heat of the afternoon sun.

At length however, for some obscure reason not yet fully understood, Pancho began to feel a vague and bothersome unease. It came from deep within him, crawling in his gut like a growing tapeworm. It was an instinctive feeling.

He shrugged philosophically, annoyed with himself for thinking like an old superstitious woman. He could taste dust, turned aside and spat. There, he felt better already.

Several of don Roberto's cowmen filed by him, grinning ruggedly at one another. They were tough riders; hard-bitten, mean, and savage-looking to an outside observer, but among themselves they were a cheerful bunch of simple-minded men dedicated to and enjoying the work they do so well.

Old Pancho gazed back at them with an amused grin.

"Aghh! Ay-yarrgh!" they cried, cracking their lariats, sombreros bobbing as the horses cantered on by.

"¡Waco! Ay-yarrh!"

The men moved on with the smelly noisy herd, sunk in a flood of heat across the plain. The hot ground churned dryly, dust smoked up, and the sun burned.

The broad hard flaming sun of Mexico.

Then *it* came …

103

Windstorm!

O nly a matter of minutes later Pancho heard an ominously raw rushing sound. He glanced up in alarm, the sun full in his eyes, and saw a colossal dust cloud in the distance. The massive dark-looking cloud was fast piling up ahead, twisting and roiling.

Within a few short moments it fell on the herd and scattered cattlemen. The old ranchero screwed up his face as a sudden blast of dry searing wind and stinging sand hit him full on.

"¡Újule! God in Heaven!" he gasped out, utterly appalled at what was coming head-on toward him.

A titanic dust spume swept with great force over the open range-land. The afternoon light began to dim, the sun obscured by a thick swirling fog of dust. Cattle lowed and bawled in bewildering confusion. Their huge heads, holding a wide horn spread, lowered to the ground, hooves kicking and stamping at the earth.

Out of the storm of dust rode Cándido, his squint eyes rounded in some alarm. "Windstorm!" he cried above the roar.

Hot gritty sand and wind raked him mercilessly as he cleaved through a hiatus of disturbed restless cattle. There was such wide-eyed bewilderment about the beasts as they bucked and stomped and jammed against one another. The air was now completely fogged with dust; a choking cloud of sullen, sulphur-yellow dust, like smoke from a forest fire. It reared high over the now slow moving herd.

"¡Ay carambas! Damn it to hell!" the old man voiced aloud.

"Sandstorm!" cried out a swing outrider, galloping furiously over the windswept plain.

Pancho ignored him, narrowed his eyes against coarse sand and grit. The wind flew over him with a dull roar like near-distant thunder. He hurriedly tied a bandanna round the lower half of his face to filter the turbulent air, giving the immediate impression of a bandit.

"Turn them! Do you hear! Mill them, damn it!" he shouted into the wind, voice rasping dryly in his windpipe.

"To the mesa?" asked another outrider.

"To the devil with that! Too late!" stormed the ranchero. He was now for some reason grinning ferociously behind the cover of his bandanna, as if enjoying this alarum. "Wheel them round in here!" he roared. "Pack them in!" – But a sudden thought hit him. " Oye, Cándido! Who's at the point?"

"José!" was instantly snapped away by the wind. "José!" repeated the young man in something like a scream.

"Right! Bueno!" Pancho turned in his saddle and shot a glance at the other man, the outrider. It was Gerardo. "You stay, hermano," he ordered. "Close them in, tight now, okay?" *Por Jesu Cristo,* he thought, we've got to keep this lot together.

. "Hey, Pancho! Oye!" called over a cowman, grinning widely. "You look just like Pancho Villa, ha-ha!" Tears streamed from the man's eyes.

"Can't hear you, hombre!"

"I said you look just like –"

C-CRACK!

104

Stampede!

A gunshot at that precise second, loud and sharp. Followed by another shot. The men heard it despite the roaring of the wind and bawling cattle. They exchanged uneasy glances.

Somewhere between left swing and flank of the herd the youth Diego had discharged his pistol. He had seen a jackrabbit running for cover, watched it belting across open ground and scrub with lightning bounds, and he could not resist the impulse which seized him. Not even thinking but acting with the instinct of the city-bred street tough, he automatically drew his Colt, fired hurriedly and without proper aim in the general direction of the rabbit's path of escape.

The herd broke at once.

Pancho started, eyes stretched wide, scalp contracted, a hot trickle of sweat running down his back. "Uuy, he's gone and done it!" he gasped, dry-mouthed.

"They're running!" cried someone in the smoke of dust.

"Look out!" gulped another. "The herd's running! Make way!" he yelled out. "Make way for God's sake!"

There was a great almighty thunder of hooves, a deep roaring and bellowing, and the ground shook like as in an earthquake. The cattle shied, careened and reeled, long horns clashed and scraped, eyes dilated with fear, nostrils flaring. They charged pell-mell in a thickening cloud of orange dust.

Macha fought at the bit, her large eyes rolling wildly in fright, whinnying and skittering among the steers. Pancho yanked the reins, spun her about to get out of the way of the stampeding herd. He was almost beside himself with helpless rage, staggered in unutterable fury. Sweat burst out in large beads on his face and chest, ran in rivulets, dark sweat stains spreading like shadow from his armpits.

"Flank them if you can! Head them off!" he thundered, strafed by wind and grit, hot dusty air scraping his lungs. By the saints in Heaven, he swore to himself. By the blessed saints – he fired that damned weapon – the lunatic! The stupid slug! He fired it, he –

And within an instant of those dreadful gunshot reports the herd was running full out over the plain of that dusty heat-burdened land. The windstorm simply made matters worse.

There's no stopping them, Pancho realised with a sickening feeling, they'll run till they fall down exhausted. But what could he and the horsemen do? Except to run with them, he decided, and somehow head them off or slow them down to a standstill.

The ground seethed beneath pounding hooves and boiling dust. Several riders frantically struggled as they mixed among the cattle with horned heads tossing; thick, hairy, wooden-like. The men fought desperately as they were tightly bunched up. Many of them, on sweating spur-bitten mounts, rode with the herd.

An outside steer veered blindly towards a large boulder, hooves enmeshed in drummings, ringing on hard stony ground. Nearer now to that high implacable chunk of rock, the ground reverberating. The animal saw it then, that solid stone barrier. It tried to angle off but was travelling too fast to check its own momentum. It carried itself inexorably forward. Smack into the boulder it went, rolling over, steam hissing from foaming nostrils. More of the steers blindly followed, crashing into a living hill of flesh and hide. Horns gored and gouged and punctured juicily into backs, bellies and hindquarters of fallen beasts.

Somewhere else in the crushed jumbled melee, one of the horsemen, a fat, heavy-set man, began to panic as he tried to swing out the path of the oncoming herd.

He cried out in inexpressible fright. His horse shied and snorted, nostrils quivering. The man had difficulty in turning his mount, savagely reining its head round. At the same instant a steer ploughed into the horse's buttock. A horn sank deep into the horse's side, sank in like a hot knife cutting dough. It neighed in terror, raised forelegs high, and bolted.

The man was thrown from the saddle, landing heavily in the dust. One foot caught in the stirrup, he was dragged over stony ground; dragged over hot, rough, rocky ground on his back for several hundred paces before his foot finally slipped freely from the stirrup.

The back of his camisa was ripped off him, his skin flayed; a searing agonised peeling.

Raw nerve-torn trembling flesh scraped and shredded in bloody excoriating pieces.

He wriggled convulsively like a speared fish hauled from a river, his eyes bulged and mouth gaped wide.

Rolled and roughly bounced across the ground, choked in dust, grit biting into his wet pulpy back.

Brought to a sudden jarring halt against a rock.

He sat there, stunned at first, then coughing dust, gulping and gasping for air.

Then the pain got to him.

He screamed, as only certain fat men can scream, a high-pitched blood-curdling feminine yell.

There he was left, sat like a mound of crushed fruit; blood and shreds of flesh and skin covering a tortured, widely lacerated back.

It was as if he were melting, salt-sweat and gore oozing from him, as though skinned alive.

He screamed, sat there in his own pool of blood. Screamed and shrieked long and piercingly.

The badly injured fat man was Emilio.

105

The Herd Runs On

The track of the stampeding herd now began heading toward a gully gashed deep and wide across the burning plain. Mountainous farstretched dustclouds rolled with the blasting wind and the herd as it charged, hurtling toward certain death. Pancho was frantic at losing half the herd in that earth wound. The responsibility was his and his alone; he could not imagine don Roberto ever forgiving him if he failed.

"Head them off!" he bawled at the top of his voice, grit raking and eating into his face.

"Ay-ay-ay-yarrh!" cried the horsemen, their figures fading in an obscurity of dust.

Uuy, this is Hell on Earth, thought the old man worriedly. He kept his mouth tight-lipped against blasts of wind and grit. The wind watered his eyes as he galloped on, eye moisture thickly collecting dust.

In the dense smoke of dust he could barely see Cándido and José close by the gully, their mounts nervously prancing. The two rancheros yelled, valiantly cracking their whips in vain hopes of re-tracking the herd. Bandannas were hastily tied over nose and mouth to filter the turbulent air. They were in danger of being crushed piecemeal at any moment by the runaway avalanche of beasts.

C-cra-ack! went their whips. "Ayí! Ay! Yarrh!" they cried.

No, no, thought Pancho, we're spitting against the wind here. "Damn it!"

He cursed to himself without a break, a deep frown furrowed above his eyes. Vitriolic wrath spewed from him : "That stupid son-of-a-bitch Diego! That drip of dog's piss! I'll string him up, uuy! I'll quarter him, the scruff rag, the leprous scab! Damned scorpion bait!"

Then, at the last possible moment the herd miraculously turned and thundered along the extreme edge of the gully. Cándido grinned with relief and José lost his sombrero as the herd swept by them, spreading out over the stone-hard ground of the plain.

One steer did not make it. A larger, cumbersome beast knocked it in the side. It toppled headlong and crashed into a gaping abyss, its neck, two legs and a rack of ribs crushed instantly against jagged rocks below.

The herd moved on at a tremendous speed, a furnace of hooves drubbing the earth. Stones have no roots and stones spun and shuddered under lightning hooves. It seemed to old Pancho that they were set to run into the middle of next week.

He put the mare once again to an all-out gallop, her ears laid back and running strongly. Still scalded with fury the ranchero uttered an expressive ranting against the one who had started this debacle : "Fired his damned pistol! The stupid burrito! The runt of cat-skin! What idiocy! Fired it after I'd – Cándido! Off that way-y! To the right!" he roared in a volcanic voice, waving his whip in the stormy air.

"They'll split at the mesa!" cried Cándido.

"God's sake don't let them! Flank them! – That young city louse! I'll skin the bastard alive, so help me God I will. I'll gut the little sewer rat, I'll break his back. I'll have him strung up, so help me – Grrrh!" He gnashed his teeth, mind in mental turmoil. And his lower back hurt from repeated thumping against the high cantle of his saddle.

It was the least of his present problems however, as he now foresaw fresh disaster looming directly ahead …

106

Diego Finds Someone

Diego in the meantime had followed at a fast run the tail-end of the stampeding herd. For a while he was utterly astonished at what he had done, wreaking such havoc. That a couple of gunshots should set to panic an entire herd of cattle; he saw at once the appalling consequences of his action and shook with fear.

He was thinking of this headlong rush of cattle, running in a blind panic. What if some were to be crushed to death in the run of madness which gripped them? The youth squirmed at the awful thought of it, and fervently hoped that the horsemen would bring the catastrophe under some control. Much harm would already be done, he realised, before that should happen.

Then he saw the injured fat man out on the plain.

Emilio was sitting as before, an almost mystical Buddha-like figure all alone before a shimmering layer of heat on the dusty windswept plain.

Diego wheeled at an abrupt angle and headed straight for the man. Bile rose in his throat at the sight of the unfortunate fellow's grisly, flayed back. A black mass of flies gorged on torn tissue and hanging shreds of skin. He got a grip on himself and quickly dismounted. Emilio looked up at him with the rounded, frightened, pleading eyes of an abandoned child. He was quietly whimpering.

"A moment, Emilio," said the youth, his falcon eyes slit against flying sand and grit. He turned on his heel and drove a hand into his saddlebag. The transistor radio was incongruously still blaring out its loud vulgar sound, and he snapped it off with an impatient twist of fingers. He found a small bottle of iodine and some grubby rolls of bandage in his pack.

"Rubbed some of the fat off you, hey, Emilio?" he said, with the unthinking callousness of youth.

Emilio tried to smile, but only managed instead a weak, pathetic grimace. The relief that help had at last came brought hot tears of self-pity. He opened and shut his mouth like a fish, obviously wanting to say something but incapable of doing so at this present time. It would hurt to speak. He gave up the idea.

Diego went to work on him at once with hurried movements of surprisingly capable hands. First, he roughly splashed the iodine over the fat man's broad back. The instant the biting liquid made contact with raw tender flesh, Emilio screamed once briefly. He sank forward in a dead faint, falling to one side in a crumpled heap. Diego bandaged him as best he could with the pitiably small supply of rolls.

The youth returned to his pony and made another search in his saddle-pack. He brought out a hip-flask of hard liquor. Back with Emilio he attempted to raise the heavy man but found the task beyond the scope of his meagre build. He put the flask to the fat man's dusty lips and by small degrees he came round to consciousness.

"Sit up if you will, if you can – here, let me help you," said Diego with unaccustomed compassion. The other groaned with pain. "Drink this, it'll do you some good I should hope," and Emilio gulped the liquor greedily, eyes rolling.

The alcohol presently alleviated a little of the man's suffering as Diego knew it would. Emilio emptied the flask in no time at all, feeling slightly light-headed as a result. At any rate it did at least put some strength back into him.

"Now, we've got to get you up and on my mount," the youth told him after a minute had passed.

"I'll get up – I can do it myself," groaned Emilio laboriously. It was a small miracle of endurance indeed for the injured man in his condition being able to mount the pony, but he managed it almost adroitly.

Shortly afterwards they followed in the wake of the stampede into a dense cloud of hot dust. Wind and grit lashed the blood-soaked bandages protecting Emilio's back. To Diego the other's vast bulk appeared somewhat top-heavy on the small-boned, short-legged pony.

Emilio of course was past all caring.

"Didn't think…" he tried to say something a little later on.

"Speak up, Emilio. What did you say?" Diego turned to face him.

"Didn't think a w-windstorm would – would rouse the herd to a r-run," Emilio articulated stutteringly. He was about to say more but the effort required was too much and he stopped himself with a sharp intake of breath.

Diego smiled to himself, and it was a credit to his conscience that the smile was made in self-mockery.

"It was me who started the herd off," he confessed, filling the pause, "I fired my pistol, you see."

Emilio had not the strength to make any comment, and they moved on, to be swallowed up by swirling dust.

107

Heading Towards Danger

Dust rolled in a hill-sized cloud, following the running herd. The steers were heading straight for the mesa, a roughly flat-topped, sheer-faced outcrop of rock which stood as large as a city block on the relatively flat plain. The herd was certainly in danger of dividing in two, Pancho clearly saw, and knew it would be pure hell to get them together again.

Cándido and José and several cattlemen turned their horses with remarkable military-like precision, broke into a fresh mad dash to head the herd away from the mesa. The mesa towered over the plain, buffeted by wind. Pancho urged his mount on, and Macha responded by running superbly, her fear evidently forgotten in the headlong, exhilarating race with the herd.

This will windbreak the horses sure enough, thought the old ranchero. It'll knock the breath and teeth right out of them, uuy. But it's the only way, he knew.

"Come on, Macha! That's it, my sweet! Ha-yarrh! Yarrh!"

"The herd's splitting!" yelled a cowman.

"¡Újule! So they are, blast them! – Cándido! Stay right there!" he commanded, hot blood thrashing in his head, every nerve tingling.

Clouds of dust like fire-smoke flurried over the moving herd as it plunged on forward in a madcap thrusting rush.

"We're losing them!" shouted someone.

"Stay there! Hold there!" repeated Pancho frantically. "Close in, hermanos. Yarrgh! Ay-yarrh!" Macha's legs went like pistons as she gradually began to outflank the splitting herd.

"Ha-yarrh!" called out the rancheros.

And there were Cándido and José – and Gerardo too popping up out of the hullabaloo. Pancho's own men. Sparks flew from kicked stones, hooves hammered the earth, pounding it, and dust spumed and roiled. The solid thudding of all those hooves made the earth shake and vibrate like a quake.

Other riders now joined in, jostled in a dense pack of men and mounts, forming a phalanx, a living restless determined barrier. They bravely held their ground in front of the oncoming storm of beasts …

"¡Waco! Ay-yarrh!"

They yelled and screamed and cracked their whips, waved sombreros – José, having lost his, waved an exotic egg-yolk-yellow bandanna – the men in danger of being impaled or crushed to death …

"On! On! ¡Waco!"

Eyes flashed and sweat dripped from them, but still they held their ground, as the herd came on, pounding the dusty, sun-scorched, wind-scoured land.

"Look out! They're coming! This is it, hermanos!"

It was a foolhardy stance but a courageous one, thought the old man with quiet pride.

"Hold fast! Hold hard, hermanos!"

And the herd came on with tossing heads and clashing horns, hooves drowning in swirling dust. Steers crossed paths, some tumbled, others crashed into them, and still they came on hurtling in a maddened, thunderous clamour …

The intrepid horsemen held firmly and defiantly to their position. The deep percussion of countless hooves resounded in their ears as the cattle rushed blindingly on in a crazed gallop, snouts blowing and snorting …

"Hold hard, amigos!"

"¡Chingada! I don't believe it," voiced Pancho to himself, big-eyed with astonishment. "¡Újule, mi cabrones! ¡Los bravados magníficos!" He was overwhelmed with emotion. "¡AY-AHUA!" he cried full-throated, chest bursting with pride as he saw what was happening.

"See that!" hollered someone exultantly. "They're turning!"

"Oh look at them go!" burst from another. "We've done it!"

"They're turning right enough." The men cheered and waved sombreros in the dust-choked air.

"Praise be…" murmured Pancho in his relief.

Then, as abruptly as it had begun, the windstorm spent itself and died down. There was left in the air a high dense bank of orange-grey dust.

"To the canyon with them!" ordered Pancho, eyes blazing with a special triumph. He was well pleased, vastly relieved, grinning and nodding at the equally happy horsemen.

"To the canyon. Ayí!" raw hoarse voices echoed him.

The old ranchero cracked his whip significantly and began to follow the herd. It was heading this time, curiously and fortuitously, toward its originally intended destination, the canyon known as Montezuma.

Montezuma was a veritable fortress, a box canyon, there being only one way in, the opposite end blocked by a landslide of loose rock and sandstone.

"Well, hermanos," grinned José, hair loose and windblown, "what did you reckon to that then, hey?"

"It was a sure close thing," responded Gerardo, wiping a hand across his wind-seared face.

"Never seen the likes of that before," commented a cowman. "A damned windstorm and the runaround with that mob of beasts, both at the same time."

"Oye, José, you look quite naked. Where's your sombrero?" joked someone. "You'll be losing your pantalones next, hey!"

"Let's go, you lot," gruffed Pancho. "Get on there. Move it! ¡Rapído!"

"Sí, señor," returned a cowman respectfully.

"Spread out there!" cried Cándido. "To your positions."

"Ay-ay-ayí! Ay-yarrh!"

And the crew slapped sombreros against their mounts' flanks, spurred them on to a fresh and further effort, though knowing that now the game was theirs and already won.

108

Montezuma Canyon

The cattle rumbled at a half-trot into the sunbaked canyon, a burning acrid stench about them. They came to a halt at last and milled crowdingly between the high canyon walls, dropping foam, sweat and dung.

Pancho dismounted and stood by the side of a boulder, following with his eyes his herd as it closed in. He felt stiff, weak, thirsty, and utterly exhausted. His face was windburned and masked in dust, eyes red-rimmed. His nose was clogged with dust and he cleared it using two fingers. He removed his bandanna and spat into the dust at his feet, then shifted his attention to José before him.

"Set the generator, hermano, if you will. We could do with a drink, eh? ¡Ay caray!"

There was a subterranean water catchment below the canyon floor, powered and pumped up by a small generator. It supplied extra water when the cattle were allowed to roam this area.

"You've got a thirst on?" grinned José. "Here, Pancho, catch this," and he threw a metal hip-flask to him. It contained mezcal which the old man would certainly prefer to water.

"Muchas gracias, compadre," he grinned back, deftly catching the flask with one hand. He unscrewed the cap and noticed that his hands were shaking slightly. He took a long pull at the torqued liquor.

"Ah-h!" he breathed in evident satisfaction, feeling better already and his hands now steady. He wiped an arm across wet lips, sniffing at his own sweat drying starchly on his dusty clothes. He did a quick and somewhat peculiar knee-bend, to ease his sore and saddle-stiffened backside.

"Where're the film people then?" he asked presently, "and that director fellow."

"No sign of them here, that's for sure," said José, rolling himself a cigarro with difficulty, as his hands too were trembling.

"Well, maybe we're a little early yet." Pancho glanced up at the sun. "I mean, we did practically run all the way here."

Cándido rode up to him.

"Anyone hurt?" the old ranchero asked at once, screwing the cap back on the flask.

"Go on, another swig, por favor," said José. "Help yourself, be my guest."

"Emilio," responded the young man. "He took a tumble a long while back."

Pancho sniffed, rubbed his nose. "Hurt badly?"

"I couldn't say. What I know is he's lost his horse somewhere, I can't say where."

"What happened?"

"Again, I couldn't tell you."

"Hmm … Gerardo! Oye, Gerardo!" the old man called over to his principal outrider, who was helping a team of men with the final drive-in of the herd. "Do you have the first-aid pack?"

"Why, I reckon so, I always do normally. Sí, I have it," making a quick check in his saddlebag.

"Bueno. Ride back to the mesa area and maybe beyond to fetch back our Emilio. He's around there somewhere, without his mount and probably hurt, I'm thinking." He turned to some cowmen nearby. "Anyone seen Emilio or his horse?" He received negative nods.

"Anyone seen my sombrero?" asked José hopefully, scratching his bare head. "I misplaced it someplace," he added with a rueful grin, only for him also to receive negative head shakes.

Pancho sniffed again, then cautiously rubbed at his saddle-battered backside. Seeing José's encouraging signal he uncapped the hip-flask once more and took another generous pull of the hard liquor.

"Just my luck," grunted Gerardo, but obediently turned his mount and galloped off at once, driving his horse with whip and expressive ranchero type yells, no doubt with the intention of impressing the gaping audience of cowmen.

"No need," Cándido commented dryly, pointing to the canyon opening where Diego came riding in at that moment at a steady walk. The fat hulk of Emilio leaned heavily against him from behind.

"Ah, he's brought him in," said the old ranchero, admitting into his harsh grating voice a decided note of approval.

He was too exhausted at present to muster up any anger. To vent his spleen now would be a waste of energy he realised; and besides, the youth Diego had had the presence of mind to pick up the injured man, instead of leaving him out on the desert plain. His head at least was cool again, thanks to the snort of liquor, and had no wish to fire up his wrath in this heat, not after that arduous run with the herd. He wagged his head with an expression on his face which had something almost affable about it. All the same it was not what he was actually feeling.

Gerardo swung round again when he saw Diego come in with the injured fat man, reined his horse to a walk. Holding a look of expectancy he joined Cándido and José, and the three of them dismounted. They put their heads together, quietly mumbling and glancing now and again at Diego with meaningful looks.

Diego rode stiffly, almost militarily, head held high and defiantly insolent in manner. Sweat sluiced down his thin chest and back. Like the others his face was ashen with dust. The corner of his mouth quirked up with a faint hint of contempt as he surveyed the silent group of men standing hostile and motionless in the thick-hanging dust.

The youth clicked his tongue for no apparent reason – perhaps he was after all afraid – and was about to dismount when a cowman rushed forward suddenly and took the reins from him, as though he might dash off and make good his escape. They stared hostilely in each other's face, then Diego dropped his eyes, fully admitting defeat and guilt.

The cowman, a burly fellow, turned to look at the tired pony, wiped a hand down its neck which was lathered with sweat and foam. He lowered his hand to the stirrup leathers and let it rest there. During these tense silent moments another man stepped forward, too late to catch Emilio who slumped to the ground like a sack of corn. The fat man was unceremoniously carried to the water pump to have his flayed back treated.

The atmosphere became heavy with tension. Stirrings of fury and a lust for vengeance rose both at the same time in the minds of the men, particularly José, Cándido and Gerardo. The old man saw at once that the situation did not permit of an act of forgiveness on his part, sensing the men would have none of it.

The rancheros stood silently as before; hard-lipped, fierce-eyed, and filled with anger or hatred or both. For some moments Pancho gazed at the youth with icy eyes. He scratched his dust-caked nose.

Then he spoke, nasal gritty voice carrying an indifferent neutrality : "What a fine brainless specimen you turned out to be. You worthless rat's tail! You damned dog turd! I reckon there's nothing in that skull of yours but corn chaff and sawdust."

The men were restless and beginning to murmur among themselves, perhaps thinking that the teenager was going to be let off with mere verbal abuse. The old man hesitated a moment. There were two possible things he could do, he was thinking : smack him across the mouth, or smack him twice across the mouth. He decided on neither. He knew what the men were thinking. They would get their turn, for he'd allow it. He went on :

"For your stupid reckless act I ought to thrash the meat right off your back – like Emilio's!" his voice rising, eyes hard like blue steel. Diego visibly flinched. "I'd do it now gladly, you skinbag of nothing. Do you hear me, you piss-drop, are you listening?"

"Sí, señor," Diego answered him in a meek, faltering half-whisper. He apparently assumed or genuinely felt some remorse.

Pancho clenched his huge fists, steely eyes riveted on the other. The fact that he was standing while the youth was still astride his mount rankled the old horseman. It seemed to give Diego a certain aspect of pride he fully did not deserve.

"Dismount!" the ranchero ordered him curtly. "Hurry it, get off that beast, you damned waste of good air!"

He said nothing more but glanced at the men, then down at his dusty boots with studied attentiveness. The affair was now entirely in the hands of the horsemen and they knew it.

Diego slid from the saddle like a snake. He stood uncertainly by the pony and shuffled his feet, breathing through his mouth and starting to sweat. A trickle of sweat ran down his cheek, and he shivered. He lifted an arm and wiped away the moisture with a slow sweep, like a little boy wiping away a tear. He seemed to have visibly wilted.

There was a deathly quietness among the men. As if some thought of devilment had prompted him, Diego looked boldly at the rancheros and gave a sneering sniff. He caught a glitter of red in the mean, cruel eyes of José, and the brief display of bravado suddenly died.

In unison the men moved slowly forward to the quaking youth. He breathed hard, fast and unevenly, involuntarily backing away with pusillanimous movements of eye and body. The morose silence was broken when a steer lowed nearby. Diego broke wind, a nervous pip of sound was all it was, and he waited with dread.

Pancho had business elsewhere. He would ride back to don Roberto's casa and find out what might be keeping the expected film people. He took Macha's rein and swung up a little heavily into the saddle. Looking the men over without expression, he took in their strained faces. He turned his mount round.

And off he went, without so much as a backward glance.

He rode at an easy canter, showing – somewhat belatedly – consideration for his horse which had earlier run so well. Rode on past the end gathering of cattle and a few scrubby thorn trees.

Out onto the wide stretch of dry smoking arcane grasslands.

Moments later, Diego's terrified screams bounced between the tall canyon walls, echoing out over the stormscaped savage land.

Part Twenty

Part Twenty

109

Recuperating

A few days following the calamitous stampede of don Roberto's long-horns, the rancheros were taking it easy and dallied about the stables. They appeared to be working but in fact exerted themselves as little as they possibly could.

There was an air of quiet somnolence about the stables and stable-yard.

Cándido was on his own in the feed-barn, resting on a bale of cornstraw. Whenever he thought he heard footsteps coming his way he quickly jumped to his feet and began pitching straw with a fork, a dedicated urge to labour hard and slavishly apparent on his face, a look almost of martyrdom plainly shown for any doubting sceptics.

Gerardo, in slow-time, slow-stepped his way along a length of horse-stalls in the main stable. Armed with a pencil and clipboard indicated that he too was working industriously like a Trojan. After shuffling to the end of a line he made a few pertinent notations on his clipboard. This was conveniently accomplished whilst sitting on a bale – for the sake of course, as he would himself have put it, for the sake of a steadier writing hand.

The clipboard notations were a load of nonsense and utterly irrelevant; he was blatantly skiving. A strained sigh following the writing in of data, as of a man being tortured on a rack, brought him in slow, lethargic motion to his feet once again. He repeated the process exactly as before, except the rests on a bale became of longer periods.

He wondered why Pancho was taking so long at *his* paperwork.

The old man was astride a wooden stool before a rickety deal-table at the wide double doorway of the stable. A pile of papers stacked before him was held from a grasping wind by the weight of a rusty horseshoe. It would appear to anyone observing him that he was just as cruelly caught up in his work. A pen was poised in his fist, one cheek resting on the topmost sheet of paper, in the manner of a schoolboy at his desk or someone near-sighted.

He was in reality enjoying a catnap. It even sounded as though he were purring, so gentle was his snoring.

Emilio made no bones about it, though he would deceive anyone who happened to look his way.

He was rigidly stood in a corner of the stable – the same one in which Gerardo shambled up and down, like a clockwork toy running down – the fat man's chin resting on the cross-bar of an unpanelled horse-stall.

It appeared as if he were checking a chestnut bay haltered within.

The injured rider was thickly mummified or rather heavily bandaged around his back, chest and neck, considerably enlarging his normal generous bulk. He stood there stiffly like a tailor's dummy or an automaton, with arms unbent and his bulging front invading the stall space, his whole frame firmly wedged between two posts.

He's awake at least, thought Gerardo, glancing over at him, one eye on the chestnut bay. Unusual for Emilio to be awake at this time, wondered Gerardo.

If he cared to look more closely however he would perhaps notice that the one eye was staring unfocused and blankly as a glass marble. All the same and to give credit where it is due, Emilio garnered singular qualities, the most notable being able to sleep in a standing position. His fellow rancheros had always maintained that he could sleep standing up. He also had the unique knack – which easily fooled Gerardo – of sometimes sleeping with one eye wide open. Emilio did this now and was indeed fast asleep, stood there at the stall and held in balance by the rigid bandaging of his upper body, legs splayed, chin firmly gripped like an anchor on the wooden cross-bar.

The only true and real movement in this waxworks-like tableau, if an eye was sharp enough to catch it, was when the simpleton stablehand Julian occasionally popped up his head in a stall, a bucket and a broom in his hands. He worked frantically at the task of scrubbing out the stalls, sloshing water about and humming to himself. A bent straw dangled from his lower lip as he toiled away as if his very life was solely dependent on it.

But there was someone missing …

110

News of a Visit

He made his presence known a few moments later, charging into the corral grounds on his dapple grey colt like one of the horsemen of the apocalypse. The stir he made was not unlike the poking of a stick in a hornet's nest.

In the feed-barn Cándido shot to his feet, trod on a prong of his pitchfork, and began hopping about on one foot. Gerardo miscalculated his sums, softly cursed, then completely forgot where he should be going, up the stalls or down them.

Pancho, startled out from his stolen slumber, jumped upright and lifted the horseshoe from the pile of papers. The papers rose and flew all over the yard, tossed and eddied in the dusty wake of José's passage. The old man slammed the horseshoe down on the deal-table, managing to catch a last remaining sheet of paper. Julian clattered out with his bucket and dropped it, in order to go chasing after the fluttering papers, snatching at them in mid-air.

Only Emilio remained immobile. He slept on blissfully; stiff, straight and solid as a stall post.

"They've started the filming at last!" José cried in some excitement, dismounting in a fog of dust. "The cameras are rolling, as they say."

"We already know that," scoffed Pancho. "You come riding in here like a damned whirlwind and start to tell us what we know already," snatching at his airborne paperwork from Julian's proffered hands.

"Sí, sí, we know it, don't we?" snarled José, barely able to constrain himself. He evidently knew much more than what he was telling at present, or so the old man conjectured as he judiciously studied the other's facial antics.

"But the big day is tomorrow," José opened up again a little, not wishing to disclose at once his precious virgin knowledge.

He passed the colt's halter to Julian, who gently led the lathered animal into the stable to be wiped down, walked a bit, fed and watered.

"Sí, tomorrow is the big day alright," repeated José with some emphasis, though nobody was biting at his bait. He seemed crestfallen over the old ranchero's response which was no response to speak of. Actually, Pancho was still a trifle groggy with sleep.

José tried again. "They're hoping for a good sunset," he offered portentously. "I was talking to one of the cameramen, and he said how important it was to have a good sunset – you know, with lots of colour. The film's in colour, you see. This hombre told me so."

"Speak in sign language, did you?" came Pancho's sarcastic response.

"What? No! The fellow's from Santa Barbara, California. Married to a Mexican. He speaks Spanish just like me and you."

He slapped dust from his chaps. "There is something else too," he said, opening the floodgates at last. "El Presidente is going to be there." José smiled with superior satisfaction.

"Of the film company?"

"No, Pancho, *el presidente de México*, that's who."

The old man was stunned for a moment. "Don Roberto never said anything about this."

"When did you last see him?" asked José. "The news is not an hour old as yet. He'll let you know all in good time I expect," he went on with unusual chirpiness.

Pancho took a pull on his moustache. "The President will be *here* tomorrow you say?"

"Arriving at 3.30 in the afternoon at the depot. Coming on the presidential train no less. Think of it, hermano, our own president coming here to don Roberto's!"

"Good God!" gasped Gerardo, catching the latter part of the conversation. "The Boss is laid up in his bed with that damned hernia problem. Who's going to do the honours?"

He meant who would be going out to the railroad junction to meet and welcome the president. There was only one possible candidate.

"Jorge can handle it well enough I reckon," said Pancho, referring to don Roberto's youngest son. "Does he know of this new arrangement?"

he asked José. "Don Roberto wasn't expecting the president's visit for two weeks or more."

"So you knew he was coming then?" said José, slightly miffed that his thunder was not all that loud after all. "Well, Jorge knows," he confirmed, "because he was there when I heard of it. Jorge told me that he wants to offer *Black Velvet* for the president to ride on. And Jorge will ride the chestnut gelding he bought only last month."

Pancho tugged at his moustache, thinking hard. "So he's here tomorrow then … el presidente." He stared meaningfully at the others. "Have you even the slightest idea what this means?" he asked at large. "The President himself coming to these parts, eh?"

The matter was now plainly in his sights. It was time to make decisions of great consequence. His first action was to despatch Gerardo to the neighbouring ranch of his friend don Fernando, in order to drum up volunteers to help build the ranks of escorts and guards.

He turned and eyed the other, said, "The President will need a security force for protection. And he should have a proper guard of honour. He will want guides to take him to the casa and on to Montezuma Canyon – or wherever they're doing the filming."

He rubbed vigorously at his jaw. "And we need to clean and smarten up some, that's for sure – Oye, Julian! Julian, to the casa with you my good little fellow, and take our best *camisas* and *pantalones*. Tell Tulia we want a handsome job done on them and in double quick time. Okay, muchacho? Off you go then. ¡Andale!"

He rubbed at his jaw some more. "Hmm … José, let's have the tub hauled out and get plenty of hot water on the go. We can all take an honest scrub and scrape in readiness for his excellency. Soak the stink of stables off us, Emilio especially." He swiftly glanced around him. "Where is he, by the by? Emilio! … EMILIO!"

The fat man's board-stiff frame convulsed a moment, his head swivelled, showing a half-gummed bleary eye. He geared himself straight into auto mode: "Specimen! Bay gelding! Grade B!" he called over dutifully. "Relegated for further training," he reeled off on a fading note.

"Ay que caray, hombre, where do you think you're at? All that was done hours ago!" Pancho plastered him. "Now listen, the President's on his way and we need to look good for him. You can go and soak your smelly feet for starters."

"The president?" blinked Emilio. "Coming here?" He lumbered stiff-gaited to the stable entranceway and peered out, scanning the lonely empty landscape. "Where?"

"Hang on a bit," smirked José, "he shouldn't be overlong. Keep your eyes peeled – and stay awake too."

"Is that true then, the president coming?"

"As the Day of the Dead falls on the Day of the Dead."

Cándido then made his appearance, partly decorated with straw confetti.

"¿Que paso?" he said, stifling a yawn, "What's all the fuss?"

"El Presidente's on his way here," Emilio told him. "I'm looking out for him."

"Daydreaming, is it, amigo? What's happening, José?"

"They've started filming at last. The cameras are going to roll. A good sunset tomorrow is the thing. Fit for a president, hee-hee!"

"If you're back in the land of the living, muchacho," Pancho said to the young man, "I'll thank you to sort out the best saddle-mounts. I want them groomed and shining till they sparkle like jewellery."

"Would someone tell me what's going on?"

"We're escorting our President to the film location tomorrow afternoon. His Excellency is coming to watch the actual shooting of the film." The old man spread his mouth in a wide grin. "You never know but we may even get a small part in the picture.

"Whatever happens, it's an important day for us lot when tomorrow comes, hmm."

Cándido gazed at him. "Now where are you off to?"

"To see Jorge and finalise the arrangements. I'll see you later."

Pancho strode happily off in the direction of the casa, swinging his massive shoulders, covering ground as light-footed as a youth, and humming to himself.

111

A Reunion

The day was radiant, sunlight bright and clear, unsullied by dust. Everything stood out with clarity and rich colours, like an oil painter's palette. A broad sky patterned by high cirrus cloud promised a spectacular sunset later.

By mid-afternoon the rail junction appeared like a scene from ancient Babylon; awash with crowds drawn from many distances around. They had been coming in since first light, on foot or by mule, horse or donkey.

Pancho and his rancheros, plus many cowmen, struggled with their mounts as they tried to maintain some order in the streaming melee about them. One bold youth set off a firecracker, causing Gerardo's horse to rear up in the crowd. The people quickly realised the folly of mixing themselves among mounted riders and backed away *en masse*.

Jorge rode up to the old ranchero, with a detached, preoccupied air. "You'll liaise with don Fernando," he said stonily. It was a command, not a question, or at least that was how old Pancho interpreted it.

"Sí, Jorge, we reckoned on that. Is the train running on time, do you know?"

"The presidential train is always punctual, wouldn't dare to be otherwise." There was an unmistakable edge to the young man's voice.

"I'll have a word with don Fernando, when he comes that is, he's not here yet. Shouldn't be long now, I guess."

"Bueno," acknowledged Jorge unsmilingly. "Let's keep one important thing in mind. Controlling this crowd. You see what I mean?" as masses of people milled and moved around with total freedom.

"That roped barricade is as much use as a string fishing line," said

Pancho, "but a roundup of mounted stallions will keep them in their place, I dare say."

"See to it then, Pancho, get your men organised."

There was a note of warning in his voice. He looked the old ranchero hard in the eye. Jorge was certainly taking his role seriously, thought Pancho, but then that was just as well.

"We need to make a good show of it today," concluded Jorge. He turned his mount, rode back to his cowmen already beginning to line up.

Pancho's keen blue eyes roved over the dress and general deportment of his men, smartly turned out in starched denim, highly polished boots and *chaparreras*. The horses too looked magnificent, perfectly groomed, coats sleek and shiny. The old ranchero was highly satisfied.

To distinguish himself from the others he had his own singular adornment. Around his waist he wore a gunbelt and holster, in which nestled a pearl-handled Colt .45.

The babel of voices increased as the minutes ticked away. Yet more people were still arriving, throngs nudged and chivvied, calling cheerily to one another. Excitement crackled like a tangible thing in the balmy air about the depot precincts – so often a lonely and desolate place; now it choked and heaved like the hub of a busy town.

"Pancho! Pancho!"

The old ranchero looked over a sea of bobbing heads, recognised the handsome chestnut bay Chapulín, then the boy Juan in the saddle. "Juanito!"

As soon as they were able to reach each other a tremendous fuss was made of it in their greetings and back-slappings. Macha and Chapulín too seemed pleased at this reunion, nuzzling and nickering in friendly horsey fashion.

"Where's your mamá?"

"She's here somewhere – we're all here!"

"¡Chihuahuas! Someone looking for me, is it?" said a warm, familiar voice from the press of people about them.

"María!"

It was indeed that good woman, elegantly attired in what must be a brand new dress for this special occasion. The old ranchero's eyes devoured her in astonishment and admiration. Doña María seemed equally taken by – even mesmerised by – the other's large revolver snugged in its holster. Pancho vainly and outrageously imagined she was looking at something quite different. He stirred and squirmed uncomfortably a moment in the saddle.

And how was she keeping? he politely enquired. Fairly well to be sure, thank you very much. How did she get here? Don Vicente kindly brought them in his cart. That lecherous old goat? Don Vicente, who had always treated her with the utmost respect. Was don Antonio in good health? He was in perfectly splendid health, and quite capable of informing him personally of the fact. For there he was, towering over everyone and stooping diffidently because of it.

Julia and Ruth jumped ecstatically at the old ranchero's stirruped feet, each vying to gain his full attention. And Cristina, blossoming in her late teenage, glanced shyly and self-consciously at everyone, having just caught the admiring stare of don Jorge.

Jorge presently conferred in whispering tones with the old man, reminding him that time was marching on and they had better prepare now to line up in readiness for the running-on-time presidential train.

"A pity old Fernando and his crew failed to make it," Jorge muttered disappointedly. "We could have done with him and his men."

"But don Fernando is here!" piped young Juan. "I saw him only a moment ago – There he is, look!"

"Make way! Stand aside, you rabble!" growled a grizzled old ranchero type on a powerfully muscled roan gelding, a solid string of mounted men hustling and manoeuvring behind him.

A great commotion ensued as the rancheros of don Fernando – and the old rancher himself – made raucous greetings and salutations among don Roberto's men. Pancho and Fernando leaned over in their saddles and warmly embraced.

More firecrackers were set off, exploding nearby. The nervous horses pawed and kicked up dust. Folk laughed and chattered, evidently enjoying themselves.

"Okay, guard of honour and escorts! Stir yourselves and get in line," commanded don Jorge in a loud no-nonsense tone.

"Jorge's a born general, to be sure," mumbled someone in the ranks.

Just like his father, thought Pancho with a grin.

The riders soon restored some semblance of order, joined up in twos and jogged raggedly in a snaking line toward the railroad depot building.

112

The Arrival

It was almost time, barely minutes to go before the train was due. A hush fell on the expectant multitude crowding the depot and railroad sidings. The only sound was that of horses' hooves clopping on hard stony ground. The riders manoeuvred their mounts into position, creating a wide avenue through which the presidential party would ride. The people watched with interest, though scores kept eyes on the single railtrack running straight as a die into a featureless distance.

A vaquero, aware of the hundreds of heads turned his way to watch his every move, rode slowly and self-consciously on toward don Jorge. He led by its bridle a magnificent black stallion with white-stocking feet. This superb beast was accoutred with a brand new light-tan saddle, immaculate snaffle and bit in shiny silver. Its tail was tied at its base with green, white and red ribbon. Don Roberto's personal horse Black Velvet. The president would be riding him to the casa. Other cowmen came forward, leading saddled mounts for the president's aides.

Time ticked inexorably on. The vast assemblage stiffened and held bated breath. Then, quite clearly and as anticipated, a locomotive whistle blew in the distance. Heads turned in the direction of its haunting, heart-pulling sound. The broad black nose of a train engine could be distinctly seen now down the track-line. White smoke puffed from its short-barrelled funnel. The whistle blew once again, a long imperative wail, a signal for the track to be clear of any encumbrance.

Behind the locomotive and tender was the presidential carriage. A second carriage accommodated his entourage of ministers, aides and privileged journalists. At the rear was a long caboose, apparently crammed with *federales*. The president had evidently thought fit to bring along his own security force.

The mighty blackfired steam engine clanked to a halt with a screech of metal wheels and clangour of piston rods. Hissing blasts of steam escaped from its massive sides. From the depot office a clock struck a puny *ting!* It was three-thirty exactly.

People craned their necks in an effort to see what was happening, which was nothing much for the first few moments. Then the federal security team exited the caboose and took station along the length of the presidential carriage.

A moment more passed. Then a uniformed porter stepped down from the first carriage, followed by two military policemen armed and helmeted. They stood rigidly to attention, all three of them, at the carriage entranceway. And another moment came on by.

The President of Mexico at last showed his august person. Folks gasped in surprise to see him wearing a short jacket, riding breeches and black leather boots. He carried a riding crop in one hand, as though ready for a hunt.

The president alighted from the train with an easy grace and broad smile, one arm waving regally to the crowds. They responded at once by wildly cheering.

Don Jorge solemnly stepped forward to welcome his father's guest, and they shook hands. The president casually introduced the most senior members of his party to the young *haciendado*. Like a flock of birds round a waterhole, a chirring of newspaper photographers snapped away at the scene.

A few whispered conversations, then the saddled horses were brought forward. Beaming a smile of self-assurance the president mounted the black stallion with flair and aplomb, though many willing hands were outstretched to assist him. The dignitaries followed suit, a few of them not properly attired for riding purposes. It was a jumbled mass of confusion for a time, until they finally settled into some formation of order.

The federal soldiers meanwhile rushed to their positions between the horses of the mounted guard of honour. Soon, the president set off at a sedate walking pace amid frantic cheering and flag waving. Young don Jorge rode proudly by his side.

Pancho, at the furthest end of the left spaced line holding back the tide of humanity, did not look the president's way, but carefully scanned the pushing surging mass of people directly opposite him. It was an effort of will to contain the crowd, he could see, as José and Cándido steadied their restive horses against the press of onlookers.

The mass of people did themselves proud in their roaring of welcome, as the cavalcade slowly made its way between the disciplined ranks of the mounted guard. The president benignly waved a hand, the other casually gripping riding crop and reins. Black Velvet did his master great honour, gently pacing his steps in an elegant and comfortable manner for his distinguished rider.

The old ranchero caught Black Velvet out the corner of his eye. But his attention was riveted on a pale-faced individual stood nearside of José's colt just opposite him. His suspicions were aroused by the man's whole demeanour; there seemed a nervous, desperate air about him. His right arm was tucked in a sarape strung loosely over one shoulder. This alone caused tiny alarm bells to jangle in the old man's mind. He had also noted a further aspect of this fellow which struck him as odd. The man was the only one in the crowd without a happy smiling face, the only one not cheering or waving. It was a particularity that somehow struck a chord in Pancho's being. It was a red-flag warning sign and he recognised it as such.

The president approached nearer to the end of lined horsemen. All eyes concentrated on his familiar figure. While the pale-faced man was now suddenly clear of the crowd and mounted men. He held an automatic gun in his hand. He swung it up in one tight movement of his arm and took aim, directly at the president's chest.

Pancho had anticipated the man, already making his own moves. He sharply heeled Macha forward, his Colt revolver cocked, gripped in his fist. The president saw at once what was about to happen. He reined in the stallion and swerved to one side. Pancho was there instantly to fill the space he had left. There was a loud report, cries from the crowd. Then another gunshot, milliseconds later. Booming out with all the power of its point 45 calibre.

The mass of humanity at once became uncontrollable; a brassy, clamorous uproar as people panicked. Passions soared in an instant, showed on angry faces, others looked shocked. Women wailed and young ones cried in bewilderment, barely understanding what had happened. The lines of horsemen broke up, their power of control overwhelmed by an onrushing surge of bodies. Federal men ran here and there in total disorder, like a disturbed ants' nest.

"He's hit!" yelled someone.

"Your excellency!" cried Jorge. "We must ride on and swiftly, get away from this crowd. Please to follow me!"

The president, quite unperturbed and still on his mount, readily agreed with his young host. They broke into a gallop at once, leaving the dignitaries trailing behind them.

Pancho was slumped over the pommel of his saddle.

113

Pancho Grounded

Cándido was first to reach the old ranchero and eased him from the saddle. José appeared and held Pancho in a sitting position on the ground. There was pandemonium all around them, the disturbed crowds jostling, and wild-eyed youngsters squalled in the noisy confusion.

The would-be assassin lay sprawled in the dust, unmoving, dead as dead, having taken a slug in the heart. He must have died instantly. A few men kicked at his corpse with booted feet. Women spat on it in disgust.

Cándido removed his bandanna and balled it. He placed it tenderly over the wound in Pancho's shoulder to staunch the flow of blood. José took over and held the cloth in place. He indicated his own bandanna – the one coloured egg-yolk-yellow of which he was so proud to own – and Cándido loosed it from his neck. He then set to in making a tourniquet.

There was a stir among the throng nearby.

"I'm a doctor! Let me through please! Let me through, damn it!" came an irate voice from the congested crowd of folk about the wounded ranchero.

A short dark-suited man pushed through a ring of onlookers surrounding the rancheros. He carried a black medical bag in one hand. He was evidently what he claimed to be; moreover, he had foreseen that his presence here in a professional capacity would ultimately be confirmed and he was pleased that it was so.

Without any preliminaries he knelt before his potential patient, assessed the damage, and attended to him with all the speed and skill of his professional training. Cándido was sent racing to the depot building for water.

Moments later doña María was there to assist the doctor and to give moral support for her old friend. The rest of the Ramos family and Pancho's fellow rancheros made a protective cordon around him. The girls put a brave face on the proceedings, trying hard to hold back the tears brimming in their eyes. Even the boy Juan was forced to swallow several times, to be rid of a choking ache in his throat, and he too managed not to cry.

In contrariness the old man appeared abundantly cheerful over his condition, giving it no second thought. He was in fact quite verbose, relating similar incidents in Mexico's bloody history.

"Sí, *hijole*, there was President Obregón, as I recall, and another time there was that —"

"Here," José interrupted him, "you'll be needing this I reckon," about to pass his hip flask to Pancho.

"Mezcal, amigo?"

"Tequila. The best."

"Thank you," said the doctor, snatching the flask from him. "It's exactly what I require right now." He helped himself to a long draught, Pancho and José looking on with pained expressions.

"Ahh! I feel ready to face anything now," declared the doctor, then turned to his patient. "It'll do you some good too," he blithely told the old man, handing the flask over at last. "Because what I'm going to do next will hurt like the devil. At all events that bullet must be removed and your wound nicely neatly cleaned up."

"Know a good prevention as they say and you won't need a cure," returned Pancho philosophically. "This will do me a treat and a treat is as good as a feast," tipping the flask to his lips. "You carry on there, doc, I'm fine," he added merrily.

Less than an hour passed by when young don Jorge returned from the casa. The crowds had long since dispersed and the corpse of the near-assassin dragged by the federales to the rail depot to be disposed of at a later time.

"Pancho!" called over the haciendado, dismounting like an acrobat from his chestnut gelding. "Are you alright?"

"I am!" declared the inveterate warrior, pulling a fierce, combative face, which did not fool doña María for one moment as she gazed fondly on him.

"The President wishes to see you, if you don't mind. He said as soon as it's convenient for you."

"Oh my!" chirped doña María. "What an honour!"

"Are you up to it, Pancho? Can you ride?"

"I can ride, damn it! Here, Cándido – José – help me up from the dust."

"We can all go on to the casa," said Jorge, addressing everyone smilingly. "The trip to Montezuma Canyon where the herd is grazing is still on, and we are the official escort."

He caught Pancho's discreet gesture indicating the doctor, who was packing his black bag.

"Doctor, you'll be our guest at my father's house, I trust. He will want to thank you personally and to pay your fee for the expert treatment I see you have performed on our dear don Francisco Ramírez."

So they all rode back to don Roberto's casa, the rancheros and the vaqueros. A half dozen of the men each carried a member of the Ramos family – Juan rode his Chapulín – and the good doctor was not forgotten either.

114

Meeting 'El Presidente'

*I*n the meantime on the hacienda the president and his followers were comfortably ensconced in deep-cushioned wicker chairs on the wide front porch of don Roberto's house. They were smoking cigars and sipping mint juleps, casually conversing among themselves.

On the president's right was an aged and silver-haired, rather distinguished looking gentleman. He wore a smart cream suit and a white sombrero. The *caballero* was suffering from a recent incapacity, for he was reclining in a wheelchair. It was the haciendado himself, Roberto Arías Zedillo.

Don Roberto, in person!

Presently a drumming of hooves sounded. The horsemen hove in sight. They slowed to a walking pace, forming a wide crescent on the open ground before the large rambling casa, then halted.

Doña María – perhaps better known as mamá – and her clan slipped unobtrusively to one side, taking the doctor with them.

Pancho and Jorge sedately walked their mounts forward several paces, and they too came to a halt. Jorge dismounted and approached the old man, whose left arm was held in a sling. He helped him off his horse, took Macha's halter. Jorge's own gelding came to him of its own accord. He held the halters of both horses and stood to attention between them.

Now the old ranchero squared his shoulders, wincing a little because of the wound, which he had almost forgotten, and strode forward with a self-conscious stiffness to his gait, aware that everyone's eyes were focused on him.

By the porch a cluster of newspapermen held their chatter out of respect for this moment. Their cameras were at the ready. Aides and ministers on the porch stubbed out cigar butts as a mark of courtesy. And they too observed a silence.

The president stepped alone from his central position and walked with slow dignity toward the man who had this day saved his life. The cluttering of journalists snapped and clicked their cameras, recording his forward progress on his own two feet.

He reached the old man, took a huge paw in his hands and warmly shook it.

"A prompt and brave action, Francisco Ramírez," he addressed him with genuine sincerity. "Your president is deeply grateful for what you did today and offers a thousand thanks."

"To be honest it was a lucky thing, your excellency," grinned Pancho in return, feeling relaxed now despite the eminent presence. "A lucky thing, because I don't normally pack a pistol or ride around armed to the teeth."

"Only in the open season perhaps, hey?" graciously smiled the president, evidently alluding with good humour to the earlier attempt that was made on his life.

"That fellow won't be bothering anybody any more, I'm thinking, your excellency."

"Fine shooting," the president's smile turned to a knowing grin, "for a trainer of horses."

He had of course taken immediate notice of the hero's left arm and shoulder bandaged and in a sling.

"If you feel up to it, Francisco," he said kindly, "I'd be honoured to be escorted by you and your fellow rancheros to the film location. It is after all what I came here for."

Pancho straightened his shoulders, wincing again slightly at the pain in one of them.

He suddenly began to realise the significance of this day's happenings, and that it would hit the front page of every national newspaper by tomorrow morning. He could not help feeling overwhelmed by a sense of history unfolding at this very moment.

And he was an integral part of it!

"The honour is all mine, your excellency," he responded proudly.

115

A Surprise

L ater toward that same evening the sunset could not have appeared more dramatic and spectacularly colourful. Don Roberto's longhorn cattle behaved admirably and on cue, stringing along in one continuous moving mass over the crest of a rise in the land. Shot in vistavision and technicolour by a major motion picture corporation.

After the successful filming of the sunset scene the president and his party left immediately for the railroad junction. He was scheduled to journey further north to visit another state. There was a sufficient number of rider escorts to return with him, so Pancho and his rancheros remained among the film crew.

José began talking with the American cameraman he had recently befriended.

Pancho took a stroll about, gazing at the western skyline. The sun was now below the distant mountain range, its glow still in the sky. The mountains looked plum-purple with a moody maroon trim of foothills. In the soft evening light, the last dying light of this eventful day.

He paused in his tracks, because he noticed the cameraman who had spoken to José was walking alone toward him. The old man waited, not a little curious.

"Señor Ramírez?" said the American in a friendly fashion, coming up to him. The stranger noted the ginger-red hair showing at the side of the other's sombrero, and the blue eyes with their glint of humour.

"That's right, I'm Ramírez." They shook hands.

"José has mentioned you," the American went on in an earnest tone, "and now I see you for myself."

He hesitated a moment, as though he wanted to choose his next words with care. "I know the name, Ramírez, from my home town of Santa Barbara in California." He gazed steadily at old Pancho. "Tell me, señor, did you – did you have a brother?"

The question took the old man completely by surprise. "I still have as far as I know," he smiled cautiously. "We haven't kept in touch, you see. As a matter of fact I have two brothers, both younger than me."

"Oh, is that so?" said the stranger. "Interesting…"

Pancho went on. "The youngest now, Rufino, he's in Sonora someplace, or at least that's where he ought to be, for I haven't set eyes on him in over twenty years.

"The other one, Eduardo –"

"Eduardo, did you say?"

"That's him. He was living in Sonora too. We originally came from Sonora. Eduardo was still there until his wife Rosaria died. And that would be nigh on twenty years ago as well. After burying his Rosaria he left straight away for a new life in California. He worked in the vine-growing business, which was picking up handsomely around that time. That was what he went for at any rate."

"Huh-huh, I see. I find that mighty interesting…"

Something told the old ranchero that there was more to this conversation than met the ear, but he continued amicably on as was his wont.

"When I say Eduardo is my younger brother, it was only by twenty minutes or so, according to our mother." He smiled disingenuously at the American stranger. "He's my twin, you understand. We are not identical look-alikes, Eduardo and me, but damn pretty close I'd say."

"Yes, I can believe it, señor Ramírez," returned the other enigmatically. He could too, for a certain reason not yet known by this old man standing before him. "Did you stay in contact with him?" he asked.

"With Eduardo? No, I'm afraid to say we didn't stay in touch, we each went our separate ways. That was how it happened in those early years … A pity I know, ay caray."

Pancho smiled a sweet nostalgic smile.

"And that is just what I figured, señor Ramírez, because I partly know your family story." The old man showed astonishment at this remark. "I suppose you didn't know he had married again?"

"No, I didn't. Eduardo hitched up again. Uuy, bless me!"

Another surprise!

"He found a new wife soon after he settled in Santa Barbara – that's where he went, Santa Barbara." The American gave a short pause. "She gave him a son about a year later."

This news hit Pancho like a hammer blow. He straightened up, eyes literally sparkling.

"A son! My little brother has a muchacho! And I'm the boy's uncle!" Old Pancho almost danced on the spot.

He made an expressive gesture with his arms, forgetting for the moment that he had one in a sling. The Californian helped him rearrange his loosened sling.

"You know," Pancho rattled on light-heartedly, face lit up with delight, "I made a fellow's day today simply by just being there and being a bit quick off the mark. And now you have made mine. You've made *my* day."

"The fellow you've mentioned there would perhaps be the president of your country? José told me about the assassination attempt on your president. You ought to be decorated for your brave act in saving him."

The American had spoken with an awkward smile. It went in an instant, only to replaced by a sombre kind of expression.

"Look, there is something else I must tell you," he went on earnestly. "I don't think you're at all aware of this … No, you can't possibly know this, señor Ramírez –"

"Francisco. Or you can call me Pancho."

"I think Francisco suits this occasion better, so Francisco it is," the other smiled rather crookedly, then resumed a solemn expression.

"Your brother Eduardo, who lived in my home town – well I'm sorry to tell you, Francisco, that he passed from this life seven years ago."

116

More Surprises

There followed a brief and awkward silence. Old Pancho was stunned. All his sudden happiness evaporated. He stared for a time with glistening eyes at the man from California.

"Eduardo? Dead?" he muttered dully. "Seven years back…"

But then, had not the old man always known it? The dream he now recalled from seven years ago. He had actually dreamt of his brother's death. When he had dismissed it from his mind, had refused to believe or accept it. It had been but a dream so he had put the matter from him and tried to forget about it. He might have known better he now realised.

"He died in Santa Barbara," the Californian told him in quiet tones. "Of kidney failure I think it was, so I was informed."

"You knew this, then? You must have known my brother?" and it was put as a question.

"No, Francisco, I only knew *of* him. I never met the guy I'm sorry to say. I wish I had known the fellow."

"Ay que caray, poor Eduardo…" murmured Pancho in a cracked voice.

The old ranchero stood there stiffly, brooding over this news.

And the dusk came down, a purple-blue dusk which steadily deepened. In the gathering dusk he thought of his brother who was no more of this earth. And the tide of dusk rolled in silently about him.

"My sincere condolences, Francisco," the American broke the silence.

Then he seemed to brighten of a sudden. He saw something or someone. He smiled again, this time full of hope and encouragement.

"Listen now my friend, do you see the young guy over there?" He pointed to a slim figure a few paces away, leaning against a boulder, gazing westward at the failing light. "He's my protégée you might say. Still at college and doing well, in his final year in fact. He's studying cinematography. A fine young man he is. I can myself vouch for that."

Old Pancho looked confused. Where was this leading to?

The American looked squarely into the old man's eyes, leaned toward him in the dimming light.

"His name is Eduardo … Eduardo Ramírez."

Pancho blinked. The other's words did not at first sink in. "I don't understand," he said at last.

The American put a reassuring hand on Pancho's undamaged shoulder, and said, "There is a distinct possibility that the young man you see not twenty feet in front of you – every possibility that he is your nephew."

He now managed a warm and compassionate smile. "In fact I'm mightily convinced that he is indeed your nephew, Francisco. He has to be! Look, why don't you go and introduce yourself?

"I'm pretty sure that you're both in for a surprise. I could guarantee it! It's alright, go to him. I need to stow away my equipment."

He took the old man's hand. "A real pleasure and honour meeting you, Francisco. You're quite a guy – a hero! I wish you every success."

"Thank you – I'm sorry but I don't know your name?"

"It's Gilhome. Ross Gilhome. I'll be seeing you around."

And he was gone, padding soundlessly into the deep soft dusk. It came over from beyond the hills and mountains in the east. It crept over smotheringly like the slow folding of a light blanket. In the shadows of silence, in the coming darkness of a young night.

The lone figure was still there by the boulder. Pancho heaved a sigh, his insides churning in turmoil, not really knowing what would come of this. He made his decision and strode resolutely to the young man, readjusting his arm in its sling.

He stopped a few paces sideways of the boulder. The youth casually turned his head with an enquiring glance. His face changed a moment later.

Old Pancho's whole attention was on this young person before him. Maybe his own flesh and blood. Even in the poor light he could see the red hair, the strikingly blue eyes. The very mirror image of his brother Eduardo as he had looked over a quarter century ago.

A spasm gripped him for a second or two, a shiver streaking down his spine.

But why such an expression as that? he wondered, seeing the young man's wide-eyed look of terror and disbelief.

"P-papá?" the youngster quavered.

"No, mi muchacho," murmured Pancho huskily, tears beginning to well in his eyes. "I am your uncle Francisco. Pancho of Sonora."

The youth still stared at him but this time large-eyed with wonder.

"You're so much like my father – when he was alive," he said at last in a pleasant tone.

"Oh, we were quite different I think," smiled the old man.

"I remember now. He spoke often of you when I was a kid. Told me all about you. How wild you were."

The young man gestured at his uncle's arm in its sling. "It seems maybe you haven't changed much," he added with a smile.

"Uuy, you can believe me or not, Eduardo, but I've learned the errors of my ways since those far off times. We were all wild then you know, hmm. Come right here my boy, let me see you…"

They embraced in the Mexican manner, carefully under the circumstances, Pancho's bandaged arm getting in the way.

And the long accumulated heat of the day came out of the stones and grasses of the earth, rising in fragrant thermal waves. Hot draughts of air stirred the dry crisp barbs of mesquite grass.

The first stars began to appear one by one, glittering and winking in the evening sky.

Eduardo Ramírez stepped back from his uncle.

"We have got a great deal to talk over, a lot of past time to cover," he said with warmth. "You have probably led a fascinating life, eh? – Uncle!"

This meaningful appellation jolted the old man.

"I wouldn't deny that one little bit, mi muchacho, and I'll tell you all about the interesting bits in good time there were many of them, ay caray."

Around them crickets sang their monotonous evening-song, and a small bat out from some secluded nook zinged closely by. A few mosquitoes whined and hummed.

There was a brief scutter of a tiny animal, probably a field mouse, in the honey-gold grass now dark and mysterious.

And other unidentifiable noises in the thickening darkness of night.

Then silence …

But only for a brief spell, for it opened up again joyously with the laughter and animated conversation between old Pancho and his newfound nephew Eduardo.

They chattered on happily through the darkling night hours, relating one to the other the experiences of their long years of separation, reliving those times far past in honest anecdote and homely tale, Pancho's crusty, nut-crunching voice as ever dominating.

The summer had all but burned itself out, the sun gradually losing its force.

And though these long summer months were now almost spent, a totally unrelated and new kind of season was beginning for old Pancho. A season forming its own and altogether different warmth …

He had family!